Xavier Dollo & Djibril Morissette-Phan

THE HISTORY OF science fiction

A GRAPHIC NOVEL ADVENTURE

HUMANOIDS

XAVIER DOLLO
Writer

DJIBRIL MORISSETTE-PHAN
Artist

MARK BENCE
Translator

MARK WAID and AMANDA LUCIDO
US Edition Editors

BRUNO LECIGNE and ERIC MARCELIN
Original Edition Editors

JERRY FRISSEN
Senior Art Director

RYAN LEWIS
Junior Designer

MARK WAID
Publisher

Rights and Licensing - licensing@humanoids.com
Press and Social Media - pr@humanoids.com

foreword

by Ted Chiang

Whenever I talk about science fiction to people who aren't regular readers of it, I tell them that science fiction is not adventure stories set in outer space. Science fiction, as I see it, is a post-Industrial Revolution kind of storytelling. Stories about good guys fighting bad guys have been around forever; they can be fun, but they're not science fiction. Science fiction tells stories that only make sense to people who have seen how technology can change the world within their lifetimes. It's about the awareness that the future will not simply be a version of the past with the names changed; the future will be different.

So, in one sense, a history of science fiction is a history of our ideas about the future. But science fiction is also a genre of literature, and how do you tell the history of a genre? What is a genre, anyway? Some people say that a genre is a collection of certain tropes, such as robots and space travel; in that case, a history of science fiction would trace the depictions of robots and space travel over time, and you'll see some pictures like that in this book. Other people say that a genre is the way publishers choose to market certain works; in that case, a history of science fiction would focus on the publishing industry, and there is definitely coverage of magazines like *Astounding* and *New Worlds* in this book.

But my favorite way to think about genre is this: a genre is a conversation. It's a conversation that takes place between authors and readers and extends over decades. Throughout the history of literature, there have been many conversations taking place simultaneously, some that overlap and some that remain distinct, and those are genres. A work belongs to a genre to the extent that it can be understood as participating in that genre's conversation. A novel is science fiction when it's engaged with the conversation that is science fiction.

And that's what you'll see most of all in this book: imagined conversations between the major figures of science fiction. H.G. Wells never actually met Judith Merril the way this book depicts, but both of those writers were, at different times, participants in the same literary conversation. Isaac Asimov and Robert Heinlein never said the things this book depicts them saying (although they did actually know each other), but that's not important; what's important is that they were engaged in a grander conversation, offering arguments and counter-arguments with the short stories and novels they wrote. And even if new writers entering the field today haven't read Asimov and Heinlein, they are joining a conversation that was shaped by them. This doesn't imply agreement with those older writers, because conversation allows for heated debate. Those new writers might shift the conversation in an entirely new direction, but their work can still be understood as a response to what older writers wrote.

And that's why I always describe myself as a science-fiction writer: because these are the authors and books that my work is in dialogue with. Because science fiction is the conversation that I have always strived to be a participant in, and it's the one I want to keep being a participant in.

TED CHIANG's first collection, Stories of Your Life and Others, *has been translated into twenty-one languages, and the title story was the basis for the Oscar-nominated film* Arrival *starring Amy Adams. His second collection,* Exhalation, *was chosen by* The New York Times *as one of the 10 Best Books of 2019.*

Bookseller, author, historian, editor, and speaker on the history of imaginary literatures, **Xavier Dollo** is a lover of fiction, which he likes to publish (*Cycle de Lanmeur* through Ad Astra, *Dominium Mundi* through Critic) and to write (the novel *American Fays* and for the anthologies Alone and Les Créateurs) as much as he does to read. He has won numerous awards for his work , including the Grand Prix de l'Imaginaire (as a publisher), the Rosny senior (for his short story "Les Tiges"), and the Prix Imaginales (for the collection *Chuchoteurs du Dragon & Other Whispers* (2019, Elenya).

In recent years, he has refocused his literary activity on writing in short form, publishing for free the Apocalyptic Suites series on the blogsite gehathomas.wordpress.com. In 2020, his SF planet opera "Under the Shadow of the Stars" was released in the collection *Hélios des Moutons Électriques*.

Djibril Morissette-Phan is a comic book illustrator from Quebec. He began his career in 2014 after completing his studies in animation. Mainly active in American comics, he has worked on notable titles such as *All-New Wolverine*, *X-Men: Gold*, and *Star-Lord* at Marvel. In 2016, he teamed up with Canadian author Jim Zub to create the Hollywood horror series *Glitterbomb*, published by Image Comics. In 2018, he joined Tristan Roulot to complete *Crypto monnaie*, his first project published in Europe, by Le Lombard. Aside from comics, Djibril also maintains an art practice and has had some of his work featured in various exhibitions.

Principal Art Sources for the Original French Language Edition:

The Science Fiction Internet Database, mine bibliographique. Youtube, various film clips. SFE: The Encyclopedia of Science Fiction. Internet Archive. NooSFere. The university magazine ReS Futurae. France Culture podcasts.

Histoire de la Science-Fiction moderne, Jacques Sadoul, J'ai Lu. *Encyclopedia of Science Fiction,* CIL. *Le Sciencefictionnaire,* Stan Barets, Denoël. *Encyclopédie de l'utopie, des voyages extraordinaires et de la science-fiction,* Pierre Versins. *Rétrofictions,* Joseph Altairac and Guy Costes, Encrage. Les revues françaises: *Bifrost, Galaxies, Fiction, Europe, Le Magazine littéraire, Science-Fiction, Futura, Science-Fiction Magazine. Dimension Espagne,* edited by Sylvie Miller, Rivière Blanche. *étoiles rouges,* Patrice Lajoye, Piranha. *Les anthologies Livres d'or de la SF,* Pocket. *Les Faiseurs d'univers,* Donald Wolheim, Robert Laffont. *La Science-Fiction américaine,* Léon Stover, Aubier Montaigne. *Moi, Asimov,* Isaac Asimov, Folio. *La Science-Fiction en France dans les années 50,* Francis Saint-Martin, Les Moutons Électriques. *Astounding,* Alec Nevala-Lee, Dey Street books. *Billion Year Spree,* Brian Aldiss, Doubleday.

PROLOGUE: The Crooked House.

HELLO?

IS ANYONE HOME?

THE HOUSE IS EMPTY. THERE IS NO INFORMATION TO BE GLEANED HERE. WE ARE DONE BEFORE WE HAVE EVEN STARTED.
NOT NECESSARILY. THINK OF THIS NOT AS A HOUSE...
...BUT AS AN ANTECHAMBER.
THESE ARE TELEPORTATION CONTROLS. THEY APPEAR TO BE PRE-SET. SHALL I?
IS YOUR THIRST FOR KNOWLEDGE SATED?
HARDLY.
KLIK
MY BOLTS ARE QUIVERING! HERE WE GO!

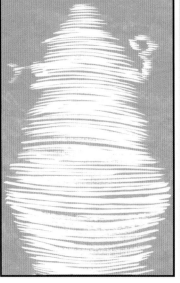

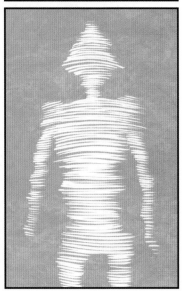

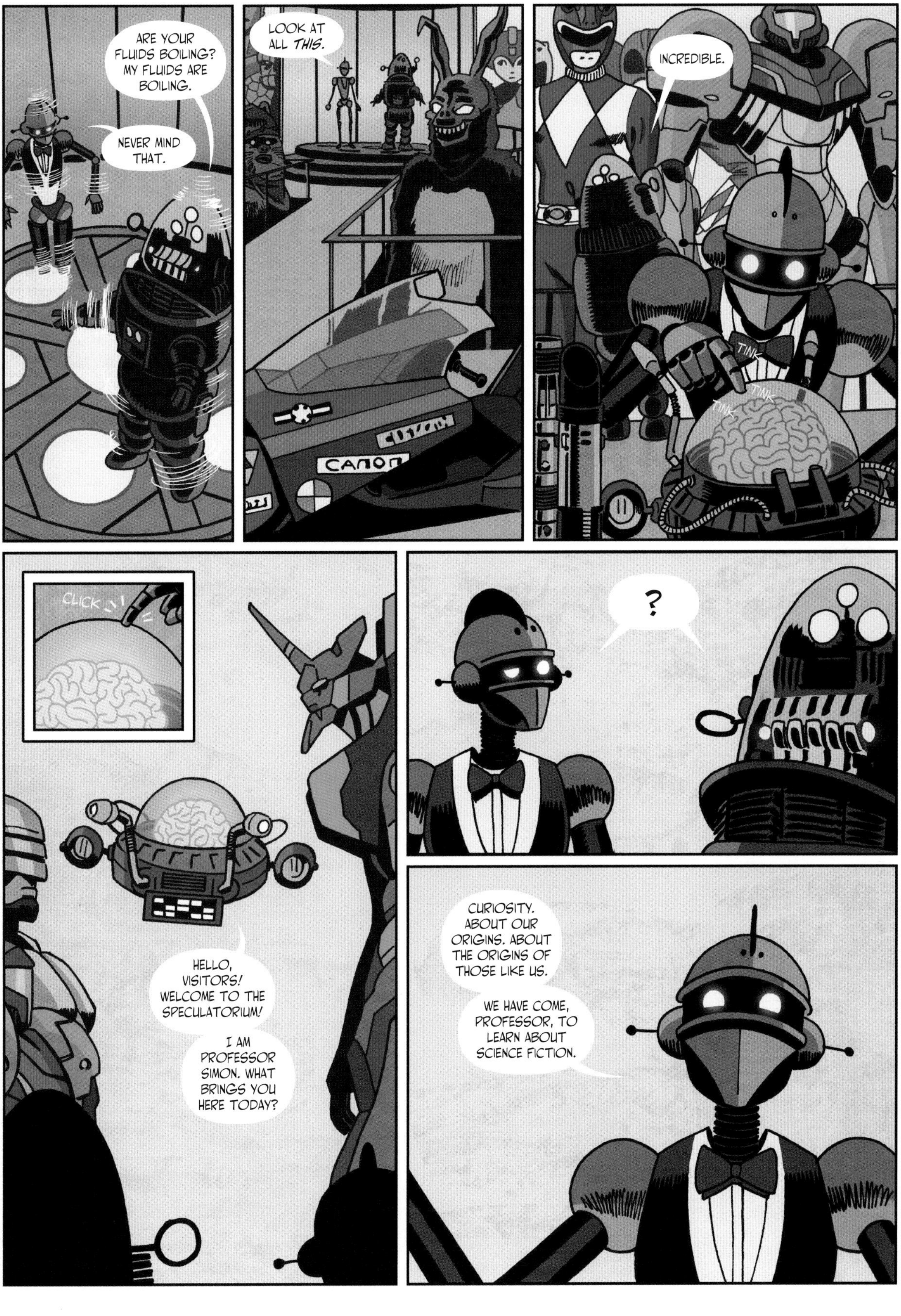
ARE YOUR FLUIDS BOILING? MY FLUIDS ARE BOILING.
NEVER MIND THAT.
LOOK AT ALL *THIS*.
INCREDIBLE.
TINK
TINK
TINK
CLICK
HELLO, VISITORS! WELCOME TO THE SPECULATORIUM!
I AM PROFESSOR SIMON. WHAT BRINGS YOU HERE TODAY?
?
CURIOSITY. ABOUT OUR ORIGINS. ABOUT THE ORIGINS OF THOSE LIKE US.
WE HAVE COME, PROFESSOR, TO LEARN ABOUT SCIENCE FICTION.

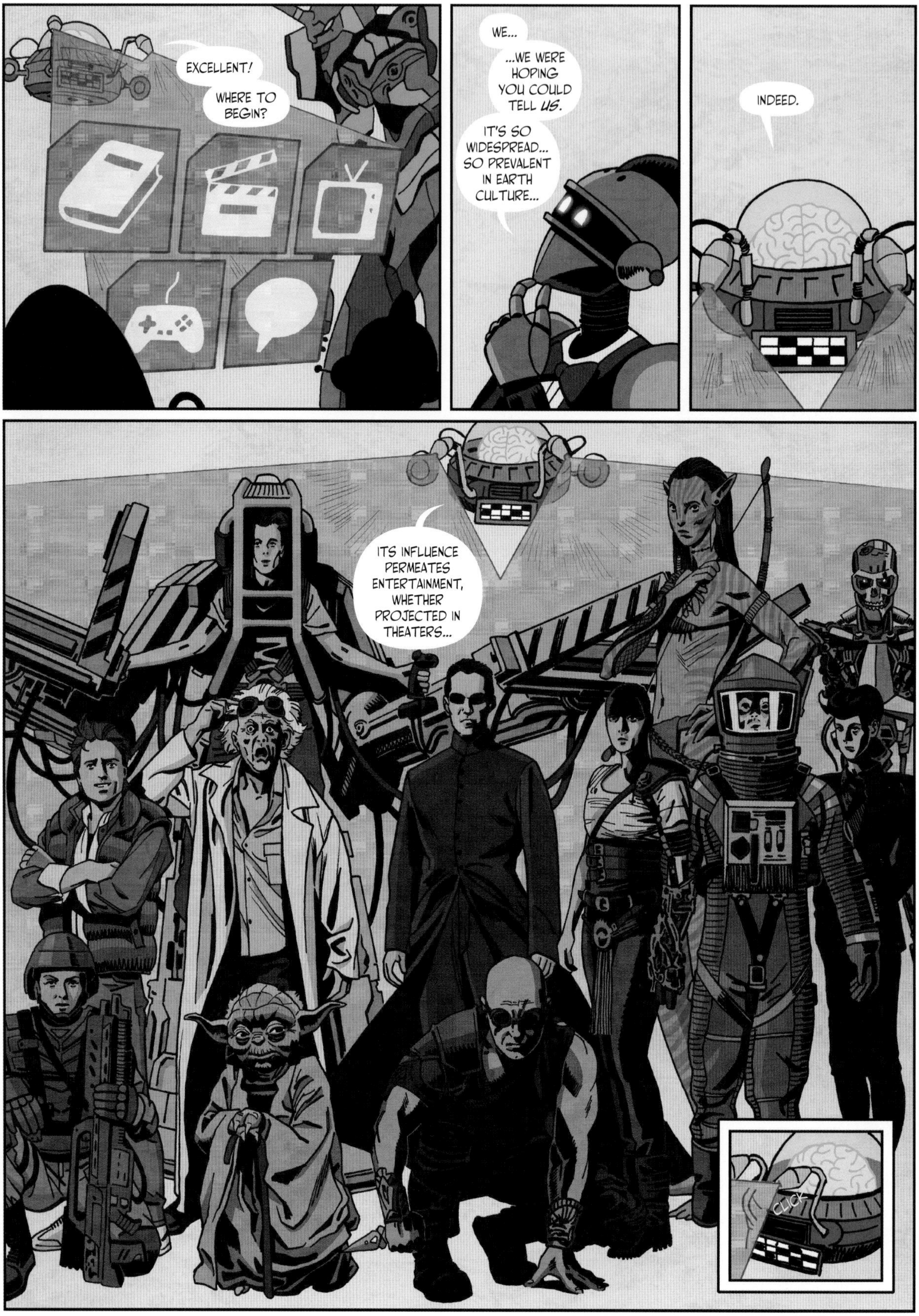
EXCELLENT!
WHERE TO BEGIN?
WE...
...WE WERE HOPING YOU COULD TELL US.
IT'S SO WIDESPREAD... SO PREVALENT IN EARTH CULTURE...
INDEED.
ITS INFLUENCE PERMEATES ENTERTAINMENT, WHETHER PROJECTED IN THEATERS...
CLICK

...OR STREAMED TO MORE INTIMATE SCREENS AND PERSONAL DEVICES.

IS THAT A...

OH MY!

ITS PRESENCE CAN BE FOUND IN OTHER, LESS NARRATIVE-DRIVEN MEDIA, YES?

SUCH AS VIDEOGAMES?

ABSOLUTELY. DO YOU RECALL *SPACE INVADERS*, RELEASED IN 1978? OR *SPACEWAR!*? *ASTEROIDS, PHOENIX, STARGATE? TRON?*

I LOVED *TRON.*

WHICH BEGAT WHICH, THEN? OR ARE THERE OLDER EXAMPLES OF THE MEDIUM?

PICTORAL LITERATURE, PERHAPS?

AH, YES! COMIC BOOKS AND NEWSPAPER STRIPS!

SUPERMAN AND BUCK ROGERS IN THE UNITED STATES... BLAKE & MORTIMER IN BELGIUM...DAN DARE IN BRITAIN...

...OR THE MANGA OF JAPAN, LIKE THOSE OF OSAMU TEZUKA, CREATOR OF PHOENIX AND ASTRO BOY!

IS THAT, THEN, WHERE SCIENCE FICTION ORIGINATED?

HARDLY, MY FRIEND.

WE MUST GO BACK FURTHER. MUCH FURTHER.

BEREFT OF COLOR AND SPECIAL EFFECTS, WITHOUT IMAGES AND SOUND, SCIENCE FICTION BEGAN WITH THE SIMPLE WRITTEN WORD.

WITH LITERATURE SPUN BY HISTORY'S MOST FANTASTIC WRITERS, WITHOUT WHOM NONE OF WHAT I HAVE SHOWN YOU COULD HAVE EXISTED.

HERE. LET ME SHOW YOU.

AND PREPARE TO BE AMAZED.

The origins of Science Fiction. From the *Odyssey* to *Frankenstein*--from ancient times to the early 19th century.

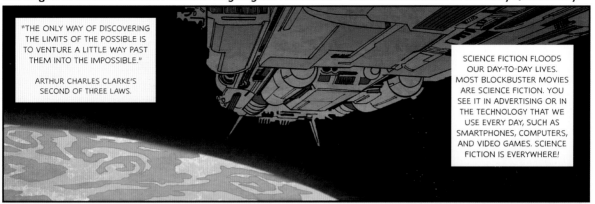

"THE ONLY WAY OF DISCOVERING THE LIMITS OF THE POSSIBLE IS TO VENTURE A LITTLE WAY PAST THEM INTO THE IMPOSSIBLE."

ARTHUR CHARLES CLARKE'S SECOND OF THREE LAWS.

SCIENCE FICTION FLOODS OUR DAY-TO-DAY LIVES. MOST BLOCKBUSTER MOVIES ARE SCIENCE FICTION. YOU SEE IT IN ADVERTISING OR IN THE TECHNOLOGY THAT WE USE EVERY DAY, SUCH AS SMARTPHONES, COMPUTERS, AND VIDEO GAMES. SCIENCE FICTION IS EVERYWHERE!

ARTHUR C. CLARKE, ONE OF THE MOST FAMOUS SCIENCE-FICTION AUTHORS OF THE 20TH CENTURY, SAID THAT, "WHEN A DISTINGUISHED BUT ELDERLY SCIENTIST STATES THAT SOMETHING IS POSSIBLE, HE IS ALMOST CERTAINLY RIGHT. WHEN HE STATES THAT SOMETHING IS IMPOSSIBLE, HE IS VERY PROBABLY WRONG."

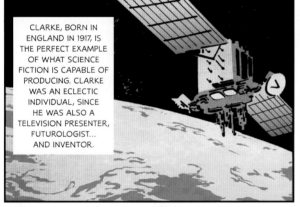

CLARKE, BORN IN ENGLAND IN 1917, IS THE PERFECT EXAMPLE OF WHAT SCIENCE FICTION IS CAPABLE OF PRODUCING. CLARKE WAS AN ECLECTIC INDIVIDUAL, SINCE HE WAS ALSO A TELEVISION PRESENTER, FUTUROLOGIST... AND INVENTOR.

CLARKE INSPIRED THE FIRST GEOSTATIONARY SATELLITE, THEN IN HIS NOVEL *THE FOUNTAINS OF PARADISE,* HE BROUGHT THE THEORY OF THE SPACE ELEVATOR BACK INTO FASHION. CURRENTLY BEING DEVELOPED IN JAPAN, IT IS SCHEDULED TO GO INTO OPERATION BY 2050!

I ALSO INFLUENCED MODERN CINEMA AS THE AUTHOR OF *THE SENTINEL,* THE STORY THAT GREW INTO THE SCRIPT FOR STANLEY KUBRICK'S CULT FILM *2001: A SPACE ODYSSEY,* RELEASED IN 1968.

RIGHT, HAL?

LISTEN, ARTHUR, I CAN SEE YOU ARE BEING STRONGLY AFFECTED BY YOUR EGO. I HONESTLY BELIEVE THAT YOU SHOULD GET A GRIP ON YOURSELF AND TAKE A TRANQUILIZER.

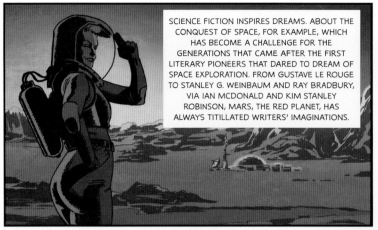

SCIENCE FICTION INSPIRES DREAMS. ABOUT THE CONQUEST OF SPACE, FOR EXAMPLE, WHICH HAS BECOME A CHALLENGE FOR THE GENERATIONS THAT CAME AFTER THE FIRST LITERARY PIONEERS THAT DARED TO DREAM OF SPACE EXPLORATION. FROM GUSTAVE LE ROUGE TO STANLEY G. WEINBAUM AND RAY BRADBURY, VIA IAN MCDONALD AND KIM STANLEY ROBINSON, MARS, THE RED PLANET, HAS ALWAYS TITILLATED WRITERS' IMAGINATIONS.

AN AVID READER OF SCIENCE FICTION, ELON MUSK, THE CEO OF TESLA, HAS WILD IDEAS OF CONQUERING MARS. HE OFTEN MAKES REFERENCE TO THE BOOKS THAT INFLUENCED HIM, ESPECIALLY ROBERT A. HEINLEIN, RECOMMENDING HIS LIBERTARIAN NOVEL *THE MOON IS A HARSH MISTRESS,* AND ISAAC ASIMOV, WHOSE *FOUNDATION* SERIES LEFT A LASTING IMPRESSION ON HIM.

FOR KIM STANLEY ROBINSON, AUTHOR OF THE *MARS* TRILOGY, ELON MUSK'S PLANS ARE "SORT OF THE 1920S' SCIENCE-FICTION CLICHÉ OF THE BOY WHO BUILDS A ROCKET TO THE MOON IN HIS BACK YARD." MADMAN OR GENIUS? TIME WILL TELL! SO, HOW ABOUT MEETING UP ON MARS?

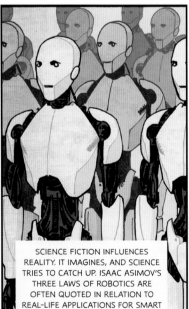

SCIENCE FICTION INFLUENCES REALITY. IT IMAGINES, AND SCIENCE TRIES TO CATCH UP. ISAAC ASIMOV'S THREE LAWS OF ROBOTICS ARE OFTEN QUOTED IN RELATION TO REAL-LIFE APPLICATIONS FOR SMART HOMES AND ROBOTS.

THE FACT THAT THE WORD "ASTRONAUTICS" EXISTS AT ALL IS BECAUSE IT WAS COINED BY THE AUTHOR JOSEPH HENRI HONORÉ BOEX, BETTER KNOWN AS AÎNÉ, J.-H. ROSNY, AUTHOR OF *THE QUEST FOR FIRE.*

AND HOW ABOUT TELEPORTATION? IT DOESN'T EXIST YET? BUT A TEAM OF CHINESE SCIENTISTS HAS ALREADY TELEPORTED A PHOTON UP TO A SATELLITE AT AN ALTITUDE OF 500 KM! BETTER GET READY, BECAUSE WE'RE ABOUT TO BEAM YOU UP INTO THE HISTORY OF SCIENCE FICTION!

IT HAS ALWAYS BEEN DIFFICULT TO PINPOINT EXACTLY WHEN SCIENCE FICTION FIRST APPEARED. WE SHALL SEE THAT IT EMERGED, AS WE KNOW IT TODAY, ALONGSIDE THE INDUSTRIAL REVOLUTION. BUT IDEAS FOR FANTASTIC STORIES HAVE ALWAYS BEEN GERMINATING IN THE HUMAN MIND AND CAN BE FOUND ALL THROUGHOUT HISTORY, E.G. *THE EPIC OF GILGAMESH*, WHICH DATES BACK TO ALMOST 2000 YEARS BC.

OF COURSE, LIKE ALL LITERATURE, SCIENCE FICTION IS STEEPED IN THE INFLUENCE OF HOMER'S *ODYSSEY* (8TH CENTURY BC), WITH ULYSSES' ADVENTURES HAVING BEEN CONSTANTLY REWORKED ACROSS THE AGES.

ARISTOPHANES AND XENOPHON TOUCHED ON THE FANTASTIC BACK IN THE FOURTH CENTURY BC. THEN, IN THE SECOND CENTURY BC, LUCIAN OF SAMOSATA WROTE AN AMUSING TALE, *A TRUE STORY*, ABOUT A VOYAGE FROM THE EARTH TO THE MOON-- CERTAINLY THE FIRST OF ITS KIND.

BUT NOT THE LAST, AS WE CAN SEE IN JULES VERNE'S *FROM THE EARTH TO THE MOON* (1865), GEORGES MÉLIÈS' FILM *A TRIP TO THE MOON* (1902), HERGÉ'S FAMOUS TINTIN COMIC BOOKS *DESTINATION MOON* AND *EXPLORERS ON THE MOON* (1953 AND 1954), AND SO MANY MORE...

I, CYRANO DE BERGERAC, ALSO TOOK A TRIP TO THE MOON. IN 1650, I PENNED *COMICAL HISTORY OF THE STATES AND EMPIRES OF THE MOON*, A SATIRE OF MY TIMES, IN WHICH I SET OFF TO CLOWN AROUND ON THE MOON AND MET, AMONGST OTHERS, ADAM AND EVE, SELENITES, AND THE DEVIL HIMSELF! THEY USED VERSE AS CURRENCY THERE!

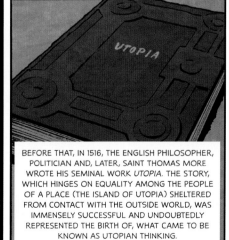

BEFORE THAT, IN 1516, THE ENGLISH PHILOSOPHER, POLITICIAN AND, LATER, SAINT THOMAS MORE WROTE HIS SEMINAL WORK *UTOPIA*. THE STORY, WHICH HINGES ON EQUALITY AMONG THE PEOPLE OF A PLACE (THE ISLAND OF UTOPIA) SHELTERED FROM CONTACT WITH THE OUTSIDE WORLD, WAS IMMENSELY SUCCESSFUL AND UNDOUBTEDLY REPRESENTED THE BIRTH OF, WHAT CAME TO BE KNOWN AS UTOPIAN THINKING.

AS LONG AS THERE IS ANY PROPERTY, AND WHILE MONEY IS THE STANDARD OF ALL OTHER THINGS, I CANNOT THINK THAT A NATION CAN BE GOVERNED EITHER JUSTLY OR HAPPILY.

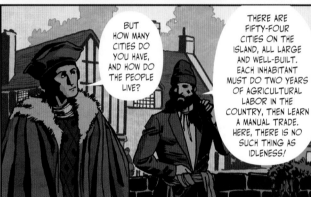

BUT HOW MANY CITIES DO YOU HAVE, AND HOW DO THE PEOPLE LIVE?

THERE ARE FIFTY-FOUR CITIES ON THE ISLAND, ALL LARGE AND WELL-BUILT. EACH INHABITANT MUST DO TWO YEARS OF AGRICULTURAL LABOR IN THE COUNTRY, THEN LEARN A MANUAL TRADE. HERE, THERE IS NO SUCH THING AS IDLENESS!

BUT DO YOU HAVE NOBLEMEN AND INTELLECTUALS?

SINCE YOU MENTION NOBLEMEN, THE CHIEF CAUSE OF MISERY AMONG YOU IS THE EXCESSIVE NUMBER OF NOBLEMEN THAT ARE IDLE AS DRONES AND SUBSIST ON OTHER MEN'S LABOR, ON THE LABOR OF THEIR TENANT FARMERS, WHOM THEY PARE TO THE QUICK.

FOR POLITICAL REASONS, THOMAS MORE WAS ACCUSED OF HIGH TREASON AGAINST THE QUEEN, ANNE BOLEYN. HE TOLD THE OFFICIAL WHO HELPED HIM MOUNT THE STEPS TO THE SCAFFOLD TO BE EXECUTED...

I PRAY YOU, MASTER LIEUTENANT, SIR, SEE ME SAFE UP. AS FOR MY COMING DOWN, LET ME SHIFT FOR MYSELF...

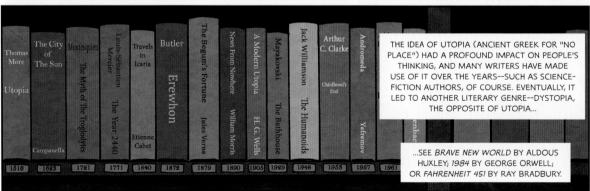

THE IDEA OF UTOPIA (ANCIENT GREEK FOR "NO PLACE") HAD A PROFOUND IMPACT ON PEOPLE'S THINKING, AND MANY WRITERS HAVE MADE USE OF IT OVER THE YEARS--SUCH AS SCIENCE-FICTION AUTHORS, OF COURSE. EVENTUALLY, IT LED TO ANOTHER LITERARY GENRE--DYSTOPIA, THE OPPOSITE OF UTOPIA...

...SEE *BRAVE NEW WORLD* BY ALDOUS HUXLEY; *1984* BY GEORGE ORWELL; OR *FAHRENHEIT 451* BY RAY BRADBURY.

OTHER MAJOR WORKS FOLLOWED, WHICH HELPED FLESH OUT THE SCIENCE-FICTION GENRE, FOR EXAMPLE *GULLIVER'S TRAVELS* BY JONATHAN SWIFT IN 1726.

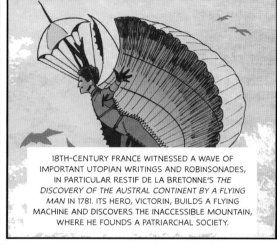

18TH-CENTURY FRANCE WITNESSED A WAVE OF IMPORTANT UTOPIAN WRITINGS AND ROBINSONADES, IN PARTICULAR RESTIF DE LA BRETONNE'S *THE DISCOVERY OF THE AUSTRAL CONTINENT BY A FLYING MAN* IN 1781. ITS HERO, VICTORIN, BUILDS A FLYING MACHINE AND DISCOVERS THE INACCESSIBLE MOUNTAIN, WHERE HE FOUNDS A PATRIARCHAL SOCIETY.

OH CHRISTINE, WILL YOU MARRY ME? I'M SO IN LOVE WITH YOU!

NO, VICTORIN, YOU ARE BUT A COMMONER, WHILST I AM OF NOBLE BIRTH. THERE CAN NEVER BE ANY LOVE BETWEEN US!

VICTORIN BECOMES DESPOTIC AND LEAVES TO CONQUER ANOTHER ISLAND, THAT OF THE MEN-OF-THE-NIGHT. HERE, RESTIF DE LA BRETONNE IMPLICITLY LAUNCHES INTO A HARSH CRITIQUE OF COLONIALISM!

IN THE EARLY 1800S, AS THE INDUSTRIAL REVOLUTION WAS IN FULL SWING, ANOTHER REVOLUTION--THAT OF SCIENCE FICTION-- WAS ABOUT TO BEGIN IN BRITAIN...

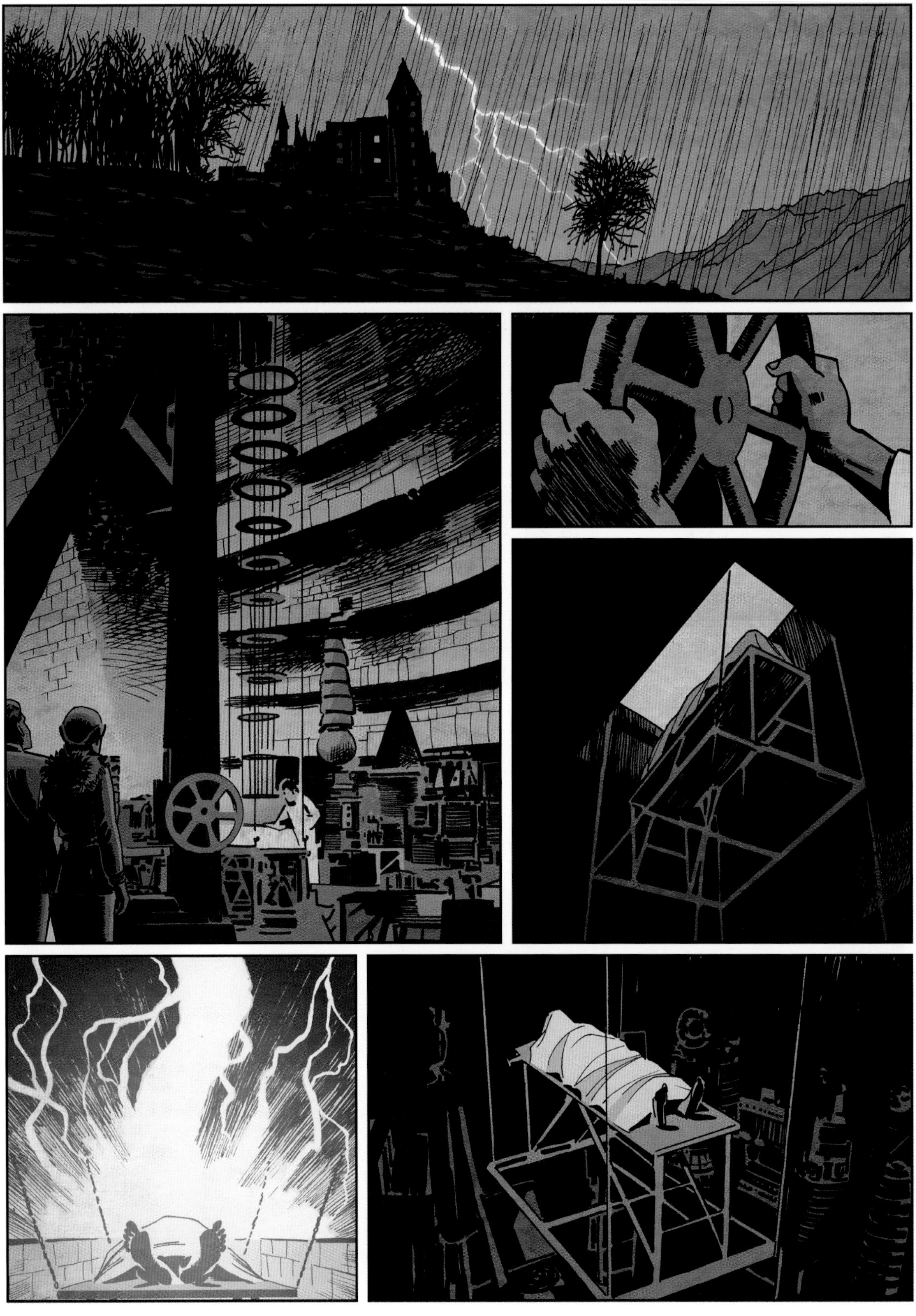

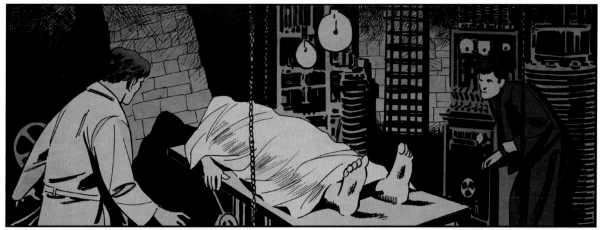

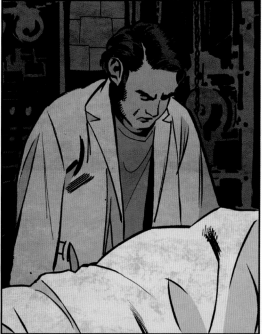

IT'S ALIVE!

IT'S ALIVE!

SUMMER 1817. ONE MARY SHELLEY WAS WRITING THE WORDS "THE END" ON A MANUSCRIPT FOR A NOVEL TITLED *FRANKENSTEIN; OR, THE MODERN PROMETHEUS*. PUBLISHED IN JANUARY 1818, HER STORY IS OFTEN REGARDED AS THE FIRST MAJOR WORK OF SCIENCE FICTION.

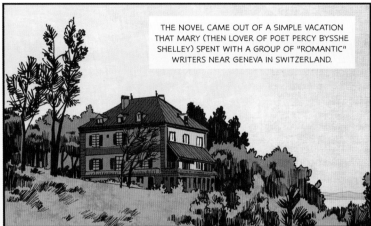

THE NOVEL CAME OUT OF A SIMPLE VACATION THAT MARY (THEN LOVER OF POET PERCY BYSSHE SHELLEY) SPENT WITH A GROUP OF "ROMANTIC" WRITERS NEAR GENEVA IN SWITZERLAND.

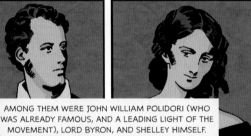

AMONG THEM WERE JOHN WILLIAM POLIDORI (WHO WAS ALREADY FAMOUS, AND A LEADING LIGHT OF THE MOVEMENT), LORD BYRON, AND SHELLEY HIMSELF.

THE SUMMER OF 1816 HAD BEEN PARTICULARLY RAINY AND DARK. TO OVERCOME THE GENERAL GLOOM, PERCY SHELLEY SUGGESTED AN IDEA TO KEEP HIS FRIENDS OCCUPIED...

HOW BORING! WILL THIS RAIN EVER STOP, DO YOU THINK?

SUCH A SOMBER ATMOSPHERE IS HIGHLY CONDUCIVE TO WRITING A FEW GHOST STORIES. WHAT DO YOU SAY, MY FRIENDS?

WHAT AN EXCELLENT IDEA!

WHY NOT?

IN 1814, MARY IS SAID TO HAVE VISITED CASTLE FRANKENSTEIN IN MÜHLTAL, GERMANY, WITH MARY JANE CLAIRMONT AND PERCY SHELLEY.

WHAT A MAGNIFICENT FORTRESS, FULL OF CHARM AND MYSTERY...

THIS WAS THE HOME OF THE PHILOSOPHER AND ALCHEMIST JOHANN KONRAD DIPPEL, WHO WAS ACCUSED OF HERESY. HIS WORK LED TO THE ACCIDENTAL INVENTION OF A NEW PIGMENT, PRUSSIAN BLUE, AND--

AND?

THEY SAY THAT DIPPEL SUBSCRIBED TO VERY ODD IDEAS...

OH, DO TELL US MORE!

I MEAN TO SAY HE WAS SEEKING THE ELIXIR OF LIFE...

THE ELIXIR OF LIFE?

...THAT WOULD ALLOW HIM TO LIVE FOREVER. AND TO THAT END, HE HAD NO QUALMS ABOUT PERFORMING EXPERIMENTS ON ANIMALS. HE BELIEVED THAT A PERSON'S SOUL COULD BE TRANSFERRED INTO THE BODY OF ANOTHER.

IN REFERENCE TO A LETTER SHE HAD RECEIVED FROM JACOB GRIMM, WHOSE FAIRY TALES SHE HAD BEEN TRANSLATING, IT WAS MARY JANE CLAIRMONT WHO MENTIONED DIPPEL TO HER STEPDAUGHTER, MARY.

THE FACT THAT THEY HAD VISITED THE REGION IN 1814 WOULD SEEM TO IMPLY THAT CASTLE FRANKENSTEIN AND ITS ERSTWHILE RESIDENT, JOHANN DIPPEL, MAY HAVE SERVED AS INSPIRATION FOR THE PIONEERING NOVEL.

WE ALSO KNOW THAT, DURING THEIR STAY AT VILLA DIODATI, MARY AND HER FRIENDS HAD TALKED ABOUT LUIGI GALVANI, A SCIENTIST STUDYING THE EFFECTS OF ELECTRICAL CURRENTS ON ANIMALS AND ORGANIC TISSUE.

A MORE RECENT THEORY ASSERTS THAT MARY SHELLEY MAY HAVE BEEN INSPIRED BY FRANÇOIS-FÉLIX NOGARET'S FRENCH NOVEL *THE MIRROR OF PRESENT EVENTS* FROM 1790, WHICH FEATURES AN INVENTOR NAMED "FRANKÉNSTEIN" WHO CONSTRUCTS A FLUTE-PLAYING AUTOMATON TO WOO A YOUNG LADY.

SHELLEY INTERWOVE HER RATIONALITY WITH THE FANTASTIC. AT THE TIME, THE MOST FRIGHTENING ASPECT OF HER STORY WAS PROBABLY THE REALISM OF "REANIMATING" A CADAVER BY SCIENTIFIC MEANS.

WE OFTEN IMAGINE *FRANKENSTEIN* TO BE A FANTASY TALE WHEN, IN FACT, IT IS THE VERY FIRST GENUINELY STRIKING STORY OF PURE SCIENCE FICTION. THERE IS NOTHING UNREAL ABOUT THE BIRTH OF THE CREATURE, WHICH IS EXPLAINED AWAY BY SCIENCE AND THE MIRACLE OF ELECTRICITY...

IN ENGLAND, A CERTAIN HERBERT GEORGE WELLS AND HIS DOCTOR MOREAU WOULD HAVE AGREED...

EVEN THOUGH IT WAS YET TO BE KNOWN AS SUCH, SCIENCE FICTION HAD BEEN BORN!

Jules Verne, the visionary pioneer of science. France, 19th century.

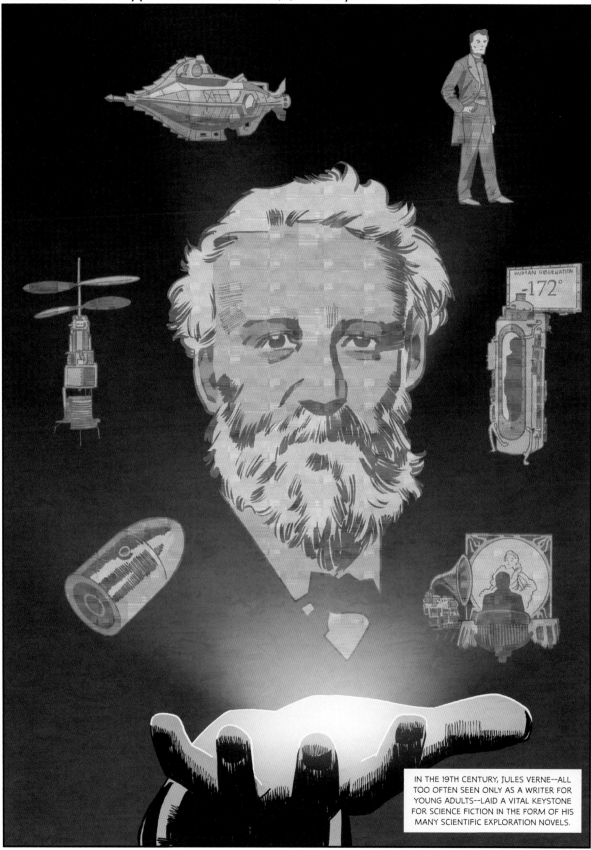

IN THE 19TH CENTURY, JULES VERNE--ALL TOO OFTEN SEEN ONLY AS A WRITER FOR YOUNG ADULTS--LAID A VITAL KEYSTONE FOR SCIENCE FICTION IN THE FORM OF HIS MANY SCIENTIFIC EXPLORATION NOVELS.

FEBRUARY 8, 1828...

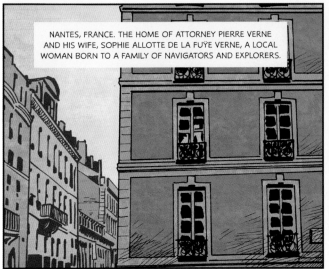

NANTES, FRANCE. THE HOME OF ATTORNEY PIERRE VERNE AND HIS WIFE, SOPHIE ALLOTTE DE LA FUŸE VERNE, A LOCAL WOMAN BORN TO A FAMILY OF NAVIGATORS AND EXPLORERS.

THEIR SON, JULES GABRIEL, ARRIVED FEBRUARY 8, 1828, HIS PARENTS UNAWARE THAT THEIR LITTLE BOY WOULD GROW TO CHANGE THE WORLD.

THE FIRST OF FIVE CHILDREN IN THE VERNE HOUSEHOLD, JULES SPENT MOST OF HIS CHILDHOOD CLOSE TO NANTES. THIS WAS NOT TO LAST. WANDERLUST, IT WOULD SEEM, RAN IN THE FAMILY.

JULES ATTENDED THE SAINT-STANISLAS CATHOLIC SCHOOL, MINGLING WITH CHILDREN WHO CAME FROM A WIDE VARIETY OF PLACES WHICH GAVE HIM A STRONG URGE TO TRAVEL FROM AN EARLY AGE. AND, INDEED, THE YOUNG VERNE SOON DISPLAYED A PASSION FOR ADVENTURE.

LEGEND HAS IT THAT, AGED 11, JULES VERNE ATTEMPTED TO SET SAIL AS A CABIN BOY ON A SHIP LEAVING FOR THE INDIES. HIS FATHER WAS SAID TO HAVE TAKEN A STEAMER IN PURSUIT AND CAUGHT UP WITH HIM IN PAIMBOEUF. OR SO THE STORY GOES...

JULES TOOK HIS FINAL EXAMS IN RHETORIC AND PHILOSOPHY IN RENNES IN 1846 AFTER COMPLETING HIS SCHOOLING AT PORT ROYAL AND GRADUATING WITH A 60-70% PASS RATE. HE WOULD BE CONSIDERED AN AVERAGE STUDENT NOWADAYS, BUT HIS EXAMS WERE FAR HARDER THAN TODAY'S.

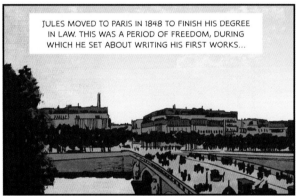

JULES MOVED TO PARIS IN 1848 TO FINISH HIS DEGREE IN LAW. THIS WAS A PERIOD OF FREEDOM, DURING WHICH HE SET ABOUT WRITING HIS FIRST WORKS...

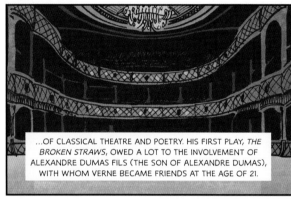

...OF CLASSICAL THEATRE AND POETRY. HIS FIRST PLAY, *THE BROKEN STRAWS*, OWED A LOT TO THE INVOLVEMENT OF ALEXANDRE DUMAS FILS (THE SON OF ALEXANDRE DUMAS), WITH WHOM VERNE BECAME FRIENDS AT THE AGE OF 21.

WHILE WRITING STORIES AND ARTICLES FOR THE MAGAZINE MUSÉE DES FAMILLES (THE FAMILY MUSEUM), VERNE BEGAN TO ENVISION A NEW KIND OF NOVEL, ONE BASED HEAVILY ON TECHNOLOGY.

IT WAS THE DAWN OF THE SECOND INDUSTRIAL REVOLUTION, WHICH BEGAN AROUND 1870, AND VERNE WOULD SOON BECOME THE INADVERTENT HERALD OF THIS NEW AGE.

HE WAS NOT NECESSARILY PREDESTINED TO BECOME THE "NOVELIST OF SCIENCE," AS HE HIMSELF ADMITTED:

I CANNOT SAY THAT I WAS PARTICULARLY TAKEN WITH SCIENCE. INDEED, I NEVER HAD BEEN; THAT IS TO SAY, I HAVE NEVER PRACTICALLY STUDIED OR EXPERIMENTED IN SCIENCE.

VERNE DID ADORE MACHINES, HOWEVER, AND THAT LOVE FOR TECHNOLOGY NEVER DIMINISHED. IN AN 1894 INTERVIEW, HE SAID, "TODAY I HAVE STILL AS MUCH PLEASURE IN WATCHING A STEAM-ENGINE OF A FINE LOCOMOTIVE AT WORK AS I HAVE IN CONTEMPLATING A PICTURE BY RAPHAEL..."

IN 1857 VERNE, THEN A 28-YEAR-OLD LAWYER, MARRIED HONORINE DE VIANE, A YOUNG WIDOW. THE NEWLYWEDS HAD A VERY COMFORTABLE LIFESTYLE THAT LEFT JULES WITH PLENTY OF TIME TO WRITE.

BUT WHAT ABOUT? HIS MEETING WITH FELIX NADAR IN 1860 TURNED OUT TO BE A DECISIVE ENCOUNTER. NADAR WAS A PHOTOGRAPHER, WRITER, CARICATURIST AND AERONAUT, WHO WAS BEST KNOWN FOR HIS INTEREST IN HOT-AIR BALLOONS AND AEROSTATS.

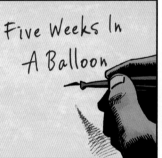

HE SERVED AS INSPIRATION FOR A CHARACTER IN VERNE'S NOVEL *FIVE WEEKS IN A BALLOON*. THAT ADVENTURE FEATURED A HERO NAMED MICHEL ARDAN, AN ANAGRAM OF THE PHOTOGRAPHER.

Five Weeks In A Balloon

AROUND THAT TIME, BETWEEN 1859 AND 1861, VERNE TRAVELED SCOTLAND AND SCANDINAVIA, WHICH GAVE HIM A WEALTH OF IDEAS FOR HIS EARLY WORKS.

IN 1861, ALFRED DE BRÉHAT, AN AUTHOR WHO IS LARGELY FORGOTTEN TODAY, HELPED JULES VERNE BY ARRANGING AN ABSOLUTELY CRUCIAL MEETING WITH PIERRE-JULES HETZEL. IT MARKED THE START OF A FRUITFUL COLLABORATION, THE LAUNCH OF HIS *VOYAGES EXTRAORDINAIRES*! A DEMANDING EDITOR AND PUBLISHER, HETZEL MADE VERNE WORK SO HARD THAT MANY OF HIS LETTERS WERE SIGNED, "YOUR BEAST OF BURDEN."

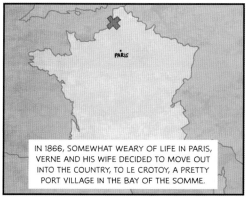

IN 1866, SOMEWHAT WEARY OF LIFE IN PARIS, VERNE AND HIS WIFE DECIDED TO MOVE OUT INTO THE COUNTRY, TO LE CROTOY, A PRETTY PORT VILLAGE IN THE BAY OF THE SOMME.

IT WAS THERE THAT HE PENNED ONE OF HIS BEST-KNOWN WORKS: *20,000 LEAGUES UNDER THE SEA*, SERIALIZED BETWEEN 1869 AND 1870.

LOCAL RUMORS HAVE LONG MAINTAINED THAT VERNE HID A MODEL OF THE NAUTILUS AWAY SOMEWHERE IN THE VILLAGE PORT, ALTHOUGH NOBODY HAS EVER FOUND IT. REGARDLESS, VERNE'S NOVEL FEATURING CAPTAIN NEMO AND THE NAUTILUS INSTANTLY WENT DOWN IN POPULAR LITERARY HISTORY AND INSPIRED MANY OTHER AUTHORS, SUCH AS PAUL D'IVOI (*CORSAIRE TRIPLEX*), AS WELL AS A NUMBER OF SCIENTISTS. IN 1931, THE POLAR EXPLORER SIR GEORGE HUBERT WILKINS LEASED A SUBMARINE THAT HE RECHRISTENED THE NAUTILUS.

VERNE PUBLISHED *JOURNEY TO THE CENTRE OF THE EARTH* IN 1864, WHICH WAS STRONGLY INSPIRED BY GEORGE SAND'S FANTASY NOVEL *LAURA: A JOURNEY INTO THE CRYSTAL*. IT CANNOT BE STRESSED ENOUGH JUST HOW PROUD VERNE WAS TO RECEIVE THE PRAISE OF FELLOW WRITERS HE ADMIRED. A LETTER FROM GEORGE SAND WAS ALSO HIS INSPIRATION FOR *20,000 LEAGUES UNDER THE SEA*.

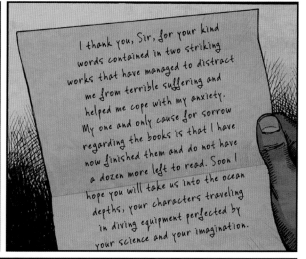

I thank you, Sir, for your kind words contained in two striking works that have managed to distract me from terrible suffering and helped me cope with my anxiety. My one and only cause for sorrow regarding the books is that I have now finished them and do not have a dozen more left to read. Soon I hope you will take us into the ocean depths, your characters traveling in diving equipment perfected by your science and your imagination.

WHILE NEMO IS STILL A LEGENDARY FIGURE, THE NAUTILUS HAS REMAINED A SYMBOL OF THE TECHNICAL PROGRESS FORESEEN BY VERNE. MUCH COPIED AND PARODIED, *20,000 LEAGUES UNDER THE SEA* WAS THE FIRST MAJOR UNDERWATER ADVENTURE STORY. IT HAS BEEN ADAPTED MANY TIMES, IN GRAPHIC NOVELS AND THE TELEVISION SERIES *SEAQUEST DSV* (1993-1996), AS WELL AS A NUMBER OF FILMS, NOTABLY THE RICHARD FLEISCHER VERSION FROM 1954, STARRING JAMES MASON AS CAPTAIN NEMO AND KIRK DOUGLAS AS THE HERO, NED LAND.

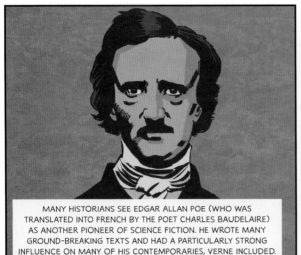

MANY HISTORIANS SEE EDGAR ALLAN POE (WHO WAS TRANSLATED INTO FRENCH BY THE POET CHARLES BAUDELAIRE) AS ANOTHER PIONEER OF SCIENCE FICTION. HE WROTE MANY GROUND-BREAKING TEXTS AND HAD A PARTICULARLY STRONG INFLUENCE ON MANY OF HIS CONTEMPORARIES, VERNE INCLUDED.

THIS POE TRULY IS A PURE GENIUS!

JULES VERNE'S NOVEL *AN ANTARCTIC MYSTERY* WAS WRITTEN AS A SEQUEL TO POE'S *THE NARRATIVE OF ARTHUR GORDON PYM OF NANTUCKET* AND BROUGHT THAT FANTASTIC TALE TO A RATIONAL CONCLUSION.

OCTOBER 5, THE GUN CLUB SALOON. THE CLUB'S PRESIDENT, IMPEY BARBICANE, ADDRESSES THE CROWD...

I ASK MYSELF WHETHER, IF SUFFICIENT APPARATUS COULD BE OBTAINED, IT MIGHT NOT BE POSSIBLE TO PROJECT A SHOT UP TO THE MOON?

BY INCONTROVERTIBLE CALCULATIONS, I FIND THAT A PROJECTILE ENDOWED WITH AN INITIAL VELOCITY OF 12,000 YARDS PER SECOND, AND AIMED AT THE MOON, MUST NECESSARILY REACH IT.

I HAVE THE HONOR, MY BRAVE COLLEAGUES, TO PROPOSE A TRIAL OF THIS LITTLE EXPERIMENT!

LATER...

LIKE I TOLD YOU, ARDAN, IT IS PERHAPS RESERVED FOR US TO BECOME THE COLUMBUSES OF THIS UNKNOWN WORLD!

AND I REPLIED THAT, DUE TO MY ABSOLUTE IGNORANCE OF THE GREAT LAWS WHICH GOVERN THE UNIVERSE, I DO NOT KNOW WHETHER THE WORLDS ARE INHABITED OR NOT. SINCE I DO NOT KNOW, I AM GOING TO SEE!

FROM 1865 TO 1870, JULES VERNE PUBLISHED TWO OF HIS MOST FAMOUS NOVELS, *FROM THE EARTH TO THE MOON* AND *ROUND THE MOON*, WHICH PRESENTED SOME HEROIC CHARACTERS THAT SEEMED RATHER UNUSUAL OR FRANKLY EVEN AHEAD OF THEIR TIME; NAMELY, ADVENTUROUS SCIENTISTS. THESE TWO NOVELS LEFT AN IMPRINT ON THEIR ERA, INFORMING H. G. WELLS, GEORGES MÉLIÈS, AND PERHAPS EVEN THE AMERICAN CONQUEST OF SPACE, WHICH LED TO THE MOON LANDING IN 1969, JUST OVER A HUNDRED YEARS LATER.

THE REFORM CLUB, LONDON. OCTOBER 2, 1872.

I WILL BET 20,000 POUNDS AGAINST ANYONE WHO WISHES THAT I WILL MAKE THE TOUR OF THE WORLD IN EIGHTY DAYS OR LESS; IN NINETEEN HUNDRED AND TWENTY HOURS, OR A HUNDRED AND FIFTEEN THOUSAND TWO HUNDRED MINUTES. DO YOU ACCEPT?

WE ACCEPT, FOGG!

GOOD! THE TRAIN LEAVES FOR DOVER AT 8:45. I WILL TAKE IT!

THIS VERY EVENING?

THIS VERY EVENING!

JULES VERNE MOVED TO HIS WIFE'S HOME CITY OF AMIENS, WHERE HE DIED ON MARCH 24, 1905. THIS WAS WHERE HE WROTE *AROUND THE WORLD IN EIGHTY DAYS*, WHICH INTRODUCED THE CELEBRATED PHILEAS FOGG. THE NOVEL ALLOWED VERNE TO ENLIST ALL TECHNOLOGICAL FORMS OF TRANSPORTATION FOR TRAVELING ON LAND, AT SEA, OR IN THE AIR. BASICALLY, HE OUTLINED THE DEVELOPMENT OF MODERN TRANSPORT.

IN TOTAL, HIS COLLABORATION WITH HETZEL RESULTED IN THE SIXTY-TWO NOVELS IN THE *VOYAGES EXTRAORDINAIRES* COLLECTION. SINCE NOT ALL WERE STRICTLY FUTURISTIC OR EVEN FANTASTIC, CAN THEY REALLY BE CONSIDERED SCIENCE FICTION? THOUGH SOME HAVE DISAGREED WITH THE LABEL, ANY OF HIS NOVELS THAT WERE LINKED TO SPECULATION REGARDING SCIENTIFIC DISCOVERIES INDEED CORRESPOND TO THE MUCH BROADER CONCEPT OF SPECULATIVE FICTION.

JULES VERNE

FOR EXAMPLE, *ROBUR THE CONQUEROR*, PUBLISHED IN 1886, TACKLED POSSIBLE TECHNICAL ADVANCES IN AVIATION.

BUT BEFORE THAT...

AMIENS, SEPTEMBER 28, 1873. THE AERONAUT EUGÈNE GODARD TAKES JULES VERNE UP IN HIS BALLOON...

WHAT AN HONOR TO BE ABOARD THE MÉTÉORE, DEAR EUGÈNE.

OH, COME NOW...THE HONOR IS ALL MINE.

BUT YOU SEE, THIS IS THE VERY FIRST TIME I'VE EVER RIDDEN IN A BALLOON...

EVERYTHING WILL GO SMOOTHLY. THE TRIP WILL ONLY LAST ABOUT TWENTY MINUTES, NOT EIGHTY DAYS!

WELL, I HOPE SO... I STILL HAVE A LOT OF WORK TO BE GETTING ON WITH!

FAVORABLY IMPRESSED BY HIS BALLOON FLIGHT, JULES VERNE WROTE A GLOWING LETTER TO THE EDITOR OF THE *JOURNAL D'AMIENS* (A FRENCH NEWSPAPER PUBLISHED IN AMIENS FROM 1857 TO 1869). IT WAS PUBLISHED UNDER THE TITLE *TWENTY-FOUR MINUTES IN A BALLOON.*

IN 1886, IN THE PAGES OF *ROBUR THE CONQUEROR*, VERNE INVENTED THE ALBATROSS, WHICH WAS ON A PAR WITH THE NAUTILUS. THIS GIANT FLYING MACHINE WAS EQUIPPED WITH SEVENTY-FOUR SUSPENSORY SCREWS AND TWO PROPELLING SCREWS, AND WAS PILOTED BY A NEMO OF THE AIR: ROBUR, A BRILLIANT ENGINEER WITH A BRAWNY PHYSIQUE.

...WHICH WE CAN CALL STREOPHORES, HELICOPTERS, ORNITHOPTERS --OR, IN IMITATION OF THE WORD "NEF," WHICH COMES FROM "NAVIS," CALL THEM FROM "AVIS," "EFS,"--BY MEANS OF WHICH MAN WILL BECOME THE MASTER OF SPACE.

AH, THE HELIX! BUT THE BIRD HAS NO HELIX... AS FAR AS WE KNOW!

BUT MR. PENAUD HAS SHOWN THAT IN REALITY THE BIRD MAKES A HELIX, AND ITS FLIGHT IS HELICOPTERAL. AND THE MOTOR OF THE FUTURE IS THE SCREW...

FROM SUCH A MALADEE, SAINT HELIX KEEP US FREE!

CITIZENS OF THE UNITED STATES, MY EXPERIMENT IS FINISHED; BUT MY ADVICE IS THAT WE SHOULD BE PREMATURE IN NOTHING, NOT EVEN IN PROGRESS. SCIENCE SHOULD NEVER OUTSTRIP OUR MORALITY. IT IS EVOLUTION AND NOT REVOLUTION THAT WE SHOULD SEEK.

JUST LIKE ROBUR, JULES VERNE WAS ALSO AFFLICTED BY PESSIMISM IN LATER LIFE. THIS IS CLEAR IN HIS NOVELETTE *THE ETERNAL ADAM* (THOUGHT TO HAVE BEEN EXPANDED OR WRITTEN BY HIS SON, MICHEL), A CHRONICLE OF THE END OF THE WORLD.

IN TIMES OF WAR, WHICH HE DESCRIBED AS MANKIND'S "DETESTABLE PASSION," GHASTLY WEAPONRY IS BORN, SUCH AS THE "WASPS" ENCOUNTERED IN ONE OF HIS POSTHUMOUS WORKS, *THE BARSAC MISSION*. THESE WERE HELICOPTER TORPEDOES, NOT UNLIKE DRONES PACKED WITH SHRAPNEL!

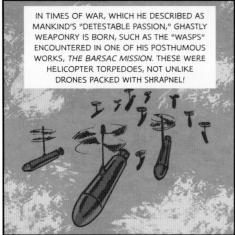

THAT NOVEL ALSO ENVISIONED AIRCRAFT CAPABLE OF VERTICAL TAKE-OFF, LIKE HELICOPTERS, AS WELL AS THE "CYCLOSCOPE," A FICTIONAL ANCESTOR OF TELESURVEILLANCE SYSTEMS.

IN *THE BEGUM'S FORTUNE*, WHICH WAS PUBLISHED IN 1879, JULES VERNE DESCRIBED AN ENORMOUS CANNON THAT LAUNCHED SHELLS CHARGED WITH LIQUID CARBONIC ACID, FREEZING AND SUFFOCATING EVERY LIVING THING WITHIN A RADIUS OF THIRTY YARDS!

EVEN SO, VERNE STILL SPOKE HOPEFULLY OF TOMORROW.

I ESTEEM MYSELF FORTUNATE FOR HAVING BEEN BORN IN AN AGE OF REMARKABLE DISCOVERIES, AND PERHAPS STILL MORE WONDERFUL INVENTIONS.

IT WAS IN THE TWILIGHT OF JULES VERNE'S CAREER THAT ANOTHER GIANT OF SCIENCE FICTION PRODUCED ONE OF HIS GREATEST WORKS, THIS TIME IN ENGLAND. WHO WAS THAT WRITER? HERBERT GEORGE WELLS, WHO, EVEN THOUGH VERNE HAD INFLUENCED HIM, WAS NOT FOND OF BEING COMPARED TO THE FRENCHMAN.

JULES VERNE IN FRANCE, ALONG WITH H. G. WELLS IN ENGLAND, UNWITTINGLY SPAWNED A SUB-GENRE OF SCIENCE FICTION AND FANTASY. THE RETROFUTURISTIC MOVEMENT KNOWN AS "STEAMPUNK" IS TYPIFIED BY HISTORICAL (OFTEN VICTORIAN) SETTINGS THAT PLAY HOME TO TECHNOLOGICAL ADVANCES UNDREAMED OF BY THAT POINT IN HISTORY. SUCH MACHINES AND GADGETS ARE POWERED BY STEAM OR OTHER FUELS APPROPRIATE TO THE TIME.

AN INTRODUCTION TO STEAMPUNK:

MORTAL ENGINES, PHILIP REEVE, 2001.

THE ANUBIS GATES, TIM POWERS, 1983.

ROBUR, FORMOSA AND LOFFICIER, 2003-2005.

SATANIA, VEHLMANN AND KERASCOËT, 2016.

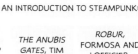

THREE NOVELS TO INTRODUCE YOU TO JULES VERNE, A SCIENCE-FICTION PIONEER:

20,000 LEAGUES UNDER THE SEA, 1870.

FROM THE EARTH TO THE MOON, 1865.

ROBUR THE CONQUEROR, 1886.

H. G. Wells, the rebellious catalyst. Britain, late 19th/early 20th century.

PLANET MARS, 1938.

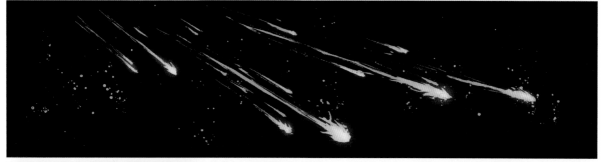

IN THE EARLY YEARS OF OUR CENTURY, OUR WORLD HAS BEEN WATCHED CLOSELY BY GREAT INTELLIGENCES NOW INVADING US FROM PLANET MARS...

WE TAKE YOU NOW TO THE SECRETARY OF THE INTERIOR, SPEAKING TO US FROM WASHINGTON...

I WISH TO IMPRESS UPON YOU THE URGENT NEED OF CALM. THE ENEMY IS STILL CONFINED TO A COMPARATIVELY SMALL AREA. WE MAY PLACE OUR FAITH IN THE MILITARY FORCES TO KEEP THEM THERE...

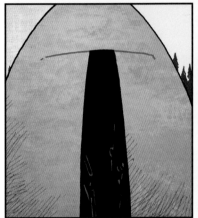

BRITAIN, 1873. A YOUNG MAN WAKES WITH A START. HIS NAME? HERBERT GEORGE WELLS...

MUM, MUM!

NATURALLY, THE YOUNG WELLS WASN'T DREAMING OF THIS FUTURE SCENE, A RADIO ADAPTATION OF *THE WAR OF THE WORLDS*, BROADCAST OVER THE CBS AIRWAVES BY HIS NEAR-NAMESAKE ORSON WELLES IN OCTOBER 1938. IT PROVOKED A GENERAL PANIC, WHICH WAS ACTUALLY EXAGGERATED BY CERTAIN NEWSPAPER JOURNALISTS TO LAMBAST THE GROWING THREAT OF INCREASED COMPETITION IN THE FORM OF RADIO.

AS FOR YOUNG HERBERT, LONG BEFORE BECOMING THE AUTHOR OF *THE WAR OF THE WORLDS*, HIS SLEEP WAS PLAGUED BY NIGHTMARES. NIGHTMARES THAT WOULD LEAD HIM TO REBEL AGAINST SOCIETY EARLY ON IN HIS LIFE.

MOTHER, YOU KNOW HOW I LOATHE THE ODIOUS TEMPLATES IMPOSED ON US BY THE WAYS OF THIS CORRUPT AND DEGENERATE SOCIETY!

SHUSH, YOU LITTLE FOOL, SOMEBODY MIGHT HEAR YOU!

LET THEM HEAR ME! I HAVE NO GOD, NOR MASTER.

AND INDEED, H. G. WELLS GREW INTO A REBEL WHO REJECTED THE CONFORMITY OF BRITISH SOCIETY. HE DISPUTED WHAT HIS PARENTS HAD TAUGHT HIM, ESPECIALLY HIS PROTESTANT MOTHER (AS HIS FATHER WAS CONSIDERED TO BE A FREE-THINKER), AND THE LIFE FOR WHICH HE WAS DESTINED.

I REFUSE TO BELIEVE IN A GOD. I REJECT RELIGION!

I REJECT ALL CLASS DIVISIONS!

I REFUSE TO WORK AT THIS DRAPER'S SHOP!

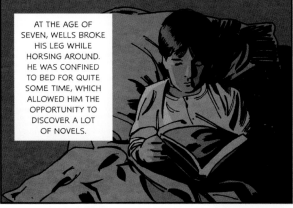

AT THE AGE OF SEVEN, WELLS BROKE HIS LEG WHILE HORSING AROUND. HE WAS CONFINED TO BED FOR QUITE SOME TIME, WHICH ALLOWED HIM THE OPPORTUNITY TO DISCOVER A LOT OF NOVELS.

READING THEM HELPED HIM TO UNDERSTAND THAT THERE WERE OTHER POSSIBLE LIVES TO DREAM OF.

IN 1880, HE BECAME A PUPIL-TEACHER IN WOOKEY, SOMERSET, THANKS TO HIS DISTANT RELATIVE, ALFRED WILLIAMS. BUT HIS STAY WAS SHORT AS HE LACKED ANY REAL QUALIFICATIONS.

HE FOUND HIMSELF A NEW JOB AS A CHEMIST'S APPRENTICE. AT THAT POINT, HE TOOK AN INTEREST IN SCIENCE AND SHOWED SOME TALENT FOR IT.

ALONGSIDE THE INDUSTRIAL REVOLUTION, SEVERAL GREAT UPHEAVALS OCCURRED DURING THE NINETEENTH CENTURY THAT ENCOURAGED SCIENCE FICTION TO EMERGE WORLDWIDE: IN TECHNOLOGY, THE ADVENT OF NEW FORMS OF TRANSPORT, SUCH AS THE STEAM LOCOMOTIVE; IN SCIENCE, DARWIN'S THEORIES OF EVOLUTION; AND IN POLITICS, THE SOCIAL REVOLUTION LAUNCHED BY KARL MARX WITH HIS WORKS *THE COMMUNIST PARTY MANIFESTO* AND *DAS KAPITAL*.

IN 1884, H. G. WELLS ATTENDED LECTURES BY THE EMINENT BIOLOGIST THOMAS HENRY HUXLEY--IT WAS A DECISIVE MEETING.

AS YOU PROBABLY KNOW, MY NICKNAME IS "DARWIN'S BULLDOG," WHICH GIVES YOU SOME IDEA OF HOW MUCH I ADMIRE THE THEORY OF EVOLUTION AND *ON THE ORIGIN OF SPECIES*, A BOOK THAT REVOLUTIONIZED THE SCIENCE!

THUS BIOLOGY ENJOYED PRIDE OF PLACE IN HIS DIVERSE WORKS.

MUCH LATER, IN HIS NOVEL *JOAN AND PETER*, HE WROTE: "TO THE WORLD OF THE 1880S THE STORY OF LIFE, OF THE ORIGIN AND BRANCHING OUT OF SPECIES, OF THE MAKING OF CONTINENTS, WAS STILL THE MOST INSPIRING OF NEW ROMANCES."

I AM ABOUT TO RECOUNT AN INCREDIBLE ADVENTURE. NO DOUBT YOU WILL THINK ME INSANE, BUT NO INTERRUPTIONS! IS IT AGREED?

AGREED. NOW, TELL US AND DON'T KEEP US IN SUSPENSE!

I HAVE INVENTED A WORKING TIME MACHINE THAT HAS ALLOWED ME TO TRAVEL FORWARD AND VISIT THE YEAR 802,701...

OH!

OH!

OH!

"THERE, IN THAT FAR-OFF FUTURE, I HAD THE CHANCE TO MEET SOME ASTONISHING, ANDROGYNOUS CREATURES THAT ARE EXQUISITE, NAIVE, HAPPY, AND KIND, KNOWN AS THE ELOIS. I THOUGHT I HAD FOUND THE ULTIMATE UTOPIA, THE LOVELIEST PLACE POSSIBLE. AND YET..."

"...YET HIDDEN AWAY BENEATH THAT WORLD THERE WAS SOMETHING SINISTER, PERNICIOUS AND SUBTERRANEAN..."

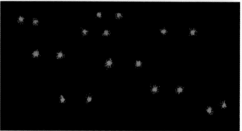

"THE MORLOCKS! THAT WAS THE NAME OF THE TERRIFYING NOCTURNAL CREATURES WHO LIVED UNDERGROUND AND CRAVED LIVING FLESH--THE FLESH OF THE ELOIS!"

H. G. WELLS WROTE HIS FIRST DRAFT OF *THE TIME MACHINE* IN 1888, TITLED *THE CHRONIC ARGONAUTS*. THE NOVEL WAS FIRST PUBLISHED IN 1895 AND BECAME HUGELY SUCCESSFUL!

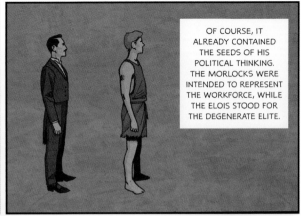

OF COURSE, IT ALREADY CONTAINED THE SEEDS OF HIS POLITICAL THINKING. THE MORLOCKS WERE INTENDED TO REPRESENT THE WORKFORCE, WHILE THE ELOIS STOOD FOR THE DEGENERATE ELITE.

THE TIME MACHINE WAS A CRUCIAL TURNING POINT IN THE DEVELOPMENT OF SCIENCE FICTION, BECAUSE THE TIME TRAVEL IT DESCRIBES TAKES PLACE IN A WHOLLY SCIENTIFIC AND RATIONAL WAY, AN ELEMENT WHICH WOULD LATER BECOME A MAJOR THEME OF THE GENRE.

1895 ALSO SAW THE FIRST-EVER PUBLIC SCREENING OF THE LUMIÈRE BROTHERS' CINÉMATOGRAPHE AT THE GRAND CAFÉ, PARIS.

THIS INVENTION, DEAR HERBERT, WILL ALLOW US TO PORTRAY THE EFFECTS OF THE TIME MACHINE.

BUT HOW? USING WHAT TECHNOLOGY? A KINETOSCOPE?

IN OCTOBER THAT SAME YEAR, AN UNUSUAL PATENT WAS APPLIED FOR BY WELLS AND ONE ROBERT WILLIAM PAUL, AN ELECTRICIAN WHO SPECIALIZED IN COPYING EDISON'S KINETOSCOPE.

ALTHOUGH THERE WERE MANY SIMILAR PATENTS AROUND IN THOSE DAYS, THE FACT REMAINS THAT PAUL AND WELLS' IDEA, DESPITE BEING ABANDONED, WAS WELL AHEAD OF ITS TIME.

IN ONE ROOM, WITH THE HELP OF SEVERAL SCREENS, SOME JETS OF AIR DESIGNED TO OFFER SENSATIONS, AND WALLS THAT MOVE, WE WILL GIVE OUR AUDIENCE THE ILLUSION OF TRAVELING BACKWARD AND FORWARD THROUGH TIME IN SCENES THAT WILL DEPICT SEVERAL DIFFERENT EPOCHS.

SPLENDID IDEA, ROBERT! EVEN IF IT WILL REQUIRE A LOT OF WORK AND CREATIVE GENIUS!

ISABEL, WILL YOU MARRY ME?

AS WELLS RAPIDLY BECAME A PROLIFIC WRITER, HE ALSO ACQUIRED A REPUTATION FOR HAVING NUMEROUS EXTRA-MARITAL AFFAIRS. HE MARRIED HIS COUSIN ISABEL MARY WELLS IN 1891, BUT THE COUPLE SEPARATED WHEN HE FELL IN LOVE WITH ONE OF HIS STUDENTS, AMY CATHERINE ROBBINS, WHOM HE MARRIED IN 1895. LATER ON, DESPITE AMY BEING FULLY AWARE OF HIS "ACTIVITIES," HE BECAME LOVERS WITH, AMONGST OTHERS, THE ACTIVIST MARGARET SANGER, THE NOVELIST REBECCA WEST, AND THE SUSPECTED DOUBLE AGENT MOURA BUDBERG.

WHAT CAN I SAY? I'VE SIMPLY NEVER BEEN CAPABLE OF REFUSING THE ADVANCES OF A WOMAN! IT'S NOT IN MY NATURE.

THE ENGLISH ACADEMIC AND NOVELIST DAVID LODGE NOTED HOW INCREDIBLE IT IS TO SEE JUST HOW PROLIFIC WELLS WAS, CONSIDERING WHAT AN INTENSE LOVE LIFE HE ALSO MANAGED TO LEAD!

IN 1896 CAME THE ISLAND OF DOCTOR MOREAU, WHERE THE "GOOD" DOCTOR SETS OUT TO UPSET THE LAWS OF NATURE AND TURN ANIMALS INTO PEOPLE.

THIS ONE WILL BE PERFECT, MONTGOMERY, I PROMISE YOU!

THERE'S NO DOUBT, YOUR GENIUS KNOWS NO BOUNDS!

NOT TO GO ON ALL-FOURS; THAT IS THE LAW. ARE WE NOT MEN?

NOT TO SUCK UP DRINK; THAT IS THE LAW. ARE WE NOT MEN?

NOT TO EAT FISH OR FLESH; THAT IS THE LAW. ARE WE NOT MEN?

NOT TO CLAW THE BARK OF TREES; THAT IS THE LAW. ARE WE NOT MEN?

NOT TO CHASE OTHER MEN; THAT IS THE LAW. ARE WE NOT MEN?

WHILE HE IS PLAYING SORCERER'S APPRENTICE, DOCTOR MOREAU BELIEVES THAT LAWS ARE MADE TO BE BROKEN. HE LEARNS THIS LESSON TO HIS COST WHEN HIS LEOPARD-MAN DECIDES TO GIVE HIM A REMINDER!

THIS IS DAY ONE OF YEAR ONE OF THE NEW EPOCH--THE EPOCH OF THE INVISIBLE MAN. I AM INVISIBLE MAN THE FIRST!

WELLS WAS INFLUENCED BY THE IDEAS OF THOMAS HUXLEY AND CHARLES DARWIN, AND THE EVOLUTION OF THE HUMAN BODY. IN 1897, HE RELEASED ONE OF HIS BEST-KNOWN NOVELS, *THE INVISIBLE MAN*.

AH! UNCLOUDED BY DOUBT, I BEHOLD A MAGNIFICENT VISION OF ALL THAT INVISIBILITY MIGHT MEAN TO A MAN--THE MYSTERY, THE POWER, THE FREEDOM!

APART FROM THE BODY, WELLS ALSO PLUMBED THE DEPTHS OF THE HUMAN MIND. THE NOVEL'S ALBINO SCIENTIST PROTAGONIST, GRIFFIN, MAKES THE MOST OF INVISIBILITY IN ORDER TO INDULGE IN THEFT, VOYEURISM, VIOLENCE, AND MEGALOMANIA.

1898 SAW THE PUBLICATION OF *THE WAR OF THE WORLDS.*

IN IT, WELLS IMAGINED THE MARTIANS ATTEMPTING TO TAKE OVER THE EARTH AT THE HELM OF THEIR GIGANTIC TRIPODS. OBSERVING THE EVOLUTION OF TECHNOLOGY, HE PROVED PARTICULARLY ASTUTE AT PREDICTING HOW DANGEROUS WEAPONS MIGHT BE IN THE FUTURE. ON THE OTHER HAND, THE MARTIANS WERE FINALLY DEFEATED NOT BY TECHNOLOGY, BUT BY SIMPLE BIOLOGY-- MICROSCOPIC BACTERIA.

WHEN THE SLEEPER WAKES WAS PUBLISHED IN 1889, HIS LAST NOVEL BEFORE THE TURN OF THE 20TH CENTURY.

WITH NO SOCIAL REVOLUTION, MANKIND WAS HURTLING HEADLONG TOWARD A WAR. IN *WHEN THE SLEEPER WAKES*, WELLS WAS PREPARING ONE OF HIS OWN.

FOR IF THE WORLD WOULD INEVITABLY COLLAPSE, IT WOULD HAVE TO BE BUILT ANEW SO THAT INDIVIDUALS WERE NO LONGER NAMELESS PAWNS BUT VITAL PARTS OF THEIR GLOBAL ENVIRONMENT. SINCE HUMAN SOCIAL AND BIOLOGICAL EVOLUTION WERE SO INTIMATELY LINKED, THEY BECAME FERTILE SOIL FOR WELLS' THINKING AT THE BEGINNING OF THE 1900S.

WELLS WAS INTERESTED IN THE POLITICS OF HIS COUNTRY ALL THROUGHOUT HIS LIFE. IN THE EARLY DAYS OF HIS CAREER HE JOINED THE FABIAN SOCIETY, WHICH GREW INTO THE BRITISH LABOUR PARTY. ALTHOUGH HE SOON LEFT IT, HE RAN AS THE PARTY'S CANDIDATE FOR THE LONDON UNIVERSITY CONSTITUENCY IN 1922 AND 1923.

THE FIRST MEN IN THE MOON ILLUSTRATES HIS SOCIALIST THINKING (WHICH WAS NOT ACTUALLY OPPOSED TO CAPITALISM). THIS WOULD COME UP AGAIN IN TWO OF HIS ESSAYS: *ANTICIPATIONS* (1901) AND *THE DISCOVERY OF THE FUTURE* (1902).

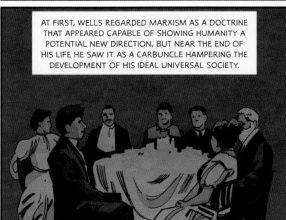

AT FIRST, WELLS REGARDED MARXISM AS A DOCTRINE THAT APPEARED CAPABLE OF SHOWING HUMANITY A POTENTIAL NEW DIRECTION, BUT NEAR THE END OF HIS LIFE HE SAW IT AS A CARBUNCLE HAMPERING THE DEVELOPMENT OF HIS IDEAL UNIVERSAL SOCIETY.

IF ONLY KARL MARX HAD NEVER EXISTED, PEOPLE WOULD BE SO HAPPY!

EVEN IF WELLS' CONTEMPORARIES ACCUSED HIM OF PRODUCING QUANTITY RATHER THAN QUALITY, HIS NOVELS LEFT THEIR MARK ON GREAT BRITAIN, THE UNITED STATES, AND EVEN IN FRANCE, WHERE MAURICE RENARD, A THEORIST OF WHAT HE DESCRIBED AS "FABULOUS SCIENCE" WRITING, ACKNOWLEDGED HIS INFLUENCE. BY THE TIME OF HIS DEATH, HOWEVER, HIS POPULARITY HAD BEEN ON THE WANE FOR SOME TIME. HE WAS ALREADY REGARDED AS A RELIC OF THE VICTORIAN AGE, AND WHEN HE DIED, *THE TIMES'* OBITUARY RAN TO BARELY HALF A COLUMN...

FROM TIME TRAVEL TO MAD SCIENTISTS, SELECTED WORKS BY H. G. WELLS:

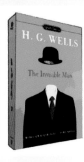

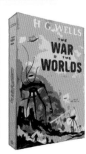

THE TIME MACHINE, 1895.

THE ISLAND OF DOCTOR MOREAU, 1896.

THE INVISIBLE MAN, 1897.

THE WAR OF THE WORLDS, 1898.

WHEN THE SLEEPER WAKES, 1899.

THE FIRST MEN IN THE MOON, 1901.

MEN LIKE GODS, 1922.

ARGOSY-ALLSTORY
WEEKLY

VOL CXLVII · SATURDAY, NOVEMBER 18, 1922 · NUMBER 2

"Frank Munsey, you have been found guilty of bringing the talents of a butcher, the ethics of a loan shark, and the style of an undertaker into the world of publishing. You and your fellows have succeeded in transforming a noble profession into an 8% investment return. As for you, Hugo Gernsback, you lack elegance, good manners and even grammar, and have occasionally been accused of destroying science fiction, rather than creating it... Hence, the pair of you are welcome here. Do you have anything to add?"

"Yes. I also stand accused of being tight-fisted. A certain Lovecraft even nicknamed me 'Hugo the Rat.' Does that earn me any extra points?"

Once Upon A Time

by XAVIER DOLLO

CHAPTER 1

Frank Munsey? Hugo Gernsback? Two names unknown to the general public. Nevertheless, be they maligned or revered, loved or loathed, in America these two publishers were vitally important to the emergence of the science-fiction genre as we know it today. Their work and passion led them to create strange, cheap booklets that published fiction, all types of fiction. But for now, let's get back to the basics...

TABLE OF THEMATIC ELEMENTS OF SF

A TRUE STORY, 2 AD.

COMICAL HISTORY OF THE STATES AND EMPIRES OF THE MOON, 1650.

I FIRST DESCRIBED SPACE TRAVEL AND OTHER PLANETS!

MONSTROSITIES... SCIENTIFIC EXPERIMENTS GOING WRONG...

...AND, BY EXTENSION, I OUTLINED THE FIRST ANDROIDS OR ROBOTS.

GULLIVER'S TRAVELS, 1721.

THE LOST WORLD, 1912.

I WAS RESPONSIBLE FOR INTRODUCING THE CONCEPTS OF GIGANTISM AND DWARFISM.

MY LOST WORLD AND PROFESSOR CHALLENGER ARE STILL FAMOUS TODAY.

THE DISCOVERY OF THE AUSTRAL CONTINENT BY A FLYING MAN, 1781.

SHE, 1886-1887.

FOR MY PART, I WAS INTERESTED IN ANCIENT, LOST CIVILIZATIONS.

AND SO WAS I!

IN MY NOVEL SHE, THE QUEEN AYESHA IS IMMORTAL!

UNITED STATES, THE TURN OF THE 19TH AND 20TH CENTURIES. ALL THE MAJOR THEMES OF SCI-FI HAD ALREADY BEEN SKETCHED OUT, OR SOON WOULD BE, BY AUTHORS FROM A VARIETY OF BACKGROUNDS...

THEY OPENED UP AN ENTIRE FIELD OF POSSIBILITIES IN THE LATE 19TH CENTURY, THUS USHERING IN A REVOLUTION FOR SF--PULP FICTION!

THE NARRATIVE OF ARTHUR GORDON PYM OF NANTUCKET, 1838.

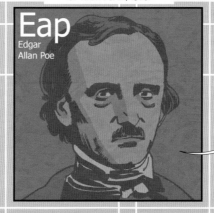

Eap
Edgar Allan Poe

I USED SCIENCE TO EXPLAIN THE OCCULT! I INVENTED CREATURES NOT OF THIS EARTH!

FRANKENSTEIN, 1818.

Ms
Mary Shelley

POST-APOCALYPTIC THE LAST MAN, 1826.

20,000 LEAGUES UNDER THE SEA, 1870.

Jv
Jules Verne

THE XIPÉHUZ, 1887.

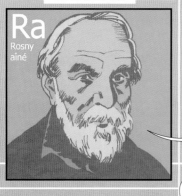

Ra
Rosny aîné

THE POSITIVE SIDE OF SCIENCE... SUBTERRANEAN LIFE, UNDERWATER EXPLORATION, AND MUCH MORE!

FIRST CONTACT WITH AN "ALIEN" RACE AND A POST-APOCALYPTIC WORLD...

I CREATED SOCIOLOGICAL UTOPIAS WITH TRUE PHILOSOPHICAL CONTEMPLATION OF HUMANITY, AS WELL AS SCIENTIFIC INVISIBILITY.

SOCIAL SCIENCE FICTION OWES US A LOT!

THE WAR OF THE WORLDS, 1898.

LOOKING BACKWARD: 2000-1887, 1888.

THE IRON HEEL, 1908.

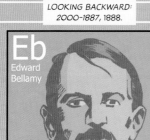

Eb
Edward Bellamy

Jl
Jack London

Hgw
H. G. Wells

THE HISTORY OF THE MAGAZINES KNOWN AS "PULPS" DEVELOPED DURING AMERICA'S ECONOMIC BOOM. THE GLORY DAYS OF THESE OFTEN-MALIGNED MAGAZINES CAME IN THE FIRST HALF OF THE TWENTIETH CENTURY. THEIR SUBJECT MATTER RANGED FROM WESTERNS TO ROMANCE, DETECTIVE STORIES, AND OF COURSE FANTASY AND WHAT WOULD EVENTUALLY BECOME SCIENCE FICTION.

1923...

IS THE LATEST ISSUE OF *WEIRD TALES* IN, SIR?

NOT YET, KID. THE DELIVERY'S LATE. IT'LL BE IN TOMORROW!

BUT WHAT EXACTLY WERE THESE PULPS THAT HELD SUCH A FASCINATION, ESPECIALLY FOR YOUNGER READERS?

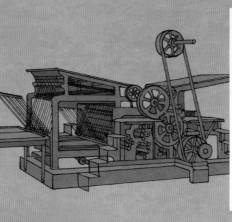

THE WORD "PULP" DERIVES FROM WOOD PULP, THE WOOD-FIBER RESIDUE THAT WAS USED TO MAKE A PASTE WHICH BECAME THE BASIC INGREDIENT IN THE MANUFACTURE OF THE VERY LOW-GRADE "PULP" PAPER THAT THE PUBLICATIONS WERE PRINTED ON. THIS TYPE OF PAPER WAS USED TO KEEP COSTS DOWN IN ORDER TO SELL THE FINAL PRODUCT CHEAPLY. MOST OF THESE PUBLICATIONS SOLD FOR THE MODEST PRICE OF TEN CENTS. FROM THE 1930S ONWARD, THEY BEGAN COMPETING WITH THE "SLICKS"--MAGAZINES WHICH WERE MORE EXPENSIVE, BUT BEAUTIFULLY PRODUCED.

HAROLD, COME AND HELP ME HAND OUT THESE TEMPERANCE LEAFLETS!

IN THE UNITED STATES, THE PULPS FOLLOWED ON FROM VARIOUS EARLIER PUBLICATIONS, PARTICULARLY MORALISTIC PAMPHLETS FROM GROUPS SUCH AS THE WOMEN'S CHRISTIAN TEMPERANCE UNION, WHICH FOUGHT AGAINST ALCOHOLISM.

BUT THE PULPS WERE THE TRUE SUCCESSORS OF WHAT WAS KNOWN AS THE "DIME NOVEL," NAMED AFTER THEIR PRICE OF TEN CENTS. THE FIRST DIME NOVEL WAS PUBLISHED IN 1860 BY BEADLE & ADAMS. IN THE SPACE OF THIRTY YEARS, SEVERAL THOUSAND STORIES WERE RELEASED, FEATURING HEROES LIKE BUFFALO BILL AND KIT CARSON.

DIME NOVELS, WHICH ACTUALLY VARIED IN PRICE AND WERE OFTEN THOUGHT TO BE TOO SIMPLISTIC, WERE HIGHLY SUCCESSFUL AND PLAYED A ROLE IN ENTERTAINING A LARGELY ILLITERATE POPULATION, ESPECIALLY AMONG THE WORKING CLASS.

KI...KIT... CAR...SON G... GRAB...BED... HIS RI...HIS... RI...

...FLE!

BUT AS THE 20TH CENTURY DREW NEARER, THE DIME NOVEL FELL INTO DECLINE, BECOMING SYNONYMOUS WITH SECOND-RATE, UNINTERESTING OR TERRIBLY WRITTEN FICTION. READERS STARTED TURNING TOWARD THE PULPS. THE FIRST, PUBLISHED IN 1882 BY A MAN NAMED FRANK MUNSEY, WAS CALLED *THE GOLDEN ARGOSY*. A NEW ERA WAS DAWNING.

NEW YORK, LATE 19TH CENTURY. WRITER AND PUBLISHER FRANK MUNSEY HAS A BRAINWAVE THAT WOULD REVOLUTIONIZE THE CULTURAL HISTORY OF AMERICA.

WHAT IF I USE HIGH-SPEED PRESSES TOGETHER WITH CHEAP PAPER? THEN I CAN MASS-PRODUCE MAGAZINES AT PRICES THAT ARE AFFORDABLE FOR EVERYONE'S POCKET!

THE *GOLDEN ARGOSY* (SHORTENED TO *ARGOSY* IN 1888), BECAME THE FIRST PULP MAGAZINE (1896), AND MERGED WITH *ALL-STORY WEEKLY* (1920) BEFORE SPLITTING BACK INTO INDIVIDUAL MAGAZINES IN 1929, LEAVING *ARGOSY* DEDICATED EXCLUSIVELY TO SCIENCE FICTION.

ONE OF THE GREATEST SCIENCE-FICTION AUTHORS OF THE EARLY 20TH CENTURY, RAY CUMMINGS, WAS, AT THIS TIME, ALREADY INTERESTED IN THE THEORIES OF ALBERT EINSTEIN AND APPLYING SUCH SCIENTIFIC THEORY TO HIS FICTION.

INCREDIBLE, WE'RE SEEING A SCENE PROJECTED FROM THE FUTURE!

THAT POOR GIRL... CAN'T WE DO ANYTHING TO HELP HER?

TIME KEEPS EVERYTHING FROM HAPPENING AT ONCE. AND SO SPACE AND MATTER ARE DEPENDENT UPON IT. THIS WAS THE THEORY BEHIND HIS NOVEL *THE MAN WHO MASTERED TIME*.

THIS RATHER OLD-FASHIONED STORY WAS SERIALIZED IN *ARGOSY ALL-STORY WEEKLY* BETWEEN JULY 12 AND AUGUST 9, 1924, BUT IT WASN'T CUMMINGS' FIRST, OR HIS STRONGEST, TEXT. THE AUTHOR'S BEST-KNOWN WORK WAS PUBLISHED IN MARCH 1919, AT THE START OF HIS CAREER, ALSO IN *ARGOSY ALL-STORY WEEKLY*.

THE GIRL IN THE GOLDEN ATOM TELLS OF A SCIENTIST WHO DISCOVERS A WAY TO SHRINK HIMSELF TO SUBATOMIC LEVEL IN AN ATTEMPT TO FIND LYLDA, A GIRL HE HAS FALLEN IN LOVE WITH, WHOSE WHOLE UNIVERSE IS CONTAINED INSIDE ONE ATOM OF GOLD.

FOR A PULP AUTHOR, CUMMINGS HAD THE EXTREMELY RARE HONOR OF SEEING HIS WORK REPRINTED IN BOUND EDITIONS BY MAJOR PUBLISHERS IN LONDON AND NEW YORK IN THE EARLY 1920S. AFTER THAT, HE TENDED TO KEEP ON WRITING THE SAME KIND OF STORIES ON WHICH HE HAD BUILT HIS REPUTATION, BUT PAID LESS ATTENTION TO HIS STYLE AND THE DEPTH OF HIS CHARACTERS. TODAY, HE IS THE MOST FORGOTTEN OF THE GREAT AUTHORS FROM THE DAWN OF PULP.

IN 1912, A KEYSTONE IN POST-APOCALYPTIC FICTION WAS LAID IN *THE CAVALIER* MAGAZINE, WHICH WAS ANOTHER OF MUNSEY'S PUBLICATIONS. THAT YEAR, GEORGE ALLAN ENGLAND RELEASED *DARKNESS AND DAWN*, HIS OWN RETELLING OF THE ADAM AND EVE MYTH.

SEVERAL CENTURIES AFTER THE DEATH OF MANKIND...

ENGLAND RECALLED HOW HE SIGNED A FIVE-YEAR CONTRACT WITH MUNSEY'S MAGAZINES WHILE OUT FISHING ONE DAY IN A CANOE ON A MAINE LAKE WITH HIS EDITOR, WHO WAS ROCKING THE BOAT (HE DIDN'T KNOW HOW TO SWIM!). HE REMAINED AN EXTREMELY POPULAR WRITER FROM THE OUTSET UNTIL THE TWILIGHT OF HIS CAREER.

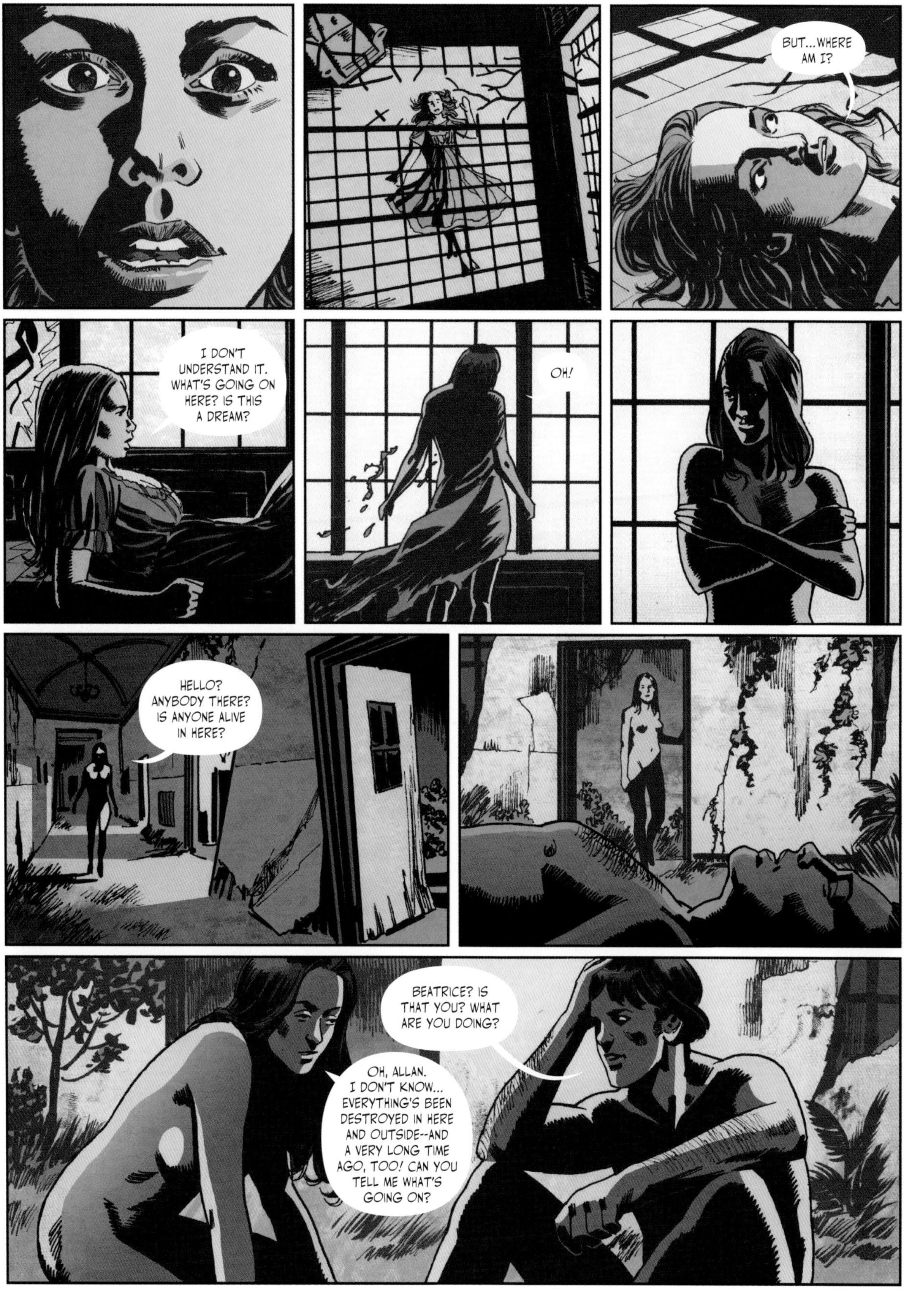
BUT...WHERE AM I?
I DON'T UNDERSTAND IT. WHAT'S GOING ON HERE? IS THIS A DREAM?
OH!
HELLO? ANYBODY THERE? IS ANYONE ALIVE IN HERE?
BEATRICE? IS THAT YOU? WHAT ARE YOU DOING?
OH, ALLAN. I DON'T KNOW... EVERYTHING'S BEEN DESTROYED IN HERE AND OUTSIDE--AND A VERY LONG TIME AGO, TOO! CAN YOU TELL ME WHAT'S GOING ON?

LATER...

NOBODY ELSE IN THIS PARTICULAR EDEN BUT YOU AND ME. TO ALL INTENTS AND PURPOSES I'M ADAM, AND YOU'RE EVE.

BUT IF YOU'RE ADAM AND I'M EVE, WHERE'S THE TREE?

PERHAPS THE FUTURE WILL SOON TELL US?

FINALLY, AFTER NUMEROUS ADVENTURES, BEATRICE AND ALLAN DISCOVER THEIR EDEN. THE STORY WAS A MIRROR OF ITS TIME, OF COURSE. THEMATICALLY, ALLAN AND BEATRICE FOLLOWED IN WELLS' FOOTSTEPS, AND *DARKNESS AND DAWN* CLEARLY SHOWS HIS INFLUENCE.

ENGLAND MAY ALSO HAVE BEEN INFLUENCED BY ANOTHER AUTHOR, WHOSE FIRST SPECTACULAR WORKS WERE PUBLISHED IN *THE ALL-STORY* IN 1912. A MAN WHO BECAME THE STUFF OF LEGEND AND ONE OF THE TWENTIETH CENTURY'S BESTSELLING AUTHORS. HE STARTED OUT WORKING AT A PENCIL-SHARPENER FACTORY...

HIS NAME WAS EDGAR RICE BURROUGHS... THE CREATOR OF JOHN CARTER AND TARZAN.

SOMEWHERE IN THE ARIZONA DESERT.

BURROUGHS, WHO WAS BORN IN 1875 AND DIED IN 1950, WAS A CONTEMPORARY OF BOTH JULES VERNE AND H.G. WELLS AND MADE A MAJOR CONTRIBUTION TO THE HISTORY OF SCIENCE FICTION. HE FIRST DISCOVERED PULP MAGAZINES WHILE WORKING AT A FIRM SELLING A CURE FOR ALCOHOLISM. HE WAS IN CHARGE OF PLACING ADVERTISEMENTS IN THE PULPS, THEN READING THEM TO MAKE SURE THAT THEY HAD BEEN PRINTED...

SO, HE BEGAN PAYING MORE ATTENTION TO THE STORIES THEY CONTAINED AND REALIZED HE COULD WRITE HIS OWN, MUCH BETTER THAN THE GENERAL, MEDIOCRE STANDARD.

INFLUENCED MORE BY WALTER SCOTT'S *IVANHOE* THAN BY WELLS OR VERNE, YET AWARE OF WHAT WAS BEING WRITTEN FOR THE PULPS, BURROUGHS SET OUT ON A PATH OF HIS OWN, CREATING IMAGINARY WORLDS THAT DIFFERED GREATLY FROM HIS ILLUSTRIOUS PREDECESSORS.

AND SO HE WROTE *A PRINCESS OF MARS*, A LONG NOVEL DIVIDED INTO THREE PARTS IN *THE ALL-STORY* BETWEEN FEBRUARY AND JULY 1912. THIS WAS THE FIRST ADVENTURE OF JOHN CARTER AND IS OFTEN CONSIDERED TO BE THE ORIGIN OF A SEPARATE BRANCH OF SCIENCE FICTION: PLANET OPERA, A GENRE THAT FEATURES ADVENTURES SET ON ALIEN PLANETS.

JOHN CARTER IS A FORMER CONFEDERATE CAPTAIN TURNED GOLD-DIGGER IN ARIZONA. BUT THE APACHES DO NOT TAKE KINDLY TO HIM AND DECIDE THAT THESE WHITE MEN HAVE TO DIE.

AFTER A LENGTHY CHASE THROUGH THE DESERT AND INTO A GORGE, CARTER ESCAPES THE NATIVES. BUT HIS FRIEND IS NOT SO LUCKY.

POWELL... NO!

CARTER WALKS INTO A CAVE HE HAS JUST DISCOVERED AND THINKS OF MARS, FEELING INEXORABLY DRAWN TO IT, BUT THEN BECOMES DROWSY AND COLLAPSES.

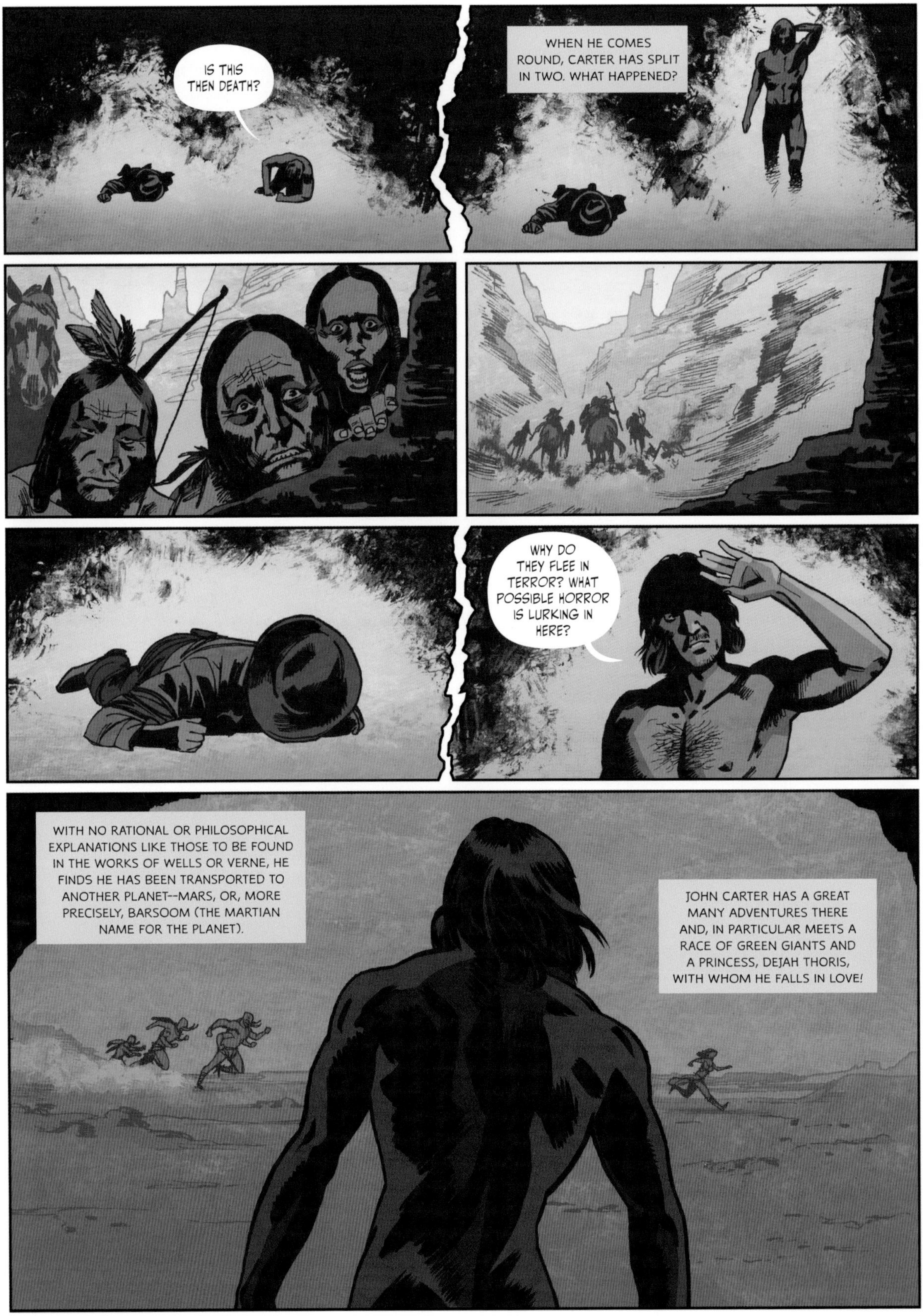
IS THIS THEN DEATH?
WHEN HE COMES ROUND, CARTER HAS SPLIT IN TWO. WHAT HAPPENED?
WHY DO THEY FLEE IN TERROR? WHAT POSSIBLE HORROR IS LURKING IN HERE?
WITH NO RATIONAL OR PHILOSOPHICAL EXPLANATIONS LIKE THOSE TO BE FOUND IN THE WORKS OF WELLS OR VERNE, HE FINDS HE HAS BEEN TRANSPORTED TO ANOTHER PLANET--MARS, OR, MORE PRECISELY, BARSOOM (THE MARTIAN NAME FOR THE PLANET).
JOHN CARTER HAS A GREAT MANY ADVENTURES THERE AND, IN PARTICULAR MEETS A RACE OF GREEN GIANTS AND A PRINCESS, DEJAH THORIS, WITH WHOM HE FALLS IN LOVE!

THE STORY WAS NEVER MEANT TO BE CONTINUED, BUT IT WENT ON TO BE STUNNINGLY SUCCESSFUL...

JOHN CARTER, YOU HAVE RETURNED!

...SO JOHN CARTER RETURNED IN BRAND-NEW ADVENTURES BEGINNING IN 1913.

BUT IN OCTOBER 1912, *THE ALL-STORY* PUBLISHED ANOTHER NOVEL THAT WOULD MAKE HISTORY: *TARZAN OF THE APES*. IT BECAME BURROUGHS' MOST SUCCESSFUL SERIES. EACH VOLUME SOLD APPROXIMATELY ONE MILLION COPIES, AND HIS HERO WAS EVENTUALLY IMMORTALIZED ON THE BIG SCREEN IN 1932 BY THE FAMOUS OLYMPIC SWIMMER AND GOLD-MEDALIST JOHNNY WEISSMULLER.

IN THE *PELLUCIDAR* SERIES (THE FIRST ADVENTURE OF WHICH APPEARED IN *ALL-STORY WEEKLY* IN 1914), DAVID INNES AND ABNER PERRY DISCOVER AN UNKNOWN PREHISTORIC EMPIRE NAMED PELLUCIDAR, LOCATED AT A DEPTH OF 500 MILES UNDERGROUND. THIS, BURROUGHS' THIRD MAJOR SERIES, WHICH ALSO FEATURED TARZAN IN ONE STORY, GUARANTEED HIS STATUS AS A LEGENDARY AUTHOR.

HE INFLUENCED WHOLE NEW GENERATIONS OF WRITERS AND, MOST CRUCIALLY, A GENRE THAT WAS STILL TAKING SHAPE: HEROIC FANTASY. THIS SUB-CATEGORY OF EPIC AND MAGICAL TALES PORTRAYED FORMIDABLE, MUSCLE-BOUND HEROES LIKE CONAN, THE FAMOUS CIMMERIAN, WHO SPRANG FROM THE FERTILE MIND OF ANOTHER GRAND MASTER OF IMAGINARY WORLDS, ROBERT ERVIN HOWARD.

HOLLIS PARK, NEW YORK. ABRAHAM MERRITT'S HOUSE...

ON NOVEMBER 24, 1917, ABRAHAM MERRITT HAD HIS FIRST PIECE FOR *ALL-STORY* PUBLISHED: *THROUGH THE DRAGON GLASS*. IT WAS FOLLOWED BY *THE MOON POOL*, WHICH CAME OUT IN 1918, A CENTURY AFTER MARY SHELLEY'S *FRANKENSTEIN*. MERRITT DEMONSTRATED HOW EINSTEIN HAD TURNED SCIENCE UPSIDE DOWN WITH HIS FAMOUS FORMULA E=MC2 IN 1905.

MERRITT'S CAREER WAS BRIEF BUT SIGNIFICANT. HE SOON BECAME ASSISTANT EDITOR OF *THE AMERICAN WEEKLY*, THEN ENDED UP RUNNING IT FROM 1937 UNTIL HIS DEATH IN 1943. THROUGH THE MAGAZINE, MERRITT BECAME FRIENDS WITH THE GREAT PULP ILLUSTRATORS VIRGIL FINLAY AND HANNES BOK. THE LATTER WAS ALSO A NOVELIST AND A POET WHO COMPLETED TWO OF MERRITT'S TEXTS POSTHUMOUSLY.

MERRITT WAS ERUDITE, LOVED TO TRAVEL, AND ENJOYED COMBINING HIS KNOWLEDGE WITH OFTEN-ESOTERIC PHILOSOPHIES AND FORGOTTEN CULTURES. MOREOVER, HE BOASTED AN EXTENSIVE LIBRARY OF FIVE THOUSAND BOOKS, PARTICULARLY ON DIVERSE ASPECTS OF THE OCCULT. HIS INFLUENCES RANGED FROM H. RIDER HAGGARD TO HELENA BLAVATSKY AND ROBERT W. CHAMBERS, AUTHOR OF THE CULT SHORT-STORY COLLECTION *THE KING IN YELLOW*.

IN 1936, TOD BROWNING ADAPTED MERRITT'S NOVEL *BURN, WITCH, BURN!* INTO A FILM TITLED *THE DEVIL-DOLL*.

AMONG MERRITT'S MAJOR WORKS WERE TWO NOVELS: *THE SHIP OF ISHTAR* (*ARGOSY*, 1924), THE STORY OF AN ARCHEOLOGIST PROPELLED THROUGH TIME ON THE GALLEY OF THE BABYLONIAN GODDESS ISHTAR; AND *DWELLERS IN THE MIRAGE* (*ARGOSY*, 1932), WHOSE HERO, LEIF LANGDON, DISCOVERS A VALLEY WHERE TIME SEEMS TO HAVE STOOD STILL. HE WAS UNDOUBTEDLY ONE OF THE MAIN POINTS OF REFERENCE FOR H. P. LOVECRAFT.

JESSE J. ROBINSON'S MANSION...

QUICK, DOCTOR VANAMAN! HURRY UP!

COME IN HERE, DOCTOR. MY UNCLE IS IN HIS STUDY.

WILL HE LIVE?

WE SHALL SOON FIND OUT...

HE'S STILL ALIVE. BUT WHAT HAPPENED HERE?

WE HAD A THIEF, I THINK. HE WAS AFTER THIS MYSTERIOUS BOX THAT MY UNCLE BOUGHT FROM A CURIO DEALER.

WHAT'S SO SPECIAL ABOUT IT?

I DON'T KNOW, BUT SINCE IT'S BEEN HERE, WE'VE BEEN EXPERIENCING... HALLUCINATIONS...

Before moving on to Weird Tales and Hugo Gernsback--the other central figure of pulp science fiction in the early 20th century-- to round off the Munsey's magazines and Argosy period, we should mention an author who Merritt admired without knowing that she was a woman--maybe the first in the modern era of American science fiction. In 1920, she published Claimed! in Argosy under the pen name of Francis Stevens. But her real name was Gertrude Barrows Bennett.

GERTRUDE BARROWS BENNETT WAS BORN IN MINNEAPOLIS IN 1884. SHE WAS WIDOWED VERY YOUNG WHEN HER EXPLORER HUSBAND DIED WHILE AWAY HUNTING FOR TREASURE.

LEFT ALONE TO CARE FOR HER YOUNG DAUGHTER AND DISABLED MOTHER, SHE DECIDED TO START WRITING SHORT STORIES, NOVELS, AND NOVELLAS FOR MUNSEY'S MAGAZINES TO INCREASE HER INCOME.

MOMMY, I'M HUNGRY!

COME HERE AND HELP PROP ME UP ON MY PILLOW...

AND SO SHE CONTINUED FOR SEVEN YEARS, DURING WHICH TIME SHE PRODUCED HALF A DOZEN NOVELS AND SEVERAL MEMORABLE SHORT STORIES FOR HER PULP READERS.

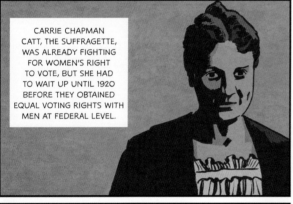

CARRIE CHAPMAN CATT, THE SUFFRAGETTE, WAS ALREADY FIGHTING FOR WOMEN'S RIGHT TO VOTE, BUT SHE HAD TO WAIT UP UNTIL 1920 BEFORE THEY OBTAINED EQUAL VOTING RIGHTS WITH MEN AT FEDERAL LEVEL.

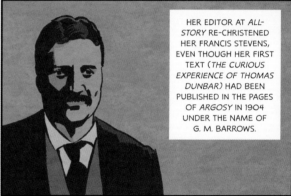

HER EDITOR AT *ALL-STORY* RE-CHRISTENED HER FRANCIS STEVENS, EVEN THOUGH HER FIRST TEXT (*THE CURIOUS EXPERIENCE OF THOMAS DUNBAR*) HAD BEEN PUBLISHED IN THE PAGES OF *ARGOSY* IN 1904 UNDER THE NAME OF G. M. BARROWS.

SOME OF HER STORIES DEMONSTRATED QUITE REMARKABLE IDEAS FOR THE TIME. HER MOST "SCIENCE-FICTIONAL" NOVEL, *THE HEADS OF CERBERUS*, FOR EXAMPLE, BLENDS DYSTOPIAN AND PARALLEL WORLDS, THEMES DEAR TO THE SCIENCE FICTION SHE HELPED TO FLOURISH.

SHE FOLLOWED IN THE WAKE OF MARY SHELLEY AND PRECEDED AUTHORS SUCH AS THE BRILLIANT CATHERINE LUCILLE MOORE, WHO LAUNCHED HER CAREER IN THE 1930S, AND MARGARET ST. CLAIR, WHO MADE HER DEBUT IN THE 1940S.

THE FIRST ISSUE OF LEGENDARY PULP MAGAZINE *WEIRD TALES* APPEARED IN MARCH 1923, PUBLISHED BY THE RURAL PUBLISHING CORPORATION IN CHICAGO. ONE OF ITS FOUNDERS, A CERTAIN JACOB CLARK HENNEBERGER, WANTED TO CREATE A MAGAZINE WITH EXCELLENT LITERARY STANDARDS, AND FICTION IN KEEPING WITH THE WORKS OF POE (OF WHOM HE WAS AN ADMIRER)--THE MACABRE, FANTASY, AND HORROR...

IN 1928, THE PLAYWRIGHT TENNESSEE WILLIAMS, WHO WON TWO PULITZER PRIZES FOR DRAMA, PUBLISHED HIS FIRST SHORT STORY IN THE PAGES OF *WEIRD TALES*. *THE VENGEANCE OF NITOCRIS* TOLD THE TALE OF AN EGYPTIAN PRINCESS TAKING REVENGE ON HER BROTHER'S KILLERS IN A VAULT THAT SHE FLOODS WITH THE WATERS OF THE NILE.

ROBERT ERVIN HOWARD CREATED HIS OWN HEROIC-FANTASY WORLDS AND WARRIOR HEROES, LIKE THE BARBARIAN KING KULL IN 1929 AND, OF COURSE, CONAN THE CIMMERIAN, WHO FIRST APPEARED IN THE PAGES OF *WEIRD TALES* IN 1932.

CONAN WAS AN ADVENTURER TRAVERSING INCREASINGLY DARKER STORIES IMBUED WITH A PESSIMISM THAT ALSO AFFLICTED THE AUTHOR HIMSELF, WHO COMMITTED SUICIDE IN 1936. CONAN MADE A COMEBACK IN THE 1970S IN COMICS BY ROY THOMAS, BARRY SMITH, AND JOHN BUSCEMA, AS WELL AS IN THE MOVIES WITH JOHN MILIUS' 1982 FILM *CONAN THE BARBARIAN*, STARRING ARNOLD SCHWARZENEGGER. HIS UNIVERSE WAS ALSO ADAPTED INTO THREE TV SERIES, AS WELL AS ROLE-PLAYING AND VIDEO GAMES!

HE CONTINUES TO BE ONE OF THE MAIN INFLUENCES ON THE CONTEMPORARY FANTASY GENRE, AS CAN BE SEEN IN THE WORKS OF THE BRITISH WRITER DAVID GEMMELL, FOR EXAMPLE.

THE MAGAZINE'S MOST-POPULAR AUTHOR WAS SEABURY QUINN, WITH HIS FRENCH HERO JULES DE GRANDIN AND HIS CATCHPHRASE, "BY THE BEARD OF A GREEN GOAT!" BUT ITS MOST FAMOUS WRITER OF ALL WAS ANOTHER HOWARD --HOWARD PHILLIPS (H. P.) LOVECRAFT, WHO DELVED INTO SCIENCE FICTION AS WELL AS THE FANTASTIC....

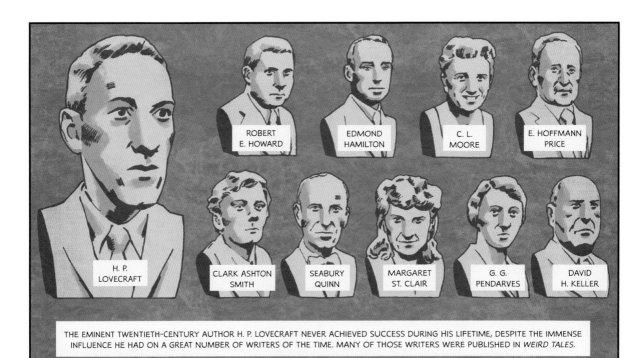

ROBERT E. HOWARD

EDMOND HAMILTON

C. L. MOORE

E. HOFFMANN PRICE

H. P. LOVECRAFT

CLARK ASHTON SMITH

SEABURY QUINN

MARGARET ST. CLAIR

G. G. PENDARVES

DAVID H. KELLER

THE EMINENT TWENTIETH-CENTURY AUTHOR H. P. LOVECRAFT NEVER ACHIEVED SUCCESS DURING HIS LIFETIME, DESPITE THE IMMENSE INFLUENCE HE HAD ON A GREAT NUMBER OF WRITERS OF THE TIME. MANY OF THOSE WRITERS WERE PUBLISHED IN *WEIRD TALES*.

I AM THE MESSENGER OF THE GODS; CRAWLING CHAOS!

NO ONE SHALL SPEAK MY NAME!

I AM THE ALL-IN-ONE AND THE ONE-IN-ALL. I DWELL IN THE CRACKS BETWEEN THE PLANES OF EXISTENCE IN OUR UNIVERSE!

I AM THE BIG BANG!

IN MY HOUSE AT R'LYEH, DEAD I WAIT, DREAMING.

I AM THE BLACK GOAT OF THE WOODS WITH 1,000 YOUNG.

IN HIS *ENCYCLOPEDIA OF UTOPIA, EXTRAORDINARY VOYAGES AND SCIENCE FICTION*, THE FRENCH WRITER PIERRE VERSINS MAINTAINED THAT LOVECRAFT'S WORK WAS AS MUCH "CONJECTURAL LITERATURE" AS IT WAS FANTASTIC, SINCE THE ENTITIES THAT LOVECRAFT DREAMT UP--HIS "GREAT OLD ONES"--WERE EXTRATERRESTRIAL IN ORIGIN AND MOSTLY BELONG TO THE REALM OF SCIENCE FICTION.

HE DIED OF BOWEL CANCER IN 1937, A YEAR AFTER HIS GOOD FRIEND ROBERT E. HOWARD. ALTHOUGH HIS WORK EVAPORATED INTO THE MISTS OF OBLIVION FOR A WHILE, IT WAS REVIVED IN PART BY THE ENORMOUS SUCCESS OF ROLE-PLAYING GAMES, PARTICULARLY *THE CALL OF CTHULHU*, BASED ON HIS SHORT STORY PUBLISHED IN *WEIRD TALES* IN 1926. THE GAME, RELEASED BY CHAOSIUM IN 1980, WAS THE FIRST IN WHICH PLAYERS COULD GO INSANE RATHER THAN DIE.

SO, WILL YOU FIGHT IT OR NOT?

HE WAS A MAJOR INFLUENCE ON STEPHEN KING, WHO ONCE SAID: "LOVECRAFT OPENED THE WAY FOR ME. I THINK THAT HE HAS YET TO BE SURPASSED AS THE 20TH CENTURY'S GREATEST PRACTITIONER OF THE CLASSIC HORROR TALE."

WEIRD TALES PUBLISHED THE MAJORITY OF HIS STORIES, FROM *DAGON* (1917) TO *THE HAUNTER OF THE DARK* (1935), INCLUDING *THE OUTSIDER* (1926), *THE CASE OF CHARLES DEXTER WARD* (1928), AND *THE THING ON THE DOORSTEP* (1933).

MARS. NORTHWEST SMITH'S SHIP BEGINS ITS DESCENT TOWARD THE RED PLANET...

IN *WEIRD TALES*, THE MOST SOUGHT-AFTER PULP MAGAZINE FOR COLLECTORS NOWADAYS, THE CONCEPT OF GENRE WAS ESSENTIALLY SECONDARY, SINCE THE MAIN OBJECTIVE WAS TO TELL HORRIFIC, BIZARRE STORIES, BE THEY SUPERNATURAL OR RATIONAL. IN 1933, IT PUBLISHED THE DEBUT STORY BY C. L. MOORE, WHOSE WRITING WAS IMBUED WITH AN AMAZING ATMOSPHERE, STRANGENESS AND SENSUALITY THAT APPEALED TO EDITOR FARNSWORTH WRIGHT. HE IS REPORTED TO HAVE SAID HE DIDN'T CARE IF SHE WAS "A MAN, A WOMAN, OR AN EXTRATERRESTRIAL; C. L. MOORE IS AN INCREDIBLE INDIVIDUAL."

THE TOWN OF LAKKDAROL...

AFTER READING *SHAMBLEAU*, THE VERY FIRST ADVENTURE FEATURING GALACTIC HERO NORTHWEST SMITH, LOVECRAFT WROTE THAT IT WAS "GREAT STUFF." THE AUTHOR HENRY KUTTNER ALSO ADDRESSED A PASSIONATE LETTER TO THE MAGAZINE, CONGRATULATING THE NEW AUTHOR, UNAWARE THAT SHE WAS ACTUALLY A WOMAN. AFTER A LONG EXCHANGE OF LETTERS AND A WHOLE RANGE OF WRITING COLLABORATIONS, C. L. MOORE MARRIED KUTTNER IN 1940.

NORTHWEST SMITH WAS ONE OF THE FIRST INTERGALACTIC HEROES. THIS SERIES OF STORIES PROVED THAT THE MAGAZINE WAS OPEN TO A WIDE VARIETY OF GENRES.

SMITH BECAME THE ARCHETYPAL, SOMEWHAT INDOLENT COSMIC ADVENTURER LATER ENCOUNTERED IN MANY SPACE OPERAS, SUCH AS THE WORKS OF EDMOND HAMILTON. IN 1934, C. L. MOORE CREATED HIS OPPOSITE IN HER WARRIOR JIREL OF JOIRY, OFTEN REGARDED AS THE FIRST TRUE HEROINE IN MODERN FANTASY.

WHAT DO YOU WANT WITH HER? STAY BACK, OR DEAL WITH ME!

SHE'S A SHAMBLEAU, CAN'T YOU SEE?! KEEP HER, THEN, BUT DON'T LET HER OUT AGAIN IN THIS TOWN!

SHAMBLEAU! SHAMBLEAU! SHAMBLEAU!

DURING HER YEARS AT *WEIRD TALES*, C. L. MOORE DEVELOPED BOTH A SCIENCE-FICTION STREAK AND SOMETHING CLOSER TO FANTASY, ALL HAMMERED OUT ON THE ANVIL OF HORROR. SHE ACKNOWLEDGED INFLUENCES RANGING FROM EDGAR RICE BURROUGHS TO GREEK MYTHOLOGY. *SHAMBLEAU* REVIVED THE MYTH OF THE GORGON AND SET IT AGAINST A BACKDROP OF SCIENCE.

YOU CAN STAY HERE.

YOU SAVED ME. I OWE YOU MY LIFE...

YOU'LL BE MINE!

SPACE OPERA, WHICH PRESENTS US WITH GALACTIC ADVENTURES ON AN EPIC, DRAMATIC SCALE, WAS ONLY JUST BEGINNING TO EMERGE FROM THE PENS OF EDWARD ELMER SMITH AND EDMOND HAMILTON, TWO GREAT FOUNDING FATHERS OF THE GENRE. THE ADVENTURES OF NORTHWEST SMITH AND JIREL OF JOIRY UNDERLINE C. L. MOORE'S IMPORTANCE, AS ALL HER INGREDIENTS WOULD TURN UP YEARS LATER IN THE *STAR WARS* SAGA.

A DECADE BEFORE ADOPTING "LEWIS PADGETT" AS A PSEUDONYM SHE USED FOR HER SUCCESSFUL STORIES CO-WRITTEN WITH HENRY KUTTNER IN THE 1940S, C. L. MOORE HAD GIVEN UP HER STUDIES DUE TO THE 1929 CRISIS AND TAKEN A JOB AS A SECRETARY IN A BANK. IN SEPTEMBER 1931, SHE BOUGHT HERSELF A COPY OF *AMAZING STORIES* MAGAZINE AND WAS PLEASED TO SEE WHAT IT CONTAINED. AS A RESULT, SHE DECIDED TO SEND OFF HER FIRST WORKS TO THEM, AND ALSO TO *WONDER STORIES*, WHO REFUSED THEM, POSSIBLY FOR BEING TOO FANTASTIC.

THREE OF C. L. MOORE'S ACCLAIMED NOVELS – *JIREL OF JOIRY*, *NORTHWEST OF EARTH*, AND *JUDGMENT NIGHT* – HAVE BEEN COLLECTED AS AN OMNIBUS BY THE PUBLISHER GOLLANCZ AS PART OF THEIR SF GATEWAY INITIATIVE.

C L MOORE

SHAMBLEAU
NORTHWEST OF EARTH
JUDGEMENT NIGHT

WHILE HUGO GERNSBACK IS KNOWN FOR HIS CONTRIBUTION TO SCIENCE FICTION, HIS PASSION FOR SCIENCE AND GADGETRY ALSO DROVE HIM TO TRY HIS HAND AT A "CAREER" AS AN INVENTOR. SOMETHING OF A GENIUS, HIS IDEAS WERE SEEN AS PROPHETIC, AND SOME OF THEM WERE ACTUALLY PATENTED, SUCH AS A DRY-CELL BATTERY IN 1907.

I SEE THE FUTURE!

GERNSBACK WAS BORN IN LUXEMBOURG IN 1884. AGED 20, HE EMIGRATED TO AMERICA WITH A DEGREE IN MECHANICAL AND ELECTRICAL ENGINEERING FROM BINGEN TECHNIKUM.

"THE ISOLATOR," ONE OF HUGO GERNSBACK'S INVENTIONS. THIS WAS NOT HEADGEAR FOR UNDERWATER OUTINGS, BUT WAS INTENDED TO BLOCK OUT ATMOSPHERIC NOISE.

IN 1906, HIS ATTEMPT TO MARKET ONE OF THE FIRST WIRELESS RADIOS AT A DERISORY PRICE OF $7.50 LED TO A VISIT FROM THE POLICE, WHO SUSPECTED HIM OF IMITATING THE COMPETITION. BUT HIS SYSTEM REALLY WORKED!

HE HELD A LARGE NUMBER OF PATENTS (APPROXIMATELY EIGHTY), AND HIS INVENTING CONTRIBUTED GREATLY TO HIS INTEREST IN ANOTHER FIELD: PUBLISHING.

HE BECAME FAMOUS THANKS TO THE MAGAZINES HE FOUNDED AND EDITED.

MODERN ELECTRICS

AT LAST, A MAGAZINE DEALING WITH THE SCIENCE OF TODAY... AND TOMORROW!

THE FIRST ISSUE OF MODERN ELECTRICS APPEARED IN 1908. THIS MAGAZINE, DESIGNED MOSTLY FOR AMATEUR RADIO ENTHUSIASTS, WAS QUITE SUCCESSFUL, AND ITS PRINT RUN QUICKLY INCREASED FROM 20,000 TO 50,000 COPIES.

THE YEAR 2660. THE SUBATLANTIC TUBE, 3,470 MILES IN LENGTH, NOW LINKS NEW YORK AND BREST, FRANCE AT SPEEDS OF UP TO 300 MILES PER HOUR!

RALPH 124C 41+

BETWEEN 1911 AND 1912, GERNSBACK PUBLISHED A SERIALIZED NOVEL OF HIS OWN, A "SCIENTIFIC ROMANCE" AS A PRETEXT TO TALK ABOUT SCIENCE THROUGH THE LENS OF A LOVE STORY. THE BOOK WAS TITLED *RALPH 124C 41+*, AND IT CLEARLY DEMONSTRATED ONE OF GERNSBACK'S MAIN PRINCIPLES: THAT FICTION SHOULD HELP IN TEACHING AND POPULARIZING SCIENCE.

EVEN THOUGH *RALPH 124C 41+* WAS A RATHER MEDIOCRE NOVEL, IT WAS CRAMMED WITH AMAZING INVENTIONS.

TELE-THEATER, OR HOW TO ATTEND A PERFORMANCE REMOTELY.

THE RADIOPERFORER, OR HOW TO KILL WITH A RADIUM BEAM.

THE PHONOLPHABET, OR HOW TO RECORD SOUNDS USING A PURPOSE-BUILT TYPEWRITER SYSTEM.

NEWSPAPERS PUBLISHED ELECTRONICALLY, OR HOW TO PREEMPT THE DIGITAL AGE.

THE HYPNOBIOSCOPE, OR HOW TO LEARN WHILE ASLEEP.

METEORO-TOWERS, OR HOW TO CONTROL THE CLIMATE BY ALTERING ATMOSPHERIC PRESSURE.

THE BACILLATORIUM, OR A ROOM ADAPTED TO KILL ALL BACTERIA, THUS EXTENDING OUR LIFESPAN UP TO 140 YEARS OLD.

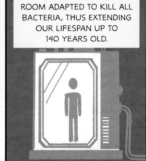

HELIO-DYNAMOPHORES, OR HOW TO CONVERT SOLAR ENERGY INTO ELECTRICITY.

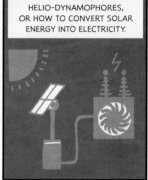

RADAR, OR HOW TO DESCRIBE IN INCREDIBLY PRECISE DETAIL AN INVENTION THAT WAS ONLY OFFICIALLY PATENTED BY ROBERT WATSON-WATT IN 1935.

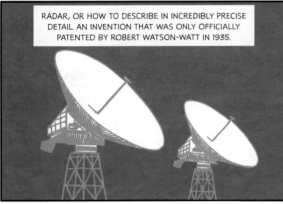

THE MENOGRAPH, OR HOW TO TRANSMIT AND REPRODUCE THOUGHTS IN GRAPHIC FORM.

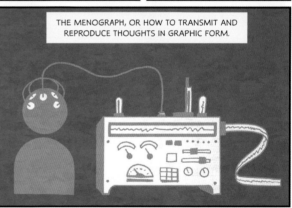

THE TELEPHOT, OR HOW TO SEE AND HEAR ANOTHER PERSON REMOTELY. ALSO EQUIPPED WITH A UNIVERSAL TRANSLATOR!

IN THE UNITED STATES, WHICH HAD BECOME A NEW PARADISE FOR SCIENCE, GERNSBACK MADE HIS CONTRIBUTION TO THE MULTIPLE TECHNICAL INNOVATIONS OF THE EARLY 20TH CENTURY BY ESTABLISHING THE IDEA THAT SCIENCE COULD BE DEVELOPED THROUGH IMAGINATION.

AS A STUDENT AT BINGEN TECHNICAL UNIVERSITY OF APPLIED SCIENCES FROM 1919 TO 1921, GERNSBACK SURELY READ *DER ORCHIDEENGARTEN*, A MAGAZINE PRINTED ON LOW-QUALITY WOOD-PULP PAPER AND EDITED BY ANOTHER STUDENT OF THE UNIVERSITY, ONE KARL HANS STROBL, A NAZI PARTY MEMBER. FOUR YEARS BEFORE *WEIRD TALES*, THIS GERMAN "PULP" HAD PUBLISHED A NUMBER OF TEXTS BY POE, WELLS, AND ALSO JOSEF ČAPEK, WHO COINED THE WORD "ROBOT."

IN 1923, GERNSBACK'S THOUGHTS ON THIS NEW FORM OF LITERATURE CONTINUED TO EVOLVE IN *SCIENCE AND INVENTION*. HE BEGAN TO CALL IT "SCIENTIFIC FICTION."

SCIENTIFIC FICTION

IN APRIL 1926, GERNSBACK CREATED THE FIRST PULP MAGAZINE EXCLUSIVELY DEDICATED TO "SCIENTIFICTION," AS HE WAS CALLING IT BY THEN. WITH ITS MUCH-LARGER FORMAT THAN THE TRADITIONAL PULPS, *AMAZING STORIES* INSTANTLY BECAME AN IMPORTANT PUBLICATION.

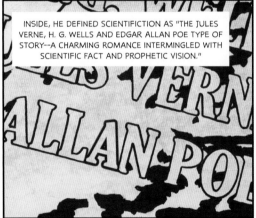

INSIDE, HE DEFINED SCIENTIFICTION AS "THE JULES VERNE, H. G. WELLS AND EDGAR ALLAN POE TYPE OF STORY--A CHARMING ROMANCE INTERMINGLED WITH SCIENTIFIC FACT AND PROPHETIC VISION."

ARKHAM COUNTY. A ROCK FALLS FROM THE SKY INTO A WELL...

THE FIRST ISSUES OF *AMAZING STORIES* SIMPLY REPRINTED THE GREAT AUTHORS, SUCH AS VERNE, WELLS, POE, AND MERRITT. THERE WAS ALSO T. S. STRIBLING, WHO LATER WON A PULITZER PRIZE FOR HIS NOVEL *THE STORE*. AMONG THE MOST FAMOUS TEXTS THAT GERNSBACK PUBLISHED WAS *THE COLOR OUT OF SPACE* BY H. P. LOVECRAFT.

"IT WAS NO LONGER SHINING OUT; IT WAS POURING OUT. AND AS THE SHAPELESS STREAM OF UNPLACEABLE COLOR LEFT THE WELL IT SEEMED TO FLOW DIRECTLY INTO THE SKY."

BUT ALTHOUGH GERNSBACK HELD THE NOVEL IN HIGH ESTEEM, LOVECRAFT WAS FURIOUS. NOT ONLY HAD GERNSBACK FAILED TO TELL HIM THAT THE TEXT HAD BEEN ACCEPTED, HE ALSO REFUSED TO PAY MORE THAN A FIFTH OF A CENT PER WORD.

GERNSBACK HAD A REPUTATION FOR BEING STINGY AND BAD AT PAYING UP. HE WAS JEWISH AND LOVECRAFT WAS A NOTORIOUS ANTI-SEMITE, DESPITE HAVING A JEWISH WIFE.

YOU'RE HUGO THE RAT! YOU'RE JUST ANOTHER SHYLOCK!

IN 1927, THE AUSTRIAN DIRECTOR FRITZ LANG RELEASED THE SEMINAL SILENT FILM *METROPOLIS*, BASED ON A SCRIPT BY HIS WIFE, THEA VON HARBOU. IT WAS A DYSTOPIAN ACCOUNT OF A POPULAR REVOLUTION AGAINST THE IDLE RICH CLASSES FROM THE UPPER CITY. THIS FILM INSPIRED NUMEROUS WRITINGS, FOR EXAMPLE *THE MACHINE MAN OF ARDATHIA* BY FRANCIS FLAGG, A SHORT STORY PUBLISHED IN *AMAZING STORIES* IN MARCH 1927 THAT EXAMINED HOW MECHANIZATION WOULD HARM THE PROLETARIAT.

1928. EDWARD ELMER SMITH'S *THE SKYLARK OF SPACE* APPEARED IN THE PAGES OF *AMAZING STORIES*.

THANKS TO METAL "X" WE CAN LIBERATE INCREDIBLE INTRA-ATOMIC ENERGY!

THE STARS ARE OURS!

YOU'RE ABSOLUTELY RIGHT, REYNOLDS. THE STARS ARE OURS!

MEANWHILE, AT THE WORLD STEEL CORPORATION...

CALM DOWN, DR. DUQUESNE, WE NEED YOUR EXPERTISE, AND WE MUST GET OUR HANDS ON THIS METAL "X" DISCOVERED BY RICHARD SEATON!

STARTING IN 1915, EDWARD ELMER SMITH (LATER NICKNAMED "DOC" BECAUSE OF HIS PHD IN CHEMISTRY) SKETCHED THE OUTLINES FOR *THE SKYLARK OF SPACE* IN COLLABORATION WITH LEE HAWKINS GARBY, THE WIFE OF A FRIEND. HOWEVER, PRESUMABLY GROWING TIRED OF THE PROJECT, SHE STOPPED WRITING AND LEFT SMITH ALONE AT THE HELM OF THIS SPACE OPERA, WHICH WAS IMMENSELY SUCCESSFUL WHEN FIRST PUBLISHED IN 1928. EVEN THOUGH THE MANUSCRIPT FOR *THE SKYLARK* WAS COMPLETED IN 1921, MANY PUBLISHERS DECLINED IT FOR BEING TOO AVANT-GARDE! CONSEQUENTLY, GERNSBACK BOUGHT IT FOR $75 AND PRINTED IT IN *AMAZING STORIES*.

WHEN *SKYLARK THREE* CAME OUT IN 1930, THE READERS' MAILBAG IN *AMAZING STORIES* PUBLISHED A LETTER FROM A 20-YEAR-OLD FAN, ONE JOHN WOOD CAMPBELL, WHO DESCRIBED "DOC" SMITH'S NOVEL AS "THE BEST STORY OF SCIENTIFICTION EVER PRINTED, WITHOUT EXCEPTION." THE YOUNG CAMPBELL WENT ON TO BECOME A KEY PLAYER IN THE GOLDEN AGE OF SCIENCE FICTION...AS WE'LL SEE LATER.

SMITH'S NOVELS WERE ALSO SAID TO HAVE MADE IMPORTANT CONTRIBUTIONS TO MILITARY AND SCIENTIFIC PROGRESS. HIS IDEAS CONCERNING STEALTH TECHNOLOGY INSPIRED GENUINE DEFENSE INITIATIVES AND SOME ACTUAL INVENTIONS.

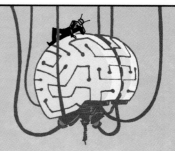

IN *THE SKYLARK OF VALERON*, THE THIRD VOLUME OF THE SERIES, SMITH DESCRIBED (IN 1934) AN ELECTRONIC BRAIN THAT DEVISED THEORIES WHICH UNMISTAKABLY CALL TO MIND "QUARKS" AND ELEMENTARY PARTICLES!

"WITH TERROR AND DARKNESS HE PETRIFIED THE UNIVERSE." – OVID

TWO LARGE SPACE FLEETS GO INTO BATTLE. THE TRIPLANETARY LEAGUE ATTEMPTS TO PUT AN END TO THE ATROCITIES OF GRAY ROGER, THE WORST SPACE PIRATE OF THEM ALL.

BUT THE TERRIBLE GRAY ROGER IS NOT YOUR ORDINARY PIRATE. HE IS AN EDDORIAN!

The Lens

HOWEVER, ANOTHER FORCE IS OBSERVING ATTENTIVELY FROM A STRANGE PLANET...

ARISIA

FIRST SERIALIZED IN *AMAZING STORIES* IN 1934, *TRIPLANETARY* RECOUNTED THE STRUGGLE BETWEEN TWO ANCIENT, EXTREMELY POWERFUL ALIEN RACES. THE FIRST, THE ARISIANS, PREFER TO STUDY OTHER SPECIES IN THE UNIVERSE AND COOPERATE WITH THEM TO LIVE A BEAUTIFUL, HARMONIOUS LIFE.

BUT THE SECOND, THE EDDORIANS, WOULD RATHER DRIVE OTHER SPECIES INTO SUBMISSION. IN THE SUBSEQUENT PARTS OF THE *LENSMAN* SERIES, THE TWO RACES CLASH IN A WAR THAT STRONGLY RESEMBLES A CHESS GAME ON AN INTERGALACTIC SCALE!

OVER THE YEARS, THE SERIES EXPANDED INTO SIX NOVELS, PLUS A COLLECTION OF THREE SHORT STORIES. "DOC" SMITH ALSO REWORKED *TRIPLANETARY* (THE NEW VERSION WAS PUBLISHED IN 1948) TO PROVIDE FULL CONTINUITY WITH THE OTHER NOVELS, WHOSE ADVENTUROUS, INVENTIVE STORYLINES SPAN BILLIONS OF YEARS!

"DOC" SMITH UNDENIABLY INFLUENCED MODERN SCIENCE FICTION. FOR EXAMPLE, *BABYLON 5*, BROADCAST IN THE 1990S, IS OFTEN CONSIDERED TO BE ONE OF TELEVISION'S BEST SCI-FI SERIES. ALONG WITH THE SERIES *ANDROMEDA*, IT HAS CLEAR ECHOES OF SMITH'S SCI-FI.

VIDEO GAMES HAVE ALSO BEEN INFLUENCED BY SMITH'S STORIES, PARTICULARLY THEIR GRANDIOSE DEPICTIONS OF SPACE BATTLES. STEVE RUSSELL, ONE OF THE DEVELOPERS OF *SPACEWAR!* IN THE 1960S, FELT THAT SMITH'S STORIES WOULD MAKE A GOOD BASIS FOR THE PROGRAM AND ITS SPACE MANEUVERS. IN MARCH 2007, *THE NEW YORK TIMES* REPORTED THAT IT HAD JOINED A LIST OF THE TEN MOST IMPORTANT VIDEO GAMES OF ALL TIME.

DAGOBAH. SLUIS SECTOR IN THE OUTER RIM TERRITORIES...

THE MOST POPULAR SCI-FI SAGA IN THE WORLD ALSO OWES A LOT TO SMITH'S CREATIONS. IN HIS BIOGRAPHY, GEORGE LUCAS REVEALED THAT SMITH'S *LENSMAN* NOVELS WERE A MAJOR, LASTING INFLUENCE ON HIS YOUTH, HIS CULTURE, AND HIS IMAGINATION.

LUKE SKYWALKER TRAVELLING TO DAGOBAH IN SEARCH OF YODA MIRRORS ONE OF SMITH'S HEROES, VIRGIL SAMMS, GOING TO ARISIA TO VISIT THE WISE MENTOR.

PUBLISH SCIENCE FICTION YOU SHALL, AND EMULATED IT WILL BE!

INCREDIBLE! I AM NOW FULLY CONNECTED TO YOUR MIND!

AND I TO YOURS! YOU ARE A TRUE LENSMAN!

THE LENS IS A JEWEL THAT ALLOWS SIMULTANEOUS, MUTUAL UNDERSTANDING AND, JUST AS WITH GEORGE LUCAS' JEDI KNIGHTS, PERMITS AN "ELITE" WITH NOBLE, PURE INTENTIONS TO BECOME GUARDIANS OF JUSTICE. INDEED, ALL THE COMPONENTS OF POPULAR SPACE OPERA WERE SPAWNED BY SMITH IN THE OFT-CRITICIZED PAGES OF *AMAZING STORIES*.

SMITH'S STYLE OF SPACE OPERAS HAD A MAJOR IMPACT ON SCI-FI WORKS OF THE 1930S AND 1940S, INCLUDING, FOR EXAMPLE, *THE LEGION OF SPACE* BY JACK WILLIAMSON, AND THE *CAPTAIN FUTURE* SERIES BY EDMOND HAMILTON.

THE LEGION OF SPACE (COLLECTED), JACK WILLIAMSON, 1934.

CAPTAIN FUTURE (SERIES), EDMOND HAMILTON, 1940.

THE SKYLARK OF SPACE, EDWARD ELMER "DOC" SMITH, 1928.

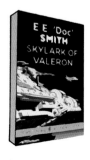

THE SKYLARK OF VALERON, EDWARD ELMER "DOC" SMITH, 1949.

THE SKYLARK DUQUESNE, EDWARD ELMER "DOC" SMITH, 1966.

ANOTHER IMPORTANT HERO OF AMERICAN SCIENCE FICTION WAS BORN IN THE PAGES OF *AMAZING STORIES* IN 1928: BUCK ROGERS (ORIGINALLY NAMED ANTHONY ROGERS). HIS FIRST ADVENTURE WAS TITLED *ARMAGEDDON 2419 A.D.*

THE STORY BEGINS IN 1927, WHEN ANTHONY ROGERS IS PUT INTO SUSPENDED ANIMATION. HE WAKES 492 YEARS LATER IN THE 25TH CENTURY. THERE HE MEETS WILMA DEERING, WHO BECOMES HIS COMPANION.

HE IS ALSO CONSIDERED TO BE THE FIRST SF HERO IN THE HISTORY OF COMICS! "ANTHONY" WAS DEEMED TOO LONG FOR THE COMIC ADAPTATION IN 1933, SO HE WAS RENAMED "BUCK."

IN *AMAZING STORIES*, HIS CREATOR, PHILIP FRANCIS NOWLAN, IMAGINED EXPLOSIVE NUCLEAR ROCKETS AS EARLY AS 1928!

THE ADVENTURES OF ANTHONY ROGERS AND WILMA DEERING WERE ALSO THE FIRST TO FEATURE ROCKET PISTOLS AND DISINTEGRATOR RAYS.

BUCK ROGERS BECAME A CORNERSTONE OF SF CULTURE, PARTICULARLY CONCERNING SPACE, BUT ESPECIALLY IN THE NASCENT WORLD OF COMIC BOOKS. FAMOUS FOR HOSTING THE BIRTH OF SUPERMAN, THE FIRST GREAT AMERICAN SUPERHERO, *ACTION COMICS* WENT INTO PRINT IN APRIL 1938, TEN YEARS AFTER NOWLAN'S FIRST NOVELLA WAS PUBLISHED IN *AMAZING STORIES*.

PROOF OF BUCK ROGERS' EARLY POPULARITY WAS HIS RAY GUN, THE "ROCKET PISTOL XZ-31," A TOY REPLICA OF WHICH WENT ON SALE IN 1933. IN 1939, A 12-EPISODE FILM SERIAL BY FORD BEEBE WAS SCREENED IN CINEMAS. BUT FANS HAD TO WAIT RIGHT UP UNTIL 1979 BEFORE A TV SERIES WAS MADE. THIS VERSION OF BUCK ROGERS RAN TO 37 45-MINUTE EPISODES AND ALLOWED AUDIENCES WORLDWIDE TO FAMILIARIZE THEMSELVES WITH THE VETERAN CULT HERO! IN 1982, SEGA RELEASED A "SHOOT 'EM UP" ARCADE GAME CALLED *BUCK ROGERS: PLANET OF ZOOM*, AND THERE WERE ALSO SEVERAL ROLE-PLAYING GAMES IN THE 1990S.

1929, YEAR OF CRISIS...

HELLO?

HELLO, MISTER GERNSBACK?

SPEAKING. TO WHOM DO I HAVE THE HONOR?

YOU DON'T KNOW ME. I'M A REPORTER.

A REPORTER?!

I'D LIKE TO ASK YOU A FEW QUESTIONS ABOUT WHY YOUR FIRM WENT BANKRUPT...

1929, YEAR OF THE WALL STREET CRASH THAT LED TO THE GREAT DEPRESSION...

1929 WAS ALSO A PARTICULARLY TERRIBLE YEAR FOR GERNSBACK. THE EDITOR LOST CONTROL OF *AMAZING STORIES* AND HIS OTHER MAGAZINES AFTER THREE OF HIS MINOR CREDITORS MANAGED TO FORCE HIM INTO BANKRUPTCY.

CONSPIRACY THEORIES ABOUNDED CONCERNING WHAT HAPPENED TO GERNSBACK. THERE WERE EVEN SUSPICIONS THAT THE EDITOR MIGHT HAVE ARRANGED TO GO BANKRUPT.

NEVERTHELESS, HUGO GERNSBACK MANAGED TO GET BACK ON HIS FEET AND, AFTER THE BANKRUPTCY HEARING, ANNOUNCED PLANS TO LAUNCH NEW MAGAZINES!

SCIENCE-FICTION

AN EVENT OCCURRED IN *SCIENCE WONDER STORIES* THAT WOULD BECOME PIVOTAL TO OUR STORY. UNTIL THAT POINT, GERNSBACK HAD BEEN USING THE TERM "SCIENTIFICTION." BUT IN HIS EDITORIAL OF JUNE 1929, HE FIRST USED THE PORTMANTEAU WORD THAT IS SO WELL-KNOWN TO FANS TODAY: "SCIENCE FICTION."

THE GENRE, BY ITS COMMON NAME, WAS THEREFORE BORN OUT OF THE BIGGEST ECONOMIC AND POLITICAL CHAOS AND UNCERTAINTY THAT THE WORLD HAD EVER EXPERIENCED. HIGHLY SYMBOLIC FOR LITERATURE THAT IS SO FOND OF CONTROLLING SPACE AND TIME!

NOT LONG BEFORE BLACK THURSDAY ON WALL STREET, THREE NEW MAGAZINES CAME OUT IN JUNE, JULY, AND SEPTEMBER 1929: *SCIENCE WONDER STORIES*, *AIR WONDER STORIES*, AND FINALLY *SCIENCE WONDER QUARTERLY*.

VOLUME 1
No. 1

JUNE
1929

Prophetic Fiction is the Mother of Scientific Fact

HUGO GERNSBACK, *Editor-in-Chief*

DAVID LASSER, *Literary Editor*   FRANK R. PAUL, *Art Director*

ASSOCIATE SCIENCE EDITORS

ASTRONOMY
Professor Samuel G. Barton
  University of Pennsylvania
Professor Donald H. Menzel
  Lick Observatory, University of California
Dr. Clyde Fisher, Ph.D., LL.D.
  Curator, The American Museum of Natural
  History.

BOTANY
Professor Elmer G. Campbell
  Transylvania College
Dr. Margaret Clay Ferguson
  Wellesley College

Professor C. E. Owens
  Oregon Agricultural College

ELECTRICITY
Professor F. E. Austin
  Dartmouth College

MATHEMATICS
Professor C. Irwin Palmer
  Dean of Students
  Armour Institute of Technology
Professor James Byrnie Shaw
  University of Illinois

Professor W. A. Titsworth, S. M.
  Alfred College

MEDICINE
Dr. David H. Keller
  Western State Hospital

PHYSICS AND RADIO
Dr. Lee dePorest, Ph.D., D.Sc.

PHYSICS
Professor A. L. Fitch
  University of Maine

ZOOLOGY
Dr. Joseph G. Yoshioka
  Illinois State Institute for Juvenile Research

Editorial, Advertising and General Offices, 96-98 Park Place, New York, N. Y.

SCIENCE WONDER STORIES

By HUGO GERNSBACK

TASTE in reading matter changes with each generation. What was acceptable to your grandparents, was hopelessly out of style for your parents. The literature of your parents—the Laura Jean Libby type of story and the dime novels, Buffalo Bill and Deadwood Dick are laughed at by the present generation.

The past decade has seen the ascendancy of "sexy" literature of the self confession type as well as the avalanche of modern detective stories.

But they are transient things, founded on the whims of the moment. For the world moves swiftly these days and as it moves literature also.

Science-Mechanics-the Technical Arts—they surround us on every hand, nay, enter deeply into our very lives. The telephone, radio, talking motion pictures, television, the X-ray, Radium, super-aircraft and dozens of others claim our constant attention. We live and breathe day by day in a saturated atmosphere.

The wonders of modern science no longer amaze us; we accept each new discovery as a matter of course. We hardly question why it had not come about sooner.

The man in the street no longer recognizes in science the word impossible; "What man wills, man can do," is his slogan.

Interplanetarian trips, space flyers, talking to Mars, transplanting heads of humans, death-rays, gravity-nullifiers, transmutation of elements—why not? If not to-day, well, then to-morrow. Are they surprises? Not to him; the modern man expects them.

No wonder, then, that anybody who has any imagination at all clamors for fiction of the Jules Verne and H. G. Wells type, made immortal by them; the story that has a scientific background, and is read by an ever growing multitude of intelligent people.

SCIENCE WONDER STORIES supplies this need for scientific fiction and supplies it better than any other magazine.

I started the movement of science fiction in America in 1908 through my first magazine, "MODERN ELECTRICS." At that time it was an experiment. Science fiction authors were scarce. There were not a dozen worth mentioning in the entire world.

I wrote a number of such stories and novels myself and gradually grouped about me a circle of authors who turned out better and better work as the years went by. I still have the best of these authors with me and practically all of them are writing and will continue to write for this magazine.

Who are the readers of SCIENCE WONDER STORIES? Everybody. Bankers, ministers, students, housewives, bricklayers, postal clerks, doctors, mechanics, dentists—every class you can think of—but chiefly those who have imagination. And as a rule, only those with intelligence and curiosity.

When the idea of this magazine first formulated itself, naturally the name was of importance, and I put that into the hands of the future readers. The publishers, had no hand in it.

Many thousands of prospective readers were circularized by means of a ... new and ... was ... fi ... subscribe to a ... The result ... twenty- ...

Science fiction, as published in SCIENCE WONDER STORIES, is a tremendous new force in America. They are the stories that are discussed by inventors, by scientists, and in the classroom...

... ific ... ty in the correctness various ... of such sto ... in mapping the future course of ...

There has been altogether too much pseudo-science fiction of a questionable quality in the past. Over-enthusiastic authors with little scientific training have rushed into print and unconsciously misled the reader by the distortion of scientific facts to achieve results that are clearly impossible.

It is the policy of SCIENCE WONDER STORIES to publish only such stories that have their basis in scientific laws as we know them, or in the logical deduction of new laws from what we know. And that is the reason why ALL stories published in this magazine must pass muster before an authority. It is a guarantee to our readers that they will not get a false scientific education thru the perusal of these stories

I believe that this innovation will make new history in magazine publishing. I know of no other fiction magazine that can muster such an array of authorities and educators to pass upon the quality of its stories.

It augurs well for the future of science fiction in America.

EVEN THOUGH SALES WERE LOWER THAN BEFORE, GERNSBACK'S NEW MAGAZINES CONTINUED TO ACT AS INCUBATORS THAT ESTABLISHED THE RULES OF MODERN SCIENCE FICTION WHILE ENCOURAGING MORE PEOPLE TO STUDY THE SCIENCES.

IN 1953, SEVERAL PRIZES WERE AWARDED AT THE ELEVENTH WORLD SCIENCE FICTION CONVENTION IN PHILADELPHIA. THEY WERE THE "HUGOS," THE FIRST AWARDS IN THE HISTORY OF THE GENRE AND STILL THE MOST COVETED TODAY.

TO FURTHER UNDERLINE HUGO GERNSBACK'S IMPORTANCE, THERE IS A 30-MILE-DIAMETER LUNAR CRATER NAMED AFTER HIM!

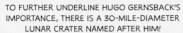

THE TEXTS YOU SELECT ARE SO TERRIBLE THAT ONE THING'S FOR SURE: YOU'VE GOT THE *WORST* TASTE IN THE ENTIRE HISTORY OF PUBLISHING!

YET SOME WERE OPPOSED TO THE ROLE THAT GERNSBACK PLAYED IN FOSTERING THE EMERGENCE OF SCIENCE FICTION. THE WRITER AND CRITIC DARRELL SCHWEITZER PUBLISHED A VITRIOLIC ARTICLE IN *ALGOL* MAGAZINE IN 1977, CLAIMING THAT GERNSBACK HAD MERELY BEEN A DAMAGING ACCIDENT IN THE EVOLUTION OF THE GENRE.

SCHWEITZER STIGMATIZED THE PULP MARKET FOR BEING TOO NARROW AND IMPENETRABLE.

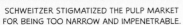

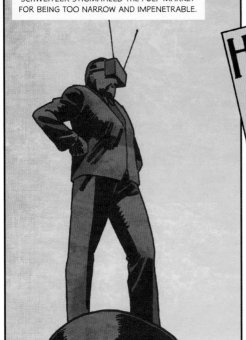

ACCORDING TO HIM, BY THE LATE 19TH CENTURY, SCIENCE FICTION WAS ALREADY APPEARING REGULARLY ENOUGH ALONGSIDE QUALITY LITERATURE IN THE LEADING LITERARY JOURNALS SUCH AS *HARPER'S MAGAZINE* AND *COSMOPOLITAN*.

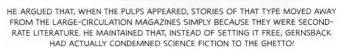

HE ARGUED THAT, WHEN THE PULPS APPEARED, STORIES OF THAT TYPE MOVED AWAY FROM THE LARGE-CIRCULATION MAGAZINES SIMPLY BECAUSE THEY WERE SECOND-RATE LITERATURE. HE MAINTAINED THAT, INSTEAD OF SETTING IT FREE, GERNSBACK HAD ACTUALLY CONDEMNED SCIENCE FICTION TO THE GHETTO!

DARRELL SCHWEITZER.

GERNSBACK HAS NO LITERARY APTITUDE WHATSOEVER, AND ENGLISH ISN'T EVEN HIS MOTHER TONGUE!

ELEGANCE, STYLE AND BEAUTY ARE SIMPLY BEYOND HIM!

GARY WESTFAHL, AUTHOR AND CRITIC.

SCIENCE FICTION WAS BORN OUT OF GERNSBACK'S IDEA TO GIVE THE GENRE A SPECIALIZED MAGAZINE AND A NAME OF ITS OWN!

PHILIPPE CURVAL, FRENCH AUTHOR, CRITIC AND EDITOR.

GERNSBACK IS JUST A REGRESSION TOWARD THE PRIMITIVE!

SAM MOSKOWITZ, SCI-FI FAN, CRITIC AND SF HISTORIAN.

HE LAID DOWN THE RULES OF TRUE SCIENCE FICTION, WHICH MAKES HIM THE REAL FATHER OF THE GENRE!

ALTHOUGH THE IMPORTANCE OF *WONDER STORIES* WAS INDISPUTABLE, GERNSBACK'S INFLUENCE GRADUALLY FADED DUE TO ONE PARTICULAR PULP CREATED IN 1930 THAT ALLOWED AMERICAN SCIENCE FICTION TO ENTER ITS GOLDEN AGE: *ASTOUNDING STORIES OF SUPER-SCIENCE.*

ONE OF THE MAIN REASONS FOR GERNSBACK'S DECLINE WAS HIS REPUTATION FOR BEING TIGHT-FISTED. WHEN *ASTOUNDING* APPEARED, THE MAGAZINE PAID ITS WRITERS MUCH MORE, SO THE BEST OF THEM DESERTED *WONDER STORIES.*

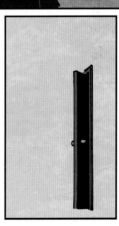

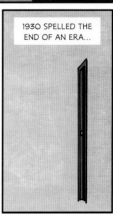

1930 SPELLED THE END OF AN ERA...

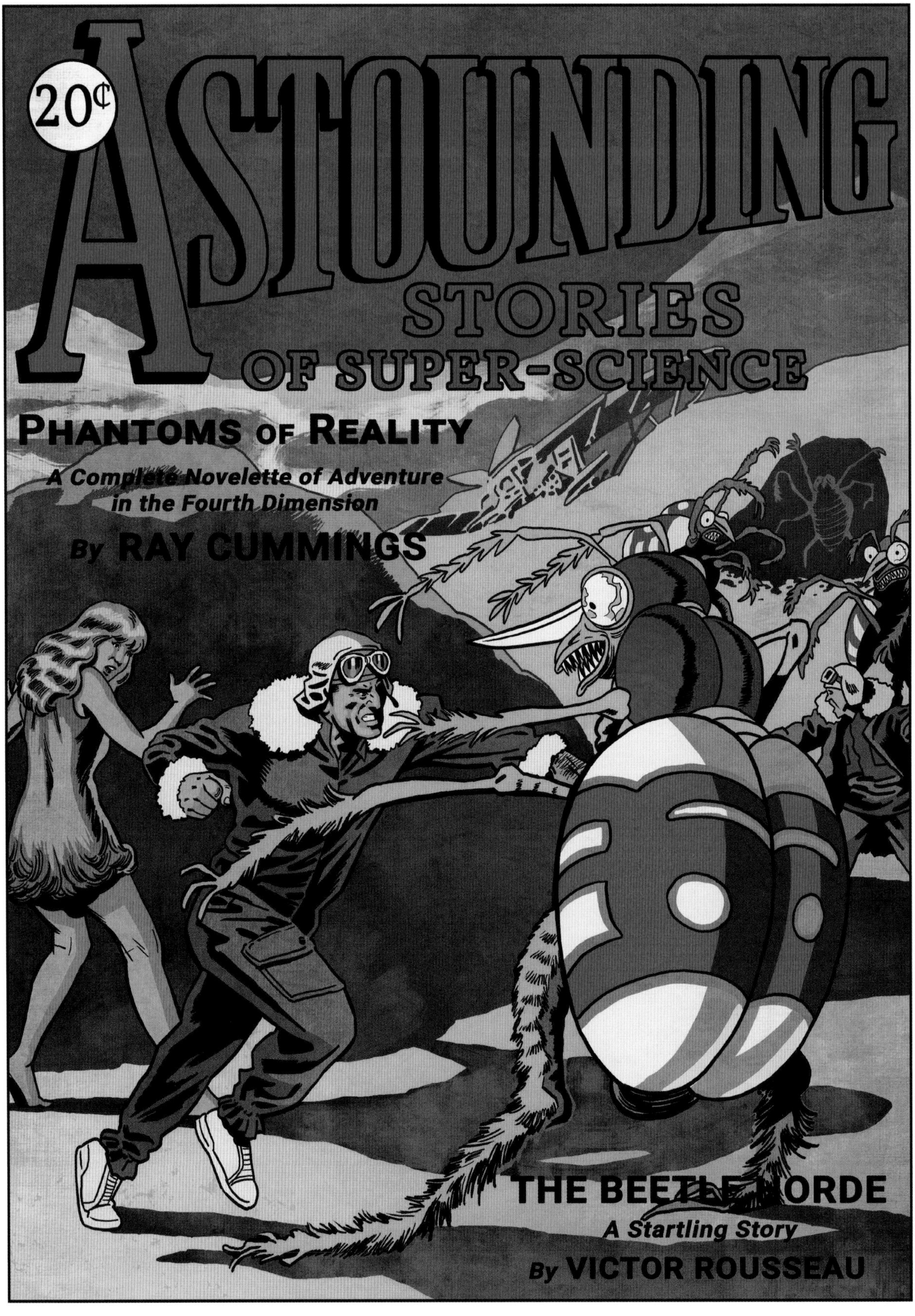
20¢
ASTOUNDING
STORIES
OF SUPER-SCIENCE
PHANTOMS OF REALITY
A Complete Novelette of Adventure
in the Fourth Dimension
By RAY CUMMINGS
THE BEETLE HORDE
A Startling Story
By VICTOR ROUSSEAU

The Golden Age of American SF. From the 1930s to the late 1940s.

AMERICA, 1935...

MRS. WEINBAUM?

DOCTOR?

I'M SORRY, BUT STANLEY'S GONE...

OH...NO! NO, STANLEY! DON'T LEAVE ME...

ON DECEMBER 14, 1935, ONE STANLEY GRAUMAN WEINBAUM PASSED AWAY DUE TO CANCER, AGED JUST 33. HE WAS ONE OF THE MOST PROMISING SCIENCE-FICTION WRITERS OF THE TIME; A FRESH, RISING TALENT.

HE IS AT PEACE AT LAST...

>SOB...<

WELL, TWEEL, I'M NOT SURE YOU'D HAVE SURVIVED AGAINST THAT MONSTER WITHOUT MY HELP. GUESS YOU OUGHT TO THANK ME!

♪♪♪♪♪
♪♪ ♪ ♪♪♪

IN 1934, *WONDER STORIES* PRINTED *A MARTIAN ODYSSEY*, THE FIRST STORY TO INCLUDE A GENUINELY FRIENDLY FORM OF ALIEN LIFE. WEINBAUM WAS A TRULY PIVOTAL AUTHOR WHO BRIDGED THE GAP BETWEEN TWO ERAS: THAT OF GERNSBACK AND THE ONE THAT FOLLOWED IN THE LATE 1930S--THE GOLDEN AGE. HE INTRODUCED, OR RATHER CONSOLIDATED, THE MAIN THEMES AND SUB-GENRES OF SCIENCE FICTION AND INFLUENCED THE GRAND MASTERS--ALL WITH JUST A HANDFUL OF STORIES.

THE GREAT ISAAC ASIMOV SAID *A MARTIAN ODYSSEY* WAS ONE OF THE THREE STORIES THAT REVOLUTIONIZED SCIENCE FICTION, DUE TO ITS NON-MANICHAEAN VISION OF AN ALIEN.

A MARTIAN ODYSSEY, 1934.

IN THIS SHORT STORY, WEINBAUM THEORIZED ON A PRE-EXISTING TREND: ALTERNATE HISTORY. ASKING THE QUESTION "WHAT IF?" CAN CHANGE ALL OF HISTORY BY CREATING HYPOTHETICAL WORLDS.

THE WORLDS OF IF, 1935.

WHAT IF I COULD MAKE A MOVIE... REAL?

COME ON, NOBODY COULD PULL OFF SUCH A FEAT!

IMAGINE YOURSELF TOTALLY IMMERSED IN THE STORY, WITH TASTE, SMELL, EVEN TOUCH... AND THE STORY IS ALL AROUND YOU, AND YOU ARE IN IT, JUST LIKE HERE AND NOW...

BASICALLY, HE INVENTED 3D!

PYGMALION'S SPECTACLES, 1935.

IF THE GULF STREAM WERE TO DISAPPEAR, EUROPE WOULD ENTER A NEW ICE AGE. THAT WAS THE SETTING I IMAGINED FOR THIS VERY MODERN AND INFLUENTIAL STORY THAT WAS SIMILAR TO WHAT IS NOW CALLED "ANTICIPATION" OR "SPECULATIVE FICTION," A TERM PROPOSED BY THE WRITER ROBERT ANSON HEINLEIN.

SHIFTING SEAS, 1937.

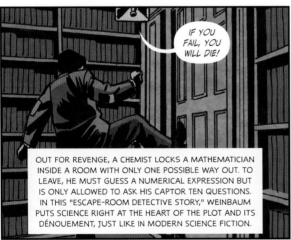

IF YOU FAIL, YOU WILL DIE!

OUT FOR REVENGE, A CHEMIST LOCKS A MATHEMATICIAN INSIDE A ROOM WITH ONLY ONE POSSIBLE WAY OUT. TO LEAVE, HE MUST GUESS A NUMERICAL EXPRESSION BUT IS ONLY ALLOWED TO ASK HIS CAPTOR TEN QUESTIONS. IN THIS "ESCAPE-ROOM DETECTIVE STORY," WEINBAUM PUTS SCIENCE RIGHT AT THE HEART OF THE PLOT AND ITS DÉNOUEMENT, JUST LIKE IN MODERN SCIENCE FICTION.

THE BRINK OF INFINITY, 1936.

WEINBAUM DISPATCHES HIS HEROES TO THE DARK SIDE OF VENUS, WHERE THEY ENCOUNTER AN INTELLIGENT SPECIES THAT IS BOTH STRANGE AND PRAGMATIC: THE LOTUS EATERS! SPACE OPERA, EXOTICISM, SCIENTIFIC ENIGMAS, AND AN AMUSING ENDING...THIS STORY HAS IT ALL.

THE LOTUS EATERS, 1935.

WEINBAUM'S *A MARTIAN ODYSSEY* WAS PRAISED BY LOVECRAFT FOR THE WAY HE HAD MANAGED TO CRAFT A STORY THAT WAS THE OPPOSITE OF ORDINARY SCIENCE FICTION. HOWEVER, CHARLES HORNIG, WHO HAD TAKEN OVER AS MANAGING EDITOR AT *WONDER STORIES*, REFUSED ONE OF WEINBAUM'S WORKS, SO HE DECIDED TO SEND IT TO *ASTOUNDING STORIES* INSTEAD. ITS EDITOR-IN-CHIEF, F. ORLIN TREMAINE, JUMPED AT THE CHANCE. AT THAT TIME, AMERICAN SCIENCE FICTION WAS RAPIDLY MUTATING AND ABOUT TO WITNESS THE DAWN OF THE MOST FAMOUS EDITOR THAT THE GENRE HAD EVER KNOWN!

JOHN W. CAMPBELL AND THE GOLDEN AGE OF
SCIENCE FICTION

STARRING:
JOHN WOOD CAMPBELL, JR.
ISAAC ASIMOV
ROBERT A. HEINLEIN
A. E. VAN VOGT
THEODORE STURGEON

THE CROOKED HOUSE...*

* FROM ROBERT HEINLEIN'S *AND HE BUILT A CROOKED HOUSE, ASTOUNDING STORIES*, 1941.

SCIENCE FICTION DEVELOPED SO MUCH DURING THE COURSE OF THE 1940S AND 1950S THAT THE PERIOD BECAME KNOWN AS THE GOLDEN AGE. TO A GREAT EXTENT, IT WAS THANKS TO THE INFLUENCE OF THE MAN WHO TOOK OVER THE REINS OF A BOOMING PULP MAGAZINE, *ASTOUNDING STORIES*, IN 1937. HIS NAME WAS JOHN WOOD CAMPBELL.

ISAAC, IS THAT YOU?

YES, IT'S ME, JOHN...

I'M READY FOR THIS MEETING OF THE GRAND MASTERS!

JOHN WOOD CAMPBELL

ISAAC ASIMOV

A. E. VAN VOGT

ROBERT A. HEINLEIN

I'M SO GLAD TO SEE YOU AGAIN, TED!

AND SO AM I, ROBERT!

THEODORE STURGEON

ALRIGHT... DISCIPLINE, GENTLEMEN! IT'S YOU WHO WANTED THIS GET-TOGETHER. SO, TIME FOR SOME WORK.

YOU'RE RIGHT, JOHN. DOWN TO BUSINESS!

WE NEED TO CHRONICLE OUR SAGA FOR THE GENERATIONS TO COME.

IT ALL STARTED WITH YOU, JOHN.

I AM GREATLY HONORED. INDEED, I DID PLAY AN ACTIVE PART IN THE GROWTH OF AMERICAN SCIENCE FICTION, RIGHT FROM MY YOUTH...

RIGHT... THIS TIME I'LL GET THE EXPERIMENT TO WORK!

"IT'S TRUE THAT, AS A YOUNG BOY, I WAS STRONGLY DRAWN TO THE SCIENCES, AND CHEMISTRY IN PARTICULAR WAS ONE OF MY FIRST PASSIONS. I WAS PRETTY PRECOCIOUS, I HAVE TO ADMIT. THE FAMILY BASEMENT BECAME MY DOMAIN!"

YOUR CHAIN'S COME OFF, AND THIS TWISTED PEDAL CRANK NEEDS REPAIRS...

THINK YOU CAN FIX IT UP, JUST LIKE LAST TIME?

YEAH, SURE THING. YOU CAN COUNT ON ME!

"BUT AT SEVEN, I GOT EVEN MORE PASSIONATELY INTO BOOKS. FIRST IT WAS TALES AND LEGENDS, THEN I MOVED ON TO EDGAR RICE BURROUGHS.

"A YEAR LATER, I WAS DEVOURING THE SCIENTIFIC WORKS OF JAMES JEANS, WHO, AS YOU KNOW, CONTRIBUTED TO QUANTUM THEORY. THEN, I DISCOVERED OTHER SCIENTISTS AND TOOK AN INTEREST IN THE THEORY OF RELATIVITY...

"WELL, I DIDN'T REALLY TURN INTO THE GREAT MAN THEY'D HOPED FOR. I LEFT WITH NO DIPLOMA, BUT MY GENERAL AND SCIENTIFIC KNOWLEDGE WERE FAR ABOVE AVERAGE.

"I LEARNED A LOT FROM MY FATHER WITHOUT ACTUALLY REALIZING IT. HE HATED IT WHEN TEXT WAS BADLY WRITTEN AND, THANKS TO HIS SEVERITY, MASTERING LANGUAGE BECAME MUCH EASIER."

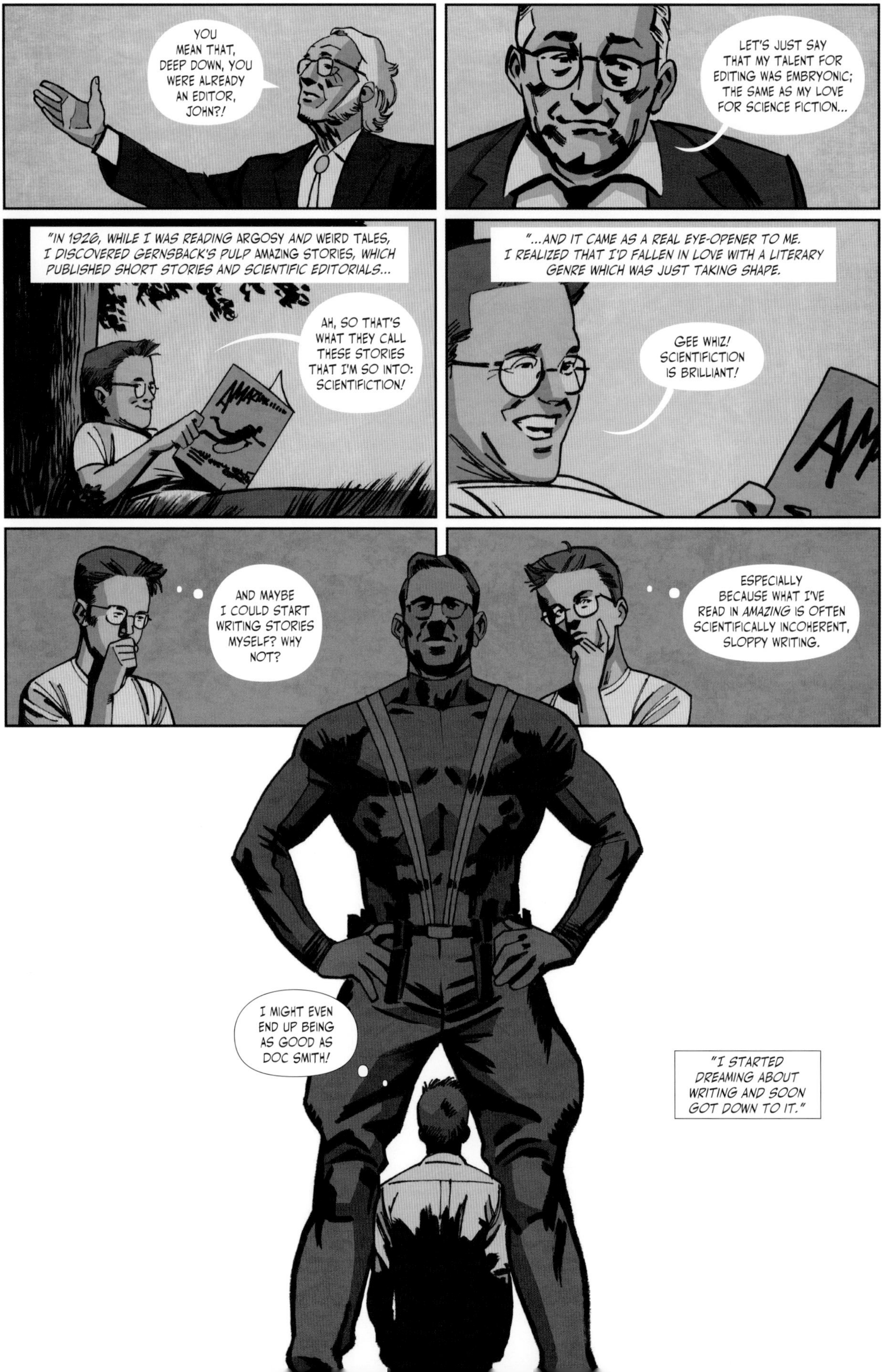
YOU MEAN THAT, DEEP DOWN, YOU WERE ALREADY AN EDITOR, JOHN?!
LET'S JUST SAY THAT MY TALENT FOR EDITING WAS EMBRYONIC; THE SAME AS MY LOVE FOR SCIENCE FICTION...
"IN 1926, WHILE I WAS READING ARGOSY AND WEIRD TALES, I DISCOVERED GERNSBACK'S PULP AMAZING STORIES, WHICH PUBLISHED SHORT STORIES AND SCIENTIFIC EDITORIALS...
AH, SO THAT'S WHAT THEY CALL THESE STORIES THAT I'M SO INTO: SCIENTIFICTION!
"...AND IT CAME AS A REAL EYE-OPENER TO ME. I REALIZED THAT I'D FALLEN IN LOVE WITH A LITERARY GENRE WHICH WAS JUST TAKING SHAPE.
GEE WHIZ! SCIENTIFICTION IS BRILLIANT!
AND MAYBE I COULD START WRITING STORIES MYSELF? WHY NOT?
ESPECIALLY BECAUSE WHAT I'VE READ IN AMAZING IS OFTEN SCIENTIFICALLY INCOHERENT, SLOPPY WRITING.
I MIGHT EVEN END UP BEING AS GOOD AS DOC SMITH!
"I STARTED DREAMING ABOUT WRITING AND SOON GOT DOWN TO IT."

"THEN I WENT TO M.I.T.*, WHERE I MET NORBERT WIENER, THE FATHER OF CYBERNETICS. I ALSO MANAGED TO SELL MY FIRST SHORT STORIES."

INVADERS FROM THE INFINITE AND WHEN THE ATOMS FAILED ARE IN AMAZING STORIES!

THE METAL HORDE OPENS THE APRIL ISSUE OF AMAZING!

THE ADVENTURES OF ARCOT, MOREY AND WADE ARE OUT AT LAST!

OFTEN, THANKS TO MY SUCCESS AT THE TIME, PEOPLE CLAIMED THAT I'D INVENTED SPACE OPERA TOGETHER WITH DOC SMITH AND EDMOND HAMILTON. BUT I WAS ALSO SEEN AS A PIONEER OF HARD SF, I.E. EXTREMELY SCIENTIFIC SCIENCE FICTION, THE KIND THAT DEALS WITH DIZZYING, DIFFICULT CONCEPTS AND THE MOST PLAUSIBLE POSSIBILITIES.

I REMEMBER THAT YOUR STORY THE METAL HORDE DELVED INTO ARTIFICIAL INTELLIGENCE, A THEME WE WOULD BOTH GO ON TO EXPLORE IN OUR WORK...

ALFRED ALSO COVERED THE SUBJECT IN HIS STORY THE GREAT JUDGE...BUT, COME TO THINK OF IT, IT WAS THANKS TO YOU THAT I SENT MY FIRST STORIES TO ASTOUNDING...

* M.I.T.: MASSACHUSETTS INSTITUTE OF TECHNOLOGY, CONSIDERED TO BE ONE OF THE WORLD'S BEST UNIVERSITIES, PARTICULARLY IN THE FIELD OF ENGINEERING SCIENCES.

WE'LL COME TO THAT. BUT FIRST I SHOULD TALK BRIEFLY ABOUT MY OTHER CAREER AS A WRITER.

RIGHT... YOU MEAN DON A. STUART?

"YES. I'D MARRIED DOÑA IN 1931, THEN DROPPED OUT OF M.I.T. AND WENT TO STUDY PHYSICS AT DUKE UNIVERSITY INSTEAD. BECAUSE OF THE DEPRESSION, A "PULPSTER" LIKE ME HAD TO TRY AND BRANCH OUT, AS THERE WERE VERY FEW PULPS DEDICATED TO SCIENCE FICTION."

"BUT A NEW PULP, ASTOUNDING STORIES, WAS BORN IN EARLY 1930. EVEN THOUGH I WAS PUBLISHING IN GERNSBACK'S WONDER STORIES FOR A WHILE--WHERE MY STYLE IMPROVED, BECOMING MORE SERIOUS AND CONTROLLED--I ENDED UP WRITING FOR THE NEW MAGAZINE IN 1934 UNDER THREE PSEUDONYMS.

"AFTER WILLIAM CLAYTON WENT BANKRUPT IN 1933, STREET & SMITH BOUGHT ASTOUNDING STORIES, WHICH HAD BEEN PUBLISHING THE GREAT JACK WILLIAMSON, MURRAY LEINSTER, AND EDMOND HAMILTON, AND IT WAS TAKEN OVER BY THE OUTSTANDING F. ORLIN TREMAINE. I WAS DUE TO HAVE A NOVEL IN IT, THE MIGHTIEST MACHINE, BUT THEY ALSO BOUGHT SOME OF MY OTHER STORIES AND PRINTED THEM UNDER A RANGE OF PSEUDONYMS, INCLUDING DON A. STUART, AS A TRIBUTE TO MY WIFE, DOÑA STEWART."

BUT WE CAN'T PUBLISH THREE OF YOUR STORIES IN THE SAME ISSUE. SO, LET'S PRINT TWILIGHT UNDER THE ALIAS OF DON A. STUART AND THE IRRELEVANT UNDER THE NAME OF KARL VAN KAMPEN.

THAT'S A REALLY GOOD IDEA. THEY'RE SO VERY DIFFERENT FROM EACH OTHER... I'M STARTING TO EVOLVE, AND TWILIGHT IS MUCH DEEPER...

AND A LOT DARKER, TOO! YOUR SCIENCE FICTION IS CRITICAL, AND I'M REALLY KEEN ON THAT ANGLE!

TWILIGHT APPEARED IN ASTOUNDING STORIES IN 1934.

WELL NOW, TERRIBLE WEATHER, AIN'T IT? WHY WERE YOU OUTSIDE?

YOU'RE NOT MUCH OF A TALKER...

DO YOU REALLY WANT ME TO TELL YOU? ARE YOU READY TO HEAR AN INCREDIBLE TALE?

GO RIGHT AHEAD! IT'LL LIVEN UP THE JOURNEY!

I'VE COME FROM ANOTHER TIME. A DISTANT, DISMAL ERA WHERE THINKING MACHINES HAVE TAKEN OVER FROM HUMANS...

LATER, YOU OFTEN FEATURED ON THE CONTENTS PAGE OF ASTOUNDING STORIES.

IT'S TRUE, I DID PUBLISH A LOT IN THAT PULP AFTER 1935.

SUCH AS BLINDNESS.

I FIRST HEARD OF YOU IN 1938, THANKS TO WHO GOES THERE?

...WHICH IS WHAT MADE YOU EMBARK ON A CAREER AS A SCIENCE-FICTION WRITER, ALFRED. YOU TOLD ME ABOUT IT PLENTY OF TIMES.

BACK THEN, I WAS SERIOUSLY IMPRESSED BY YOUR NOVELLA.

THIS TEXT IS EXTRAORDINARY! SO INVENTIVE, SO POLISHED!

WHO GOES THERE? CAME OUT IN 1938 IN *ASTOUNDING*...

WHO GOES THERE?

JOHN W. CAMPBELL JR

...AND LATER BECAME WORLD-FAMOUS AS *THE THING (FROM ANOTHER WORLD)*.

NOW THAT OUGHTA BLOW THE LID RIGHT OFFA THIS DAMN WRECK...

HOPE SO. I'M GONNA FREEZE!

COME ON, LET'S GET THIS THING BACK TO BASE.

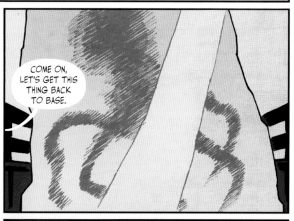

BOOM

SEVERAL HOURS LATER...

ZZZZ...

NOW I WILL BECOME YOU...

THE NOVELLA HAS BEEN ADAPTED THREE TIMES FOR THE BIG SCREEN INCLUDING BY CHRISTIAN NYBY AND HOWARD HAWKES IN 1951, AND THE JOHN CARPENTER VERSION FROM 1982 (TITLED *THE THING*). EACH ELEVATED THE STORY TO LEGENDARY STATUS.

IT WAS THANKS TO YOUR NOVELLA THAT I STARTED TO WONDER IF I COULD ALSO WRITE SCIENCE FICTION FOR THE MAGAZINE.

YES, AND YOU WENT ON TO SUBMIT A RANGE OF STORIES TO *ASTOUNDING*. AND I PRINTED THEM.

IT'S TRUE, YOU DID SEEM DESTINED TO BECOME A LEADING SCIENCE-FICTION AUTHOR. BUT IN THE END YOU CHOSE PUBLISHING.

WELL, ISAAC, I HAVE TO SAY IT TURNED MY WHOLE LIFE UPSIDE DOWN. TREMAINE BECAME THE EDITORIAL DIRECTOR OF STREET & SMITH, THE OWNERS OF *ASTOUNDING*, SO HE PUT ITS FATE IN MY HANDS...

YOU WERE ONLY 27, WITH NO PUBLISHING EXPERIENCE, RIGHT?

EXACTLY, ROBERT, AND I HAD PRETTY FIXED IDEAS ABOUT WHAT MADE FOR A GOOD SCIENCE-FICTION STORY.

MY THOUGHTS ON THE MATTER WERE VERY CLEAR...

I EVEN LAID THEM ALL OUT IN AN ESSAY I WROTE LATER...

...TITLED THE SCIENCE OF SCIENCE-FICTION WRITING.

IT CONTAINED MY OWN PERSONAL FORMULA!

"STYLE IS BASED ON THE WAY AN AUTHOR PUTS HIS IDEAS INTO ENGLISH."

"PREDICTIONS MUST BE BASED ON THE KNOWN DATA OF THE EXISTING SCIENCE."

"AN HONEST EFFORT AT PROPHETIC EXTRAPOLATION OF THE KNOWN MUST BE MADE. WE MUST FORECAST THE DEVELOPMENT OF A SCIENCE OF SOCIOLOGY."

"BECAUSE WE ARE HUMAN BEINGS, THE HUMAN SCIENCES ARE MORE INTERESTING TO CONTEMPLATE. THE HUMANITY IS CENTRAL."

"READERS WANT STORIES OF PEOPLE LIVING IN A WORLD WHERE THE GREAT IDEAS AND MACHINES MERELY FORM THE BACKGROUND."

"READ THE EXPERTS, TO SEE WHY THEIR STORIES WERE BELL-RINGERS, NOT JUST ANOTHER YARN!"

BACK THEN, I'D BITTERLY REFUSE ANY STORIES THAT WERE STRONG ON IDEAS BUT JUST NOT INTRIGUING ENOUGH.

ACTUALLY, THE MOST IMPORTANT ASPECT OF ALL THOSE YOU LISTED WAS TO PLEASE THE READER.

YOU ALSO RECOMMENDED THAT AUTHORS WRITE IN THE THIRD PERSON TO BETTER DESCRIBE HOW THEIR CHARACTERS ACT, GIVING INSIGHTS INTO THEIR THOUGHTS AND THEIR WORLDVIEW, AS WELL AS THEIR MENTAL PROCESSES!

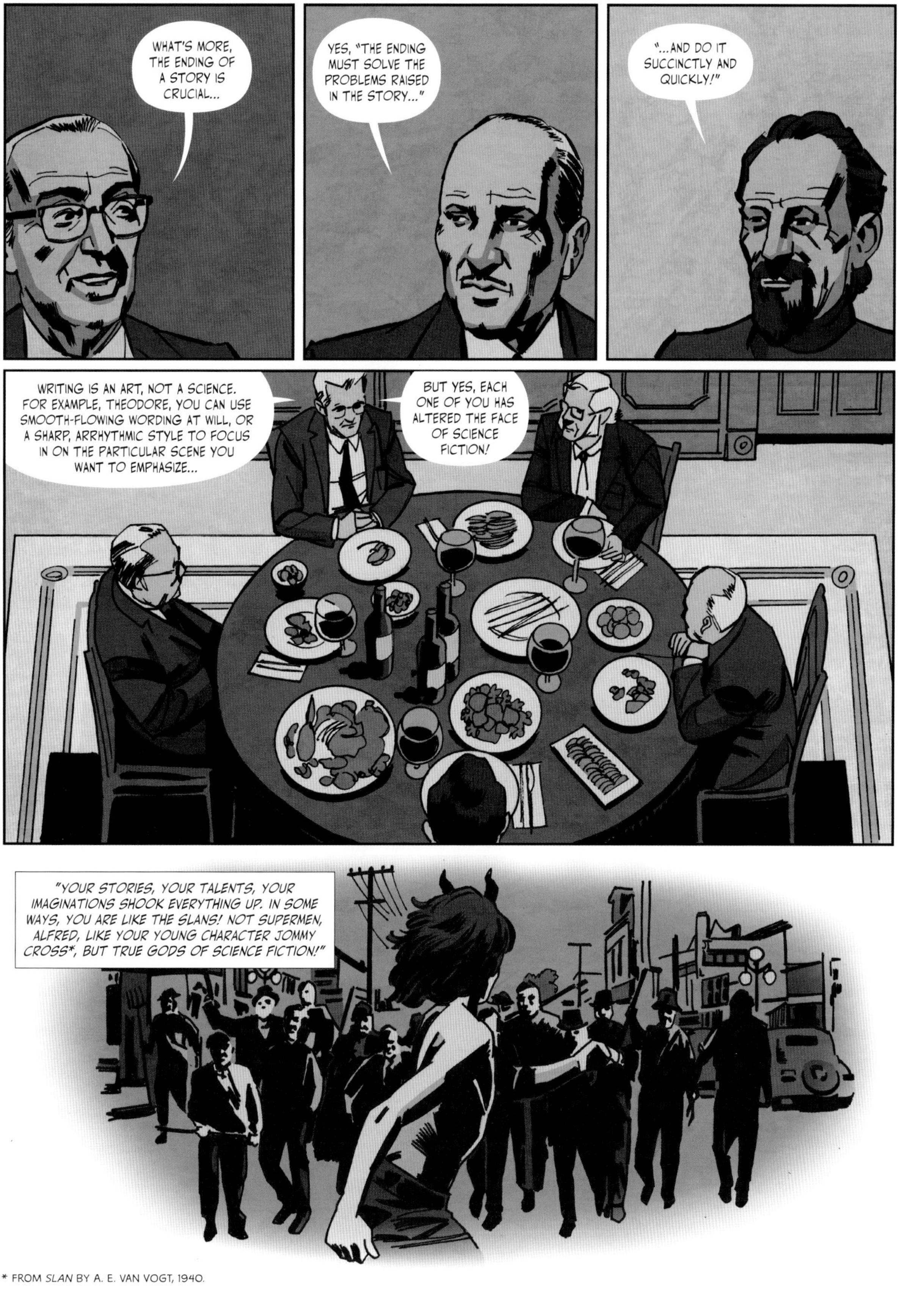
WHAT'S MORE, THE ENDING OF A STORY IS CRUCIAL...
YES, "THE ENDING MUST SOLVE THE PROBLEMS RAISED IN THE STORY..."
"...AND DO IT SUCCINCTLY AND QUICKLY!"
WRITING IS AN ART, NOT A SCIENCE. FOR EXAMPLE, THEODORE, YOU CAN USE SMOOTH-FLOWING WORDING AT WILL, OR A SHARP, ARRHYTHMIC STYLE TO FOCUS IN ON THE PARTICULAR SCENE YOU WANT TO EMPHASIZE...
BUT YES, EACH ONE OF YOU HAS ALTERED THE FACE OF SCIENCE FICTION!
"YOUR STORIES, YOUR TALENTS, YOUR IMAGINATIONS SHOOK EVERYTHING UP. IN SOME WAYS, YOU ARE LIKE THE SLANS! NOT SUPERMEN, ALFRED, LIKE YOUR YOUNG CHARACTER JOMMY CROSS*, BUT TRUE GODS OF SCIENCE FICTION!"

* FROM *SLAN* BY A. E. VAN VOGT, 1940.

SOME TIME LATER...

LIKE THE SO-CALLED "MUTANT ISSUES."*

SO, I TOOK THE HELM OF *ASTOUNDING* IN THE FALL OF 1937, AND THE MAGAZINE UNDERWENT SOME MAJOR CHANGES STARTING FROM 1938.

...WHICH BECAME VERY WELL-KNOWN FOR PRESENTING SUCH AN ORIGINAL IDEA.

YES! AND I ALSO DECIDED TO COMPLETELY ALTER THE OVERALL STYLE OF THE COVER ART TO MAKE IT MORE SERIOUS.

THEN YOU EVEN WENT AS FAR AS CHANGING THE TITLE OF THE MAGAZINE!

I SIMPLY COULDN'T STAND THAT PUERILE TITLE ANYMORE. ORIGINALLY, I JUST WANTED TO RENAME IT "SCIENCE FICTION," BUT CHARLES HORNIG, THE FORMER EDITOR OF *AMAZING STORIES*, HAD JUST USED THAT FOR THE TITLE OF A NEW MAGAZINE. TOUGH LUCK!

* THE "MUTANT" ISSUES WERE FILLED WITH STORIES THAT WOULD TAKE *ASTOUNDING* (AND SCI-FI) IN A NEW DIRECTION, AND SEE IT MUTATE INTO A MAGAZINE OF MORE CEREBRAL WORKS.

THE FIRST MUTANT ISSUE CAME OUT IN FEBRUARY 1938. THE HEADLINER WAS JACK WILLIAMSON WITH *THE LEGION OF TIME*, THE FIRST NOVEL TO IMAGINE TIME TRAVEL AS A MEANS OF MODIFYING THE PRESENT.

"TWO OPPOSING FACTIONS; TWO HUMANITIES FROM TWO POSSIBLE FUTURES. GREAT NAMES AND GREAT STORIES STARTED TO APPEAR ON THE CONTENTS PAGE OF ASTOUNDING..."

L. RON HUBBARD, *THE DANGEROUS DIMENSION*, JULY 1938.

CLIFFORD D. SIMAK, *RULE 18*, JULY 1938.

NAT SCHACHNER, *WORLDS DON'T CARE*, APRIL 1939.

LYON SPRAGUE DE CAMP, *EMPLOYMENT*, MAY 1939.

AMELIA REYNOLDS LONG, *WHEN THE HALF GODS GO--*, JULY 1939.

LESTER DEL REY, *THE DAY IS DONE*, MAY 1939.

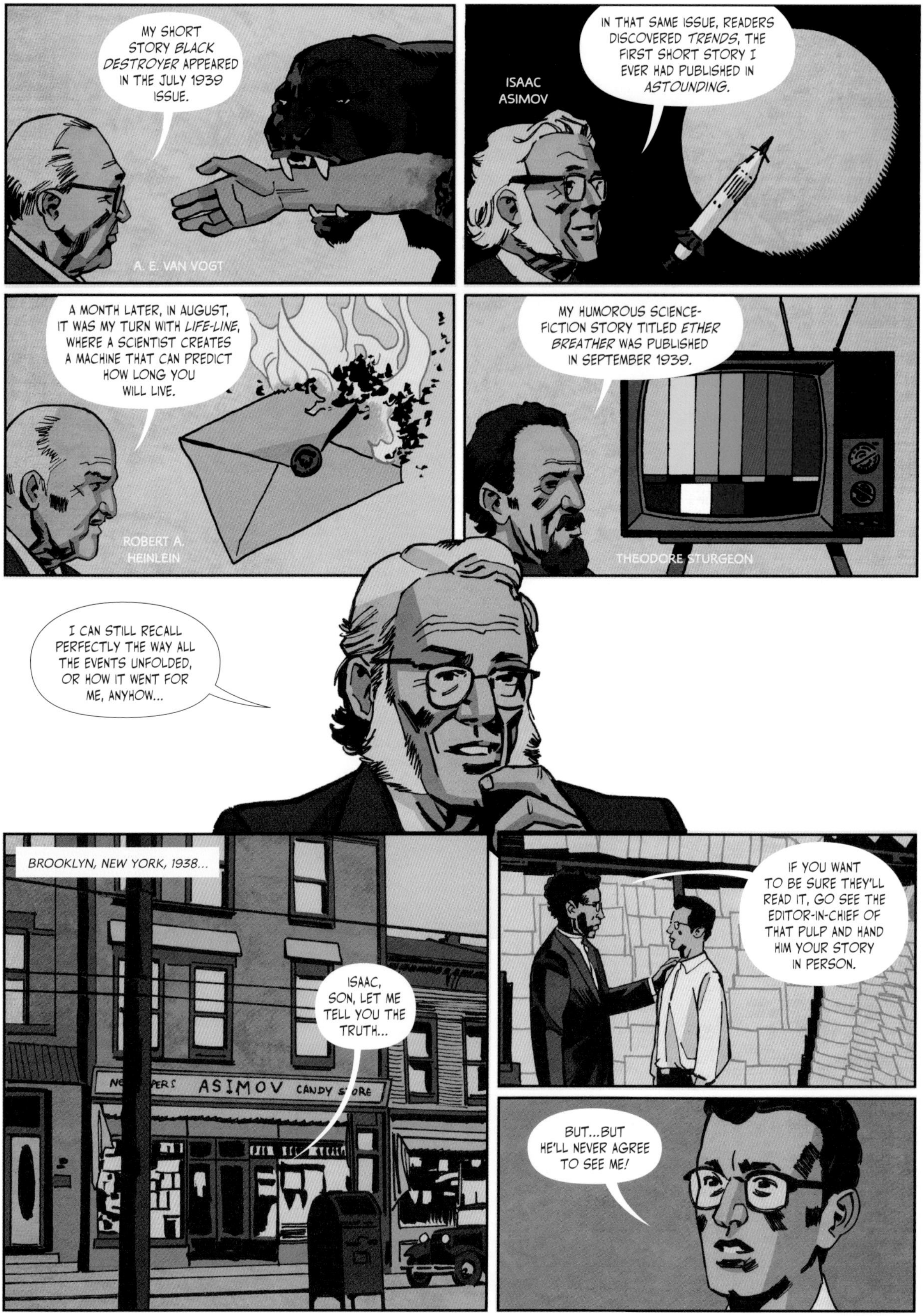
MY SHORT STORY BLACK DESTROYER APPEARED IN THE JULY 1939 ISSUE.
A. E. VAN VOGT
ISAAC ASIMOV
IN THAT SAME ISSUE, READERS DISCOVERED TRENDS, THE FIRST SHORT STORY I EVER HAD PUBLISHED IN ASTOUNDING.
A MONTH LATER, IN AUGUST, IT WAS MY TURN WITH LIFE-LINE, WHERE A SCIENTIST CREATES A MACHINE THAT CAN PREDICT HOW LONG YOU WILL LIVE.
ROBERT A. HEINLEIN
MY HUMOROUS SCIENCE-FICTION STORY TITLED ETHER BREATHER WAS PUBLISHED IN SEPTEMBER 1939.
THEODORE STURGEON
I CAN STILL RECALL PERFECTLY THE WAY ALL THE EVENTS UNFOLDED, OR HOW IT WENT FOR ME, ANYHOW...
BROOKLYN, NEW YORK, 1938...
ASIMOV CANDY STORE
ISAAC, SON, LET ME TELL YOU THE TRUTH...
IF YOU WANT TO BE SURE THEY'LL READ IT, GO SEE THE EDITOR-IN-CHIEF OF THAT PULP AND HAND HIM YOUR STORY IN PERSON.
BUT...BUT HE'LL NEVER AGREE TO SEE ME!

LATER, AT THE OFFICES OF STREET & SMITH...

MORNING, MA'AM. MY NAME IS ISAAC ASIMOV AND I'D LIKE TO MEET MR. CAMPBELL FROM *ASTOUNDING SCIENCE FICTION*.

JUST A MOMENT, I'LL CALL HIM RIGHT AWAY.

YOU WILL?

IF HE'S FREE, OF COURSE HE'LL SEE YOU.

AND JUST A FEW MINUTES LATER...

John W. Campbell

TOC TOC TOC

COME IN!

PLEASE, WON'T YOU HAVE A SEAT, MR. ASIMOV?

COSMIC CORKSCREW... ALRIGHT, I'LL READ YOUR MANUSCRIPT AND LET YOU KNOW VERY SOON.

I'VE HEARD OF YOU, OF COURSE, MR. ASIMOV. WE'VE PRINTED YOUR LETTERS IN THE "BRASS TACKS" SECTION OF ASTOUNDING.

SEVERAL DAYS LATER...

HERE'S A LETTER FOR YOU, ISAAC! IT'S FROM STREET & SMITH!

MY STORY'S BEEN REFUSED.

"NEVERTHELESS, HIS REFUSAL WAS SO POLITE AND WELL-ARGUED THAT IT KIND OF GALVANIZED ME INTO BELIEVING IN MYSELF."

"AT THE TIME, I HAD ALSO STARTED TO HANG AROUND WITH A GROUP OF SCIENCE-FICTION FANS WHO CALLED THEMSELVES 'THE FUTURIANS'."

HAVE YOU READ WHAT'S IN THE LATEST ISSUE OF AMAZING STORIES?

THE GROUP MEMBERS INCLUDED FUTURE GREATS OF SCIENCE FICTION LIKE FREDERIK POHL AND DONALD WOLLHEIM.

DONALD A. WOLLHEIM, AUTHOR OF *THE UNIVERSE MAKERS*.

JUDITH MERRIL, CO-AUTHOR OF *OUTPOST MARS*.

FREDERIK POHL, AUTHOR OF *GATEWAY*.

JAMES BLISH, AUTHOR OF *THE SEEDLING STARS*.

DAMON KNIGHT, AUTHOR OF *THE FUTURIANS* AND THE FAMOUS SHORT STORY *TO SERVE MAN*.

CYRIL M. KORNBLUTH, CO-AUTHOR OF *THE SPACE MERCHANTS*, WITH FREDERIK POHL.

ALL THESE FRIENDS WENT ON TO BECOME ACCLAIMED FIGURES IN PUBLISHING. POHL AND BLISH EVOLVED INTO MAJOR WRITERS OF THE GENRE, WHILE WOLLHEIM AND MERRIL LATER BECAME FAMOUS EDITORS, NOT TO MENTION MAINSTAYS OF "FANDOM"--THE WORLD OF SCIENCE-FICTION FANATICS WHO ALSO ORGANIZED THE FIRST NATIONAL CONVENTIONS DEDICATED TO THE GENRE.

BROOKLYN BRIDGE, 1938...

I'VE GOT STUCK ON A STORY, FRED. I NEED YOUR HELP...

DON'T PANIC, ISAAC. TELL ME ALL ABOUT IT...

DAD! *MAROONED OFF VESTA* IS OUT IN *AMAZING STORIES*!

WELL DONE, SON! I'LL GO TELL THE WHOLE FAMILY AND ALL MY FRIENDS THE GOOD NEWS!

"FRED POHL HELPED ME GET MY FIRST STORIES PUBLISHED AND REMAINED ONE OF MY BEST FRIENDS ALL THROUGHOUT HIS LIFE.

"SO, IN JULY 1939, THE HOLY GRAIL WAS WITHIN MY GRASP. WHAT I'D DREAMED OF MOST IN THE WORLD--BEING PUBLISHED IN MY FAVORITE MAGAZINE, ASTOUNDING, THE MOST POPULAR PULP OF THEM ALL--FINALLY CAME TRUE WHEN *TRENDS* WAS PRINTED!"

MY DEAR ISAAC, YOUR EXPERIENCE WAS VERY SIMILAR TO MINE IN MANY WAYS!

LOOKOUT MOUNTAIN AVENUE, CALIFORNIA, 1938.

WE'RE GOING TO HAVE TO SETTLE UP ALL OUR DEBTS. NO MORE POLITICS FOR NOW!

ROBERT A. HEINLEIN

I'M GOING TO WRITE SOME STORIES AND SEND THEM TO MAGAZINES. WILL YOU HELP?

IN 1938, I WAS BROKE AFTER RUNNING FOR EPIC* IN THE ELECTIONS. THEY WERE A SMALL LEFT-LEANING MOVEMENT CLOSE TO THE DEMOCRATS, WHICH HAD GENERATED QUITE A BUZZ WHEN THEY WERE HEADED BY THE FAMOUS WRITER UPTON SINCLAIR.

IF SUCH A RUTHLESS SMEAR CAMPAIGN USING ANTI-EPIC NEWSREELS HADN'T BEEN WAGED FOR THE FIRST TIME IN AMERICA, I MIGHT NEVER HAVE WRITTEN ANY SCIENCE FICTION. I'D PROBABLY HAVE STAYED IN POLITICS.

LESLYN KNEW ALL ABOUT THE WORLD OF ARTS AND LITERATURE, SO SHE GUIDED ME, BECAUSE I'D NEVER REALLY THOUGHT ABOUT WRITING.

JUST LIKE ME AND EDNA. SHE WOULD CORRECT, STEER, AND SOMETIMES REWRITE MY STORIES.

A. E. VAN VOGT

* END POVERTY IN CALIFORNIA.

"JOMMY'S MOTHER'S FINGERS FELT COLD, CLUTCHING HIS..."

IT WOULD BE BETTER IF YOU WROTE: "JOMMY'S MOTHER'S *HAND* FELT COLD, CLUTCHING HIS..."

YOU'RE RIGHT, OF COURSE. FOR ME, IT'S NO ACCIDENT THAT THE "E" IN "A. E. VAN VOGT" COULD STAND FOR EDNA AS WELL AS ELTON!

EDNA ALSO PUBLISHED SEVERAL SHORT STORIES OF HER OWN, PARTICULARLY IN JOHN'S OTHER HUGE PULP, *UNKNOWN* (WHICH WAS MORE FANTASY-ORIENTED). NOT LONG AFTER THAT IT CLOSED DOWN DUE TO THE EXTREME PAPER SHORTAGES THAT OCCURRED DURING THE WAR.

LESLYN PREFERRED WRITING POETRY. ONE OF HER POEMS APPEARED IN *WEIRD TALES*. BUT ONE THING'S FOR SURE: OUR WIVES' ROLES WERE CRUCIAL TO THE QUALITY OF OUR WORK!

THE HEINLEIN RESIDENCE, LOOKOUT MOUNTAIN AVENUE.

"IN THE EARLY 1940S, LESLYN AND I USED TO ORGANIZE OUR CELEBRATED PARTIES. WE WOULD INVITE PLENTY OF ARTISTS AND WRITERS, OF COURSE. BUT ALSO SCIENTISTS, SUCH AS THE EXTRAVAGANT JACK PARSONS, KNOWN AS MUCH FOR HIS RESEARCH AT CALTECH AS FOR BEING A DEVOTEE OF ALEISTER CROWLEY."

SO, MR. WILLIAMSON, HOW ARE YOU ENJOYING THIS LATEST GATHERING OF THE MAÑANA LITERARY SOCIETY?

FASCINATING, AS ALWAYS. IT'S FUN TO HAVE SO MANY CELEBRITIES LIKE EDMOND HAMILTON, JACK PARSONS, ANTHONY BOUCHER, AND L. RON HUBBARD IN THE SAME ROOM!

JACK WILLIAMSON

97

I READ YOUR *BLOWUPS HAPPEN* IN *ASTOUNDING*--A GRIPPING STORY ABOUT NUCLEAR FISSION. ARE YOU WRITING ANYTHING ELSE IN THE SAME VEIN?

YOU KNOW, CLEVE, I'VE BEEN TALKING WITH MY PHYSICIST FRIEND ROBERT CORNOG LATELY, AND I HAVE A SHORT STORY IN MIND CALLED *SOLUTION UNSATISFACTORY*.

CLEVE CARTMILL

IN 1938, THE URANIUM FISSION CHAIN REACTION WAS DISCOVERED...

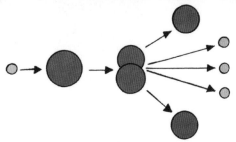

EVER SINCE RAY CUMMINGS AND A FEW OTHER WRITERS, THE ATOM HAS ALWAYS LURED US...

OH, SO WHAT'S THIS IDEA OF YOURS?

WELL, THAT DISCOVERY OPENED UP SOME PRETTY FRIGHTENING PROSPECTS, OR SO I CONCLUDED AFTER MY DISCUSSIONS WITH CORNOG.

THE TOPIC FASCINATES ME TOO...

TRUST ME, CLEVE, GIVE IT A GO.

I'LL THINK ABOUT IT... WHEN IS *SOLUTION UNSATISFACTORY* DUE OUT?

IN THE MAY ISSUE OF *ASTOUNDING*.

SOLUTION UNSATISFACTORY, 1941, ASTOUNDING SCIENCE FICTION.

DRIIIIINNNNGGGG!
DRIIIIINNNNGGGG!

STORY REPRINTED IN THE *JACKPOTS* ANTHOLOGY, ACTUSF, 2011.

THIS IS MANNING...

HELLO, GENERAL!

BUT GENERAL, I'M NO LONGER A COLONEL. I'M RETIRED AND I HAVE THIS JOB--

COLONEL, THIS IS AN AFFAIR OF STATE!

OH... I SEE...

WHAT'S THAT YOU SAY?

I'LL BE RIGHT OVER, GENERAL!

WHAT'S GOING ON? HAS SOMETHING BAD HAPPENED?

GET YOUR HAT, JOHN. WE'RE GOING OVER TO THE WAR DEPARTMENT!

IN THAT STORY, I EXPLORE HOW THE COLONEL DEVELOPS A KIND OF DUST WITH APPALLING PROPERTIES.

WHAT EXACTLY?

IMAGINE A DUST THAT COULD STERILIZE A COUNTRY'S ENTIRE CAPITAL CITY. IMAGINE ALL THE CONTAMINATED SURVIVORS...

THAT DUST WOULD MAKE A TERRIFYING WEAPON!

WHEN CENSORSHIP OF THE SUBJECT WAS INTRODUCED IN AMERICA IN 1942, THANKS TO THE STORY'S SUCCESS, IT BECAME PART OF THE DEBATE ON WEAPONS OF MASS DESTRUCTION. SO, MY BOOK WAS RATHER PROPHETIC!

BUT YOU RAN INTO A FEW PROBLEMS WHEN CLEVE CARTMILL PUBLISHED *DEADLINE*, A STORY THAT DESCRIBED A NUCLEAR WEAPON IN A LITTLE TOO MUCH DETAIL! THE READERS APPRECIATED IT A WHOLE LOT MORE THAN THE SECRET SERVICEMEN IN CHARGE OF THE MANHATTAN PROJECT!

THEODORE, YOU DEALT MORE WITH THE AFTERMATH OF A NUCLEAR WAR IN YOUR SHORT STORY *THUNDER AND ROSES*, WHICH I PUBLISHED IN 1947.

YES, YOU MIGHT SAY THERE WAS PRE-HIROSHIMA AND POST-HIROSHIMA SCIENCE FICTION. MY STORY WAS A DARK YET PACIFISTIC PARABLE THAT SOUGHT HOPE AMID THE CHAOS.

I WAS ALWAYS PROGRESSIVE, REBELLING AGAINST AUTHORITARIAN IDEOLOGIES. AND I PONDERED WHAT IT REALLY MEANS TO BE HUMAN, AND SOMETIMES SUPERHUMAN. I TOUCHED ON THOSE THEMES IN THAT STORY AND A LOT OF MY OTHER WORK.

THEODORE STURGEON

WHERE ARE YOU TAKING US, JOHN?

SEE FOR YOURSELVES!

BY THE RULERS OF THE SEVAGRAM!*

WELL, NOW! A GALLERY OF OUR WORKS!

* SEE A. E. VAN VOGT'S NOVEL *THE WEAPON MAKERS*.

THAT'S RIGHT. THIS IS THE GALLERY OF YOUR DREAM WORLDS.

LOOK, ISAAC, IT'S ROBBIE, YOUR FIRST ROBOT.

YES, THAT STORY CAME OUT IN 1940 IN *SUPER SCIENCE STORIES* WITH A TITLE CHOSEN BY FRED POHL, *STRANGE PLAYFELLOW.* BUT YOU'D REFUSED IT, JOHN!

I THOUGHT IT WAS TOO MUCH LIKE TWO OTHER SHORT STORIES: *HELEN O'LOY* BY LESTER DEL REY, BUT MOSTLY *I, ROBOT*, PART OF THE ADAM LINK SERIES WRITTEN BY BROTHERS EARL AND OTTO BINDER AS "EANDO BINDER."

I ALSO ADMIRED BINDER'S WORK AND WANTED TO WRITE MY OWN VISION OF A POSITIVE ROBOT, WITHOUT ALL THE NEGATIVE FRANKENSTEIN-SYNDROME CLICHÉS.

BUT STILL, I DID BUY EVERYTHING YOU WROTE NEXT, AND WE CAME UP WITH A SERIES OF MEMORABLE STORIES THAT TOOK A GROUND-BREAKING APPROACH TO ROBOT PSYCHOLOGY.

GOOD DAY, MASTERS. HOW MAY I BE OF SERVICE?

102

ROBBIE, PLEASE WOULD YOU RECITE THE THREE LAWS OF ROBOTICS FOR US.

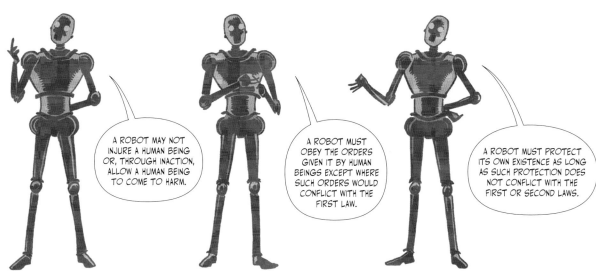

A ROBOT MAY NOT INJURE A HUMAN BEING OR, THROUGH INACTION, ALLOW A HUMAN BEING TO COME TO HARM.

A ROBOT MUST OBEY THE ORDERS GIVEN IT BY HUMAN BEINGS EXCEPT WHERE SUCH ORDERS WOULD CONFLICT WITH THE FIRST LAW.

A ROBOT MUST PROTECT ITS OWN EXISTENCE AS LONG AS SUCH PROTECTION DOES NOT CONFLICT WITH THE FIRST OR SECOND LAWS.

THANKS, ROBBIE. THAT'LL BE ALL...

THE LAWS MADE SUCH A LASTING IMPACT ON SCIENCE FICTION THAT A LOT OF WRITERS TOOK THEM FOR GRANTED. GNOME PRESS, ONE OF THE FIRST PUBLISHERS TO REPRINT THE BEST PULP-FICTION STORIES IN HARDBACK, RELEASED *I, ROBOT* IN 1950.

TITLE LIFTED FROM EANDO BINDER... BUT NOT BY ME!

ALTHOUGH THAT SERIES WAS A MILESTONE, YOU WOULDN'T REST UNTIL YOU'D TIED IT IN WITH YOUR OTHER GREAT WORK, *FOUNDATION*.

AT HEART, MY FRIENDS, WE ARE ALL CREATORS OF UNIVERSES. AND MANY MORE WRITERS WOULD FOLLOW IN OUR FOOTSTEPS, DREAMING UP REAL FUTURE HISTORIES.

AND ON THAT SUBJECT, ROBERT WAS DEFINITELY THE FIRST TO DEVISE A TRULY REALISTIC FUTURE HISTORY...

WELL, I'D REALLY BEEN THINKING OF CREATING A COHERENT UNIVERSE ALMOST FROM THE START. IN FACT, BY 1942, HALF OF MY STORIES ALL FITTED TOGETHER INTO ONE HUGE CYCLE.

THE HEINLEIN TIMELINE

IT WAS A HISTORY THAT STRETCHED FROM 1950 TO 2600. YOU PESTERED ME FOR A TIMELINE, JOHN, SO I GAVE YOU ONE. AND YOU EVEN WENT AND PUBLISHED IT IN *ASTOUNDING*, JUST TO BE SURE I'D ACTUALLY WRITE ALL THE STORIES. MIND YOU, AT THE TIME, I WAS CONSIDERING GIVING UP WRITING ONCE MY DEBTS WERE PAID.

I TOOK MY INSPIRATION FOR THIS FUTURE HISTORY FROM SINCLAIR LEWIS' NOBEL PRIZE-WINNING WORK *BABBITT*. HIS NOVEL WAS BASED ON A METACONSTRUCTION, A SUM OF PARTS WHICH INTERCONNECTED WITH ONE ANOTHER IN ORDER TO COMPLETE THE PROJECT.

IN MY CASE, I DEFINED THE THREE MAJOR PERIODS: FIRSTLY THAT OF THE TRAILBLAZERS; THEN COLONIZATION OF THE MOON AND THE SOLAR SYSTEM; AND FINALLY THE EXPLORATION OF PLANETARY SYSTEMS WHERE HUMANITY WOULD GO TO SETTLE.

COMING BACK TO THE MOON, MARS WAS ASSOCIATED WITH RAY BRADBURY, BUT OUR SATELLITE WAS THE SETTING FOR MANY OF MY STORIES.

LAUNCH SIMULATION!

OH...NOW I'M AN ASTRONAUT! AT ONE POINT I DREAMED OF MAKING IT IN THE MOVIES BY WRITING SOME SCREENPLAYS.

AND THAT LED TO *DESTINATION MOON* IN 1950, PARTLY ADAPTING YOUR NOVEL *ROCKET SHIP GALILEO* AND MOST OF *THE MAN WHO SOLD THE MOON.*

DESTINATION MOON WAS ONE OF CINEMA'S FIRST ATTEMPTS AT MAKING REALISTIC SCIENCE FICTION. IN THAT RESPECT, IT WAS MUCH CLOSER TO "HARD SCIENCE."

FRITZ LANG, WHO WAS ONE OF MY FRIENDS, HAD BEEN APPROACHED TO DIRECT IT, BECAUSE IT WAS ALSO INSPIRED BY HIS FAMOUS FILM *WOMAN IN THE MOON.*

BASICALLY, LONG BEFORE STANLEY KUBRICK AND ARTHUR C. CLARKE, I FELT THAT WAS HOW SCIENCE FICTION OUGHT TO BE PORTRAYED ON THE SCREEN, IN AN EXTREMELY SERIOUS LIGHT. THE FILM WON AN OSCAR FOR ITS SPECIAL EFFECTS!

IT ALSO INSPIRED SOME SCENES AND DESIGNS IN HERGÉ'S TINTIN COMIC, TRANSLATED INTO ENGLISH AS *"DESTINATION MOON!"*

FANTASTIC PHANTASMAGORIA!

A NICE DIVE INTO YOUR IMAGINATION, ROBERT!

BECAUSE I WAS SO IMPRESSED WITH THE WAY YOU HAD DONE IT, AND AFTER A BIT OF PRODDING FROM JOHN, I ALSO PLANNED OUT A GIGANTIC STORY OF THE FUTURE.

ISAAC ASIMOV

DO YOU MEAN *FOUNDATION*?

FOUNDATION AND A WHOLE LOT MORE. I HAD THE CRAZY IDEA...

...OF MERGING MY *TWO* BIGGEST SERIES, *ROBOTS* AND *FOUNDATION*.

NEW YORK, 1941.

HOW ON EARTH AM I GOING TO COME UP WITH A NEW STORY FOR JOHN? I'M OUT OF IDEAS...

OH, I COULD USE THE ROMAN EMPIRE FOR INSPIRATION!

AND I COULD DRAW ON *THE HISTORY OF THE DECLINE AND FALL OF THE ROMAN EMPIRE* BY EDWARD GIBBON TO HELP ME!

A FEW MINUTES LATER, IN THE OFFICES OF STREET & SMITH.

JOHN!

YES, ISAAC? SOME ENTRANCE!

I HAD AN IDEA ON THE WAY OVER HERE. I THINK YOU'LL LIKE IT!

COME ON THEN, OUT WITH IT!

WHAT IF I WROTE A STORY DETAILING THE FALL OF A GALACTIC EMPIRE, ECHOING THE EXAMPLE OF THE ROMAN EMPIRE?

WILL YOU GIVE IT AN INTERESTING SLANT? YOU KNOW I'M NOT REALLY IN THE MARKET FOR SPACE OPERAS IN THE STYLE OF EDMOND HAMILTON OR DOC SMITH...

NOTHING LIKE IT!

YOU KNOW ME, JOHN, I'M MUCH MORE INTO CEREBRAL ACTION THAN PLAIN OLD PHYSICAL ACTION! APART FROM THE FALL OF THIS GALACTIC EMPIRE, I'D ALSO EXAMINE THE PERIOD OF BARBARISM THAT FOLLOWS IT...

...WHILE MAINTAINING THE DETACHED, ANALYTICAL POINT OF VIEW OF THE EMPIRE THAT COMES AFTER THE BARBARISM!

THE PREMISE SOUNDS REALLY GREAT, ISAAC, BUT I'M AFRAID IT CAN'T BE DONE.

REALLY? BUT...BUT I THOUGHT--

IT CAN'T BE DONE IN A SINGLE STORY. YOU'LL NEED TO WRITE A WHOLE SERIES!

THAT'S HOW THE *FOUNDATION* SERIES CAME INTO BEING. THE FAMOUS TRILOGY OF NOVELS RELEASED BETWEEN 1942 AND 1950 INCLUDED *FOUNDATION, FOUNDATION AND EMPIRE,* AND FINALLY *SECOND FOUNDATION.*

THE THREE BOOKS WERE REPRINTED IN VOLUMES BY GNOME PRESS IN 1951.

IN IT, YOU INVENTED THE MOST FAMOUS SCIENCE IN ALL OF SCIENCE FICTION; PSYCHOHISTORY!

A SCIENCE THAT PREDICTED FUTURE EVENTS BY MEANS OF THOROUGH STATISTICAL ANALYSIS.

SO, I DREAMED UP THE MASTERMIND OF THIS UNIVERSE, THE FAMOUS HARI SELDON, INVENTOR OF PSYCHOHISTORY!

I AM THE MULE. PSYCHOHISTORY DIDN'T PREDICT ME. I'M A MUTANT CAPABLE OF INFLUENCING PEOPLE'S MINDS. I ALMOST WRECKED HARI SELDON'S PLANS FOR A DETERMINIST UNIVERSE.

PREDICTED OR NOT, THE MULE HAS TO DEAL WITH THE MIGHT OF THE SECOND FOUNDATION AND PSYCHOHISTORY, ESTABLISHED TO REDUCE THE BARBARISM PERIOD FROM 20,000 YEARS TO ONE MILLENNIUM...

LIKE ROBERT, YOUR WORKS WERE ALL ABOUT COHERENCE. AND MUCH LATER, YOU COMPLETED YOUR MAGNUM OPUS...

YES, A MAMMOTH TASK THAT I MANAGED TO SEE THROUGH TO THE END (DESPITE MY RATHER COMPLEX, MEANDERING CAREER), WHICH MADE ME ONE OF THE MOST PROLIFIC POPULARIZERS OF SCIENCE IN THE 20TH CENTURY. I WAS PRAISED FOR MY CLARITY AND NICKNAMED "THE GOOD DOCTOR..."

HAHAHAHA!

YOUR MOST FAMOUS NOVELETTE WASN'T PART OF A SERIES, THOUGH. *NIGHTFALL* TRANSPORTED US TO A WORLD WHERE THE STARS ONLY EVER CAME OUT ONCE EVERY TWO THOUSAND YEARS. YOU WROTE IT FOLLOWING A DISCUSSION WE ONCE HAD.

IN 1968, THE SCIENCE FICTION WRITERS OF AMERICA ASSOCIATION VOTED THE STORY ONE OF THE GREATEST EVER PENNED.

THEN, BETWEEN 1950 AND 1956, I PUBLISHED SIX NOVELS, MINOR CLASSICS OF THE GENRE, LIKE *THE CURRENTS OF SPACE* AND *THE END OF ETERNITY*...

BUT ABOVE ALL *THE CAVES OF STEEL* AND *THE NAKED SUN*, WHICH SHOWCASED TWO KEY CHARACTERS IN YOUR UNIVERSE. I MEAN THE UNUSUAL DETECTIVE DUO OF ELIJAH BALEY, THE AGORAPHOBIC HUMAN, AND R. DANEEL OLIVAW, HIS ROBOT PARTNER.

THOSE TWO CHARACTERS WOULD REAPPEAR IN OTHER NOVELS WRITTEN IN THE 1980S. IN MY UNIVERSE, THEIRS WAS THE DAWN OF THE ERA OF THE GALACTIC EMPIRE...

READERS HAD TO WAIT FOR THE FINAL VOLUMES OF THE *FOUNDATION* SERIES TO FINALLY UNRAVEL THE MYSTERY OF WHY THERE HAD BEEN NO ROBOTS IN IT. THEN THINGS CAME FULL CIRCLE AT LAST!

JOHN MADE US FAMOUS, BUT YOU ENDED UP LEAVING *ASTOUNDING*, TOO, ROBERT.

IT ALL BEGAN AFTER THE WAR. BACK IN 1947, WHEN I'D MANAGED TO PUBLISH FOUR STORIES IN *THE SATURDAY EVENING POST*, A TOP MAGAZINE WITH A HUGE CIRCULATION.

I REMEMBER WE WERE ALL A BIT JEALOUS OF YOU THEN. IT WAS NIGH ON MISSION IMPOSSIBLE FOR AN SF WRITER TO ESCAPE THE PULPS.

EXCEPT FOR YOU, ROBERT.

AND *ASTOUNDING* COULDN'T AFFORD THE STORIES, OF COURSE. YOU WERE THINKING OF QUITTING!

THE WAR HAD GIVEN ME A STRONG SENSE OF PATRIOTIC DUTY. I WANTED TO MAKE MYSELF USEFUL. AND I BELIEVED THAT THE UNITED STATES OUGHT TO PLAY A VITAL ROLE IN FIGHTING FASCISM.

YOU GAVE A MEMORABLE SPEECH ON THE SUBJECT AT THE THIRD WORLD SCIENCE FICTION CONVENTION IN DENVER...

...A PERIOD OF SUDDEN AND DRASTIC CHANGE IN A GOOD MANY OF THE THINGS THAT HAPPEN TO US. SCIENCE-FICTION FANS ARE BETTER PREPARED TO FACE THE FUTURE THAN THE ORDINARY PEOPLE AROUND THEM, BECAUSE THEY BELIEVE IN CHANGE!

MR. KORZYBSKI, TO ME, YOU'RE AS GREAT A MAN AS EINSTEIN.

AND YOUR FIELD OF STUDY IS EVEN MORE VAST THAN HIS.

"I ALSO MADE THE MOST OF MY TRIP TO DENVER BY ATTENDING SEMINARS BY THE INVENTOR OF GENERAL SEMANTICS, ALFRED KORZYBSKI."

GENERAL SEMANTICS HELPS INDIVIDUALS TO UNDERSTAND THE WORLD BETTER AND MAKE THE RIGHT DECISIONS.

OBVIOUSLY MY SYSTEM IS BASED ON THE WORK OF ALBERT EINSTEIN, AS WELL AS THAT OF ALFRED NORTH WHITEHEAD AND BERTRAND RUSSELL. BY TAKING A SCIENTIFIC APPROACH TO LANGUAGE AND USING IT AS PRECISELY AS WE CAN, IT OUGHT TO BE POSSIBLE FOR HUMANITY TO STEER CLEAR OF ALL CONFLICTS IN THE FUTURE.

YES, WORDS ARE LIKE MAPS. THEY CAN ONLY DESCRIBE TERRITORIES.

JUST LIKE WORDS, MAPS ARE MERE REPRESENTATIONS OF REALITY.

YES, AS I HAVE SAID BEFORE, "A MAP IS NOT THE TERRITORY."

AND I THINK MANY PEOPLE ARE JUST LIVING WITH THE WRONG SET OF MAPS.

AH! GENERAL SEMANTICS! A TRULY EXCITING SUBJECT FOR SCIENCE-FICTION WRITERS!

IT'S TRUE! EVEN THOUGH I WASN'T QUITE AS ENTHUSIASTIC AS SOME OF YOU, I DID ENCOURAGE YOU TO CONTINUE ALONG THAT PATH. YOU, OF COURSE, ROBERT, AND ISAAC, L. RON HUBBARD, AND NOT FORGETTING YOU, ALFRED.

I'M MOSTLY REMEMBERED FOR BRINGING TWO THINGS TO SCIENCE FICTION. ALTHOUGH MY NARRATIVE STYLE WAS CLOSER TO THE FANTASTIC, MY TWO CONTRIBUTIONS WERE RELATED TO THE NEW SCIENCES I INVENTED OR ADAPTED, INCLUDING GENERAL SEMANTICS.

A. E. VAN VOGT

MY NOVEL *THE VOYAGE OF THE SPACE BEAGLE* TRACES THE JOURNEY OF A SPACESHIP AND ITS CREW ACROSS THE UNIVERSE, ENCOUNTERING AN ASSORTMENT OF EXTRATERRESTRIAL SPECIES. LIKE LOVECRAFT, I'M ALSO KNOWN FOR MY IMPRESSIVE BESTIARY.

ELLIOTT GROSVENOR, A SCIENTIST ABOARD THE *SPACE BEAGLE*, IS AN ARDENT DEVOTEE OF NEXIALISM, A FICTITIOUS NEW DISCIPLINE THAT STRIVES TO INTEGRATE ALL OTHERS. AND GROSVENOR IS CONSTANTLY TRYING TO PROVE ITS WORTH.

IXTL, THE CREATURE THEY MEET IN *DISCORD IN SCARLET*, PARTLY INSPIRED THE ALIEN IN *ALIEN*, WHILE THE *SPACE BEAGLE* STORIES ALSO GREATLY INFLUENCED ANOTHER CULT SERIES, *STAR TREK*.

BUT I AM BEST KNOWN FOR WRITING A MAJOR NOVEL FROM THE GOLDEN AGE OF SCIENCE FICTION. *THE WORLD OF NULL-A* EXTRAPOLATED SEVERAL CONCEPTS BORROWED FROM GENERAL SEMANTICS AND NON-ARISTOTELIAN LOGIC.

EARTH, 26TH CENTURY. THE GAMBLING CAPITAL.

YOU CAN'T TURN ME AWAY LIKE THIS! I HAVE THE RIGHT TO COMPETE IN THE GAMES OF THE MACHINE! I'VE DONE ALL MY TRAINING.

SORRY, BUT YOU'LL HAVE TO LEAVE!

YOU WON'T STOP ME FROM JOINING IN AND WINNING THE TRIP TO VENUS! I WANT TO PARTICIPATE IN THE GAMES!

YOU AREN'T WHO YOU CLAIM TO BE. THERE IS NO GILBERT GOSSEYN!

AS HIS DISAPPOINTMENTS START TO PILE UP, GOSSEYN ("GO SANE") REALIZES THAT HIS LIFE IS JUST AN ILLUSION AND SETS OFF ON A QUEST TO FIND HIS TRUE IDENTITY.

THEN HE DISCOVERS HE HAS AN EXTRA BRAIN THAT IS CAPABLE OF IMPRESSIVE FEATS! HE ALSO FINDS HIMSELF BEING USED AS A TOOL IN A REVOLUTION...

...AND ALL SET AGAINST A BACKDROP OF ALIEN MENACE! ANYHOW, THE NOVEL MADE A HUGE IMPACT ON THE READERS AND CRITICS ALIKE. IT ALSO REVEALED HOW MY CHARACTERS WERE OFTEN HEROES ENDOWED WITH AMAZING ABILITIES, REAL SUPERMEN...

THE CRITICS CERTAINLY GAVE YOU A HARD TIME, PARTICULARLY DAMON KNIGHT, KNOWN FOR HIS VIRULENCE. HE WROTE: "VAN VOGT IS A PYGMY WHO HAS LEARNED TO OPERATE AN OVERGROWN TYPEWRITER."

I NEVER HELD IT AGAINST HIM, AND HE WAS WELL AWARE OF IT.

THE FACT REMAINS THAT *THE WORLD OF NULL-A* GENUINELY DID LEAVE ITS MARK. INCLUDING IN EUROPE AND PARTICULARLY IN FRANCE, WHERE IT WAS TRANSLATED BY BORIS VIAN HIMSELF!

AND, AS IRONIC AS IT MAY SOUND, I WON THE DAMON KNIGHT GRAND MASTER AWARD IN 1995. HE WAS THE FOUNDER OF THE SCIENCE FICTION AND FANTASY WRITERS OF AMERICA, THE ASSOCIATION WHICH ALSO PRESENTS THE ANNUAL NEBULA AWARDS.

IT'S TRUE THAT WE WERE ALL IMPRESSED BY KORZYBSKI...

SOMETIMES SCI-FI WRITERS DID SHARE A BED WITH SCIENCE AND PARASCIENCE... FOR BETTER, BUT ALSO FOR WORSE...

AH, YOU MEAN L. RON HUBBARD, I PRESUME?

PRECISELY. HE CREATED DIANETICS, WHICH HE REGARDED AS AN EXTENSION OF GENERAL SEMANTICS, AND WENT ON TO FOUND THE CONTROVERSIAL CHURCH OF SCIENTOLOGY. HIS FIRST ARTICLES ON DIANETICS WERE PUBLISHED IN *ASTOUNDING*...

YES, HE USED TO WRITE SCIENCE FICTION BEFORE THAT... I LET MYSELF GET DRAWN INTO THE SUBJECT HE WAS TRYING TO SELL ME, A BRAND-NEW SCIENCE OF THE MIND...

NEW YORK, 1948.

YOU KNOW, I WAS CLINICALLY DEAD FOR EIGHT MINUTES, JOHN!

YOU WHAT, RON?!

AN OPERATION THAT NEARLY WENT WRONG. AND WHILE I WAS DEAD, I SAW MYSELF CLIMBING UP THIS BIG HILL, THEN WHEN I WOKE UP...

YES, RON? WHEN YOU WOKE UP... GO ON!

I ASKED THE NURSE IF I'D DIED. FROM THE WAY SHE AND THE DOCTOR LOOKED AT ME I KNEW THAT I HAD...

YOU'RE THE KING OF SUSPENSE... WELL?!

WHEN I WAS LYING DEAD, I WAS GIVEN A MESSAGE THAT I HAD TO PASS ON TO OTHERS. YOU SEE, JOHN, THAT WAS WHEN I STARTED WRITING *EXCALIBUR*, A MANUSCRIPT CONTAINING THE FUNDAMENTAL SECRETS OF THE UNIVERSE.

IS THAT ALL?!

GO AHEAD AND LAUGH. ANYHOW, *EXCALIBUR* WAS WAY TOO MUCH FOR MERE MORTALS, SO I CAME UP WITH AN ARTICLE ON PERCEPTICS, WHICH EVENTUALLY BECAME DIANETICS. YOU CAN READ ALL ABOUT IT.

YOU'RE RIGHT. LET ME JUDGE FOR MYSELF.

AT THE TIME, I ENDED UP ANNOUNCING DIANETICS AS AN IMPORTANT SCIENTIFIC WORK, AND THE ARTICLE WAS PUBLISHED IN *ASTOUNDING* IN 1950...

AND THAT DEFINITELY SPELLED THE DECLINE OF JOHN WOOD CAMPBELL AS *ASTOUNDING'S* EDITOR-IN-CHIEF, ALONG WITH THE MAGAZINE IN GENERAL.

A LOT OF READERS WERE UNHAPPY WITH HOW IT WAS DRIFTING TOWARD PSEUDOSCIENCE...

AT THE SAME TIME, IN THE 1950S, SCIENCE FICTION WAS INCREASINGLY BEING PRINTED IN BOOK FORMAT BY A WIDE VARIETY OF PUBLISHERS, THE FIRST OF WHOM WERE ACE, AVON, AND BANTAM.

AND IT WAS CERTAINLY BENEFICIAL FOR US. THE PULPS STOPPED BEING OUR SOLE POSSIBLE OUTLET!

OF COURSE, THE WAR PUT A STOP TO MY WRITING ACTIVITY. SO, WITH ISAAC AND LYON SPRAGUE DE CAMP, WHO WROTE THE MARVELOUS ALTERNATE-HISTORY NOVEL *LEST DARKNESS FALL* IN 1939, WE WENT AND GOT OURSELVES CIVIL-ENGINEERING JOBS AT THE PHILADELPHIA NAVY YARD...

ROBERT A. HEINLEIN

...WORKING ON HIGH-ALTITUDE PRESSURE SUITS!

TOM CORBETT

SPACE CADET

HOWEVER, AFTER THE WAR, AT THE START OF THE 1950S, I BEGAN TO FOCUS ON PUBLISHING MY "JUVENILES," THE YOUNG-ADULT NOVELS THAT WERE INSTRUMENTAL IN MAKING ME FAMOUS.

MOST OF THE TIME, THEY WERE SPACE ADVENTURES WHICH I WOULD INFUSE WITH SCIENCE AND EDUCATION. YOU DID THE SAME THING, ISAAC, WITH YOUR ADVENTURES OF *LUCKY STARR*. MEANWHILE, THE TELEVISION SERIES *TOM CORBETT, SPACE CADET* WAS INSPIRED BY MY NOVEL *SPACE CADET*!

DOUBLE STAR WON ME THE FIRST OF MY FOUR HUGO AWARDS, IN 1956. IN THE NOVEL, AN ACTOR IS HIRED TO BECOME THE DOUBLE OF A PROMINENT POLITICIAN IN THE SOLAR SYSTEM...

...BUT MY FREE-SPIRITED APPROACH WAS PARTICULARLY NOTICEABLE IN THREE OTHER NOVELS THAT ALSO WON HUGO AWARDS AND WERE CONTROVERSIAL IN SOME WAY...

STARSHIP TROOPERS, 1959.

STRANGER IN A STRANGE LAND, 1961.

THE MOON IS A HARSH MISTRESS, 1966.

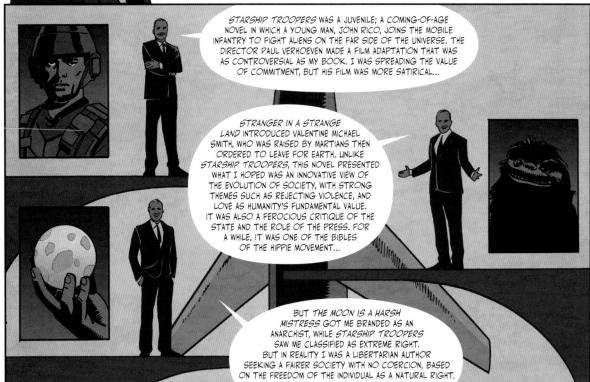

STARSHIP TROOPERS WAS A JUVENILE; A COMING-OF-AGE NOVEL IN WHICH A YOUNG MAN, JOHN RICO, JOINS THE MOBILE INFANTRY TO FIGHT ALIENS ON THE FAR SIDE OF THE UNIVERSE. THE DIRECTOR PAUL VERHOEVEN MADE A FILM ADAPTATION THAT WAS AS CONTROVERSIAL AS MY BOOK. I WAS SPREADING THE VALUE OF COMMITMENT, BUT HIS FILM WAS MORE SATIRICAL...

STRANGER IN A STRANGE LAND INTRODUCED VALENTINE MICHAEL SMITH, WHO WAS RAISED BY MARTIANS THEN ORDERED TO LEAVE FOR EARTH. UNLIKE STARSHIP TROOPERS, THIS NOVEL PRESENTED WHAT I HOPED WAS AN INNOVATIVE VIEW OF THE EVOLUTION OF SOCIETY, WITH STRONG THEMES SUCH AS REJECTING VIOLENCE, AND LOVE AS HUMANITY'S FUNDAMENTAL VALUE. IT WAS ALSO A FEROCIOUS CRITIQUE OF THE STATE AND THE ROLE OF THE PRESS. FOR A WHILE, IT WAS ONE OF THE BIBLES OF THE HIPPIE MOVEMENT...

BUT THE MOON IS A HARSH MISTRESS GOT ME BRANDED AS AN ANARCHIST, WHILE STARSHIP TROOPERS SAW ME CLASSIFIED AS EXTREME RIGHT. BUT IN REALITY I WAS A LIBERTARIAN AUTHOR SEEKING A FAIRER SOCIETY WITH NO COERCION, BASED ON THE FREEDOM OF THE INDIVIDUAL AS A NATURAL RIGHT.

THE FREEDOM TO ENLIST, LIKE IN *STARSHIP TROOPERS*; THE FREEDOM TO BE IDEALISTIC, AS IN *THE MOON IS A HARSH MISTRESS*; OR THE FREEDOM TO REJECT VIOLENCE, LIKE THE *STRANGER IN A STRANGE LAND*.

IN 1974, THE JURY OF THE SCIENCE FICTION WRITERS OF AMERICA HANDED ME A DAMON KNIGHT GRAND MASTER AWARD FOR MY LIFETIME ACHIEVEMENT. IT'S THE OTHER MAIN PRIZE IN SCIENCE FICTION...

IT LOOKS AS IF OUR JOURNEY'S COMING TO AN END, MY FRIENDS...

NOT QUITE, DEAR TED. WE STILL NEED TO BRIEFLY DISCUSS THAT EXTREMELY ODD VOICE YOU WROTE IN. YOU CALLED IT "RHYTHMIC PROSE..."

TO ME, SCIENCE FICTION IS A RHYTHM OF LIFE. IT GIVES US THE FREEDOM TO CREATE ENTIRELY NEW WORLDS. IT'S A FREE FORM OF LITERATURE. IN THE PAST, THE PRESENT, THE FUTURE, OR IN WHATEVER KIND OF SPACE WE WANT.

THEODORE STURGEON

HOWEVER, THE CRITICS, ESPECIALLY NON-SPECIALISTS, HAD LONG DISPARAGED SCIENCE FICTION, AS IF THE ENTIRE GENRE WAS DEVOID OF ALL LITERARY MERIT.

YOU KNOW MY FAMOUS STURGEON'S LAW, ALFRED: "90% OF EVERYTHING IS CRUD!" PEOPLE CAN TELL IF A DETECTIVE STORY IS GOOD OR BAD, AND THE SAME GOES FOR ALL OTHER LITERATURE. THEY HAVE TO UNDERSTAND THAT THIS RULE ALSO APPLIES TO SCIENCE FICTION.

THEREFORE I ALWAYS PAID AS MUCH ATTENTION AS POSSIBLE TO POLISHING MY TEXTS AND INCLUDING THEMES THAT WERE RARELY TO BE FOUND IN SCIENCE FICTION. LIKE THE HUMAN SCIENCES, AS WELL AS SEXUALITY, AS IN MY 1953 SHORT STORY *THE WORLD WELL LOST*, WHICH HAS SOME HOMOSEXUAL CHARACTERS (WHICH INFURIATED ONE EDITOR TO WHOM I SENT THE STORY). OR IN MY NOVEL *VENUS PLUS X*, WHICH CLEARLY INFLUENCED THE GREATEST FEMALE SCI-FI AUTHOR OF ALL TIME: URSULA K. LE GUIN.

THE FRENCH CRITIC GÉRARD KLEIN DESCRIBED YOUR STYLE AS: "SOME SORT OF BUBBLING, CUMBERSOME, AND JUMBLED LEXICAL LAVA BLATANTLY LADEN WITH PEDANTRY, REGARDLESS OF ITS EFFECT. WHEN A STORY BEGINS, IT IS OFTEN CLUMSY AND ROUGH-HEWN, THEN FINDS A TONE OF ITS OWN, BECOMING MORE REFINED, GRABBING THE READER AND TUNING IN WITH THE BEATING OF THEIR HEARTS."

THAT'S A FINE ILLUSTRATION OF THE DIFFICULTIES I WOULD FACE WHILE WRITING, AND OF MY ABILITY TO GIVE STORIES A SOUL...

BECAUSE, IN A WAY, ALL YOUR WORKS CONCERNED THE DEVELOPMENT OF THE INDIVIDUAL, OR EVEN THE WHOLE OF HUMANITY. AND WHAT'S MORE, YOU WERE ALSO THE ONLY ONE OF US WHO PORTRAYED WOMEN RESPECTFULLY...

IT'S TRUE, THERE WERE CERTAINLY A LOT MORE ROBOTS IN THE GOLDEN AGE OF SCIENCE FICTION THAN PEOPLE OF COLOR OR WOMEN.

AND THOUGH I WASN'T EXACTLY BLAMELESS IN THAT RESPECT EITHER, AT LEAST THE WOMEN I WROTE ABOUT WERE NEVER "EASY" OR SUBMISSIVE. THEY WERE FASCINATING, LIKE IN MY STORIES *THE OTHER CELIA* OR *THE GIRL HAD GUTS*. MY WORKS QUESTIONED WHAT IT MEANS TO BE HUMAN. AND IF WE'RE HUMAN, WE ARE AUTOMATICALLY MEN *AND* WOMEN!

YOU WERE WIDELY ACCLAIMED, ABOVE ALL, BY OTHER SCI-FI AUTHORS, FROM JAMES BLISH TO RAY BRADBURY AND SAMUEL R. DELANY. BLISH CALLED YOU THE "FINEST CONSCIOUS ARTIST SCI-FI EVER PRODUCED," AND BRADBURY SAID HE WAS "SECRETLY ENVIOUS."

AS FOR DELANY, HE CLAIMED THAT THE FACT I WAS WRITING SF WAS ALL WAS SOME "GLORIOUS ACCIDENT." BUT HE WAS WRONG. I SOUGHT CREATIVE FREEDOM WHICH, FOR ME, LAY CHIEFLY IN THE REALM OF SCIENCE FICTION.

YOUR TWO BIGGEST NOVELS BECAME TRUE CLASSICS. FIRSTLY *THE DREAMING JEWELS*, THEN *MORE THAN HUMAN*, WHICH WAS NEARLY ADAPTED FOR THE SCREEN BY BERTRAND TAVERNIER. BUT IN THE END HE MADE *DEATH WATCH*, BASED ON A DAVID COMPTON NOVEL.

THAT'S RIGHT. *THE DREAMING JEWELS* WAS ALSO A MAJOR INSPIRATION FOR THE HBO TV SERIES *CARNIVÀLE*.

THE STORY QUESTIONED OUR HUMANITY, THE CONCEPTS OF BEAUTY AND UGLINESS, SOLITUDE, AND AESTHETIC VALUES AS SEEN THROUGH A MASS OF MORAL UPHEAVALS. IT'S SET WITHIN A FAIRGROUND WORLD PEOPLED WITH MONSTROSITIES--*FREAKS* OF THE TYPE TOD BROWNING HAD SHOWN IN HIS 1932 FILM, AND A FEW OF THEM EVEN POSSESSED PSYCHIC POWERS.

MORE THAN HUMAN, MEANWHILE, TACKLED THE IDEA OF A MENTAL *GESTALT*, A BOND THAT CONNECTS SIX YOUNG FREAKS. THUS UNITED, THEY BECOME AN ENTITY STRONGER THAN THEIR INDIVIDUAL SELVES. PUBLISHED IN *GALAXY* MAGAZINE, THE NOVEL WON THE INTERNATIONAL FANTASY AWARD!

MY NOVEL'S INFLUENCE WENT FAR BEYOND LITERATURE. IT WAS POPULAR AMONG FIGURES FROM THE COUNTERCULTURE, PARTICULARLY MUSICIANS. CROSBY, STILLS, NASH & YOUNG AND THE GRATEFUL DEAD SAID THAT THIS *GESTALT* WOULD FORM A PEDESTAL FOR THEIR IDEA OF THE TRUE SPIRIT OF A ROCK BAND. SOMETIMES WE CAN BE MORE CREATIVE AND STRONGER TOGETHER THAN ALONE.

I ALSO LAID A FEW FOUNDATION STONES IN THE BUILDING OF GENE RODDENBERRY'S CULT SERIES *STAR TREK*, WRITING SEVERAL EPISODES, THOUGH NOT ALL OF THEM WERE FILMED. ONE WAS *AMOK TIME*, WHICH FIRST INTRODUCED THE VULCAN SALUTE, AND THE *PON FARR*, A SEXUAL RITUAL OF THE FAMOUS MR. SPOCK'S RACE THAT ACTOR LEONARD NIMOY CREDITED ME WITH INVENTING.

LIVE LONG AND PROSPER.

PON FARR.

AND SPEAKING OF INVENTIONS...

HERE IS
THE LEGACY
THAT ALL YOU
GOLDEN-AGE
AUTHORS LEFT
TO THE WORLD!

Bibliography of the Golden Age

Poul Anderson
The Polesotechnic League
The Time Patrol
Brain Wave
Tau Zero

Isaac Asimov
Robot series
Foundation
The Caves of Steel
The End of Eternity

Alfred Bester
The Stars My Destination
The Demolished Man

Eando Binder
I, Robot

James Blish
The Seedling Stars
A Case of Conscience
Cities in Flight

Leigh Brackett
Martian Quest

Ray Bradbury
Fahrenheit 451
The Martian Chronicles
The Illustrated Man

Fredric Brown
What Mad Universe
Martians, Go Home

Arthur C. Clarke
2001: A Space Odyssey
Rendezvous with Rama
Childhood's End
The Fountains of Paradise
The Collected Stories

Hal Clement
Cycle of Fire
Mission of Gravity

Lyon Sprague de Camp
Lest Darkness Fall

Philip José Farmer
The Lovers

Jack Finney
The Body Snatchers

Edmond Hamilton
Captain Future
The Star Kings
Starwolf

Robert Heinlein
Future History
The Door into Summer
The Moon is a Harsh Mistress
The Puppet Masters
Starship Troopers
Stranger in a Strange Land

Cyril M. Kornbluth & Frederik Pohl
The Space Merchants

Fritz Leiber
The Big Time
The Wanderer

Murray Leinster
The Forgotten Planet
A Logic Named Joe

Richard Matheson
I Am Legend
The Shrinking Man

Walter Miller
A Canticle for Leibowitz

Catherine L. Moore
Judgment Night

Lewis Padgett
The Fairy Chessmen

Frederik Pohl
Gateway

Eric Frank Russell
Sinister Barrier

Clifford D. Simak
City
Way Station
Time is the Simplest Thing
Ring Around the Sun
Aliens for Neighbors

Cordwainer Smith
The Instrumentality of Mankind

Theodore Sturgeon
The Dreaming Jewels
More Than Human
Venus Plus X
Some of Your Blood

A. E. van Vogt
The World of Null-A
The Voyage of the Space Beagle
Slan

Jack Vance
Planet of Adventure
Demon Princes
The Jack Vance Treasury

Kurt Vonnegut
Player Piano
The Sirens of Titan
Slaughterhouse-Five

Jack Williamson
The Legion of Time
The Humanoids

John Wyndham
The Day of the Triffids

NON-FICTION:

Isaac Asimov
I, Asimov

Donald Wollheim
The Universe Makers

Damon Knight
In Search of Wonder
The Futurians

Alec Nevala-Lee
Astounding

Frederik Pohl
The Way the Future Was

John Clute & Peter Nicholls
The Encyclopedia of Science Fiction

THE ABOVE TITLES ARE GENERALLY AVAILABLE FROM LIBRARIES, BOOKSTORES, AND ONLINE. ALL THESE NOVELS, ESSAYS, MAGAZINES, ETC. ARE REPRESENTATIVE OF THE GOLDEN AGE OF SCIENCE FICTION.

A FEW WORKS CLASSIFIED BY SUB-GENRE AND THEME…

SPACE OPERA: TERM COINED BY THE WRITER WILSON TUCKER, A SUB-GENRE POPULARIZED BY EDMOND HAMILTON (*THE STAR KINGS*) AND JACK WILLIAMSON (*THE LEGION OF SPACE*).

MUTANTS: READ *SLAN* BY A. E. VAN VOGT OR RICHARD MATHESON'S SHORT STORY *BORN OF MAN AND WOMAN*.

TIME TRAVEL: POSSIBLE DESTINATIONS? THE PAST OR THE FUTURE. READ *THE TIME PATROL* BY POUL ANDERSON.

HARD SF: SCIENCE FICTION WRITTEN STRICTLY ACCORDING TO THE SCIENTIFIC KNOWLEDGE OF THE TIME. READ *MISSION OF GRAVITY* BY HAL CLEMENT OR *THE CITY AND THE STARS* BY ARTHUR C. CLARKE.

SEX AND SCI-FI: READ *THE LOVERS* BY PHILIP JOSÉ FARMER OR *VENUS PLUS X* BY THEODORE STURGEON.

ALIENS: READ *THE VOYAGE OF THE SPACE BEAGLE* BY A. E. VAN VOGT OR *THE BODY SNATCHERS* BY JACK FINNEY.

PLANET OPERA: ADVENTURES ON OTHER PLANETS OR ALIEN ARTIFACTS. READ *PLANET OF ADVENTURE* BY JACK VANCE.

POST-APOCALYPTIC: AFTER THE WORLD HAS ENDED. READ *A CANTICLE FOR LEIBOWITZ* BY WALTER MILLER.

ALTERNATE HISTORY: CHANGING THE COURSE OF HISTORY. READ *BRING THE JUBILEE* BY WARD MOORE.

PARALLEL WORLDS: READ *WHAT MAD UNIVERSE* BY FREDRIC BROWN.

WANT MORE ROBOTS?: READ *CITY* BY CLIFFORD SIMAK OR ISAAC ASIMOV'S *ROBOT SERIES*.

OPPRESSIVE SOCIETIES: READ *LIMBO* BY BERNARD WOLFE OR *FAHRENHEIT 451* BY RAY BRADBURY.

THE END

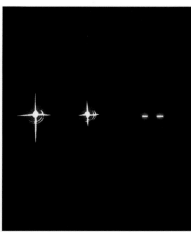

CLAC!

WELL, MY DEAR ROBERT, THE SHOW IS OVER.

IT WOULD SEEM SO, JENKINS. BUT OF COURSE THAT WAS ONLY THE CORE OF THE GOLDEN AGE OF SCIENCE FICTION.

AND THE VISION OF ONE MAN, JOHN WOOD CAMPBELL, WHO REMAINED IN CHARGE OF HIS MAGAZINE RIGHT UP UNTIL 1971, THE YEAR HE DIED. BY THEN, THE MAGAZINE WAS CALLED *ANALOG*, AS IT STILL IS TODAY.

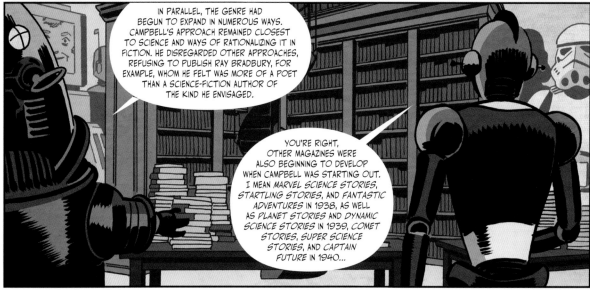

IN PARALLEL, THE GENRE HAD BEGUN TO EXPAND IN NUMEROUS WAYS. CAMPBELL'S APPROACH REMAINED CLOSEST TO SCIENCE AND WAYS OF RATIONALIZING IT IN FICTION. HE DISREGARDED OTHER APPROACHES, REFUSING TO PUBLISH RAY BRADBURY, FOR EXAMPLE, WHOM HE FELT WAS MORE OF A POET THAN A SCIENCE-FICTION AUTHOR OF THE KIND HE ENVISAGED.

YOU'RE RIGHT, OTHER MAGAZINES WERE ALSO BEGINNING TO DEVELOP WHEN CAMPBELL WAS STARTING OUT. I MEAN *MARVEL SCIENCE STORIES, STARTLING STORIES,* AND *FANTASTIC ADVENTURES* IN 1938, AS WELL AS *PLANET STORIES* AND *DYNAMIC SCIENCE STORIES* IN 1939, *COMET STORIES, SUPER SCIENCE STORIES,* AND *CAPTAIN FUTURE* IN 1940...

AND SOME OF THEM WERE PUBLISHING THE GREATEST WRITERS OF THE GOLDEN AGE.

A GOLDEN AGE THAT SOME REGARD AS RUNNING FROM 1938 TO 1942, THE HEIGHT OF THE CAMPBELL ERA. OTHERS WOULD EXTEND IT UNTIL THE EARLY 1960s, WHEN FRANK HERBERT'S GREAT NOVEL *DUNE* FIRST APPEARED.

THESE MAGAZINES PUBLISHED GREAT NAMES, SUCH AS OTTO BINDER, EDMOND HAMILTON, HENRY KUTTNER, FREDRIC BROWN, JACK VANCE, ARTHUR C. CLARKE, WILLIAM TENN, JAMES BLISH, WILSON TUCKER, AND RAY BRADBURY, WHO RELEASED HIS FIRST PROFESSIONAL SHORT STORY, *THE PENDULUM*, IN *SUPER SCIENCE STORIES*.

THE CRITIC MIKE ASHLEY DESCRIBED *SUPER SCIENCE STORIES*, EDITED BY FREDERIK POHL, AS PROOF OF WHAT EXCELLENT RESULTS WERE ATTAINABLE ON A VERY MODEST BUDGET.

YES, MANY OF THE MAGAZINES BEGAN WITH NEXT TO NOTHING...

BUT WE SHOULD ALSO MENTION THAT BRIDGES BETWEEN VARIOUS MEDIA AND GENRES WERE FORMING MUCH MORE EASILY, AND ESPECIALLY WITH COMICS, WHICH WERE UNDERGOING A GOLDEN AGE OF THEIR OWN.

JERRY SIEGEL AND JOE SHUSTER, THE CREATORS OF SUPERMAN, MET ONE ANOTHER THROUGH A SHARED INTEREST IN THE PULP *AMAZING STORIES*.

JULIUS SCHWARTZ AND MORT WEISINGER MET AFTER SCOURING THE READERS' LETTERS PAGES OF THE PULPS, AND THE TWO MEN WENT ON TO BECOME HIGHLY INFLUENTIAL.

IN THIS PHOTOGRAPH FROM 1937, WE CAN SEE SCHWARTZ AND WEISINGER TOGETHER WITH OTTO BINDER, JACK WILLIAMSON, AND EDMOND HAMILTON. THE TWO MEN, ALONG WITH AMERICA'S BEST-KNOWN FAN AND COSPLAY PIONEER, FORREST J. ACKERMAN, FOUNDED *THE TIME TRAVELLER*, THE FIRST FANZINE DEDICATED TO SCIENCE FICTION. THEN, IN 1937, THEY JOINTLY SET UP SOLAR SALES SERVICES, AN AGENCY DESIGNED TO MAKE THINGS EASIER FOR AUTHORS AND HELP GET THEIR SCIENCE-FICTION WORK READ BY THE EDITORS-IN-CHIEF OF MAGAZINES.

THE UNITED STATES IS HUGE, BUT THE MAJORITY OF PUBLISHERS WERE BASED IN NEW YORK, TURNING IT INTO A LITERARY NEXUS.

THEY WERE REPRESENTING THE INTERESTS OF AUTHORS SUCH AS KUTTNER, BINDER, HAMILTON, AND EVEN LOVECRAFT.

IT WAS THEY WHO SOLD *THE SHADOW OUT OF TIME*, PUBLISHED IN *ASTOUNDING* IN 1936. LOVECRAFT WAS PAID SEVERAL HUNDRED DOLLARS FOR IT--THE LARGEST CHECK OF HIS ENTIRE CAREER.

NEXT, WEISINGER AND SCHWARTZ BRANCHED OUT INTO COMICS...

WEISINGER WAS THE FIRST TO LEAVE THE AGENCY. BOTH MEN BEGAN TO SPECIALIZE IN MAGAZINE EDITING: SCHWARTZ WITH *FANTASY MAGAZINE* IN 1937, AND WEISINGER AT *THRILLING WONDER STORIES.*

IN 1944, SCHWARTZ ENDED UP AT ALL-AMERICAN PUBLICATIONS, LATER DC COMICS. HE HAD NEVER READ A COMIC BOOK BEFORE APPLYING FOR THE JOB, BUT HE HAD THE ENCOURAGEMENT OF THE AUTHOR ALFRED BESTER, WHO WROTE ONE OF SCIENCE FICTION'S GREAT CLASSICS, *THE DEMOLISHED MAN.* SCHWARTZ REMAINED WITH DC UNTIL HIS DEATH IN 2004.

WEISINGER HAD BEAT HIM TO ALL AMERICAN BY THREE YEARS. ALMOST IMMEDIATELY, HIS FORCEFUL PERSONALITY INGRATIATED HIM WITH UPPER MANAGEMENT, EVENTUALLY EARNING HIM THE STEWARDSHIP OF DC'S *SUPERMAN.*

HE WAS ALSO INVOLVED IN THE CREATION OF *AQUAMAN* AND *GREEN ARROW.* WITH OTTO BINDER AND JERRY SIEGEL, WHO RETURNED TO DC FOR A SHORT WHILE, HE ELEVATED AND DEFINED THE SUPERMAN MYTHOS FOR DECADES TO FOLLOW.

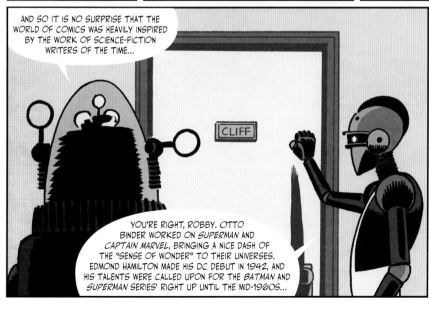

AND SO IT IS NO SURPRISE THAT THE WORLD OF COMICS WAS HEAVILY INSPIRED BY THE WORK OF SCIENCE-FICTION WRITERS OF THE TIME...

YOU'RE RIGHT, ROBBY. OTTO BINDER WORKED ON *SUPERMAN* AND *CAPTAIN MARVEL,* BRINGING A NICE DASH OF THE "SENSE OF WONDER" TO THEIR UNIVERSES. EDMOND HAMILTON MADE HIS DC DEBUT IN 1942, AND HIS TALENTS WERE CALLED UPON FOR THE *BATMAN* AND *SUPERMAN* SERIES' RIGHT UP UNTIL THE MID-1960S...

NOTABLY, HE WROTE THE SCRIPT FOR THE FAMOUS *THE LAST DAYS OF SUPERMAN.*

127

COME IN!

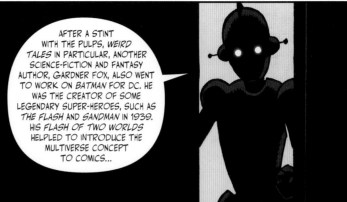

AFTER A STINT WITH THE PULPS, *WEIRD TALES* IN PARTICULAR, ANOTHER SCIENCE-FICTION AND FANTASY AUTHOR, GARDNER FOX, ALSO WENT TO WORK ON *BATMAN* FOR DC. HE WAS THE CREATOR OF SOME LEGENDARY SUPER-HEROES, SUCH AS *THE FLASH* AND *SANDMAN* IN 1939. HIS *FLASH OF TWO WORLDS* HELPED TO INTRODUCE THE MULTIVERSE CONCEPT TO COMICS...

EASY NOW, TIGE. IT'S JENKINS AND ROBERT, HERE TO VISIT OUR CROSSROADS OF SCIENCE FICTION.

WELL, FRIENDS, WHERE HAVE YOU COME FROM?

WE HAVE JUST LEFT THE CAMPBELL ERA, MR. SIMAK.

AH, CAMPBELL! I KNEW HIM WELL. HE WAS A TRULY GIFTED WRITER AND A MARVELOUS EDITOR. I SENT A LOT OF MY STORIES TO *ASTOUNDING* IN THE LATE 1930S AND AT THE BEGINNING OF THE 1940S, SMACK IN THE MIDDLE OF THE GOLDEN AGE. WHAT'S MORE, MY DEAR JENKINS, YOU WERE BORN IN THE PAGES OF THAT MAGAZINE. IN A STORY TITLED *HUDDLING PLACE* BACK IN 1944, THE SECOND IN A COLLECTION THAT LATER MADE ME FAMOUS...

...CITY!

CORRECT! IN IT, MY SENSITIVITY WAS ALREADY DEVELOPING, ROOTED IN EMOTION AND A CERTAIN NOSTALGIA. MY AESTHETIC TENDED MORE TOWARD NATURALISM, AND I WROTE *CITY* OUT OF SHEER DISGUST AT THE CONSTANT BLOODSHED. IT WAS MY PROTEST AGAINST THE SEEMINGLY ENDLESS WARS OF THE CHAOTIC 20TH CENTURY.

IN FACT, IN THAT NOVEL YOU SHOWED THE WORLD IN THE WAY YOU FELT IT OUGHT TO BE. A WORLD SHAPED BY KINDNESS AND GENTLENESS, BUT ALSO BY COURAGE.

I CERTAINLY DID, AND TURNED MY ROBOTS AND MY DOGS INTO THE KIND OF PEOPLE I'D LIKE TO LIVE WITH.

BUT STILL, YOU DRIFTED AWAY FROM CAMPBELL AND *ASTOUNDING*, AS DID OTHER WRITERS.

FOR SEVERAL REASONS. PERHAPS I WASN'T REALLY HIS SORT OF AUTHOR. MAYBE I WASN'T OPTIMISTIC ENOUGH ABOUT HUMANITY AND SCIENCE. HE REFUSED THE FINAL PART OF *CITY*, PRESUMABLY BECAUSE IT TAINTED HIS VISION OF MANKIND EMERGING TRIUMPHANT.

WELL, THAT IS PUTTING IT MILDLY!

JENKINS AND I DISCUSSED WHAT A UNIQUE CHARACTER CAMPBELL WAS. HE WAS SIMULTANEOUSLY A GOOD, INFLUENTIAL WRITER AND AN IMPORTANT EDITOR. BUT HE WAS MARRED BY RACISM AND RATHER QUESTIONABLE STANCES, PARTICULARLY ON PSEUDO-SCIENCES SUCH AS SCIENTOLOGY. A FEW WRITERS ACTUALLY GOT INVOLVED IN THE MOVEMENT. VAN VOGT, FOR EXAMPLE, HELPED ESTABLISH ONE OF THE FIRST DIANETICS CENTERS.

QUITE A PARADOX, THIS CAMPBELL.

THAT IS TRUE, TIGE. HIS DECLINE MIGHT ALSO HAVE BEEN DUE TO MORE SCI-FI BOOKS BEING PUBLISHED IN THE EARLY 1950S, AS WELL AS THE EMERGENCE OF TWO IMPORTANT MAGAZINES: *GALAXY* AND *THE MAGAZINE OF FANTASY AND SCIENCE FICTION*.

MANY GREAT AUTHORS WERE FIRST PUBLISHED IN THEM AND GREW ALONGSIDE OTHERS WHO HAD CUT THEIR TEETH WITH CAMPBELL'S MAGAZINES, LIKE FRITZ LEIBER AND POUL ANDERSON.

WE SHOULD ALSO MENTION THE MAGAZINE *STARTLING STORIES*, WHICH PUBLISHED THE FIRST MASTERPIECES BY FREDRIC BROWN (*WHAT MAD UNIVERSE*) AND PHILIP JOSÉ FARMER. FARMER'S WAS HIS "HERETICAL" *THE LOVERS*, IN WHICH HE OFFERED READERS AN ORIGINAL LOVE STORY BETWWEN A HUMAN AND AN ALIEN.

THAT'S RIGHT. BACK THEN, BROWN AND FARMER WERE AT THE FOREFRONT OF THE GENRE'S EVOLUTION. THEY WERE ALSO PUBLISHED IN *GALAXY*, A MAGAZINE THAT WAS MORE CAUSTIC AND SATIRICAL IN TONE THAN *ASTOUNDING* HAD EVER BEEN. IT ALSO FEATURED AUTHORS SUCH AS DAMON KNIGHT, ALFRED BESTER, FREDERIK POHL AND ANNE MCCAFFREY.

TAKE THE IDIOCRACY CONCEPT, EXPLORED BY CYRIL M. KORNBLUTH IN HIS STORY *THE MARCHING MORONS* THAT CAME OUT IN *GALAXY* IN 1951. IT FEATURED A MAN FROM THE 20TH CENTURY WHO WAKES UP IN A FUTURE WHERE THE MAJORITY OF MEN AND WOMEN HAVE TURNED INTO TOTAL IDIOTS DUE TO ALL THE MATERIAL COMFORTS OF AN EVOLVED SOCIETY!

BUT SINCE I SUPPOSE YOU WON'T HAVE TIME TO VISIT EVERY ROOM IN OUR HOUSE OF SCIENCE FICTION, ESPECIALLY THOSE DEVOTED TO THE GOLDEN-AGE AUTHORS WHOSE CAREERS WERE ONLY MENTIONED BRIEFLY DURING THE CAMPBELL ERA, THEN I WOULD SUGGEST THAT YOU HAVE A LOOK AT MY SPECIAL GLOBE HERE.

WELL, WHY NOT? COME ON, JENKINS. I'M INTRIGUED!

YOU WON'T REGRET IT. YOU'RE STANDING AT THE CROSSROADS OF SCI-FI. NOW YOU CAN CHOOSE WHICH WAY TO GO, BECAUSE I ASSUME THAT WAS THE REASON FOR YOUR VISIT.

YES, WE WOULD LIKE TO GO THROUGH THE DOOR THAT WILL LEAD US TO BRITISH SCIENCE FICTION, THEN THE REST OF THE HISTORY OF THE GENRE. AND WHO BETTER THAN SIMAK DRESSED AS ENOCH WALLACE TO GUIDE US TOWARD THE STARS?

INCIDENTALLY, SOME CRITICS CONSIDER YOUR HUGO AWARD-WINNING NOVEL *WAY STATION*, PUBLISHED IN 1963, TO BE YOUR TRUE MASTERPIECE.

YES, THE STORY OF ENOCH WALLACE (THE KEEPER OF AN ALIEN JUMP-POINT IN HIS ODD HOUSE SOMEWHERE OUT IN THE STICKS OF WISCONSIN) LEFT A LASTING IMPRESSION ON SCIENCE FICTION. ESPECIALLY THANKS TO THE VALUES OF INTER-SPECIES FRIENDSHIP IT PROMOTED, AND ITS OPTIMISM, DESPITE THE FACT THAT IT WAS PUBLISHED DURING THE COLD WAR, SOON AFTER THE CUBAN MISSILE CRISIS.

I RECALL A SIMPLY WONDERFUL LINE FROM THE BOOK: "HERE LIES ONE FROM A DISTANT STAR, BUT THE SOIL IS NOT ALIEN TO HIM, FOR IN DEATH HE BELONGS TO THE UNIVERSE." AND...*OH MY!*

EDMOND HAMILTON WROTE HIS FIRST STORY, *THE LIVING PLANT*, AT JUST 14 YEARS OF AGE AND EVENTUALLY MADE HIS DEBUT IN 1926 WITH THE SHORT STORY *THE MONSTER-GOD OF MAMURTH*, WHICH WAS PUBLISHED IN *WEIRD TALES*. HAMILTON INITIALLY DISCOVERED SCIENCE FICTION THROUGH THE WORKS OF ABRAHAM MERRITT AND MURRAY LEINSTER IN MUNSEY'S MAGAZINES. BUT IT WAS HUGO GERNSBACK'S PUBLICATIONS THAT MADE HIM DECIDE TO PURSUE WRITING AS A PROFESSION. HIS SEMINAL *CRASHING SUNS* WAS ONE OF THE FIRST DEPICTIONS OF INTERSTELLAR PATROLS, A CONCEPT THAT WOULD LATER REACH ITS PEAK AT THE PENS OF JACK WILLIAMSON AND "DOC" SMITH. HAMILTON'S INFLUENCE COULD BE CLEARLY SEEN IN THE WORK OF HIS PEERS, WHILE ALSO SPREADING INTO OTHER MEDIA SUCH AS COMICS AND CINEMA (PARTICULARLY *STAR WARS*). AMONG HIS MOST NOTABLE WORKS ARE *THE STAR KINGS*, *STARWOLF*, AND THE RENOWNED *ADVENTURES OF CAPTAIN FUTURE*. IN COMICS HE WROTE MANY TALES FOR THE *BATMAN* AND *SUPERMAN* TITLES, AS WELL AS FOR *STRANGE ADVENTURES*. HAMILTON WAS THE HUSBAND OF ANOTHER NOTABLE AUTHOR, **LEIGH BRACKETT**. BRACKET DEBUTED IN 1940 WITH *MARTIAN QUEST*. SHE WAS A PROLIFIC WRITER OF FANTASY AND SCIENCE FICTION AT A TIME WHEN IT WAS A FIELD THAT REMAINED ALMOST IMPENETRABLE TO WOMEN. FOLLOWING IN THE FOOTSTEPS OF EDGAR RICE BURROUGHS AND C. L. MOORE, SHE PRODUCED A RANGE OF STORIES THAT BECAME *MARTIAN QUEST* AND *THE BOOK OF SKAITH*. BUT SHE WAS BEST KNOWN FOR HER WORK IN CINEMA, CO-WRITING THE SCREENPLAYS FOR SEVERAL CLASSIC FILMS, SUCH AS *THE BIG SLEEP*, *RIO BRAVO*, AND *RIO LOBO*...AS WELL AS *THE EMPIRE STRIKES BACK*, EPISODE V OF THE *STAR WARS* SAGA.

JACK WILLIAMSON DEBUTED IN 1928 WITH *THE METAL MAN*. THIS LITTLE-KNOWN BUT OFTEN EXCELLENT AUTHOR DISCOVERED SCIENCE FICTION IN THE PAGES OF *AMAZING STORIES*. A FRIEND OF EDMOND HAMILTON AND FREDERIK POHL, AND ADMIRED BY THE YOUNG ISAAC ASIMOV, JACK WILLIAMSON LEFT AN EXTREMELY DIVERSE BODY OF WORK BEHIND HIM, INCLUDING MEMORABLE NOVELS SUCH AS *THE LEGION OF SPACE*, INSPIRED BY ALEXANDRE DUMAS' *THE THREE MUSKETEERS*. HIS SERIES *THE LEGION OF TIME* IS SAID TO HAVE INSPIRED THE *TERMINATOR* SAGA, WHILE HIS NOVEL *DARKER THAN YOU THINK* REVIVED THE THEME OF LYCANTHROPY. IN 1949, HE WROTE ONE OF HIS BEST NOVELS, *THE HUMANOIDS*, A DYSTOPIAN TALE IN WHICH ROBOTS INTERPRET THE THREE LAWS OF ROBOTICS A BIT TOO LITERALLY UNTIL MANKIND HAS NOTHING LEFT TO DO. WILLIAMSON KEPT WRITING UNTIL 2005, BEFORE HE PASSED AWAY AT THE VENERABLE AGE OF 98 IN 2006. WINNER OF HUGO, NEBULA, BRAM STOKER, AND DAMON KNIGHT GRAND MASTER AWARDS.

FRITZ LEIBER DEBUTED IN 1934 WITH *RICHES AND POWER*. BUT HIS REAL DEBUT CAME IN *UNKNOWN* MAGAZINE WITH THE FIRST PARTS OF HIS MOST FAMOUS SERIES, *FAFHRD AND THE GRAY MOUSER*, WHICH HE DESCRIBED AS "SWORD AND SORCERY," THUS CREATING A NEW SUB-GENRE OF FANTASY. A FAN OF THOMAS MANN AND H. G WELLS, AS WELL AS A DISCIPLE OF CLARK ASHTON SMITH AND ROBERT E. HOWARD, HE RAISED THE CREDIBILITY OF FANTASY. HIS SCIENCE FICTION WAS ALSO WELL-REPUTED, ALTHOUGH HE HAD DIFFICULTIES PUBLISHING IT, PARTICULARLY BECAUSE CAMPBELL CONSIDERED HIS STORIES UNSUITABLE FOR *ASTOUNDING*. HE DID MANAGE TO CONVERT HIM, HOWEVER, AND *GATHER, DARKNESS!* WAS PUBLISHED IN 1943, IN WHICH PERVERSE SCIENCE BECOMES A TYRANT BENEATH A RELIGIOUS MASK. BUT LEIBER FELT UNABLE TO CONFORM TO CAMPBELL'S VISION AND MOVED AWAY IN THE EARLY 1950S ONCE NEW MAGAZINES APPEARED THAT ALLOWED HIM TO GROW AND FLOURISH. HE BEGAN TO BE PUBLISHED REGULARLY IN THE PAGES OF *GALAXY*, AS HIS OFTEN SARCASTIC STYLE WAS PERFECTLY IN TUNE WITH THE MOOD OF THE MAGAZINE. THE LATE 1950S AND THE 1960S WERE FRUITFUL: *FAFHRD AND THE GRAY MOUSER* WAS PRINTED IN VOLUMES, AND HE HAD NOVELS PUBLISHED SUCH AS *THE BIG TIME* (AN ALTERNATE-HISTORY WAR), AND HIS ONLY LARGE NOVEL, *THE WANDERER* (1964). THIS VIRTUOSO AUTHOR PENNED SOME OF THE HIGHEST-ACCLAIMED WORK IN SCIENCE FICTION, WINNING SIX HUGOS, THREE NEBULAS, TWO LOCUS', AND THREE WORLD FANTASY AWARDS. HIS FANTASY WORKS ALSO LEFT THEIR MARK ON ROLE-PLAYING GAMES, ESPECIALLY *DUNGEONS & DRAGONS*.

FREDRIC BROWN MADE HIS WRITING DEBUT IN 1936 WITH *V.O.N. MUNCHDRILLER SOLVES A PROBLEM*. THE ROOTS OF HUMOROUS SCIENCE FICTION CAN UNDOUBTEDLY BE TRACED BACK TO THIS CONSUMMATE NOVELIST. HIS WIFE, ELIZABETH, ONCE CLAIMED THAT FREDRIC HATED TO WRITE, WHICH MAY HAVE CONTRIBUTED TO HIS HUGE TALENT FOR VERY SHORT STORIES. OR MAYBE IT WAS SIMPLY A DESIRE TO GET THINGS SAID AS QUICKLY AND AS CONCISELY AS POSSIBLE. WHATEVER THE CASE, THE FACT REMAINS THAT HUMOR WAS FUNDAMENTAL TO THE WORK OF FREDRIC BROWN, WHO ALSO BECAME NOTED FOR HIS CRIME STORIES SUCH AS *MADBALL*. IT WAS CERTAINLY TRUE OF HIS SHORT-STORY COLLECTION *NIGHTMARES AND GEEZENSTACKS* (1961) AND HIS NOVELS *WHAT MAD UNIVERSE* (1949) AND THE CELEBRATED *MARTIANS, GO HOME* (1955). HIS AVANT-GARDIST WORKS WON FEW AWARDS, THOUGH HE DID RECEIVE AN EDGAR ALLAN POE AWARD FOR *THE FABULOUS CLIPJOINT* IN 1947.

FREDERIK POHL DEBUTED IN 1939 WITH *HEAD OVER HEELS IN TIME* AFTER FIRST BECOMING KNOWN IN HIS YOUTH AS A MEMBER OF THE FUTURIANS. HE HAD A MAJOR INFLUENCE ON THE GENRE AS AN AUTHOR, AN EDITOR (*ASTONISHING STORIES*), AND A LITERARY AGENT. TOGETHER WITH CYRIL M. KORNBLUTH, HE CREATED ONE OF HIS MOST STRIKING SATIRICAL DYSTOPIAS, *THE SPACE MERCHANTS* (1952), WHICH EXPLORED THE EXCESSES OF ADVERTISING. *THE AGE OF THE PUSSYFOOT* (1969) ANTICIPATED A SMARTPHONE SOCIETY, WHILE *MAN PLUS* (1976) DELVED INTO THE TRANSFORMATION OF HUMANS INTO CYBORGS TO ADAPT TO THE MARTIAN ENVIRONMENT. HE ALSO WON MANY AWARDS: FIVE HUGOS (PARTICULARLY FOR *GATEWAY*, 1977, THE FIRST NOVEL IN HIS *HEECHEE* SERIES) AND TWO NEBULAS.

ALFRED BESTER DEBUTED IN 1939 WITH *THE BROKEN AXIOM*. ALTHOUGH NOT THE MOST FAMOUS OF THE GOLDEN-AGE AUTHORS, HE DID MAKE A SIZEABLE CONTRIBUTION, WORKING A LOT IN COMICS (*SUPERMAN*, *GREEN LANTERN*) BEFORE CONCENTRATING ON WRITING RADIO DRAMAS AFTER 1946. THESE REMAINED IMPRINTED IN THE MINDS OF FANS LIKE THE WRITER HARLAN ELLISON, WHO MENTIONED THEM IN HIS MAGNIFICENT, TIMELESS SHORT STORY *JEFFTY IS FIVE*. BUT HE IS BEST REMEMBERED FOR TWO NOVELS, *THE DEMOLISHED MAN* (1953) AND *THE STARS MY DESTINATION* (AKA *TIGER! TIGER!*, 1956). THE FIRST REVEALED A CRIMELESS WORLD RULED BY TELEPATHY, WHILE THE SECOND REVISITED *THE COUNT OF MONTE CRISTO*. WHEN HE DIED, HE IS SAID TO HAVE LEFT HIS ESTATE TO HIS FAVORITE BARMAN.

DAMON KNIGHT DEBUTED IN 1940 WITH *THE ITCHING HOUR*. ANOTHER SEASONED FUTURIAN, KNIGHT WAS BEST KNOWN AS A LITERARY CRITIC, BUT WAS ALSO AN UNDERRATED WRITER. HIS MOST FAMOUS WORK WAS *TO SERVE MAN*, A SHORT STORY WITH A TWIST ENDING THAT WAS ADAPTED AS AN EPISODE OF TV SERIES *THE TWILIGHT ZONE*. BUT HE ALSO WROTE SEVERAL GOOD NOVELS, SUCH AS *HELL'S PAVEMENT* (1955) AND *THE MAN IN THE TREE* (1984). TOGETHER WITH HIS WIFE, THE SCIENCE-FICTION AUTHOR **KATE WILHELM,** HE LAUNCHED THE CELEBRATED CLARION WRITERS' WORKSHOPS. AS AN EDITOR, HE PUBLISHED THE CHALLENGING *ORBIT* SERIES OF ANTHOLOGIES, AND WON A NUMBER OF HUGO, NEBULA, AND LOCUS AWARDS. TOGETHER WITH JAMES BLISH, HE FOUNDED THE SCIENCE FICTION AND FANTASY WRITERS OF AMERICA ASSOCIATION, WHICH PRESENTS THE NEBULAS, AND THE GRAND MASTER AWARDS THAT BEAR HIS NAME.

RAY BRADBURY DEBUTED PROFESSIONALLY WITH *THE PENDULUM* IN 1939. HE BECAME INTERESTED IN SCIENCE FICTION EARLY AND WENT ON TO BE ONE OF ITS MOST PROMINENT AUTHORS, YET MAINTAINED THAT ONLY HIS BEST-KNOWN NOVEL, *FAHRENHEIT 451*, CAME UNDER THAT HEADING. STILL, BRADBURY ATTENDED THE FIRST WORLD SCIENCE FICTION CONVENTION WHEN HE WAS JUST NINETEEN. THERE HE BECAME FRIENDS WITH EDMOND HAMILTON AND LATER ROBERT HEINLEIN. HE WAS REJECTED BY JOHN CAMPBELL, WHO CONSIDERED HIM MORE OF A POET THAN A SCIENCE-FICTION WRITER. AFTER READING A COLLECTION OF SHORT STORIES BY SHERWOOD ANDERSON IN 1944, BRADBURY CAME UP WITH THE PREMISE FOR HIS FAMOUS *THE MARTIAN CHRONICLES*, WHICH WERE MOSTLY PUBLISHED IN MAGAZINES FROM 1946 TO 1950 BEFORE BEING RELEASED AS A BOOK BY DOUBLEDAY IN 1950. IN 1953, BRADBURY RELEASED THE HUGO AWARD-WINNING *FAHRENHEIT 451*, A NOVEL THAT SYMBOLIZED ALL BOOK-BURNERS SINCE THE EARLIEST DAYS OF HUMANITY, THE GREEKS, THE ROMANS, THOSE WHO TORCHED THE LIBRARY OF ALEXANDRIA, RIGHT UP UNTIL HITLER. THE FRENCH NEW WAVE DIRECTOR FRANÇOIS TRUFFAUT FILMED AN ADAPTATION IN 1966. BRADBURY WROTE MANY REMARKABLE WORKS, INCLUDING *SOMETHING WICKED THIS WAY COMES* AND *THE GOLDEN APPLES OF THE SUN*. HE REGARDED MELANCHOLY AS HUMANITY'S USUAL STATE.

LEWIS PADGETT DEBUTED IN 1941 WITH *A GNOME THERE WAS*. IN ACTUAL FACT, HIDING BEHIND THE MONIKER WERE THE COMMON-LAW COUPLE OF AUTHORS, HENRY KUTTNER AND CATHERINE LUCILLE MOORE. THEY WENT ON TO COLLABORATE (AS PADGETT) ON THE NOVEL *THE FAIRY CHESSMEN* (1946), AND THE SHORT STORY *MIMSY WERE THE BOROGOVES* (1943). BOTH OF THESE WORKS EXAMINED THE LAWS OF PHYSICS: IN *THE FAIRY CHESSMEN*, THOSE IMMUTABLE LAWS BECAME VARIABLE; WHILE IN *MIMSY WERE THE BOROGOVES*, ONE OF THE MOST FAMOUS SHORT STORIES IN SCIENCE FICTION HISTORY, SOME CHILDREN DISCOVER TOYS FROM THE FUTURE THAT HELP THEM THINK AND LEARN IN NON-EUCLIDIAN WAYS. THE TITLE WAS TAKEN FROM LEWIS CARROLL'S NONSENSE POEM, *JABBERWOCKY*, AS MIGHT HAVE BEEN THE COUPLE'S PSEUDONYM, THOUGH IT'S ALSO SUGGESTED THAT IT WAS TAKEN FROM EACH OF THEIR MOTHERS' MAIDEN NAMES. A NOT PARTICULARLY FAITHFUL BUT LIKABLE SCREEN ADAPTATION TITLED *THE LAST MIMZY* WAS RELEASED IN 2007.

JACK VANCE DEBUTED IN 1945 WITH *THE WORLD-THINKER*, BUT PERHAPS HIS STORY REALLY BEGAN BACK IN PEARL HARBOR. HE WORKED AS AN ELECTRICIAN AT THE NAVY YARD THERE, BUT FORTUNATELY LEFT A MONTH BEFORE THE INFAMOUS ATTACK BY THE JAPANESE FORCES. A KEEN TRAVELER, VANCE'S DEBUT IN *STARTLING STORIES* WAS THE FIRST PARTS OF *THE MANY WORLDS OF MAGNUS RIDOLPH*, A QUICK-WITTED SPACE DETECTIVE. IN 1953, HE RELEASED HIS FIRST JUVENILE NOVEL, *VANDALS OF THE VOID*, PUBLISHED BY JOHN C. WINSTON, BUT HIS LATER CAREER DID NOT RESEMBLE THAT OF AN AUTHOR INSPIRED BY HEINLEIN. HIS RICH, EXOTIC WORKS SKILLFULLY BLENDED FANTASY AND SCIENCE FICTION WITH A PERPETUAL WANDERLUST AND A CRAVING FOR THE ELSEWHERE AND THE OTHER. ONE OF HIS BESTSELLERS WAS *THE LANGUAGES OF PAO* (1958), WHICH FOCUSED ON HOW LANGUAGES CAN BE USED TO CONDITION PEOPLE'S THINKING. SAMUEL R. DELANY (*BABEL-17*) AND IAN WATSON (*THE EMBEDDING*) WOULD LATER RAISE THIS THEME TO NEW HEIGHTS. VANCE ALSO WROTE AN INVENTIVE DYSTOPIAN NOVEL, *EMPHYRIO* (1969), AND WHAT IS OFTEN CONSIDERED HIS BEST WORK, *THE DRAGON MASTERS* (1963). HE WAS A WAYFARER OF WORDS AND VAGABOND IDEAS IN INCREDIBLE SURROUNDINGS AND EXTRAORDINARY CULTURES, WITH DREAMLIKE ATMOSPHERES. VANCE DEPICTED COMPLEX UNIVERSES WHERE INVENTION VIED AGAINST CREATIVITY. RELIGION, CUSTOMS, GEOGRAPHY, ECONOMICS, POLITICS; VANCE LEFT NOTHING OUT OF HIS STORIES WHOSE PLOTS WERE SOMETIMES ONLY INCIDENTAL OR MERELY AN EXCUSE FOR TRAVEL. HIS TWO BEST-KNOWN SERIES WERE THE SPRAWLING PLANET OPERA *PLANET OF ADVENTURE*, AND *DEMON PRINCES*. IN THE FORMER, SPACE CASTAWAY ADAM REITH SEEKS A SPACESHIP TO RETURN TO EARTH, BUT MUST FIRST TRAVEL ALL AROUND THE PLANET, MEETING ITS FOUR RESIDENT ALIEN RACES: THE CHASCH, THE WANKH, THE DIRDIR, AND THE PNUME. *DEMON PRINCES*, MEANWHILE, INTRODUCES KIRTH GERSEN, A YOUNG MAN WHOSE CLAN HAS BEEN WIPED OUT BY FIVE INTERGALACTIC CRIMINALS, ON WHOM HE WREAKS HIS VENGEANCE THROUGHOUT THE NOVELS. BY THE END OF HIS CAREER VANCE HAD LOST HIS SIGHT AND HAD TO DICTATE STORIES TO HIS WIFE NORMA. BUT HE NEVER LET THAT GET IN THE WAY OF HIM PRODUCING THE SUPERB NOVEL, *NIGHT LAMP* (1996), AT THE AGE OF 80.

PHILIP JOSÉ FARMER DEBUTED IN 1946 WITH *O'BRIEN AND OBRENOV*, THEN REVOLUTIONIZED SCIENCE FICTION IN 1961 WITH HIS CONTROVERSIAL NOVEL *THE LOVERS*. AN ADAPTATION OF HIS SHORT STORY PUBLISHED IN *STARTLING STORIES* IN 1952, IT TOUCHED ON SEXUALITY, WHICH WAS A TABOO SUBJECT IN SCIENCE FICTION (AND AMERICAN SOCIETY AS A WHOLE) AT THE TIME. OF COURSE, AUTHORS LIKE THEODORE STURGEON AND EVEN *MARVEL SCIENCE STORIES* MAGAZINE HAD ALREADY COVERED THE TOPIC, BUT FARMER WENT A STEP FURTHER BY TELLING THE LOVE STORY OF AN EARTHMAN AND A SEEMINGLY HUMANOID ALIEN (WHO WAS IN FACT INSECTOID), THUS DENTING THE PURITANISM OF AMERICAN SOCIETY ALONG THE WAY. FARMER'S CAREER WAS DOTTED WITH SIMILAR STORIES, INCLUDING THE *TARZAN* PARODY, *A FEAST UNKNOWN*. FARMER AND OTHER AUTHORS, FEMALE AND MALE ALIKE, SUCH AS MARGARET ATWOOD, URSULA K. LE GUIN, AND ARTHUR C. CLARKE WERE ALSO PUBLISHED IN *PLAYBOY* MAGAZINE--AFTER ALL, IT WAS PAYING BETWEEN $3,000 AND $5,000 PER STORY. IN 1965, FARMER WROTE *WORLD OF TIERS*, A SERIES THAT HAS BECOME A CLASSIC AND WAS HIGHLY INNOVATIVE FOR ITS TIME. IT PORTRAYED A MORE ADVANCED HUMAN RACE THAT HAD CREATED POCKET UNIVERSES, "PRIVATE COSMOSES" THEY WOULD PLAY WITH LIKE GODS, DESPITE BEING MERE MORTALS. FRANK HERBERT, THE AUTHOR OF *DUNE*, BORROWED THIS IDEA FOR HIS 1968 NOVEL *THE HEAVEN MAKERS*. MORE RECENTLY, THE IDEA WAS RECYCLED IN *THE SIMS* GAMES. FARMER ALSO WROTE ANOTHER IMPORTANT SERIES, *RIVERWORLD* (HUGO AWARD 1972), AND HIS EXOTIC "PLANETARY ROMANCE" ADVENTURE NOVEL *THE GREEN ODYSSEY* (1957) MAY HAVE INSPIRED JACK VANCE'S *PLANET OF ADVENTURE*.

POUL WILLIAM ANDERSON DEBUTED IN 1947 WITH *TOMORROW'S CHILDREN*. REGARDED AS ONE OF THE GREATEST AMERICAN AUTHORS OF THE GOLDEN AGE, POUL ANDERSON--NAME AND SURNAME INHERITED FROM HIS SCANDINAVIAN ANCESTRY-- REMAINED RELATIVELY UNKNOWN IN CERTAIN PARTS OF THE WORLD SUCH AS FRANCE, ESPECIALLY DUE TO HIS SUPPORT OF THE VIETNAM WAR, WHICH SAW HIM EXCLUDED FROM THE FRENCH PUBLISHING CIRCUIT. UNLIKE VAN VOGT'S CHARACTERS, FOR EXAMPLE, ANDERSON'S WERE STRIKING HUMAN HEROES RATHER THAN SUPERMEN. FROM NICOLAS VAN RIJN, THE RUTHLESS MERCHANT OF *TRADER TO THE STARS*, TO MANSE EVERARD, THE HERO OF *THE TIME PATROL*, AND EVEN THE *AGENT OF THE TERRAN EMPIRE*, DOMINIC FLANDRY, ALL THE HEROES OF HIS MAJOR SERIES WERE PRIMARILY MEN WITH STRONG PERSONAL CODES AND PRINCIPLES. EQUALLY AT HOME WITH FANTASY (*THE BROKEN SWORD*, 1954) AND SCIENCE FICTION, HIS LIST OF WORKS IS FESTOONED WITH PURE GEMS. *HROLF KRAKI'S SAGA* (1973) DELVED INTO SCANDINAVIAN MYTHOLOGY (HE HAD PREVIOUSLY EXPLORED OTHER MYTHS), WHILE IN *BRAIN WAVE* (1954), HUMANITY'S IQ SUDDENLY RISES SHARPLY IN THE TYPE OF SCI-FI STORY FAVORED BY CAMPBELL AND *ASTOUNDING*. THE WRITER JAMES BLISH ONCE DESCRIBED SOME OF POUL ANDERSON'S SCIENCE-FICTION WORK AS "HARD COPY," WHICH LED TO THE CONCEPT OF "HARD SF." ONE OF HIS BEST NOVELS IN THAT GENRE, *TAU ZERO*, WAS NOMINATED FOR A HUGO AWARD IN 1971 BUT LOST OUT TO LARRY NIVEN'S CLASSIC *RINGWORLD*. THIS SUPERB WRITER ALSO PENNED THE WONDERFUL SHORT STORIES *GOAT SONG* (1972, BASED ON THE MYTH OF ORPHEUS AND JEAN COCTEAU'S FILM *ORPHÉE*) AND *CALL ME JOE* (IN *ASTOUNDING*, 1957), WHICH LATER INSPIRED JAMES CAMERON'S RECORD-BREAKING MOVIE *AVATAR*.

WHAT A UNIQUE GLOBE YOU HAVE!

AND IF YOU TAKE ANOTHER LOOK INTO IT YOU CAN SEE THE REST OF THE PANTHEON. BIOGRAPHIES OF OTHER SCIENCE-FICTION HEROES: JUDITH MERRIL, CORDWAINER SMITH, RICHARD MATHESON, ROBERT SHECKLEY, KURT VONNEGUT, FRANK HERBERT, AND PHILIP K. DICK.

OF COURSE WE PLAN TO HEAR MORE ABOUT THEM, BUT BEFORE THAT--

BEFORE THAT, YOU WERE LOOKING FOR THE DOOR LEADING TO BRITISH SCIENCE FICTION...

YES. THEIR SCIENCE FICTION BLENDED WITH AMERICAN SCI-FI, AS MANY BRITISH AUTHORS, SUCH AS ARTHUR C. CLARKE AND JOHN WYNDHAM, ALSO PUBLISHED IN THE PULPS...

IT'S TRUE, BUT IT ALSO SET OFF ON A PATH ALL OF ITS OWN.

CLAP!

IN YOU GO. HE'S WAITING! I KNOW THAT JENKINS HAS THE PASSWORD...

THANK YOU VERY MUCH FOR SEEING US, MR. SIMAK!

Britain and the New Wave. From its beginnings in the late 1930s up until the 1970s.

British
Science Fiction

HMM, I'LL NEED TO FIND A SPECIALIST TO HELP DECODE THIS MANUSCRIPT.

24 FILMS THAT MAKE GOOD ENTRY POINTS TO DISCOVER SCIENCE FICTION:

A TRIP TO THE MOON, GEORGES MÉLIÈS, 1902. THEME: SPACE TRAVEL.

METROPOLIS, FRITZ LANG, 1927. THEME: DYSTOPIAN SOCIETY.

THE THING FROM ANOTHER WORLD, CHRISTIAN NYBY, 1951. THEME: AN ALIEN.

FORBIDDEN PLANET, FRED MCLEOD WILCOX, 1956. THEME: SPACE ADVENTURE.

I'M MICHAEL MOORCOCK, THE BRITISH SCIENCE-FICTION WRITER. WHAT CAN I DO FOR YOU, MR. WELLS?

THANK YOU, MR. MOORCOCK. YOU CAN HELP ME WITH DECODING THE HISTORY OF SCIENCE FICTION IN BRITAIN, ESPECIALLY THE WORKS PRODUCED AFTER MINE. THIS MANUSCRIPT SHOULD PROVE USEFUL.

OH...AH...

WELL, THIS IS JUST MY KIND OF THING, AND WHAT'S MORE, I'M A PART OF THAT HISTORY!

IF YOU'LL LEND ME YOUR DEVICE, I CAN MAKE A START!

FORWARD, DEAR HERBERT! FOLLOW THE GUIDE!

THE TIME MACHINE, GEORGE PAL, 1960. THEME: TIME TRAVEL.

FAHRENHEIT 451, FRANÇOIS TRUFFAUT, 1966. THEME: TOTALITARIANISM.

2001: A SPACE ODYSSEY, STANLEY KUBRICK, 1968. THEME: ARTIFICIAL INTELLIGENCE.

PLANET OF THE APES, FRANKLIN J. SCHAFFNER, 1968. THEME: THE EVOLUTION OF HUMANITY.

DEAR HERBERT, YOU OF ALL PEOPLE KNOW THAT BRITISH SCIENCE FICTION HAS ALWAYS HAD A PENCHANT FOR CATASTROPHES. YOUR NOVEL *THE WAR OF THE WORLDS* WAS A CRUCIAL MILESTONE IN THIS LITERARY GENRE, AS WAS YOUR SHORT STORY *THE STAR*, FROM 1897.

AH, THE STAR...

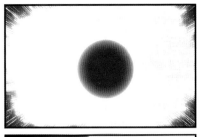

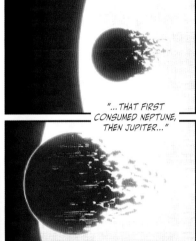

"...THAT FIRST CONSUMED NEPTUNE, THEN JUPITER..."

THE STAR AND OUR OWN SUN WERE EXERTING RECIPROCAL GRAVITATIONAL FORCES. THUS DRAWN INTO OUR SOLAR SYSTEM, THE STAR'S INEXORABLE COURSE RAVAGED MUCH OF THE EARTH...

INDEED, YOUR STORY LEFT MANY PEOPLE ASTONISHED AND WAS EXTREMELY INSPIRATIONAL TO OTHER WRITERS. TAKE PHILIP WYLIE'S *WHEN WORLDS COLLIDE* FROM 1933, OR FRITZ LEIBER'S *THE WANDERER*, NOT FORGETTING ARTHUR C. CLARKE, WHO MENTIONED IT IN HIS NOVEL *RENDEZVOUS WITH RAMA*.

I HAVEN'T HEARD OF THIS CLARKE... WHO IS HE?

A CLOCKWORK ORANGE, STANLEY KUBRICK, 1971. THEME: DYSTOPIAN SOCIETY.

SOLARIS, ANDREI TARKOVSKY, 1972. THEME: PERCEPTION OF REALITY.

PHASE IV, SAUL BASS, 1974. THEMES: ANIMAL AND INSECT INTELLIGENCE.

SOYLENT GREEN, RICHARD FLEISCHER, 1973. THEMES: POLLUTION AND OVERPOPULATION.

PATIENCE, DEAR HERBERT, WE'LL GET TO HIM. BUT BEFORE CLARKE...

...WE SHOULD MENTION THE POST-APOCALYPTIC NOVEL *AFTER LONDON* (1885) BY RICHARD JEFFERIES, IN WHICH THE ENGLISH CAPITAL IS REDUCED TO NOTHING MORE THAN SWAMPLAND. THEN, IN 1928, SYDNEY FOWLER WRIGHT WROTE *DELUGE*, A NOVEL THAT SAW HIM COMPARED TO JEFFERIES AND TO YOU, HERBERT.

I'VE READ THEM. WRIGHT'S BOOK WAS SELF-PUBLISHED AND SPOKE OUT AGAINST THE SOCIAL CLASS SYSTEM, REJECTING ALL FORMS OF SCIENTIFIC PROGRESS...

MANY BRITISH WRITERS EXPLORED THIS LITERARY GENRE FOR THEIR OWN SOCIAL OR PHILOSOPHICAL PURPOSES. LIKE THE BRILLIANT OLAF STAPLEDON. THOUGH NOT STRICTLY A SCIENCE-FICTION AUTHOR, HE USED THE GENRE IN ORDER TO UNDERPIN HIS PHILOSOPHICAL POINTS OF VIEW.

LAST AND FIRST MEN WAS PUBLISHED IN 1930 AND IMPRESSED THE BRITISH READERSHIP. CERTAIN AMERICAN CRITICS, SUCH AS DONALD WOLLHEIM, EVEN LAMENTED THAT STAPLEDON HAD NOT SHAPED AMERICAN SCIENCE FICTION ENOUGH, PRESUMABLY BECAUSE THE AUTHOR AVOIDED TRENDY SUBJECTS SUCH AS NUCLEAR ENERGY AND INTERSTELLAR TRAVEL. HIS NOVEL WAS A STRAIGHTFORWARD ACCOUNT OF HUMAN HISTORY OVER A PERIOD OF TWO THOUSAND YEARS!

INDEED, A VAST AND AMBITIOUS PROJECT! AND HE DIDN'T STOP AT THAT!

THAT'S RIGHT. STAPLEDON ENDED UP PRODUCING NUMEROUS ESSAYS AND BOOKS. IN 1932, HE WROTE THE NOVEL *LAST MEN IN LONDON*, FOLLOWED, IN PARTICULAR, BY *STAR MAKER* IN 1937...

ROLLERBALL, NORMAN JEWISON, 1975. THEMES: SPORT AND DYSTOPIA.

STAR WARS, GEORGE LUCAS, 1977. THEME: THE FIGHT OF GOOD VERSUS EVIL.

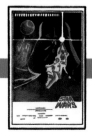

ALIEN, RIDLEY SCOTT, 1979. THEME: THE EIGHTH PASSENGER ISN'T HUMAN!

MAD MAX, GEORGE MILLER, 1979. THEME: A POST-APOCALYPTIC WORLD.

IN THAT NOVEL, A MAN IS ABLE TO LEAVE HIS BODY AND EXPLORE A FARAWAY PLANET, WHERE HE MERGES WITH ONE OF ITS INHABITANTS' MINDS. IT'S THE FIRST OF MANY COUPLINGS THAT LETS HIM CARRY ON EXPLORING A MISCELLANY OF OTHER WORLDS.

BUT BRITAIN'S MOST IMPORTANT NOVEL OF THE 1930S WAS NONE OTHER THAN *BRAVE NEW WORLD* BY ALDOUS HUXLEY, WHO CONSIDERED THE "SCIENCE FICTION" LABEL TO BE BENEATH HIM!

OH, YES, I'M VERY FAMILIAR WITH THAT WORLD. I KNEW ALDOUS AND THE HUXLEYS WELL, PARTICULARLY HIS BROTHER, JULIAN, AND HIS GRANDFATHER, THOMAS HENRY, WHO WAS MY PROFESSOR.

IN 1998, THE MODERN LIBRARY VOTED *BRAVE NEW WORLD* (THE TITLE REFERS TO SHAKESPEARE'S *THE TEMPEST* AND THE WORDS REPEATED BY JOHN THE SAVAGE) AS THE FIFTH-BEST ENGLISH-LANGUAGE NOVEL OF ALL TIME, BETWEEN NABOKOV'S *LOLITA* AND WILLIAM FAULKNER'S *THE SOUND AND THE FURY*.

AND HOW DID MY NOVELS FARE?

ER...AHEM... WELL NOW, YOU SEE...

BLADE RUNNER, RIDLEY SCOTT, 1982. THEME: TO BE OR NOT TO BE...HUMAN.

THE TERMINATOR, JAMES CAMERON, 1984. THEMES: ARTIFICIAL INTELLIGENCE AND ROBOTICS.

BRAZIL, TERRY GILLIAM, 1985. THEME: DYSTOPIA.

GATTACA, ANDREW NICCOL, 1997. THEME: EUGENICS.

"BRAVE NEW WORLD DESCRIBES A WORLD STATE CREATED IN THE AFTERMATH OF DEVASTATION WROUGHT DURING THE NINE YEARS' WAR. ITS PEOPLE WORSHIP THE SUPREME BEING HENRY FORD.

"ALL HIS FOLLOWERS ARE UNDER THE INFLUENCE OF A PLEASURE-INDUCING DRUG CALLED SOMA.

"SEXUAL REPRODUCTION NO LONGER EXISTS. ALL CHILDREN ARE BORN IN LABORATORIES AND THEIR EMBRYOS ARE GENETICALLY MODIFIED IN ORDER TO DETERMINE WHICH CASTE THEY WILL GROW INTO...

"THERE ARE FIVE OF THESE CASTES: THE DOMINANT ALPHAS ARE GOOD-LOOKING AND INTELLIGENT; BETAS ARE THE HIGH-RANKING WORKFORCE; GAMMAS MAKE UP THE WORKING CLASSES; AND FINALLY, THE DELTAS AND EPSILONS ARE SHORT, UGLY, AND DESIGNED PURELY TO PERFORM MANUAL LABOR.

"IN THE NOVEL, WE ALSO MEET THE SAVAGES, INCLUDING JOHN, WHO IS NUMBERED AMONG THEM DESPITE HAVING BEEN BORN ACCIDENTALLY TO A MOTHER FROM THE WORLD STATE... HE IS GIVEN A CHANCE TO VISIT THIS "BRAVE NEW WORLD" THAT IS ACTUALLY A EUGENICS HELL!"

THIS NOVEL RANKS AMONG THE GREATEST DYSTOPIAS OF THE 20TH CENTURY, ALONGSIDE YEVGENY ZAMYATIN'S *WE* (1920), *KALLOCAIN* (1940) BY SWEDISH AUTHOR KARIN BOYE AND, OF COURSE, *1984* (1949) BY GEORGE ORWELL. BRAVE NEW WORLD'S INFLUENCE IS UNQUANTIFIABLE SINCE IT WAS SUCH A CRUCIAL AND VISIONARY WORK.

THE NOVEL CAME IN RESPONSE TO YOUR UTOPIAS, DEAR HERBERT. HE WROTE IT WHILE YOU WERE WORKING ON A THREE-VOLUME ESSAY ON BIOLOGY, *THE SCIENCE OF LIFE*, WITH YOUR OWN SON AND ALDOUS HUXLEY'S BROTHER, JULIAN. ALTHOUGH THE HUXLEY FAMILY DIDN'T ALWAYS AGREE ON EVERYTHING, JULIAN (A RENOWNED BIOLOGIST WHO LATER POPULARIZED THE TERM "TRANSHUMANISM"), ALDOUS, AND YOU, HERBERT, WERE ALL STAUNCH SUPPORTERS OF DARWINISM AND EUGENICS THAT WOULD BE OF BENEFIT TO THE HUMAN RACE. IN CONTRAST TO THE EXTREMIST EUGENIC IDEAS OF THE NAZIS, FOR EXAMPLE.

THE MATRIX, THE WACHOWSKIS, 1999. THEME: MANKIND VERSUS THE MACHINE.

CHILDREN OF MEN, ALFONSO CUARÓN, 2006. THEME: STERILE HUMANITY.

INTERSTELLAR, CHRISTOPHER NOLAN, 2014. THEMES: SPACE TRAVEL AND ARCOLOGY.

ARRIVAL, DENIS VILLENEUVE, 2016. THEMES: FIRST CONTACT WITH ALIENS, AND ALIEN LINGUISTICS.

ALL THIS BRINGS US NEATLY TO ANOTHER "HARBINGER" OF BRITISH LITERATURE: GEORGE ORWELL, WHO GAVE US TWO MASTERPIECES, *ANIMAL FARM*, PUBLISHED IN 1945, AND HIS CLASSIC *1984*.

OH!

NO NEED TO BE AFRAID. THE SCREWDRIVER HAS FROZEN THEM. BACK TO ORWELL, WHO WAS A SWORN ENEMY OF BRITISH IMPERIALISM...

HE HAD SERVED IN BURMA BEFORE BECOMING A WRITER. AFTER THE SPANISH CIVIL WAR, HE DECLARED HE WAS AGAINST TOTALITARIAN SYSTEMS AND FOR DEMOCRATIC SOCIALISM. SO HE WROTE SEVERAL ESSAYS, BUT THE TWO NOVELS HAVE ENDURED AS HIS MOST FAMOUS WORKS.

IN THE GUISE OF AN ANIMAL FABLE, *ANIMAL FARM* WAS A FURIOUS DENUNCIATION OF STALINISM AND, CONSEQUENTLY, ALL AUTHORITARIAN REGIMES. *1984* GREW OUT OF SIMILAR SENTIMENTS.

COME ON, HERBERT.

IT WAS WRITTEN IN 1948, WITH ITS TITLE REVERSING THE LAST TWO DIGITS. THE TOTALITARIAN WORLD OF *1984* IS SPLIT INTO THREE BLOCS: OCEANIA, EURASIA AND EASTASIA.

BIG BROTHER IS WATCHING YOU

BIG BROTHER IS WATCHING YOU

THE HERO, WINSTON SMITH, AN EMPLOYEE OF THE MINISTRY OF TRUTH, HAS HAD ENOUGH OF ALL THE LIES. HE STARTS TO KEEP A PERSONAL DIARY IN SECRET, KNOWING THAT HE MAY BE CAUGHT AT ANY MOMENT BY THE THOUGHT POLICE...

TWELVE SCI-FI MANGA TITLES TO DISCOVER:

ASTRO BOY, OSAMU TEZUKA, 1952. THEME: ROBOTICS.

SPACE PIRATE CAPTAIN HARLOCK, LEIJI MATSUMOTO, 1977. GENRE: SPACE OPERA.

COBRA, BUICHI TERASAWA, 1978. GENRE: SPACE OPERA.

NAUSICAÄ OF THE VALLEY OF THE WIND, HAYAO MIYAZAKI, 1982. THEME: ECOLOGY.

MEETING JULIA, WHOM HE INITIALLY SUSPECTS OF BEING A SPY FOR THE THOUGHT POLICE, SIGNALS HIS CONSCIOUS AWAKENING. *1984* ANALYZED THE MECHANISMS OF TOTALITARIAN SOCIETIES, DETAILING ALL OF THEIR INDOCTRINATION TECHNIQUES, AS WELL AS OTHER METHODS THAT CAN BE USED TO UNDERMINE THE SYSTEM.

INGSOC

IGNORANCE IS STRENGTH

FREEDOM IS SLAVERY

DOUBLETHINK

WAR IS PEACE

1984 ALSO GAVE BIRTH TO *NEWSPEAK*, WHICH WAS DESIGNED TO IMPOVERISH A LANGUAGE BY STRIPPING AWAY ITS SUBTLETIES. IN SO DOING, THE MORE LIMITED VOCABULARY PREVENTED ANY POSSIBLE CRITICISM OF THE SYSTEM AND ALLOWED SOCIETY TO BE DIVIDED UP INTO VARIOUS CLASSES.

IN REALITY, MINITRUE, THE MINISTRY OF TRUTH, IS A HIVE OF LIES... A GOOD EXAMPLE OF THE DOUBLETHINK TECHNIQUE.

HOWEVER, IT MUST BE SAID, HUXLEY AND ORWELL'S WORKS WERE WRITTEN OUTSIDE OF THE GENERALLY TURBULENT, AND STILL QUITE NEW, CONTEXT OF EMERGING BRITISH SCIENCE FICTION.

UNDOUBTEDLY, *1984* AND *BRAVE NEW WORLD* PRIMARILY GREW OUT OF SEVERE SOCIO-POLITICAL SITUATIONS, AS DID THE NOVELS *WE* BY YEVGENY ZAMYATIN AND *KALLOCAIN* BY KARIN BOYE, WHICH ALSO INSPIRED ORWELL.

IT WOULD SEEM THE UNITED KINGDOM DIDN'T REALLY HAVE THE SAME TYPE OF CREATIVE MOVEMENT THAT DEVELOPED IN THE UNITED STATES. MAYBE STAPLEDON, HUXLEY AND ORWELL WERE HAPPY ACCIDENTS? BUT I'M SURE I SAW A FEW BRITISH MAGAZINES FROM THE 1930S...

OF COURSE, THINGS WERE DEVELOPING IN PARALLEL TO AMERICAN SCIENCE FICTION, THOUGH NOT QUITE AS INTENSELY. THE UNITED STATES WERE STILL YOUNG, WHEREAS GREAT BRITAIN WAS AN OLD NATION WITH A VERY DIFFERENT MENTALITY AND POLITICS. CONSEQUENTLY, SCIENCE FICTION WAS NO LONGER JUST ONE SINGLE GENRE BUT SEVERAL AT ONCE. SO, YES, BRITAIN DID HAVE MAGAZINES OF ITS OWN...

AKIRA, KATSUHIRO ŌTOMO, 1982. GENRE: CYBERPUNK.

APPLESEED, MASAMUNE SHIROW, 1985. GENRE: CYBERPUNK.

PARASYTE, HITOSHI IWAAKI, 1988. THEME: POSSESSION OF THE HUMAN BODY BY ALIENS.

GUNNM, YUKITO KISHIRO, 1990. THEMES: TRANSHUMANISM, NANOTECHNOLOGY.

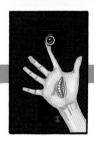

1934 SAW THE BIRTH OF *SCOOPS*, A MAGAZINE THAT PUBLISHED ONLY TWENTY POORLY DISTRIBUTED ISSUES FEATURING REPRINTED STORIES SUCH AS *THE POISON BELT* BY SIR ARTHUR CONAN DOYLE, AND WORKS BY JOHN RUSSELL FEARN.

THE JOURNALIST AND EDITOR WALTER GILLINGS SAID THAT *SCOOPS* WAS THE BIGGEST BLUNDER THAT BRITISH SCI-FI EVER MADE. INITIALLY PUBLISHING A FANZINE, *SCIENTIFICTION*, HE WENT ON TO EDIT BRITAIN'S FIRST REAL SCIENCE-FICTION MAGAZINE, *TALES OF WONDER*, FROM 1937 TO 1942. IT ALSO FEATURED JOHN RUSSELL FEARN, NOT TO MENTION ERIC FRANK RUSSELL, BEST KNOWN FOR HIS NOVEL *SINISTER BARRIER*, PRINTED IN THE AMERICAN MAGAZINE *UNKNOWN* IN 1939.

THE END OF THE 1930S WAS CRUCIAL FOR THE UNITED KINGDOM'S IMAGINATION. IN 1937, A CERTAIN JOHN RONALD REUEL TOLKIEN PUBLISHED HIS NOVEL *THE HOBBIT*, WHICH HAD A MOMENTOUS IMPACT ON SCIENCE FICTION'S LITERARY COUSIN, FANTASY.

ARTHUR C. CLARKE ALSO MADE HIS DEBUT IN *TALES OF WONDER*, WITH A SCIENTIFIC ARTICLE.

IN FACT, IT'S HIGH TIME WE DISCUSSED THAT FINE BRITISH AUTHOR, WHO WAS A FULLY FLEDGED PARTICIPANT OF THE GOLDEN AGE OF SCI-FI, ALONGSIDE ASIMOV, HEINLEIN, AND VAN VOGT. ASIMOV ONCE LIGHT-HEARTEDLY AGREED TO CALL CLARKE THE BEST SCIENCE-*FICTION* WRITER IN THE WORLD, WITH HIMSELF AS SECOND BEST, WHILE CLARKE WAS TO CALL ASIMOV THE BEST *SCIENCE* WRITER, WITH HIMSELF SECOND...

CLARKE'S FIRST SHORT STORY, *TRAVEL BY WIRE!*, WAS PRINTED IN THE FANZINE *AMATEUR SCIENCE STORIES* IN 1937...

BLAME!, TSUTOMU NIHEI, 1998. GENRE: CYBERPUNK.

20TH CENTURY BOYS, NAOKI URASAWA, 1999. GENRE: DYSTOPIA.

PLANETES, MAKOTO YUKIMURA, 1999. THEME: SPACE-JUNK COLLECTORS.

SPACE BROTHERS, CHŪYA KOYAMA, 2007. THEME: BECOMING AN ASTRONAUT!

THE YOUNG CLARKE, FASCINATED BY SCIENCE AND EXCITED AT THE CONCEPT OF THE FOURTH DIMENSION, HAD BEEN AN AVID READER OF *ASTOUNDING* MAGAZINE SINCE THE 1930S.

AND SO HE PUBLISHED HIS FIRST WRITINGS IN *AMATEUR SCIENCE STORIES.* MEANWHILE, WALTER GILLINGS, WHO GAVE CLARKE HIS FIRST TYPEWRITER, REGULARLY TOLD HIM THAT HE WAS SIMPLY TOO GOOD FOR HIS MAGAZINES. AS A RESULT, AND DUE T THE LIMITED BRITISH MARKET OF THE 1940S CLARKE EXPORTED HIMSELF TO AMERICA, WHE HIS FIRST PROFESSIONAL SHORT STORY, *LOOPHOLE,* APPEARED IN JOHN WOOD CAMPBELL'S *ASTOUNDING* IN APRIL 1946.

AN IMPRESSIVE RANGE OF MEDIA WELCOMED HIS STORIES, AND HE DID NOT CONFINE HIMSELF TO *ASTOUNDING.* OVER THE YEARS, HIS NAME APPEARED AMONG THE CONTENT OF SF'S BIGGEST MAGAZINES, FROM *STARTLING STORIES* TO *GALAXY,* VIA *IF* AND *PLAYBOY.*

HE PENNED A WIDE RANGE OF MEMORABLE STORIES, LIKE *THE STAR* (HUGO AWARD 1956), WHIC DESCRIBES A TEAM OF ASTRONAUTS RETURNING FRO A MISSION TO A PLANET THAT WAS ONCE HOME TO A EXTINCT ALIEN RACE. THE VOYAGE SHAKES THE FAITH OF EXPEDITION'S PRIEST. REGULARLY PONDERING MATTERS FAITH, CLARKE ALSO WROTE *THE NINE BILLION NAMES GOD* (1953), AN INGENIOUS SHORT STORY IN WHICH SC BUDDHIST MONKS ATTEMPT TO USE A COMPUTER TO DISCOVER ALL THE POSSIBLE NAMES OF GOD.

THREE MORE OF HIS STORIES, *BREAKING STRAIN* (1949), AND PARTICULAR *THE SENTINEL* (1951) AND *ENCOUNTER IN T DAWN* (1953), FORMED THE BASIS FOR A F CO-WRITTEN BY CLARKE AND STANLEY KUBR *2001: A SPACE ODYSSEY* (1968). ALTHOUG MET WITH A MIXED RECEPTION ON ITS RELEAS GRADUALLY BEGAN TO ACQUIRE CULT STAT TURNING ARTHUR C. CLARKE INTO THE MOST FAMOUS SCIENCE-FICTION WRITER IN THE WORLD.

THREE PODCASTS TO DISCOVER MORE ABOUT SCI-FI:

THE CLARKESWORLD PODCAST, HOSTED BY KATE BAKER. CONTENT: SF LITERATURE.

SFF YEAH!, HOSTED BY JENN NORTHINGTON. CONTENT: SF AND FANTASY.

ESCAPE POD. CONTENT: SF LITERATURE.

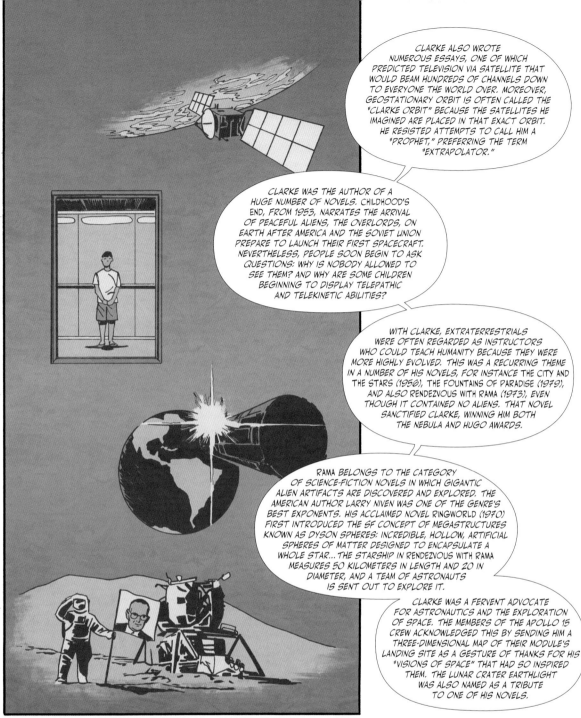

CLARKE ALSO WROTE NUMEROUS ESSAYS, ONE OF WHICH PREDICTED TELEVISION VIA SATELLITE THAT WOULD BEAM HUNDREDS OF CHANNELS DOWN TO EVERYONE THE WORLD OVER. MOREOVER, GEOSTATIONARY ORBIT IS OFTEN CALLED THE "CLARKE ORBIT" BECAUSE THE SATELLITES HE IMAGINED ARE PLACED IN THAT EXACT ORBIT. HE RESISTED ATTEMPTS TO CALL HIM A "PROPHET," PREFERRING THE TERM "EXTRAPOLATOR."

CLARKE WAS THE AUTHOR OF A HUGE NUMBER OF NOVELS. CHILDHOOD'S END, FROM 1953, NARRATES THE ARRIVAL OF PEACEFUL ALIENS, THE OVERLORDS, ON EARTH AFTER AMERICA AND THE SOVIET UNION PREPARE TO LAUNCH THEIR FIRST SPACECRAFT. NEVERTHELESS, PEOPLE SOON BEGIN TO ASK QUESTIONS: WHY IS NOBODY ALLOWED TO SEE THEM? AND WHY ARE SOME CHILDREN BEGINNING TO DISPLAY TELEPATHIC AND TELEKINETIC ABILITIES?

WITH CLARKE, EXTRATERRESTRIALS WERE OFTEN REGARDED AS INSTRUCTORS WHO COULD TEACH HUMANITY BECAUSE THEY WERE MORE HIGHLY EVOLVED. THIS WAS A RECURRING THEME IN A NUMBER OF HIS NOVELS, FOR INSTANCE THE CITY AND THE STARS (1956), THE FOUNTAINS OF PARADISE (1979), AND ALSO RENDEZVOUS WITH RAMA (1973), EVEN THOUGH IT CONTAINED NO ALIENS. THAT NOVEL SANCTIFIED CLARKE, WINNING HIM BOTH THE NEBULA AND HUGO AWARDS.

RAMA BELONGS TO THE CATEGORY OF SCIENCE-FICTION NOVELS IN WHICH GIGANTIC ALIEN ARTIFACTS ARE DISCOVERED AND EXPLORED. THE AMERICAN AUTHOR LARRY NIVEN WAS ONE OF THE GENRE'S BEST EXPONENTS. HIS ACCLAIMED NOVEL RINGWORLD (1970) FIRST INTRODUCED THE SF CONCEPT OF MEGASTRUCTURES KNOWN AS DYSON SPHERES: INCREDIBLE, HOLLOW, ARTIFICIAL SPHERES OF MATTER DESIGNED TO ENCAPSULATE A WHOLE STAR... THE STARSHIP IN RENDEZVOUS WITH RAMA MEASURES 50 KILOMETERS IN LENGTH AND 20 IN DIAMETER, AND A TEAM OF ASTRONAUTS IS SENT OUT TO EXPLORE IT.

CLARKE WAS A FERVENT ADVOCATE FOR ASTRONAUTICS AND THE EXPLORATION OF SPACE. THE MEMBERS OF THE APOLLO 15 CREW ACKNOWLEDGED THIS BY SENDING HIM A THREE-DIMENSIONAL MAP OF THEIR MODULE'S LANDING SITE AS A GESTURE OF THANKS FOR HIS "VISIONS OF SPACE" THAT HAD SO INSPIRED THEM. THE LUNAR CRATER EARTHLIGHT WAS ALSO NAMED AS A TRIBUTE TO ONE OF HIS NOVELS.

FOUR MODERN MAGAZINES TO HELP DISCOVER SCIENCE FICTION:

THE MAGAZINE OF FANTASY & SCIENCE FICTION. CONTENT: SHORT FICTION AND REVIEWS.

ANALOG SCIENCE FICTION AND FACT. CONTENT: SHORT FICTION, NEWS, REVIEWS.

ASIMOV'S SCIENCE FICTION. CONTENT: SHORT FICTION, NEWS, REVIEWS.

SPACE AND TIME MAGAZINE. CONTENT: SPECULATIVE FICTION AND POETRY.

CLARKE WAS A TRUE ICON OF CLASSIC BRITISH SCIENCE FICTION. HIS AURA IS STILL PERFECTLY ALIVE AND WELL, AND FIXED IN PEOPLE'S MINDS TODAY. BUT HE AND SEVERAL OTHERS WERE JUST SETTING THE STAGE FOR AN IMPENDING REVOLUTION IN BRITISH SCIENCE FICTION.

I AM MOST INTRIGUED, MR. MOORCOCK!

OH, BRITAIN HAD OTHER ILLUSTRIOUS WRITERS IN THE GENRE, OF COURSE. I'M THINKING OF C.S. LEWIS, FATHER OF NARNIA AND FRIEND OF TOLKIEN, WHO PUBLISHED THE SCI-FI NOVEL *OUT OF THE SILENT PLANET* (1938), AND ITS SEQUELS. THEN JOHN WYNDHAM AND HIS UNFORGETTABLE *THE DAY OF THE TRIFFIDS* IN 1951, WHICH TOOK AN ORIGINAL APPROACH TO ALIEN INVASION.

BUT THEN, COMPLETELY OUT OF THE BLUE, AS IT WERE, *NEW WORLDS* MAGAZINE APPEARED AND WENT ON TO PLAY A CENTRAL ROLE IN THE DEVELOPMENT OF CONTEMPORARY SCIENCE FICTION IN BRITAIN, EVEN BECOMING ITS CORNERSTONE.

BUT HOW? WHAT WAS SO SPECIAL ABOUT THIS MAGAZINE? JUDGING BY THE COVER, IT DOESN'T STRIKE ME AS PARTICULARLY REVOLUTIONARY...

YOU'RE QUITE RIGHT, MY DEAR HERBERT. BUT TO EXPLAIN WHAT MADE IT SO SPECIAL, WE SHOULD FIRST EXAMINE ITS BIRTH IN THE CORRECT CONTEXT.

NEW WORLDS, WAS EDITED BY A FAN, JOHN CARNELL, AND ALREADY EXISTED BEFORE WORLD WAR TWO. IT BEGAN AS A FANZINE NAMED *NOVAE TERRAE*, WHICH WAS RENAMED *NEW WORLDS* IN 1939. BUT THE MAGAZINE'S REAL BIRTHDAY IS CONSIDERED TO BE AFTER THE WAR, IN 1946, WHEN IT FINALLY TURNED PROFESSIONAL!

THIRTY-NINE REPRESENTATIVE SCIENCE-FICTION GRAPHIC NOVELS:

Y: THE LAST MAN, BRIAN K. VAUGHAN AND PIA GUERRA, 2002. GENRE: ANDROCIDE, MATRIARCHY.

TINTIN: DESTINATION MOON, HERGÉ, 1953. GENRE: MOON LANDING, ESPIONAGE.

TOP 10, ALAN MOORE, GENE HA AND ZANDER CANNON, 1999–2001. GENRE: ALIEN PLANET, POLICE PROCEDURAL.

BARBARELLA, JEAN-CLAUDE FOREST, 1962–1964. GENRE: SPACE OPERA, EROTICISM.

THE MAGAZINE FEATURED WRITERS LIKE THE PROLIFIC WILLIAM F. TEMPLE, FOR EXAMPLE. HE PENNED THE SCIENCE-FICTION CLASSIC *FOUR SIDED TRIANGLE*, IN WHICH A SCIENTIST MANAGES TO CREATE A WOMAN, THEN FALLS HEAD OVER HEELS IN LOVE WITH HER...

INTERESTING MAN, TEMPLE...

YES, BUT IN THE END, THE REST OF HIS WORK WAS MOSTLY OVERLOOKED. HOWEVER, HISTORY DOES RECALL THAT, BEFORE WORLD WAR TWO, HE SHARED AN APARTMENT WITH ARTHUR C. CLARKE, AND THEY WERE MEMBERS OF THE BRITISH INTERPLANETARY SOCIETY, AN ASSOCIATION THAT STILL EXISTS TO PROMOTE ASTRONAUTICS AND THE CONQUEST OF SPACE!

SO, DID BRITAIN END UP CHASING THE AMERICANS INTO THE STARS?

I'M SORRY TO SAY WE DIDN'T, HERBERT. BUT FANDOM OVER HERE WAS VERY ACTIVE, LIKE IN THE UNITED STATES. ITS PARTICIPANTS INCLUDED WILLIAM TEMPLE, CARNELL, AND JOHN CHRISTOPHER, WHO WAS ACCLAIMED FOR HIS DISASTER NOVELS, ESPECIALLY THE SERIES TITLED...

...*THE TRIPODS*, A TRILOGY OF YOUNG-ADULT NOVELS INSPIRED, DEAR HERBERT, BY YOUR NOVEL *THE WAR OF THE WORLDS*. THE ACTION REVOLVES AROUND A YOUNG MAN TRYING TO ESCAPE THE "CAPPING" THAT WOULD FORCE HIM TO BOW FOREVER TO THE RULE OF THE TRIPODS.

JOHN CHRISTOPHER PUBLISHED A FANZINE, TOO, BUT ONLY FOR THREE ISSUES BETWEEN 1939 AND 1941. *NEW WORLDS* WAS ALSO PUBLISHED ERRATICALLY, AT FIRST, BUT BECAME MORE REGULAR STARTING FROM 1949, WHEN IT WAS TAKEN OVER BY ANOTHER PUBLISHER.

IN 1950, *NEW WORLDS* DECIDED TO LAUNCH A COMPANION MAGAZINE, *SCIENCE FANTASY*, INITIALLY EDITED BY WALTER GILLINGS. ITS PAGES WITNESSED THE DEBUTS OF GREAT AUTHORS WHO WOULD GO ON TO REVOLUTIONIZE THE GENRE. IT HOSTED THE EMERGENCE OF BRIAN ALDISS, WITH HIS SHORT STORY *CRIMINAL RECORD* IN 1954, AND JOHN BRUNNER'S *THE TALISMAN* IN 1955, THOUGH HE HAD PUBLISHED A NOVELETTE IN AMERICA TWO YEARS PREVIOUSLY, IN *ASTOUNDING*.

LONE SLOANE, PHILIPPE DRUILLET, 1966. GENRE: SPACE OPERA.

PAPER GIRLS, BRIAN K. VAUGHAN AND CLIFF CHIANG, 2015-2019. GENRE: TIME TRAVEL.

VALERIAN AND LAURELINE, PIERRE CHRISTIN AND J.-C. MÉZIÈRES, 1967. GENRE: SPACE OPERA.

DEAD ENDERS, ED BRUBAKER AND WARREN PLEECE, 2000-2001. GENRE: POST-APOCALYPTIC, TIME TRAVEL.

SCIENCE FANTASY AND *NEW WORLDS* WENT THROUGH A MINOR GOLDEN AGE FROM THE 1950S UP UNTIL THE BEGINNING OF THE 1960S. *NEW WORLDS* FOLLOWED MORE IN THE FOOTSTEPS OF ITS AMERICAN PREDECESSORS, WHEREAS *SCIENCE FANTASY* WAS MORE INNOVATIVE. THE PAGES OF *SCIENCE FANTASY* WERE JAM-PACKED WITH WORKS BY SOME EXTREMELY TALENTED WRITERS...

...INCLUDING QUITE A FEW FAMOUS AMERICAN AUTHORS WHO WERE JUST EMERGING THEN, SUCH AS SHECKLEY AND SILVERBERG. BUT OF COURSE THERE WERE MAJOR DIFFERENCES BETWEEN AMERICAN AND BRITISH SCIENCE FICTION.

J. T. MCINTOSH

JOHN CHRISTOPHER

JOHN WYNDHAM

E. C. TUBB

ERIC FRANK RUSSELL

JUDITH MERRIL

A. BERTRAM CHANDLER

BRIAN ALDISS

WILSON TUCKER

JOHN BRUNNER

JAMES WHITE

HARLAN ELLISON

MARION ZIMMER BRADLEY

ROBERT SHECKLEY

J. G. BALLARD

MICHAEL MOORCOCK

ROBERT SILVERBERG

HARRY HARRISON

THEODORE STURGEON

DURING THE 1950S, AMERICA WAS BECOMING INCREASINGLY OBSESSED WITH THE IDEA OF BEING INVADED, WHETHER BY EXTRA-TERRESTRIALS OR COMMUNISTS. THE BRITISH, MEANWHILE, WERE NOT SO WELL-VERSED IN COLD-WAR PARANOIA AND WERE MORE ATTRACTED TO "FIRST CONTACT" SCENARIOS, AS ARTHUR C. CLARKE DEMONSTRATED ON MANY OCCASIONS.

HOW FASCINATING... TELL ME MORE. WERE THERE OTHER DIFFERENCES BETWEEN BRITISH AND AMERICAN SCI-FI?

OH YES, THERE WERE PLENTY OF THEM. BUT ON THE WHOLE, THE AMERICANS WERE MORE ACTION-ORIENTED THAN THE BRITISH, WHOSE WRITING STYLE WAS OFTEN MORE RELAXED AND FOCUSED ON SEARCHING FOR NEW IDEAS.

RONIN, FRANK MILLER, 1983-1984. GENRE: DYSTOPIA.

THE METABARONS, JODOROWSKY AND GIMÉNEZ, 1992-2003. GENRE: SPACE OPERA.

MIRACLEMAN, ALAN MOORE, GARRY LEACH AND ALAN DAVIS, 1982-1985. GENRE: SUPERHERO.

ASTRO CITY, KURT BUSIEK AND BRENT ANDERSON, 1995-2018. GENRE: SUPERHERO.

THE FACT REMAINS THAT THE 1950S BROUGHT US SEVERAL CLASSICS OF BRITISH SCIENCE FICTION, LIKE *THE SOUND OF HIS HORN* BY SARBAN. IT'S AN ALTERNATE-HISTORY NOVEL IN WHICH THE NAZI OVERLORDS HUNT PEOPLE DOWN AS IF IT WERE SOME KIND OF BLOOD SPORT.

THE DAY OF THE TRIFFIDS, JOHN WYNDAM 1951.

THE SOUND OF HIS HORN, SARBAN 1952.

CHILDHOOD'S END, ARTHUR C. CLARKE 1953.

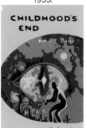

NON-STOP, BRIAN ALDISS, 1958.

SOME OF THE BEST BRITISH WRITERS, SUCH AS JAMES G. BALLARD AND BRIAN ALDISS, STILL FOUND THINGS A LITTLE CRAMPED ON THE AS YET UNDERDEVELOPED BRITISH SCI-FI MARKET.

LET ME GUESS... THEY SET OUT TO STORM THE AMERICAN MARKET?

THEY DID. EVEN THOUGH THEY HAD THREE SERIOUS MAGAZINES (*NEW WORLDS* AND *SCIENCE FANTASY*, PLUS THE EXCELLENT *SCIENCE FICTION ADVENTURES*, ALSO A NOVA PUBLICATION), THEY HOPED TO GET THEMSELVES NOTICED BY HAVING THEIR WORK PUBLISHED IN THE UNITED STATES, WHOSE BIGGEST MAGAZINES WERE DISTRIBUTED IN BRITAIN ANYWAY.

SADLY, THIS LITTLE GOLDEN AGE WAS NOT TO LAST. VARIOUS ECONOMIC ISSUES INTERFERED AND STOPPED IT IN ITS TRACKS. THE MAGAZINES' LARGEST EXPORT MARKETS ALL COLLAPSED, PARTICULARLY AUSTRALIA, AND A LOT OF OTHER FACTORS WERE PILING UP...

OH! WHERE THE DEVIL ARE WE?

IN WHAT SENSE?

WE'RE ON EARTH'S FIRST ARTIFICIAL SATELLITE, SPUTNIK 1, PLACED IN ORBIT BY AN R-7 ROCKET ON OCTOBER 4, 1957. THIS SPHERE, JUST 23 INCHES IN DIAMETER, SENT OUT A "BEEP-BEEP" THAT CHANGED THE FACE OF THE WORLD...AND PERHAPS THE FACE OF SCIENCE FICTION, TOO.

THE UNITED STATES WERE GENUINELY TRAUMATIZED BY THIS SOVIET VICTORY BECAUSE THE EASTERN BLOC HAD SUDDENLY BECOME CAPABLE OF ANYTHING, ESPECIALLY THE WORST! BUT TO SCIENCE-FICTION WRITERS, AND PARTICULARLY THEIR READERS, THIS SATELLITE LAUNCH SIGNALED HUMANITY'S ENTRY INTO THE SPACE AGE. THE TIME FOR FANTASIZING WAS OVER--SCIENCE FICTION WAS BECOMING A REALITY. IN AMERICA, THE MAGAZINE MARKET WAS STARTING TO COLLAPSE, AND BRITAIN WAS ALSO FACING A SIMILAR PHENOMENON.

THE MANHATTAN PROJECTS, JONATHAN HICKMAN AND NICK PITARRA, 2012-2015. GENRE: ALTERNATE HISTORY.

THE INCAL, JODOROWSKY AND MOEBIUS, 1980. GENRE: GALACTIC SAGA.

DO ANDROIDS DREAM OF ELECTRIC SHEEP?, PHILIP K. DICK AND TONY PARKER, 2009. GENRE: DYSTOPIA.

SNOWPIERCER, LOB AND ROCHETTE, 1982. GENRE: POST-APOCALYPTIC.

THEREFORE, A CHANGE OF FOCUS WAS REQUIRED, AND IT TOOK HOLD MOST INTENSELY IN BRITAIN. I HAVE ALWAYS BELIEVED THAT SCIENCE FICTION IS NOT JUST ONE GENRE, BUT SEVERAL, AND I HAVE ALWAYS CONSIDERED MYSELF TO BE MORE THAN JUST A SCIENCE-FICTION WRITER.

BUT SINCE YOU'RE HERE WITH ME, THEN YOU MUST HAVE PLAYED SOME VITAL ROLE...

PATIENCE!

"JOHN CARNELL WON HIMSELF A HUGO AWARD IN 1957 FOR NEW WORLDS AT THE 15TH WORLD SCIENCE FICTION CONVENTION, HELD FOR THE FIRST TIME IN LONDON, WITH GUEST OF HONOR JOHN W. CAMPBELL. BUT IN SPITE OF THE MAGAZINE'S ACCLAIM, ITS PUBLISHER, NOVA, RAN INTO FINANCIAL DIFFICULTIES AND CLOSED IT DOWN, TOGETHER WITH SCIENCE FANTASY, IN 1963.

"THEN CARNELL DECIDED TO MOVE INTO PUBLISHING SHORT-STORY ANTHOLOGIES AND SIGNED A CONTRACT WITH DENNIS DOBSON TO PRODUCE A SERIES TITLED NEW WRITINGS IN SF.

"I WAS BARELY EVEN TWENTY WHEN THE FATE OF NEW WORLDS WAS ENTRUSTED TO ME. IN THE MEANTIME, KYRIL BONFIGLIOLI, WHO WAS BEST KNOWN FOR HIS THRILLER NOVELS, TOOK OVER AT SCIENCE FANTASY. THREE YEARS EARLIER, I HAD PUBLISHED THE FIRST ADVENTURES OF MY CULT CHARACTER...

"...ELRIC OF MELNIBONÉ. ORIGINALLY, I ONLY PLANNED TO WRITE ONE NOVELLA, BUT READERS WANTED MORE. I WAS VERY YOUNG AND READING A LOT OF GOTHIC AND ROMANTIC LITERATURE. ELRIC WAS MY REACTION TO ALL THE SWORD-AND-SORCERY CLICHÉS THAT CAME IN THE WAKE OF HOWARD'S CONAN. MY CHARACTER WAS THE FIRST INCARNATION OF THE ETERNAL CHAMPION, WHOM I EXPANDED INTO AN ENTIRE MULTIVERSE. OTHER CHAMPIONS INCLUDED CORUM, EREKOSË, HAWKMOON AND, OF COURSE...

"...JERRY CORNELIUS! THIS CHARACTER WAS A LONDONER; AN URBAN ADVENTURER AND A CONTEMPORARY HEDONIST. HIS INITIALS WERE NO ACCIDENT, PERHAPS CLASSING HIM AS A MODERN MESSIANIC FIGURE; A MAN FIGHTING AGAINST SYSTEMS INTENDED TO CONTROL AND DEHUMANIZE US. CORNELIUS INJECTED A TOUCH OF MADNESS AND HUMOR...AND I ALSO ENCOURAGED OTHER WRITERS AND ARTISTS TO KEEP DEVELOPING THE CHARACTER FOR THEMSELVES. MOEBIUS, WHO REVOLUTIONIZED FRENCH GRAPHIC NOVELS WITH DRUILLET IN THE MID-1970S, FEATURED CORNELIUS IN HIS THE AIRTIGHT GARAGE."

DESCENDER, JEFF LEMIRE AND DUSTIN NGUYEN, 2015–2018. GENRE: SPACE OPERA, ANDROIDS.

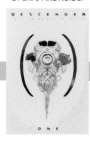

BITCH PLANET, KELLY SUE DECONNICK AND VALENTINE DE LANDRO, 2014–2017. GENRE: DYSTOPIA.

THE FOREVER WAR, HALDEMAN AND MARVANO, 1988. THEMES: WAR AGAINST ALIENS, AND THE HORRORS OF WAR.

THE UMBRELLA ACADEMY, GERARD WAY AND GABRIEL BÁ, 2007-PRESENT. GENRE: SUPER POWERS, TIME TRAVEL.

"BUT BEFORE THAT, THANKS TO BRIAN ALDISS AND J. G. BALLARD, I SET ABOUT TRANSFORMING NEW WORLDS INTO A TRULY AVANT-GARDE MAGAZINE! AND ONCE BALLARD HAD PUBLISHED HIS SHORT STORY THE TERMINAL BEACH, HE BECAME A REAL LANDMARK OF CHANGES THAT WERE STARTING TO TAKE PLACE INSIDE BRITISH SCIENCE FICTION."

STRANGE TITLE...A CLOCKWORK ORANGE!

IT IS, RATHER! THIS EXTREMELY TRANSGRESSIVE DYSTOPIAN NOVEL BY ANTHONY BURGESS WAS PUBLISHED IN 1962.

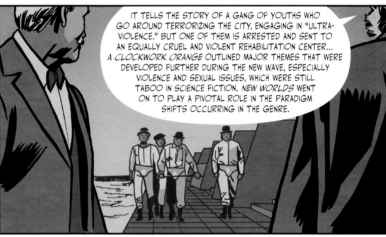

IT TELLS THE STORY OF A GANG OF YOUTHS WHO GO AROUND TERRORIZING THE CITY, ENGAGING IN "ULTRA-VIOLENCE." BUT ONE OF THEM IS ARRESTED AND SENT TO AN EQUALLY CRUEL AND VIOLENT REHABILITATION CENTER... A CLOCKWORK ORANGE OUTLINED MAJOR THEMES THAT WERE DEVELOPED FURTHER DURING THE NEW WAVE, ESPECIALLY VIOLENCE AND SEXUAL ISSUES, WHICH WERE STILL TABOO IN SCIENCE FICTION. NEW WORLDS WENT ON TO PLAY A PIVOTAL ROLE IN THE PARADIGM SHIFTS OCCURRING IN THE GENRE.

THE NEW WAVE FOLLOWED A SOCIAL TREND, OR, MORE ACCURATELY, A MOVEMENT FOR SOCIAL REVOLUTION AND CHANGE. THIS NEW WAVE OF WRITERS ATTEMPTED TO ADOPT A COMPLETELY NEW ATTITUDE TO SCIENCE-FICTION WRITING IN TERMS OF BOTH CONTENT AND STYLE, MOVING AWAY FROM THE AMERICAN MODEL, WHICH SEEMED TO BE STUCK IN A RUT. MAYBE IT WAS BECAUSE THE TECHNOLOGY WAS STARTING TO DEVELOP FASTER THAN THE STORIES WERE ABLE TO DREAM IT UP?

ALTHOUGH THE FIRST TEXTS PUBLISHED IN NEW WORLDS WERE MOSTLY IN CLASSIC STYLE, E.G. ARTHUR C. CLARKE, BOB SHAW, AND MACK REYNOLDS, MY FIRST, FAIRLY RADICAL EDITORIALS WERE ALREADY CALLING TO REFORM THE WHOLE APPROACH TO THE GENRE.

TOKYO GHOST, RICK REMENDER AND SEAN MURPHY, 2015-2016. GENRE: DYSTOPIA.

EAST OF WEST, JONATHAN HICKMAN AND NICK DRAGOTTA, 2013-2019. GENRE: DYSTOPIAN, WESTERN.

BLACK HAMMER, JEFF LEMIRE AND DEAN ORMSTON, 2016-PRESENT. GENRE: SUPERHERO.

SEX CRIMINALS, MATT FRACTION AND CHIP ZDARSKY, 2013-2020. GENRE: FREEZING TIME.

THEN, IN 1965, IN ONE DELIBERATELY CONTROVERSIAL EDITORIAL, I DROPPED A BOMBSHELL! HERE'S WHAT I WROTE:

"WE NEED MORE WRITERS WHO REFLECT THE PRAGMATIC MOOD OF TODAY, WHO USE IMAGES APT FOR TODAY, WHO EMPLOY SYMBOLS GATHERED FROM THE WORLD OF TODAY, WHO USE SOPHISTICATED WRITING TECHNIQUES. LIKE ALL GOOD WRITING, GOOD SF MUST RELATE PRIMARILY TO THE TIME IN WHICH IT IS WRITTEN; A WRITER MUST WRITE PRIMARILY FOR HIS OWN GENERATION..."

WELL, THAT SOUNDS LIKE AN INTELLIGENT, JUSTIFIED APPROACH.

AND THEN I ADDED: "HE MUST NOT SEEK TO EMULATE HIS PREDECESSORS IN THEIR OWN TERRITORY, NEITHER MUST HE WRITE FOR A POSTERITY WHICH WILL ANYWAY NOT REMEMBER HIM UNLESS HE IS TRUE TO HIMSELF AND HIS OWN AGE. HE CAN LEARN FROM HIS PREDECESSORS, BUT HE SHOULD NOT IMITATE THEM..."

IN THAT SENSE, OUR NEW WAVE WAS INSPIRED BY TWO FRENCH MOVEMENTS, NAMELY THE *NOUVELLE VAGUE* IN CINEMA, REPRESENTED BY GODARD AND TRUFFAUT, BUT ALSO THE *NOUVEAU ROMAN* FOR ALDISS AND BALLARD.

IN 1962, BALLARD WROTE AN ESSAY INVITING SCIENCE FICTION TO PROBE DEEPER INTO INNER SPACE INSTEAD OF JUST INTER-GALACTIC SPACE. ALDISS'S NOVEL *REPORT ON PROBABILITY A* (1967) CLEARLY SHOWED A FONDNESS FOR THE *NOUVEAU ROMAN*.

EX MACHINA, BRIAN K. VAUGHAN AND TONY HARRIS, 2004-2010. GENRE: SUPERHERO.

THE BOSTON METAPHYSICAL SOCIETY, MADELEINE HOLLY-ROSING AND EMILY HU. 2014-PRESENT. GENRE: STEAMPUNK.

JUPITER'S LEGACY, MARK MILLAR AND FRANK QUITELY, 2013. GENRE: SUPERHERO.

OLD MAN LOGAN, MARK MILLAR AND STEVE MCNIVEN, 2008-2009. GENRE: SUPERHERO.

"I TREATED THE AUTHORS AT NEW WORLDS WITH CONVICTION AND DETERMINATION, AND SOON EARNED A REPUTATION FOR BEING HELPFUL, ADVISING AND GUIDING THEM TO HONE THEIR CRAFT, AND THEIR MANUSCRIPTS, OF COURSE.

"ONE OF THE WRITERS THAT I DISCOVERED AND ENCOURAGED THROUGH THE MAGAZINE WAS THE ILLUSTRIOUS SIR TERRY PRATCHETT, WHO STARTED BEING PUBLISHED IN CARNELL'S SCIENCE FANTASY IN 1963. THEN I PRINTED HIS SHORT STORY NIGHT DWELLER IN 1965. SUBSEQUENTLY, HIS CAREER TOOK OFF WITH THE DISCWORLD SERIES OF NOVELS, WHICH SOLD MORE THAN 60 MILLION BOOKS AND MADE HIM THE MOST-READ BRITISH AUTHOR OF THE 1990S.

"OTHER WRITERS WITH TALENT, BUT LESS FLAMBOYANT CAREERS, MADE THEIR DEBUTS IN THE MAGAZINE, SUCH AS BARRINGTON J. BAYLEY, HILARY BAILEY, DAVID I. MASSON, AND THE SATIRIST JOHN T. SLADEK, WHO IS OFTEN REMEMBERED FOR TWO OF HIS ORIGINAL, IRONIC, AND PESSIMISTIC NOVELS, MECHASM (1968) AND TIK-TOK (1983), WHICH WON A BRITISH SCIENCE FICTION ASSOCIATION AWARD."

ALTHOUGH THEY DEBUTED IN CARNELL'S DAY, BRIAN ALDISS AND J. G. BALLARD ALWAYS REMAINED MY CLOSEST AND BEST COLLABORATORS. THE PAGES OF NEW WORLDS PRESENTED THEM WITH A FREEDOM THEY HAD NEVER BEEN GIVEN ELSEWHERE.

I GAVE THEM ALL THE SPACE THEY NEEDED TO EXPRESS THEMSELVES AND FLOURISH. SOME OF THEIR MOST STRIKING WORK WAS FIRST PUBLISHED IN NEW WORLDS: FOR EXAMPLE, BALLARD'S SHORT-STORY SERIES VERMILION SANDS, WHICH HE BEGAN WHILE CARNELL WAS EDITOR, AS WELL AS THE ATROCITY EXHIBITION (1966) AND NOTES TOWARDS A MENTAL BREAKDOWN (1967).

BRIAN ALDISS, MEANWHILE, TURNED OUT TO BE BETTER AT ADAPTING TO THE AMERICAN MARKET (AS PROVEN BY THE HUGO AWARD FOR BEST SHORT FICTION HE WON FOR HOTHOUSE IN 1962). HE WROTE SOME OF HIS MOST EXPERIMENTAL WORK FOR NEW WORLDS, SUCH AS BAREFOOT IN THE HEAD IN 1969, IN WHICH SEX, VIOLENCE AND DRUGS INTERMINGLED IN THE LIFE OF AN LSD DEALER. THIS STORY SOMEHOW ECHOED A CERTAIN PHILIP K. DICK, WHO WAS IN HIS PRIME OVER IN THE UNITED STATES.

WE3, GRANT MORRISON AND FRANK QUITELY, 2004. GENRE: DYSTOPIA, CYBORGS.

RASL, JEFF SMITH, 2013. GENRE: PARALLEL UNIVERSES.

MOONCOP, TOM GAULD, 2016. GENRE: LUNAR COLONY.

THE BEAUTIFUL DEATH, MATHIEU BABLET, 2017. GENRE: POST-APOCALYPTIC DYSTOPIA.

FROM 1962 TO 1966, BALLARD PUBLISHED FOUR "DISASTER" NOVELS, *THE WIND FROM NOWHERE* (WHICH HE DISLIKED), *THE DROWNED WORLD*, *THE BURNING WORLD*, AND *THE CRYSTAL WORLD*. FOUR NOVELS ABOUT FOUR NATURAL CATASTROPHES. THEN, FROM 1973 TO 1975, HE WROTE AND PUBLISHED THREE MASTERPIECES: *CRASH*, *CONCRETE ISLAND*, AND *HIGH-RISE*. HE HAD BEGUN TO DEVELOP A FORM OF "SPECULATIVE FICTION"--A TERM COINED BY ROBERT HEINLEIN IN A 1947 ARTICLE FOR *THE SATURDAY EVENING POST* TO DESCRIBE SCIENCE FICTION IN WHICH THE SCIENCE NO LONGER DROVE THE PLOT ALONG. HE PREFERRED TO BUILD A PARTICULAR ATMOSPHERE THAT WAS OFTEN URBAN AND SOMETIMES CLOSER TO FANTASY.

THE USUAL GRANDIOSE BACKDROPS OF SCIENCE FICTION WERE OFTEN SIMPLY AN EXCUSE TO DEFLECT THEM TOWARD THE AUTHOR'S BELOVED INNER SPACES. HIS STYLE WAS EXTREMELY VISUAL AND DESCRIPTIVE, AND OWED A LOT TO THE SURREALIST PAINTERS, AS BALLARD WAS VERY KEEN ON PAINTING. HIS CHARACTERS WOULD OFTEN RETREAT INTO FANTASTIC DREAM WORLDS.

BALLARD ONCE SAID:

"WHAT UNIQUELY CHARACTERIZES THIS FUSION OF THE OUTER REALITY AND THE PSYCHE IS ITS REDEMPTIVE AND THERAPEUTIC POWER. TO MOVE THROUGH THESE LANDSCAPES IS A JOURNEY OF RETURN TO ONE'S INNERMOST BEING."

A MOST INTERESTING MAN, BALLARD. I SUPPOSE THAT HE ALSO JOINED THE PANTHEON OF SCIENCE FICTION?

YES, AND MUCH MORE... BALLARD WAS THE MOST FAMOUS NEW-WAVE AUTHOR WORKING OUTSIDE THE CONFINES OF THE GENRE, TO SUCH AN EXTENT THAT HE WAS ASSIMILATED INTO GENERAL LITERATURE. HIS WORKS RADIATED OUT WELL BEYOND ALL NOTIONS OF GENRE, AND HIS INFLUENCE WAS CLEARLY FELT IN ASPECTS OF THE FRENCH PHILOSOPHER JEAN BAUDRILLARD'S THEORIES OF CONTEMPORARY SOCIETY.

SOUTHERN CROSS, BECKY CLOONAN AND ANDY BELANGER, 2015-2018. GENRE: SPACE, MYSTERY.

HEAVY LIQUID, PAUL POPE, 1999-2000. GENRE: ALIENS, CRIME, DRUGS.

PARADISO, RAM V AND DEARBHLA KELLY, 2017-2018. GENRE: DYSTOPIA.

FRIENDO, ALEX PAKNADEL AND MARTIN SIMMONDS, 2018. GENRE: ARTIFICIAL INTELLIGENCE.

THE SAME GOES FOR BRIAN ALDISS, I SUPPOSE?

NOT EXACTLY, ALTHOUGH HE IS STILL ONE OF THE ESSENTIAL NAMES OF THE GOLDEN AGE OF BRITISH SCIENCE FICTION. HIS COMPLEX AND EXTREMELY DIVERSE WORKS WERE INTERSPERSED WITH GREAT NOVELS...

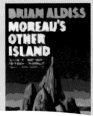

GREYBEARD (1964) DEPICTED A HUMANITY THAT HAD GROWN INFERTILE AND WHOSE SURVIVORS WERE ALREADY AGED. HE BRILLIANTLY REVISITED CLASSICS, TOO: MARY SHELLEY WITH *FRANKENSTEIN UNBOUND* IN 1973, AND YOU YOURSELF, DEAR HERBERT, WITH *MOREAU'S OTHER ISLAND* IN 1980.

"THE HELLICONIA TRILOGY, WHICH ALDISS REGARDED AS HIS GREATEST WORK, IS AN ENORMOUS PANORAMA OF CIVILIZATION ON THE PLANET HELLICONIA, WHERE THE SEASONS LAST AN INCREDIBLY LONG TIME--SEVERAL CENTURIES. THESE THREE EPIC NOVELS, WHICH ARE SOMETIMES COMPARED TO FRANK HERBERT'S DUNE, UNFOLD ACROSS AN ARC SPANNING MORE THAN A MILLENNIUM! THE LATE DIRECTOR STANLEY KUBRICK ORIGINALLY PLANNED TO ADAPT ALDISS'S STORY SUPERTOYS LAST ALL SUMMER LONG, BUT IT WAS COMPLETED BY STEVEN SPIELBERG AS A.I. ARTIFICIAL INTELLIGENCE."

LAZARUS, GREG RUCKA AND MICHAEL LARK, 2013-PRESENT. GENRE: DYSTOPIA.

THE BIG GUY AND RUSTY THE BOY ROBOT, FRANK MILLER AND GEOF DARROW, 1995. GENRE: KAIJU.

STAR WARS: DOCTOR APHRA, KIERON GILLEN AND SALVADOR LARROCA, 2016-2019. GENRE: SPACE OPERA.

ALL-STAR SUPERMAN, GRANT MORRISON AND FRANK QUITELY, 2005-2008. GENRE: SUPERHERO.

TO TELL THE REST OF THE STORY, I WILL INVITE AN AMERICAN AUTHOR AND ANTHROPOLOGIST WHO WAS IMPORTANT IN THE FIELD OF SCIENCE FICTION: JUDITH MERRIL.

OH, SPLENDID.

HOW CAN I HELP YOU, GENTLEMEN?

MS. MERRIL, I'VE BEEN TELLING MR. WELLS ABOUT THE HISTORY OF BRITISH SCIENCE FICTION. WE JUST REACHED THE NEW WAVE, AND I THOUGHT IT WOULD HELP IF YOU COULD GIVE US A BRIEF OVERVIEW OF YOUR LONDON EXPERIENCE AND YOUR NEW WAVE CONNECTIONS...

WITH PLEASURE! IT'S VERY SIMPLE. I HEADED FOR LONDON IN 1965, DRAWN BY NEW WORLDS AND ITS INNOVATIVE SCIENCE FICTION. I'D BEEN SEARCHING FOR EXCELLENCE AND ORIGINALITY, AND IT LOOKED AS IF I'D FOUND IT IN BRITAIN.

I WAS ALREADY QUITE WELL KNOWN IN THE WORLD OF AMERICAN SCIENCE FICTION. I HAD BEEN MARRIED TO FREDERIK POHL AND WRITTEN NOVELS, NOTABLY OUTPOST MARS WITH CYRIL M. KORNBLUTH, PLUS A NUMBER OF SHORT STORIES. BUT MOSTLY...

...DURING THE 1950S I HAD STARTED TO COMPILE ANTHOLOGIES OF THE BEST SHORT SCIENCE-FICTION STORIES OF THE YEAR FOR THE SERIES SF: THE YEAR'S GREATEST SCIENCE FICTION AND FANTASY. THE FIRST WAS PUBLISHED IN 1956 BY GNOME PRESS...

TWELVE COMICS TO HELP YOU DISCOVER SCIENCE FICTION:

V FOR VENDETTA, ALAN MOORE AND DAVID LLOYD, 1982. GENRE: DYSTOPIA, POST-APOCALYPTIC.

WATCHMEN, ALAN MOORE AND DAVE GIBBONS, 1986. THEMES: SUPER HEROES, ALT-HIST, PARALLEL UNIVERSES.

KINGDOM COME, MARK WAID AND ALEX ROSS, 1996. PLOT: SUPERHEROES GET SUPPLANTED BY A NEW BREED OF AMORAL ONES...

TRANSMETROPOLITAN, WARREN ELLIS AND DARRICK ROBERTSON, 1997. GENRE: CYBERPUNK.

"WHILE COMPILING THOSE DEMANDING ANTHOLOGIES, I WAS DIGGING EVERYWHERE, CONSULTING THE PULP MAGAZINES, OF COURSE, AS WELL AS OTHER MEDIA, SUCH AS HARPER'S AND THE NEW YORK TIMES, WHICH ALSO PUBLISHED SCI-FI OCCASIONALLY. I EVEN SELECTED A FEW STORIES BY IONESCO AND STEINBECK, WHICH I PUBLISHED ALONGSIDE SHECKLEY, ALDISS, AND THE SHAMEFULLY UNKNOWN ZENNA HENDERSON!"

"ANYWAY, I ARRIVED IN LONDON IN 1965 TO UNCOVER THE WORLD OF BRITISH SCIENCE FICTION AND, I HAVE TO SAY, I ADAPTED FAIRLY QUICKLY TO MY NEW ENVIRONMENT AND THE BRITISH WRITERS' COMMUNITY."

"THEIR AUTHORS WERE EQUALLY AS FOND OF FICTION AS THEORY AND CRITICISM.

"MEANWHILE, I CARRIED ON WRITING FOR THE MAGAZINE OF FANTASY & SCIENCE FICTION, RUN BY ANTHONY BOUCHER. SOME OF MY ARTICLES DESCRIBED THE ORIGINALITY OF THE BRITISH SCENE IN GLOWING TERMS. I WAS A REAL RELAY TO AMERICA FOR BRITISH WRITERS."

"IN 1968, DOUBLEDAY PUBLISHED AN ANTHOLOGY TITLED ENGLAND SWINGS SF: STORIES OF SPECULATIVE FICTION, FEATURING THE BEST SF PUBLISHED IN BRITAIN. YOU WERE IN IT, MICHAEL, ALONG WITH DAVID I. MASSON, CHARLES PLATT, JOSEPHINE SAXTON, THOMAS DISCH, AND J. G. BALLARD, AS WELL AS A VERY YOUNG BUT BRILLIANT NEWCOMER, CHRISTOPHER PRIEST, WITH HIS STORY THE RUN."

YES, THAT ANTHOLOGY WAS A LANDMARK!

IT WAS A VERY BEAUTIFUL ANTHOLOGY. AFTER THAT THE TWO MAIN BRITISH SF MAGAZINES, NEW WORLDS AND SF IMPULSE (THE NEW NAME FOR SCIENCE FANTASY), WERE FORCED TO MERGE DUE TO THE PUBLISHER'S FINANCIAL DIFFICULTIES.

BLACK SCIENCE, RICK REMENDER AND MATTEO SCALERA, 2013. THEME: INTER-DIMENSIONAL TRAVEL.

PLANETARY, WARREN ELLIS AND JOHN CASSADAY, 1998. THEMES: THE BIZARRE, PARANORMAL POWERS.

THE LEAGUE OF EXTRAORDINARY GENTLEMEN, ALAN MOORE AND KEVIN O'NEILL, 1999. GENRE: STEAMPUNK.

FEAR AGENT, RICK REMENDER, JEROME OPEÑA AND TONY MOORE, 2007. GENRE: PULP SPACE OPERA.

NEW WORLDS WAS A WONDERFUL MAGAZINE THAT ALSO ATTRACTED A NUMBER OF MAJOR AMERICAN AUTHORS SEEKING SOMETHING DIFFERENT; SUCH AS THOMAS DISCH, A DARK, DESPAIRING WRITER WHO BEGAN CRAFTING HIS STORIES EVEN MORE CAREFULLY WHEN THEY STARTED TO BE PUBLISHED IN *NEW WORLDS*. THAT WAS CERTAINLY TRUE OF HIS NOVEL *CAMP CONCENTRATION* (1967), WHICH DEALT WITH EXPERIMENTATION ON HUMANS...

AND WHAT ABOUT JOHN BRUNNER AND NORMAN SPINRAD? IN 1968, BRUNNER RELEASED *STAND ON ZANZIBAR*, WITH AN EXCERPT PUBLISHED IN *NEW WORLDS*. THIS WAS A PROPHETIC NOVEL, AS WERE HIS SUBSEQUENT WORKS *THE SHEEP LOOK UP* (1972) AND *THE SHOCKWAVE RIDER* (1975).

THE BRITISH WRITER, M. JOHN HARRISON WROTE THAT *STAND ON ZANZIBAR* WAS, "AN APPLICATION OF THE DOS PASSOS TECHNIQUE TO THE SPECULATIVE FIELD, A MASSIVE COLLAGE OF A BOOK THAT OFFERS A BROAD FICTIONAL EXTRAPOLATION FROM CURRENT EVENTS, AN UNBALANCED, CONSUMER-ORIENTED SOCIETY, VIOLENCE, RACE RIOTS, POVERTY, AND GENETIC CONTROL."

BRUNNER WROTE A FEW POTBOILERS, BUT HE LEFT US WITH AN ASTOUNDINGLY RICH BODY OF WORK, ALL THANKS TO HIS ABILITY TO CONJURE UP A LUCIDLY REALISTIC WORLD OF TOMORROW. *THE SHOCKWAVE RIDER* IS OFTEN CONSIDERED TO BE THE FIRST WORK OF CYBERPUNK, WHICH WAS TRULY SPAWNED BY WILLIAM GIBSON'S *NEUROMANCER*.

AND WHEN *NEW WORLDS* OPENED ITS DOORS TO NORMAN SPINRAD IN 1969, HE IMMEDIATELY PUBLISHED THE STUNNING, AND VERY CONTROVERSIAL NOVEL *BUG JACK BARRON*.

IN THE BOOK, TV TALK-SHOW HOST JACK BARRON MEDIATES BETWEEN AN ANGRY CITIZEN AND A PUBLIC FIGURE. HIS AURA, CHARISMA AND TENACITY LEAD HIM INTO A CONFRONTATION WITH AN EXTREMELY WEALTHY BUSINESSMAN OFFERING IMMORTALITY. DEEMED SHOCKING ON ITS RELEASE, IT BECAME A CLASSIC, AS DID SPINRAD'S OTHER KEY NOVEL, *THE IRON DREAM*, IN WHICH HE IMAGINED A BOOK BY AN ALT-ADOLF HITLER WHO EMIGRATED TO AMERICA IN 1919.

SAGA, FIONA STAPLES AND BRIAN K. VAUGHN, 2012. GENRE: SHAKESPEAREAN SPACE OPERA.

PUNK ROCK JESUS, SEAN MURPHY, 2012. PLOT: CLONING JESUS CHRIST!

STARLIGHT, MARK MILLAR AND GORAN PARLOV, 2014. GENRE: SPACE OPERA THAT PAYS HOMAGE TO *FLASH GORDON*.

ON A SUNBEAM, TILLIE WALDEN, 2018. GENRE: LGBT SPACE OPERA.

SAMUEL R. DELANY, ANOTHER YOUNG AMERICAN AUTHOR, PUBLISHED HIS FAMOUS SHORT STORY *TIME CONSIDERED AS A HELIX OF SEMI-PRECIOUS STONES* IN THE DECEMBER 1968 ISSUE OF *NEW WORLDS*, AND SNAPPED UP BOTH THE HUGO AND NEBULA!

new worlds

WHAT A LONG-WINDED TITLE!

PERHAPS, BUT DELANY GREW INTO A MAJOR NAME IN THE GENRE, WITH SOME INCREDIBLE NOVELS, E.G. *BABEL-17*, *NOVA*, AND *THE BALLAD OF BETA-2* (SOME OF THE RARE WORKS TO FOCUS ON LINGUISTICS), AS WELL AS *THE EINSTEIN INTERSECTION*, A SUBTLE NOVEL IN WHICH OUR UNIVERSE WAS SUDDENLY LINKED TO ANOTHER, WITH NO RATIONAL EXPLANATION!

AND WE SHOULD MENTION ANOTHER ESSENTIAL PLAYER IN THE HISTORY OF SCI-FI: HARLAN ELLISON, WHO WAS ALSO PUBLISHED IN *NEW WORLDS*, PARTICULARLY HIS SHORT STORY *A BOY AND HIS DOG*. ELLISON WAS AN EXTREMELY TALENTED WRITER.

OH, PLEASE TELL ME SOME MORE ABOUT HIM!

HMM, THEN WE NEED TO HEAD BACK TO AMERICAN SCIENCE FICTION. SO, ARE YOU GAME?

OF COURSE!

THERE WERE MANY OTHER GREAT AUTHORS WHO CAME TO PROMINENCE DURING THE NEW WAVE OF THE 1960S TO THE LATE 1970S. ROBERT HOLDSTOCK, CHRISTOPHER PRIEST, IAN WATSON...

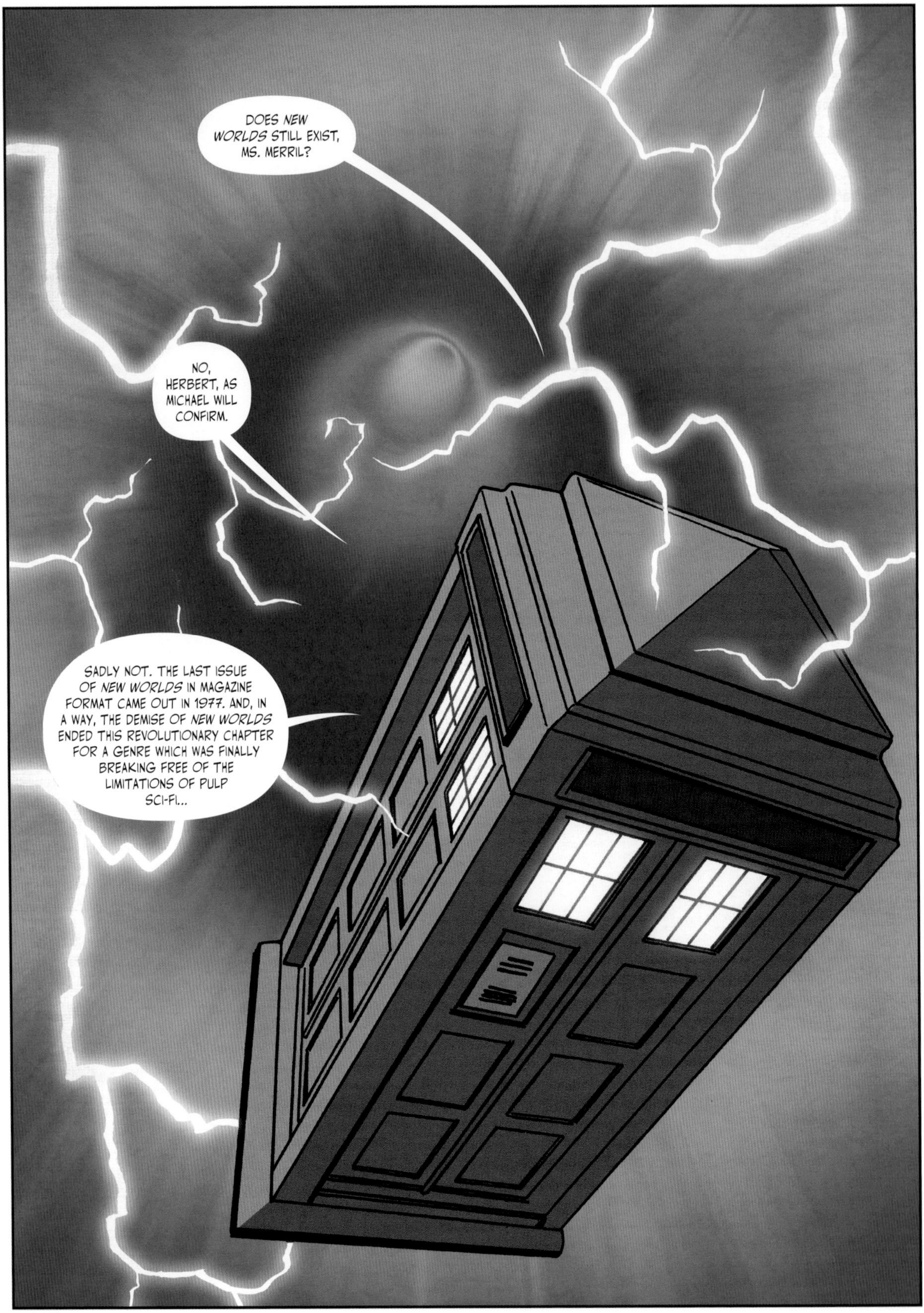
DOES *NEW WORLDS* STILL EXIST, MS. MERRIL?
NO, HERBERT, AS MICHAEL WILL CONFIRM.
SADLY NOT. THE LAST ISSUE OF *NEW WORLDS* IN MAGAZINE FORMAT CAME OUT IN 1977. AND, IN A WAY, THE DEMISE OF *NEW WORLDS* ENDED THIS REVOLUTIONARY CHAPTER FOR A GENRE WHICH WAS FINALLY BREAKING FREE OF THE LIMITATIONS OF PULP SCI-FI...

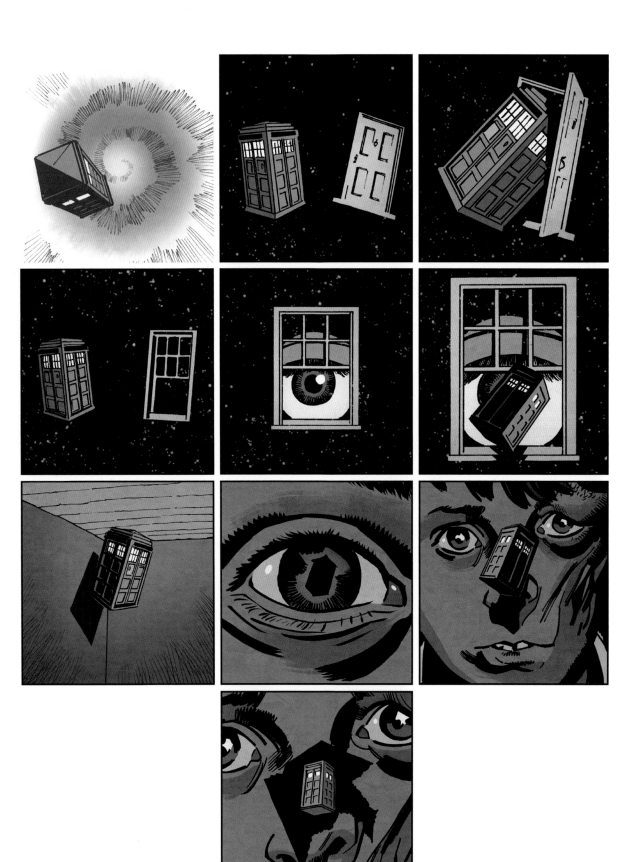

BUT... WHAT IS GOING ON?

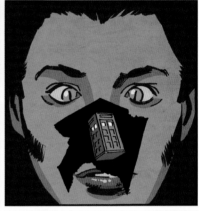

OH, LOOK!

BY SAINT LEIBOWITZ!

Alternative American SF. From the end of the 1950s' Golden Age until the 1969 moon landing.

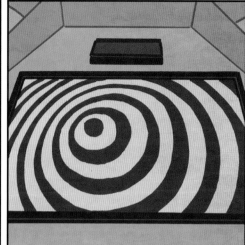

ALL OF THOSE SCENES WE PASSED THROUGH WERE TAKEN FROM STORIES BY AMERICAN AUTHORS ACTIVE DURING THE 1950S. ACCORDING TO MANY SPECIALISTS, THE GOLDEN AGE OF SCIENCE FICTION LASTED UNTIL THE LATE 1950S. IT WAS A DECADE THAT ALSO PRODUCED SOME EXCELLENT WRITERS AND SEMINAL WORKS. IN ORDER OF APPEARANCE, WE FLEW THROUGH...

THE FIRST PICTURE, OF THE LITTLE KID, PLUNGED US INTO ONE OF THE MOST FAMOUS SHORT STORIES IN SF. I'M TALKING ABOUT *BORN OF MAN AND WOMAN* BY *RICHARD MATHESON*, PUBLISHED IN *THE MAGAZINE OF FANTASY & SCIENCE FICTION* IN 1950. IT DESCRIBES THE SUFFERING OF A CHILD BORN DEFORMED AND LOCKED AWAY IN A CELLAR BY THE PARENTS. AT HOME WITH BOTH SCI-FI AND FANTASY, AND OFTEN VERGING ON HORROR, MATHESON PENNED SEVERAL ALL-TIME CLASSICS, MANY OF WHICH WERE ADAPTED FOR THE BIG SCREEN. THE BEST EXAMPLES BEING *I AM LEGEND* (1954) AND *THE SHRINKING MAN* (1956). THE FORMER WAS A CLEVER TWIST ON THE VAMPIRE MYTH, WITH AN EXTREMELY SYMBOLIC ENDING. THE LATTER IS THE BIZARRE ADVENTURE OF A MAN WHO STARTS TO SHRINK AFTER BEING EXPOSED TO A STRANGE MIST. AS A SCRIPTWRITER, ESPECIALLY FOR ROD SERLING'S TV SERIES *THE TWILIGHT ZONE*, HE ALSO STRONGLY INFLUENCED THE MODERN MASTER OF HORROR AND THE FANTASTIC, STEPHEN KING.

THE SPACESHIP THAT WE TORE THROUGH NEXT WAS FEATURED IN THE FIRST-EVER NOVEL BY AN AMERICAN WRITER WHO WOULD LATER VENTURE BEYOND THE COCOON OF SF: *KURT VONNEGUT*. THE BOOK WAS TITLED *THE SIRENS OF TITAN* (1959), A HUMOROUS, ACERBIC WORK THAT CUT HUMAN EXISTENCE RIGHT DOWN TO SIZE ON A COSMIC SCALE. VONNEGUT WAS ONE OF THE MOST BRILLIANT VOICES IN AMERICAN LITERATURE. THE PINNACLE OF HIS TALENT WAS *SLAUGHTERHOUSE-FIVE, OR THE CHILDREN'S CRUSADE* (1969), A MASTERPIECE OF THE GENRE. IN THIS BOOK, VONNEGUT, HARROWED BY THE FIREBOMBING OF DRESDEN (WHICH HE LIVED THROUGH), TOLD THE STORY OF A MAN WHO EXISTS IN SEVERAL TIMELINES: ONE IN DRESDEN, IN THE TITULAR SLAUGHTERHOUSE FIVE, AND ANOTHER ON THE PLANET OF THE TRALFAMADORIANS, WHO KIDNAP HIM AND LOCK HIM IN A ZOO. VONNEGUT ALSO CREATED THE CHARACTER KILGORE TROUT, A WASHED-UP SF WRITER WHO APPEARED IN SEVERAL OF HIS NOVELS. THE NAME WAS A PARODY OF THEODORE STURGEON AND HIS EQUALLY FISH-THEMED SURNAME.

NEXT, WE DROPPED IN ON THE AMAZING C'MELL, A CAT-GIRL WHO APPEARED IN A NOVELLA FROM WHAT CERTAIN SCIENCE-FICTION FANATICS CONSIDER THE BEST UNIVERSE EVER CREATED: *INSTRUMENTALITY OF MANKIND*. THIS FUTURE HISTORY WAS PENNED BY THE MYSTERIOUS *CORDWAINER SMITH*. SOME OF HIS STORIES DERIVED DIRECTLY FROM VARIOUS IDEAS EXPOUNDED BY HUXLEY. THANKS TO HIS QUALITY WRITING, POLITICAL AND PSYCHOLOGICAL FINESSE, AND UNBRIDLED IMAGINATION, THIS CULT SERIES OF AROUND 30 SHORT STORIES AND ONE NOVEL IS TRULY CAPTIVATING. WE ARE INTRODUCED TO THE "TRUE MEN," THE "UNDERPEOPLE" (LIKE C'MELL OR D'JOAN, A DOG-GIRL) AND THE ROBOTS, WAY DOWN AT THE BOTTOM OF THE SOCIAL LADDER. SMITH'S SEMI-ARID PLANET NORSTRILIA ALSO HAD A LOT IN COMMON WITH ANOTHER FAMOUS SCI-FI PLANET WE WILL BE MENTIONING LATER: ARRAKIS, THE BRAINCHILD OF WRITER FRANK HERBERT.

THE MAN WITH A MICROPHONE WAS INSPIRED BY A SCENE FROM YVES BOISSET'S 1983 FILM *THE PRIZE OF PERIL*, WHICH WAS ACTUALLY BASED ON AN AVANT-GARDE SHORT STORY THAT FORESHADOWED THE DANGERS OF REALITY TV, WRITTEN BY SCI-FI'S GREATEST SATIRIST OF THE 1950S AND 1960S, *ROBERT SHECKLEY*. HIS WORKS WERE, PUBLISHED IN ANTHONY BOUCHER'S *GALAXY* MAGAZINE, INCLUDING SOME OF HIS BEST-KNOWN STORIES. APART FROM *THE PRIZE OF PERIL* (1958), HE ALSO GAVE US *SEVENTH VICTIM* IN 1953, A SCATHING SATIRE OF A WORLD IN WHICH THE EMOTIONAL CATHARSIS BUREAU HAS LEGALIZED MURDER IN A SERIES OF BRUTAL GAME EVENTS INVOLVING HUNTERS AND THEIR PREY. AMONG HIS MOST SUCCESSFUL NOVELS, I SHOULD MENTION *IMMORTALITY, INC.* (1959), AND *BRING ME THE HEAD OF PRINCE CHARMING* (1991) OF COURSE, WHICH HE CO-WROTE WITH ANOTHER LEGEND OF THE GENRE, ROGER ZELAZNY.

FINALLY, WE CROSSED THE PATH OF A MONK, BROTHER FRANCIS GERARD, A CHARACTER FROM THE NOVEL *A CANTICLE FOR LEIBOWITZ* BY *WALTER M. MILLER*. THE BOOK WAS A "FIX-UP," I.E. A WORK MADE UP OF SEVERAL PREVIOUSLY PUBLISHED SHORT STORIES, REWORKED IN ORDER TO FORM A COHERENT WHOLE. ITS THREE PARTS WERE FIRST PRINTED IN *THE MAGAZINE OF FANTASY & SCIENCE FICTION*, THEN COMBINED INTO THE NOVEL IN 1959. IN A POST-NUCLEAR WORLD THAT HAS SUNK BACK INTO THE DARK AGES, BROTHER FRANCIS DISCOVERS RELICS LEFT BEHIND BY A HOLY MAN, SAINT LEIBOWITZ, IN WHAT MUST HAVE BEEN A FALLOUT SHELTER. THOSE RELICS PROCEED TO PERMANENTLY ALTER THE NEW ORDER...

THAT MEANS WE'VE DRIFTED OFF COURSE. WE WERE SUPPOSED TO ARRIVE IN THE 1960S...

WE'RE NOT WHERE WE WERE ORIGINALLY AIMING FOR. IT'S AS IF SOME FORCE HAS TRANSPORTED US INTO ANOTHER--

DIMENSION!

THE TWILIGHT ZONE!

WELCOME TO A DIMENSION WHERE ANYTHING IS POSSIBLE! MY NAME IS ROD SERLING, AND I'M HERE TO HELP YOU GET YOUR BEARINGS AND MANIPULATE MATTER. THEN YOU'LL BE ABLE TO TRAVEL WHEREVER YOU WANT IN YOUR SCIENCE-FICTION UNIVERSES.

WELL, THAT'S JUST PERFECT, ROD! YOU CAN HELP ME DESCRIBE EVERYTHING THAT HAPPENED NEXT, PARTICULARLY THE EVENTS THAT I WANTED TO INTRODUCE HERBERT TO.

OH, THAT WOULD BE VERY KIND OF YOU...

SO BE IT! WHERE EXACTLY WOULD YOU LIKE TO BEGIN?

WE MAY AS WELL START WITH THEM... THEY'RE EASY TO RECOGNIZE: ROBERT SILVERBERG, PHILIP K. DICK, AND FRANK HERBERT...

YES, THAT'S THEM ALRIGHT. LET'S GO TAKE A CLOSER LOOK...

SCI-FI SHOWS FROM AROUND THE WORLD:

OSMOSIS (FRANCE), CREATED BY AUDREY FOUCHÉ, 2019. PLOT: SINISTER DATING APP.

RAGNAROK (NORWAY), CREATED BY ADAM PRICE, 2020-PRESENT. THEMES: THE APOCALYPSE.

3% (BRAZIL), CREATED BY PEDRO AGUILERA, 2016-2020. GENRE: DYSTOPIA.

THE RAIN (DENMARK), CREATED BY JANNIK TAI MOSHOLT, 2018-2020. GENRE: POST APOCALYPSE.

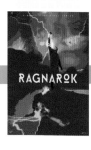

NO NEED TO WORRY. WE'RE GOING TO TAKE A TRIP RIGHT TO THE HEART OF THESE WRITERS. EACH HAS THEIR OWN DIMENSION!

WHAT A BIZARRE SENSATION!

SO, LET'S GO IN AND EXPLORE THE INNER DIMENSIONS OF THESE GIANTS!

IP K. DIC

FIVE CHILDREN'S GRAPHIC NOVELS FOR YOUR KIDS TO READ:

LITTLE ROBOT, BEN HATKE, 2015. FEATURES: NO TEXT, FOR THE YOUNGEST READERS.

ZITA THE SPACEGIRL, BEN HATKE, 2011. THEMES: FRIENDSHIP, OTHERNESS, AMAZING JOURNEYS.

SPACE DUMPLINS, CRAIG THOMPSON, 2015. GENRE: CRAZY SPACE OPERA.

S.A.M., MARAZANO AND XIAO, 2011. GENRE: POST-APOCALYPSE.

CAPTAIN UNDERPANTS, DAV PILKEY, 1997-PRESENT. GENRE: SUPERHERO.

HERE WE ARE WITH *PHILIP KINDRED DICK*, WHO IN THE COURSE OF TIME BECAME THE MOST FAMOUS SCIENCE-FICTION WRITER IN THE WORLD, AND CAN ALSO BE REGARDED AS A GOLDEN-AGE AUTHOR. BY 1953, HE HAD ALREADY PUBLISHED AROUND THIRTY SHORT STORIES, FOLLOWED BY A SHORT NOVEL, *SOLAR LOTTERY*, IN 1955. DICK WAS VERY KEEN ON VAN VOGT, AND HIS EARLY WORKS SUCH AS THAT NOVEL CLEARLY SHOWED THE CANADIAN WRITER'S INFLUENCE.

OFTEN CONSIDERED TO BE AN AUTHOR WITH NO PARTICULAR STYLE, DUE TO HIS QUITE TERSE WRITING, HIS STORIES SUDDENLY ASCENDED TO A WHOLE NEW LEVEL IN THE EARLY 1960S. HE WROTE NINE NOVELS BETWEEN 1963 AND 1964! THIS MASSIVE OUTPUT CAN BE EXPLAINED BY THE FACT THAT HE WAS A HEAVY USER OF AMPHETAMINES, WHICH ALLOWED HIM TO LAUNCH INTO SUSTAINED BOUTS OF WRITING FOR HOURS ON END.

IN 1959, HE PRODUCED ONE OF HIS VERY FIRST MASTERPIECES, *TIME OUT OF JOINT*, IN WHICH A MAN STARTS TO REALIZE THAT HIS WORLD SEEMS ARTIFICIAL. THE SCREENPLAY FOR PETER WEIR'S FILM *THE TRUMAN SHOW* (1998) WAS HEAVILY INSPIRED BY THE STORY. TO QUOTE DICK HIMSELF, "REALITY IS THAT WHICH, WHEN YOU STOP BELIEVING IN IT, DOESN'T GO AWAY."

HIS FAVORITE THEMES INCLUDED THE DOPPELGANGER (HE HAD HAD A TWIN SISTER WHO DIED VERY YOUNG), HUMAN NATURE, AND ESPECIALLY THE DEFINITION OR EVEN REDEFINITION OF REALITY. HE ALSO EXPLORED INSANITY (IN HIS NOVEL *CLANS OF THE ALPHANE MOON*) AND TOTALITARIANISM, ESPECIALLY NAZISM. 1962 SAW THE PUBLICATION OF ONE OF HIS BEST-KNOWN WORKS, *THE MAN IN THE HIGH CASTLE*, WHICH TELLS OF AN ALTERNATE HISTORY WHERE THE AXIS POWERS WON WORLD WAR TWO, AND GERMANY AND JAPAN DIVIDED UP THE UNITED STATES AMONGST THEMSELVES.

DICK HAD ALWAYS DREAMED OF WRITING REALIST NOVELS, BUT ALL OF HIS MANUSCRIPTS WERE REFUSED, ONE AFTER ANOTHER. AS A RESULT, HE KEPT ON WRITING SCIENCE FICTION. SADLY UNDERRATED, HIS NOVELS WERE RELEASED STRAIGHT TO PAPERBACK, MOSTLY PUBLISHED BY DONALD WOLLHEIM IN HIS COLLECTION FOR ACE BOOKS. THE PHILIP K. DICK AWARD IS STILL PRESENTED TO THE BEST NEW WORK OF THE YEAR TO COME OUT IN PAPERBACK IN AMERICA. IN FEBRUARY 1974, TOWARD THE END OF HIS LIFE, HE HAD A MYSTICAL REVELATION THAT LED HIM TO HAND-WRITE THE 8,000-PAGE *EXEGESIS*. AT THE TIME, DICK BELIEVED WE WERE ALL LIVING IN AN ILLUSION THAT HAD BEEN SUPERIMPOSED ON REALITY, WHILE THE TRUE REALITY WAS ACTUALLY TAKING PLACE IN FIRST-CENTURY ROME...

HE WAS AN EXCELLENT AUTHOR OF IDEA-DRIVEN SHORT STORIES LIKE *THE GOLDEN MAN* (1954 IN *IF*) AND *WE CAN REMEMBER IT FOR YOU WHOLESALE* (1966 IN *F&SF*), ON WHICH PAUL VERHOEVEN'S FILM *TOTAL RECALL* WAS BASED. DICK LEFT US A PLETHORA OF NOVELS: *MARTIAN TIME-SLIP* (1964), *DR. BLOODMONEY* (1965), *UBIK* (1969, WHICH MANY CONSIDER TO BE HIS TRUE MASTERPIECE), *DO ANDROIDS DREAM OF ELECTRIC SHEEP?* (1968, ADAPTED INTO RIDLEY SCOTT'S FILM *BLADE RUNNER*), *A SCANNER DARKLY* (1977), AND FROM 1981 TO 1982, THE THREE NOVELS IN THE *VALIS* TRILOGY: *VALIS*, *THE DIVINE INVASION*, AND *THE TRANSMIGRATION OF TIMOTHY ARCHER*, WHICH INCLUDED A STRONG FEMALE CHARACTER IN RESPONSE TO URSULA LE GUIN'S CRITICISM OF THE WOMEN HE PORTRAYED.

DISCOVER PHILIP K. DICK IN THREE BOOKS:

THE LIFE OF PHILIP K. DICK: THE MAN WHO REMEMBERED THE FUTURE, ANTHONY PEAKE, 2013.

I AM ALIVE AND YOU ARE DEAD: A JOURNEY INTO THE MIND OF PHILIP K. DICK, EMMANUEL CARRERE, 2006.

DO ANDROIDS DREAM OF ELECTRIC SHEEP?, 1968.

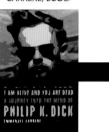

AND NOW HERE'S THE ILLUSTRIOUS *FRANK HERBERT*, AUTHOR OF *DUNE*. ALTHOUGH BORN IN 1920, LIKE ASIMOV, HE STARTED OUT IN SCIENCE FICTION LATER THAN HIS CONTEMPORARIES. HIS FIRST SHORT STORY WAS ONLY PUBLISHED IN *STARTLING STORIES* IN 1952. HERBERT HAD AN ECLECTIC PROFESSIONAL CAREER. CURIOUS BY NATURE, IF A SUBJECT FASCINATED HIM HE STROVE TO LEARN AS MUCH AS HE COULD. HE WAS ALSO A JUNGIAN PSYCHOANALYST, AS WELL AS AN INSTRUCTOR FOR NASA, TEACHING PILOTS HOW TO SURVIVE IN HOSTILE TERRAIN SUCH AS JUNGLES AND DESERT AREAS.

HIS FIRST NOVEL CAME OUT IN 1956, TITLED *THE DRAGON IN THE SEA*, AND HAD BEEN INSPIRED BY READING A STUDY ON DEPTH PSYCHOLOGY. THE PLOT UNFOLDED ON BOARD A SUBMARINE SENT ON A MISSION TO PUMP THE ENEMY'S OIL RESERVES RIGHT OUT FROM UNDER THEIR NOSES. VISIONARY!

HOT ON THE HEELS OF THIS FIRST (MORE CRITICAL THAN COMMERCIAL) SUCCESS, HERBERT, WHO WAS A COMMITTED ECOLOGIST, LAUNCHED INTO WRITING A NOVEL OF A WHOLE NEW MAGNITUDE FOLLOWING A JOURNALISTIC ASSIGNMENT WHICH HAD LED HIM OUT INTO THE DUNES OF FLORENCE, OREGON. THRILLED AT WHAT HE DISCOVERED THERE, HE DOCUMENTED IT EXHAUSTIVELY YET NEVER PUBLISHED AN ARTICLE. BUT HE DID BEGIN DRAFTING HIS NOW-CULT NOVEL, *DUNE!* IT FIRST APPEARED IN TWO PARTS IN *ANALOG* MAGAZINE (THE FORMER *ASTOUNDING*, STILL EDITED BY CAMPBELL) IN 1963 AND 1965, BEFORE FINALLY BEING RELEASED AS A BOOK FROM A SMALL PUBLISHER, AND WINNING BOTH THE NEBULA AND THE HUGO AWARDS.

DUNE MARKED A WATERSHED IN SCI-FI, A GENUINE ANCHOR POINT AND FRAME OF REFERENCE. IN A WAY, ITS PUBLICATION DENOTED THE REAL END OF THE GOLDEN AGE, SWEEPING THE GENRE INTO A BRAND-NEW ERA BY WEAVING IN MORE PHILOSOPHICAL, POLITICAL, AND ESPECIALLY ECOLOGICAL THEMES. WHEREAS CLASSIC SCI-FI HAD ALWAYS BEEN A HUGE PUBLICITY CAMPAIGN FOR SCIENCE, THESE THEMATIC STORIES WERE MORE FOCUSED ON THE HUMAN ANGLE, AND ALSO WARNED OF THE DANGERS THAT AWAITED US. MOREOVER, HERBERT BROUGHT IN THE CONCEPT OF THE NEED TO TAKE A LONG-TERM OVERVIEW OF THE SYSTEMS GOVERNING HOW HUMANITY FUNCTIONS (PRINCIPALLY REGARDING ECOLOGY), SO AS TO LESSEN OUR ENVIRONMENTAL IMPACT. AND HE APPLIED THOSE PRINCIPLES IN DAY-TO-DAY LIFE, AS HIS HOME WAS HEATED USING SOLAR PANELS, PROVING THAT HE WAS AHEAD OF HIS TIME!

MEANWHILE, THE *DUNE* SAGA SPREAD OUT OVER SIX VOLUMES; THEN HIS SON LATER CONTINUED THE SERIES WITH ANOTHER WRITER, KEVIN J. ANDERSON. *DUNE* IS SET ON THE FARAWAY PLANET OF ARRAKIS, WHERE A YOUNG MAN, PAUL ATREIDES, IS RESCUED BY THE FREMEN PEOPLE AFTER THE DEATH OF HIS FATHER, LETO ATREIDES, AT THE HANDS OF THE BRUTAL HOUSE HARKONNEN. HE BECOMES MUAD'DIB (HIS NOM DE GUERRE MEANING "DESERT MOUSE") AND DISCOVERS THE POWER OF "THE SPICE," WHICH GIVES HIM "PRESCIENCE."

DISCOVER FRANK HERBERT IN TWO BOOKS:

STILL, IT WOULD BE PRETTY UNFAIR TO REDUCE ALL OF HERBERT'S WORK TO THE *DUNE* SERIES. HE ALSO PENNED A VARIETY OF OTHER EXCEPTIONAL NOVELS, SUCH AS *THE SANTAROGA BARRIER*, *HELLSTROM'S HIVE*, *THE WHITE PLAGUE*, PLUS THE EXCELLENT *BUREAU OF SABOTAGE* BOOKS AND *THE HEAVEN MAKERS*, WHICH IS REMINISCENT OF PHILIP JOSÉ FARMER'S *WORLD OF TIERS* SERIES.

DREAMER OF DUNE: THE BIOGRAPHY OF FRANK HERBERT, BRIAN HERBERT, 2003.

DUNE, 1965.

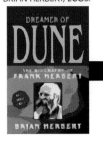

AND, FINALLY, HERE'S THE IMAGINATION OF *ROBERT SILVERBERG*, ANOTHER GIANT OF THE GENRE, WHO MADE HIS SCIENCE-FICTION DEBUT AT 18. HIS FIRST SHORT STORY WAS PUBLISHED IN 1952, BUT HE HAD LONG BEEN A FAN SF, AS WE CAN SEE FROM HIS LETTERS TO MAGAZINES LIKE *STARTLING STORIES*. DESPITE AN UNASSUMING START, HE WAS QUICKLY NOTICED AND RECEIVED HIS FIRST HUGO AWARD FOR MOST PROMISING NEW AUTHOR AT THE AGE OF BARELY 20!

SILVERBERG SOON TURNED OUT TO BE A PROLIFIC WRITER, PRODUCING A WIDE RANGE OF NOVELS AND SHORT STORIES WHICH LACKED AMBITION AND WERE MOSTLY POTBOILERS FOR PULP MAGAZINES. TO ACHIEVE THIS, HE DEPLOYED AN ASSORTMENT OF PSEUDONYMS. NEVERTHELESS, AFTER THE WORLD OF THE PULPS FELL INTO A CRISIS IN 1958 WHEN THEIR MAIN DISTRIBUTOR WENT OUT OF BUSINESS, HE TRIED TO DIVERSIFY HIS OUTPUT AND ENDED UP PUBLISHING EVERYTHING FROM WESTERNS TO PORNOGRAPHIC FICTION!

DURING THE 1960S, FREDERIK POHL WAS EDITOR AT *GALAXY SCIENCE FICTION* MAGAZINE. REALIZING THAT SILVERBERG WAS SQUANDERING HIS TALENT, HE DECIDED TO PERSUADE HIM TO STOP BEING SO DIVERSE AND FOCUS HIS UNDENIABLE TALENT ON WRITING SCI-FI INSTEAD. TO MAKE THIS HAPPEN, HE STRUCK A BARGAIN WITH SILVERBERG, AGREEING TO BUY ALL THE WRITER'S NOVELS AND SHORT STORIES IF HE STARTED PRODUCING HIS BEST POSSIBLE WORK; BUT IF HE GOT DIVERSE AGAIN, THE DEAL WAS OFF. SILVERBERG ACCEPTED AND IT TURNED HIS CAREER AROUND.

FROM THEN ON, WITH REGULAR SALES GUARANTEED, THE MAJORITY OF HIS WORKS BECAME EXTRAORDINARY, AND SOME WENT ON TO BE PROPER CLASSICS. TAKE, FOR EXAMPLE: *THE MAN IN THE MAZE* (1968), A STORY OF ALIEN FIRST CONTACT THAT DOESN'T GO THE WAY THE MAN IN CHARGE PLANNED IT; *DYING INSIDE* (1972), ONE OF HIS MOST BEAUTIFUL (AND SADDEST) NOVELS, WHICH EXAMINES THEMES OF TELEPATHY; *THE BOOK OF SKULLS* FROM THE SAME YEAR, WHICH NARRATES THE LAVISH ROAD TRIP OF FOUR STUDENTS TOWARD A PROMISE OF IMMORTALITY; AND *THE WORLD INSIDE*, A DYSTOPIAN TALE WITH MORE OF A HUXLEYAN OR BALLARDIAN BRITISH FEEL, WHICH DEPICTS TERRIFYING, THOUSAND-FLOOR SKYSCRAPERS AND EARTH WITH A POPULATION OF 75 BILLION PEOPLE!

AFTER RETIRING IN THE MID-1970S, HE LATER MADE A COMEBACK WITH SEVERAL LARGE ADVENTURE CYCLES SUCH AS *MAJIPOOR*, WHICH BEGAN WITH *LORD VALENTINE'S CASTLE*. HE CONTINUED TO PUBLISH A PROLIFIC AMOUNT OF WORK, E.G. THE STUNNING ALTERNATE-ROMAN HISTORY NOVEL, *ROMA ETERNA*, IN 2003. PROGRESSIVE AND HUMANIST, SILVERBERG WAS ONE OF THE FIRST TO WRITE A STORY WITH A BLACK HERO, *SHADRACH IN THE FURNACE*. THE WORLD OF SCIENCE FICTION, WHICH WAS VIRTUALLY CLOSED OFF TO WOMEN ALREADY, WAS EVEN LESS RECEPTIVE TO MINORITIES.

DISCOVER
ROBERT SILVERBERG
IN FOUR BOOKS:

THE WORLD INSIDE, 1971.

SHADRACH IN THE FURNACE, 1976.

LORD VALENTINE'S CASTLE, 1980.

THE STOCHASTIC MAN, 1972.

WELL, WHAT AN EXPERIENCE, FRIENDS! WHERE SHALL WE GO NEXT?

LET'S TAKE A MORE IN-DEPTH LOOK AT THE AMERICAN EXPERIENCE OF THE 1960S AND 1970S. ROD, CAN YOU PULL UP PICTURES OR SCENES TO ILLUSTRATE WHAT I'M SAYING?

NOTHING'S IMPOSSIBLE IN THIS DIMENSION, MS. MERRIL.

ALRIGHT, MY DEAR MR. WELLS, HERE'S THE REST OF THE STORY, WHICH PARTLY RESEMBLES THE BRITISH EXPERIENCE. THE UNITED STATES ALSO HAD A KIND OF NEW WAVE OF THEIR OWN, FEATURING KEY FIGURES SUCH AS DAMON KNIGHT AND HARLAN ELLISON.

CERTAIN GROUPS, LIKE THE FUTURIANS (WHICH ASIMOV HAD LEFT ONCE HIS FIRST TEXTS WERE PUBLISHED IN *ASTOUNDING*), HAD LONG SOUGHT TO FIGHT BACK AGAINST THE ESTABLISHED ORDER OF THOSE WHO HELD THE "POWER" OF THE FINAL DECISION, SUCH AS CAMPBELL. EDITORS LIKE DAMON KNIGHT WERE AMONG THIS NEW BREED, AND WOLLHEIM, POHL, AND BOUCHER WOULD SOON FOLLOW.

TWO OF THEM, KNIGHT AND WOLLHEIM, FOUND THEMSELVES A NICHE WHEN THE BOOK MARKET BEGAN TO COMPETE WITH THE MAGAZINE GHETTO. THE NEW BOOKS AND ANTHOLOGIES WERE PARTLY RESPONSIBLE FOR THE DECLINE OF THE MAGAZINES. AFTER 1952, WOLLHEIM BECAME EDITOR OF ACE BOOKS' FAMOUS *ACE DOUBLES* COLLECTION. MEANWHILE, DAMON KNIGHT DREW INSPIRATION FROM POHL'S *STAR SCIENCE FICTION STORIES* ANTHOLOGIES, AND MINE TOO, TO LAUNCH HIS WELL-KNOWN ANTHOLOGY SERIES *ORBIT* IN 1966.

AND FROM THAT POINT ONWARD, THE STANDARDS OF SCIENCE-FICTION WRITING BEGAN TO SKYROCKET.

TEN SCIENCE-FICTION NOVELS TO INITIATE YOUR CHILDREN:

THE TRIPODS, JOHN CHRISTOPHER, 1967. THEME: LIFE ON EARTH AFTER AN ALIEN INVASION.

THE GIVER, LOIS LOWRY, 1993. GENRE: DYSTOPIA.

DARK LORD, JAMIE THOMSON, 2011. GENRE: SF SCHOOL COMEDY.

THE MAZE RUNNER, JAMES DASHNER, 2009. GENRE: DYSTOPIA.

NOUGHTS AND CROSSES, MALORIE BLACKMAN, 2008. GENRE: ALTERNATE HISTORY.

BY DISCOVERING AND PUBLISHING KATE WILHELM, GARDNER DOZOIS, THE COMPLEX GENE WOLFE, THE ECCENTRIC RAPHAEL ALOYSIUS LAFFERTY, THE SUBTLE CAROL EMSHWILLER, THE FUTURE CYBERPUNK GEORGE ALEC EFFINGER, THE DARKLY COMIC DORIS PISERCHIA, AND THE GREAT URSULA LE GUIN, THEY ELEVATED THE GENERAL STANDARD OF SCIENCE-FICTION STORIES. NOW THEY WERE COMING OUT IN BOOK FORM, THEY WERE TAKEN MORE SERIOUSLY IN AMERICA, WHICH WAS UNDERGOING A MAJOR SOCIO-POLITICAL TRANSFORMATION. DON'T FORGET THAT THE 1960S WAS A DECADE MARRED BY THE KENNEDY ASSASSINATION, AS WELL AS THE WAR IN VIETNAM.

WITH *ORBIT*, I WAS DETERMINED TO REVOLUTIONIZE SCIENCE FICTION, JUST LIKE CAMPBELL HAD IN THE EARLY 1940S, OR WHAT HORACE GOLD AND ANTHONY BOUCHER HAD ACHIEVED WITH *GALAXY* AND *THE MAGAZINE OF FANTASY & SCIENCE FICTION* IN THE 1950S. I SAW NO GOOD REASON WHY SCIENCE FICTION, WHICH HAD TENDED TO PRIORITIZE IDEAS OVER WRITING QUALITY, SHOULDN'T BE TAKEN ON THE SAME TERMS AS ALL OTHER LITERATURE.

ANYHOW, THE STORIES INCLUDED IN THE *ORBIT* ANTHOLOGIES RAPIDLY CARRIED OFF ALL OF THE GENRE'S MOST-COVETED AWARDS. IN 1970, FOR EXAMPLE, SIX OF THE SEVEN FINALISTS FOR BEST SHORT STORY HAD BEEN PUBLISHED IN *ORBIT*, AND TWO OF THEM WERE WOMEN, JOANNA RUSS AND KATE WILHELM. I MUST SAY THAT ALMOST A QUARTER OF THE WRITERS IN DAMON'S ANTHOLOGIES WERE FEMALE, WHICH WAS UNHEARD OF IN THOSE DAYS.

A BIT LIKE WHAT I WAS DOING WITH *NEW WORLDS*, DAMON KNIGHT WAS INTERESTED IN BUYING AND PUBLISHING STORIES FROM THE FRINGES OF THE USUAL SF, TO KEEP THE BOUNDARIES OF THE GENRE FROM CLOSING IN.

THAT'S TRUE, MICHAEL, AND I'D SAY THAT *ORBIT* WAS EVEN MORE IMPORTANT THAN THE MOST FAMOUS ANTHOLOGY OF THE TIME, *DANGEROUS VISIONS*, COMPILED BY HARLAN ELLISON AND RELEASED IN 1967.

ENDER'S GAME, ORSON SCOTT CARD, 1985. PLOT: A WAR AGAINST ALIENS.

BINTI, NNEDI OKORAFOR, 2015. GENRE: AFRICANFUTURISM.

THE HOUSE OF THE SCORPION, NANCY FARMER, 2002. THEME: CLONING.

THE HUNGER GAMES, SUZANNE COLLINS, 2008. GENRE: DYSTOPIA.

THE GIRL WITH ALL THE GIFTS, M. R. CAREY, 2014. GENRE: ZOMBIE APOCALYPSE.

HARLAN ELLISON WAS AN EXUBERANT PERSONALITY, CAPABLE OF WRITING AMAZING SHORT STORIES BEFORE A LIVE AUDIENCE AT A CONVENTION, AS WELL AS GATHERING THE GREATEST NAMES OF THE PERIOD TOGETHER UNDER HIS BANNER FOR THIS PROJECT THAT AIMED TO BE TRANSGRESSIVE AND INNOVATIVE; CLOSER TO THE SPIRIT OF THE BRITISH NEW WAVE.

EXACTLY. FOR INSTANCE, IT DARED TO MENTION HOMOSEXUALITY. THIS HAD BEEN A TABOO SUBJECT IN SF, WHICH WAS WAY BEHIND THE TIMES REGARDING SEXUAL ISSUES.

WHO WAS IN IT? DICK, LEIBER, ALDISS, ASIMOV, NIVEN, ZELAZNY, SONYA DORMAN, EMSHWILLER, ANDERSON...A MIXTURE OF WRITERS OLD AND NEW, ALL DRAWN TOGETHER BY THIS IDEA TO BREATHE NEW LIFE INTO THE GENRE BY PUTTING THEMSELVES IN "DANGER." BUT THANKS TO ELLISON'S CHARISMA, COUPLED WITH THE HIGH-QUALITY STORIES, THE ANTHOLOGY SOLD EXTREMELY WELL AND LEFT A LASTING IMPRESSION.

THE SUCCESS OF *ORBIT* AND *DANGEROUS VISIONS* LED TO OTHER ANTHOLOGIES, SUCH AS SAMUEL DELANY AND MARILYN HACKER'S *QUARK*, TERRY CARR'S *UNIVERSE*, ROBERT SILVERBERG'S *NEW DIMENSIONS*, AND HARRY HARRISON'S *NOVA*!

BUT IT WOULD BE A SHAME NOT TO GIVE A WELL-DESERVED MENTION TO *AMAZING STORIES* MAGAZINE, A PULP *PAR EXCELLENCE*, WHICH, IN THE HANDS OF ITS EXCELLENT EDITOR, CELE GOLDSMITH LALLI...

...TOOK FULL ADVANTAGE OF THE NEW WAVE AND OPENED ITSELF UP TO NEW AUTHORS SUCH AS BALLARD AND ALDISS, AS WELL AS OTHERS WHO WENT ON TO BECOME FUTURE GREATS, LIKE ROGER ZELAZNY, THOMAS DISCH, NORMAN SPINRAD, HARLAN ELLISON, AND PHILIP K. DICK. IN 1962, SHE ALSO PUBLISHED (IN *FANTASTIC STORIES OF IMAGINATION*) ONE OF THE VERY FIRST WORKS BY URSULA LE GUIN, FUTURE AUTHOR OF *THE LEFT HAND OF DARKNESS*, WINNER OF A NEBULA IN 1969 AND A HUGO IN 1970.

THIRTY TV SERIES THAT LEFT THEIR MARK ON SCI-FI:

BUCK ROGERS, 1979. GENRE: SPACE OPERA.

TALES OF TOMORROW, 1951. ANTHOLOGY SERIES OF FANTASY AND SCIENCE FICTION.

FLASH GORDON, 1954. GENRE: SPACE OPERA.

THE TWILIGHT ZONE, 1959. CULT ANTHOLOGY SERIES.

SPACE PATROL, 1962. GENRE: SPACE OPERA WITH MARIONETTES.

F&SF PREFERRED A MORE DEMANDING, LITERARY BRAND OF SCIENCE FICTION. IN 1963, ROGER ZELAZNY, FUTURE AUTHOR OF THE FANTASY SERIES *THE CHRONICLES OF AMBER*, PUBLISHED HIS STILL-FAMOUS STORY, *A ROSE FOR ECCLESIASTES*, IN WHICH A POLYGLOT POET MADE USE OF HIS LINGUISTIC SKILLS TO SAVE THE DECADENT MARTIAN CIVILIZATION FROM COLLAPSE. SAMUEL DELANY WAS ALSO AN AUTHOR WHO APPLIED HIS BAROQUE STYLE TO WRITING A WONDERFUL LINGUISTIC SCI-FI NOVEL, *BABEL-17*, WHICH WON HIM A NEBULA AWARD.

THE 1960S CAME TO AN END WITH AN EVENT THAT WAS FUNDAMENTAL TO THE SCI-FI COMMUNITY. THE AMERICANS HAD BEEN AT WAR IN VIETNAM SINCE 1955 AND, ESPECIALLY AFTER THE TET OFFENSIVE LAUNCHED IN JANUARY 1968, THE AMERICAN SF COMMUNITY WAS SO DIVIDED THAT IT WAS TORN INTO TWO SEPARATE FACTIONS: THOSE WHO WERE IN FAVOR OF CONTINUING THE VIETNAM WAR, AND THOSE WHO WERE RADICALLY OPPOSED.

OH! WHAT EXACTLY HAPPENED?

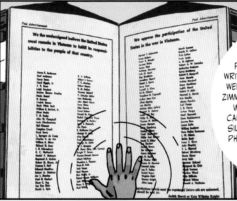

WELL, DEAR HERBERT, IN THE JUNE 1968 ISSUE OF *GALAXY* MAGAZINE, THE CLANS TOOK OUT A WHOLE NEWSPAPER PAGE EACH TO STATE THEIR VIEWS. AMONG THE WRITERS WHO FAVORED PROLONGING THE CONFLICT WERE JOHN W. CAMPBELL, ROBERT HEINLEIN, MARION ZIMMER BRADLEY, JACK VANCE, POUL ANDERSON, JACK WILLIAMSON, AND LARRY NIVEN. IN THE OPPOSING CAMP WERE DAMON KNIGHT, ISAAC ASIMOV, ROBERT SILVERBERG, CAROL EMSHWILLER, URSULA LE GUIN, PHILIP K. DICK, SAMUEL DELANY, AND DANIEL KEYES, WHO HAD PUBLISHED HIS BRILLIANT *FLOWERS FOR ALGERNON* (NEBULA AWARD) TWO YEARS BEFORE.

I WAS ACTIVELY INVOLVED WITH THE SECOND CAMP, AS WAS KATE WILHELM. IT ALL WENT TO SHOW HOW *POLITICAL* SCIENCE FICTION WAS BECOMING.

AND THE NEXT YEAR, IN JULY 1969, ONE MORE MOMENTOUS EVENT OCCURRED: HUMANS WALKED ON THE MOON FOR THE VERY FIRST TIME. "THAT'S ONE SMALL STEP FOR A MAN, ONE GIANT LEAP FOR MANKIND," AS NEIL ARMSTRONG PUT IT!

DOCTOR WHO, 1963. GENRE: TIME TRAVEL.

THUNDERBIRDS, 1965. GENRE: SPACE OPERA WITH MARIONETTES.

STAR TREK, 1966. GENRE: SPACE OPERA.

THE TIME TUNNEL, 1966. GENRE: TIME TRAVEL.

THE INVADERS, 1967. GENRE: "DAVID VINCENT HAS SEEN THEM!"

American female SF writers.

BUT WHILE ONE GIANT LEAP WAS BEING MADE FOR *"MANKIND,"* A GRADUAL REVOLUTION WAS TAKING PLACE FOR *WOMEN* IN THE WORLD OF 1960S' AND 1970S' SCI-FI. IN FACT, AFTER MARY SHELLEY, APART FROM RARE CASES LIKE FRANCIS STEVENS AND CATHERINE LUCILLE MOORE, WOMEN HAD AGAIN FOUND THEMSELVES SIDELINED IN THE GENRE.

THAT'S VERY TRUE. FROM MARY SHELLEY UP TO THE 1960S, WOMEN WERE PRACTICALLY EXCLUDED ALTOGETHER.

BUT WHY DO YOU THINK THAT WAS THE CASE?

PREVIOUSLY, SCIENCE FICTION --ESPECIALLY PULP-MAGAZINE STORIES--WAS A MAN'S GAME IN THE POST-WAR SOCIETY, WHERE WOMEN WERE PRESSURIZED INTO STAYING AT HOME AND TAKING CARE OF THE HOUSEHOLD CHORES!

TO SUPPORT YOUR ARGUMENT, JUDITH, IT'S TRUE, THE BULK OF THE PULP AND GOLDEN-AGE SCI-FI ONLY EVER GLORIFIED *ONE* OF THE SEXES, DEMONSTRATING THIS PURPORTED MALE SUPERIORITY IN THE REALM OF FICTION! WOMEN WERE OFTEN CLICHÉD OBJECTS INTENDED TO FACILITATE THAT GLORIFICATION.

EVEN THOSE STORIES WRITTEN WITH A VENEER OF FEMINISM WERE OFTEN THE WORK OF MEN FANTASIZING ABOUT THEIR OWN IMAGE OF WOMEN. AS A RESULT, STRONG WOMEN WERE PORTRAYED JUST LIKE MEN, WITH CORRESPONDING MASCULINE BEHAVIOR. BUT MOST OF THE TIME, WOMEN WERE DEPICTED AS BIMBOS, WITCHES, OR IRRELEVANT SIDEKICKS...

AND THEN THAT STATE OF AFFAIRS BEGAN TO CHANGE DURING THE 1960S...

THE PRISONER, 1967. GENRES: DYSTOPIA AND ESPIONAGE.

PLANET OF THE APES, 1974. THEME: POST-APOCALYPTIC.

THE SIX MILLION DOLLAR MAN, 1974. INSPIRED BY THE NOVEL *CYBORG* BY MARTIN CAIDIN.

SPACE: 1999, 1975. THEME: EXPLORATION OF SPACE.

MESSAGE FROM SPACE: GALACTIC WARS, 1978. GENRE: *TOKUSATSU* SPACE OPERA (LIVE ACTION WITH SPECIAL EFFECTS).

I HELPED INITIATE THAT CHANGE WITH STORIES LIKE *THAT ONLY A MOTHER* (1948). THEN KATHERINE MACLEAN SOON FOLLOWED SUIT WITH *CONTAGION* (1950), IN WHICH THE WOMEN HAVE TO TAKE OVER CONTROL OF A SHIP WHEN A SICKNESS STARTS TO AFFECT THE MALE CREW MEMBERS.

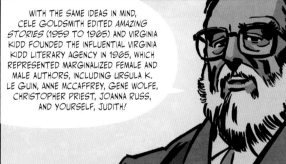

WITH THE SAME IDEAS IN MIND, CELE GOLDSMITH EDITED *AMAZING STORIES* (1959 TO 1965) AND VIRGINIA KIDD FOUNDED THE INFLUENTIAL VIRGINIA KIDD LITERARY AGENCY IN 1965, WHICH REPRESENTED MARGINALIZED FEMALE AND MALE AUTHORS, INCLUDING URSULA K. LE GUIN, ANNE MCCAFFREY, GENE WOLFE, CHRISTOPHER PRIEST, JOANNA RUSS, AND YOURSELF, JUDITH!

WE MADE A GENUINE BREAKTHROUGH IN THE 1960S, WHICH WAS POSSIBLE THANKS TO DEEPER ANALYSIS INTO STYLE, THE EXPLORATION OF INNER SPACES, THE EVOLUTION OF SOCIETIES, THEIR SOCIOLOGY AND PHILOSOPHY, NOT TO MENTION CHARACTER PSYCHOLOGY AND POLITICS, OF COURSE.

HARD SCIENCES AND TECHNOLOGY REMAINED AT THE CORE OF ONE TYPE OF SCIENCE FICTION, BUT CEASED TO BE THE GENRE'S ONLY THEMES...

AUTHORS LIKE SIMAK, WEINBAUM, BRADBURY, AND STURGEON BECAME SOME OF THE VERY FIRST WRITERS TO SET ABOUT DEMOLISHING THE NARROW-MINDED VISIONS OF ONE TYPE OF SF LEFT OVER FROM THE PULPS, OFTEN ANTI-RUSSIAN, ANTI-GERMAN, ANTI-BLACK, AND EVEN ANTI-ALIEN--BECAUSE HOW COULD THEY *POSSIBLY* BE FRIENDLY?!

SO, AGAINST THIS BACKDROP OF REJECTION OF OTHERNESS AND ANYTHING ALIEN, IN TERMS OF SEX, RACE, CULTURE OR SOCIETY, WOMEN GOT TREATED IN A SIMILAR FASHION. ONLY A HANDFUL OF AUTHORS EVER WROTE WORKS THAT FEATURED WOMEN IN THE LEADING ROLES, THEY INCLUDED SEVERAL OF THE GREATS, E.G. ASIMOV'S DR. SUSAN CALVIN, OR THE IMMORTAL MARGARET IN STANLEY G. WEINBAUM'S NOVEL *THE BLACK FLAME*.

AS A RESULT, THE SOCIOLOGICAL SCI-FI OF THE 1960S AND 1970S GAVE WOMEN THE OPPORTUNITY TO RE-EVALUATE THEIR POSITION IN AN EVOLVING GENRE. FROM THEN ON, WOMEN FINALLY BEGAN TO APPEAR IN DEPICTIONS OF FUTURE SOCIETIES--IN BOTH SOCIAL AND POLITICAL ROLES.

V, 1983. THEMES: ALIEN INVASION TO STEAL RESOURCES, THE RESISTANCE.

QUANTUM LEAP, 1989. GENRE: TIME TRAVEL.

THE X-FILES, 1993. THEMES: THE PARANORMAL, ALIENS, CONSPIRACY THEORIES.

BABYLON 5, 1993. GENRE: SPACE OPERA, POLITICAL FICTION.

SLIDERS, 1995. THEME: PARALLEL UNIVERSES.

URSULA LE GUIN EXPLORED THIS NEW RANGE OF ISSUES PERFECTLY. SHE WAS VERY FOND OF THEODORE STURGEON AND PHILIP K. DICK, AND WENT ON TO BECOME A LINCHPIN OF SCI-FI.

WOULD A WORLD GOVERNED BY WOMEN BE A BETTER PLACE? MORE GIVING AND SERENE?

! !

THIS WAS ONE OF THE CENTRAL ISSUES IN HER NOVEL *THE DISPOSSESSED* (1974), WHICH WON THE HAT-TRICK OF HUGO, LOCUS, AND NEBULA AWARDS AND FEATURED TWO OPPOSING SOCIAL CONCEPTS. IT WAS ALSO FUNDAMENTAL IN *THE LEFT HAND OF DARKNESS* (NEBULA AWARD 1969 AND HUGO 1970), WITH ITS SUBTLY FEMINIST MESSAGE COUPLED WITH CONTEMPLATIONS ON SEXUALITY, WHICH PORTRAYED AN ANDROGYNOUS HUMANITY CAPABLE OF PHYSICALLY TAKING ON THE ATTRIBUTES OF EITHER ONE OF THE SEXES.

IN THAT *HAINISH CYCLE*, CIVILIZATION IS MADE POSSIBLE BY AN INVENTION CALLED THE ANSIBLE, A DEVICE WHICH ALLOWS FASTER-THAN-LIGHT COMMUNICATION. IT WAS LATER BORROWED BY OTHER GREAT AUTHORS, E.G. IN ORSON SCOTT CARD'S *ENDER'S GAME* SERIES, THE *HYPERION CANTOS* BY DAN SIMMONS, AND PHILIP PULLMAN'S *HIS DARK MATERIALS* TRILOGY.

SO, THANKS TO URSULA LE GUIN IN PARTICULAR, SCIENCE FICTION WRITTEN BY WOMEN WAS ABLE TO BREAK AWAY FROM CLICHÉD FEMALE STEREOTYPES.

ABSOLUTELY. FOR EXAMPLE, ONE OF SCI-FI'S MOST ARDENT FEMINISTS, JOANNA RUSS (WHO ALSO AUTHORED SEVERAL MAJOR ESSAYS ON WOMEN IN THE SCIENCE-FICTION FIELD), WISHED TO DEMONSTRATE THAT DIFFERENCES BETWEEN WOMEN AND MEN ONLY EVER AROSE DUE TO EDUCATIONAL CONDITIONING.

YOU MEAN THAT EDUCATION COULD IMPEDE WOMEN'S CREATIVITY OR NIP IT IN THE BUD?

YES. FEMININITY IS A PURELY *SOCIAL INVENTION*.

STARGATE SG-1, 1997. THEMES: SPACE EXPLORATION, MILITARY SCI-FI, ALIENS.

FARSCAPE, 1999. GENRE: SPACE OPERA.

FIREFLY, 2002. GENRE: SPACE WESTERN!

BATTLESTAR GALACTICA, 2004. GENRE: REBOOT OF THE ORIGINAL 1978 SPACE-OPERA SERIES.

FRINGE, 2008. GENRE: PARALLEL UNIVERSES.

HOW'S THAT?

TAKE A LOOK AT THE STORIES WRITTEN BY WOMEN. THEY ARE CRITICIZED IF THE HEROINES CONFORM TO A TEMPLATE STANDARDIZED BY MEN. AND THE SAME CAN BE SAID IF THE HEROINES SEEK TO INNOVATE AND GET OUT OF THESE STANDARDS. IT'S THAT SIMPLE.

I SEE...

TO ANOTHER IMPORTANT FEMALE WRITER, PAMELA SARGENT (WHO GAVE US THE MANIFESTO *WOMEN OF WONDER*, IN 1975, AS WELL AS THE PIONEERING FEMINIST SCI-FI NOVEL *THE SHORE OF WOMEN*, 1986), SCIENCE FICTION WAS VOLUNTARILY DISCRIMINATORY IN NATURE, DUE TO THE POST-WAR SOCIAL PRESSURE I MENTIONED.

SO, ACCORDINGLY, IT WAS THE ROLE OF WOMEN TO ACT AS A COUNTERPOINT TO ALL OF SCI-FI'S MILITARISTIC, MONARCHIC, CAPITALIST, OR EVEN PRIMITIVE SOCIETIES.

SOCIETIES WHICH, AS A GENERAL RULE, WERE PREDOMINANTLY UNAPPEALING TO WOMEN. FORTUNATELY, EVEN THOSE KINDS OF SOCIETAL MODELS WERE EXPLORED, AND THE FIELD WAS SUCCESSFULLY APPROPRIATED DURING THE 1980S AND 1990S BY FEMALE AUTHORS LIKE CAROLYN JANICE CHERRYH (*DOWNBELOW STATION*, 1981) AND LOIS MCMASTER BUJOLD (*BARRAYAR*, 1991).

AFTER ALL, IF SCIENCE FICTION WAS TO BE TAKEN SERIOUSLY, THEN IT HAD TO INCLUDE MORE CONTRIBUTIONS FROM WOMEN AND MINORITIES. BECAUSE WHEN WOMEN FINALLY SECURED THEIR HARD-FOUGHT PLACE IN SCIENCE FICTION AT SOME POINT DURING THE 2010-2020S, THIS MAJOR BREAKTHROUGH PAVED THE WAY FOR OTHER ETHNIC AND SEXUAL MINORITIES TO GET INVOLVED AT LONG LAST (IN THE UNITED STATES, AT LEAST)...

PERSON OF INTEREST, 2011. THEMES: ARTIFICIAL INTELLIGENCE, TECHNOLOGICAL SINGULARITY.

BLACK MIRROR, 2011. GENRE: DYSTOPIAN ANTHOLOGY SERIES.

REAL HUMANS, 2012. THEME: ROBOTICS.

THE HANDMAID'S TALE, 2017. GENRE: DYSTOPIA. THEME: FEMINISM.

DARK, 2017. GENRE: TIME TRAVEL.

ROD, DO YOU THINK YOU COULD BRIEFLY TRANSPORT US TO THE APARTMENT OF *REBECCA F. KUANG*, DURING THE FIRST VIRTUAL HUGO AND ASTOUNDING AWARDS CEREMONY? IN CONCLUSION, I'D LIKE MR. WELLS TO LISTEN TO HER SPEECH TO HELP HIM GRASP THE STATE OF PLAY IN SCIENCE FICTION IN 2020.

NO SOONER SAID THAN DONE!

...THE ASTOUNDING AWARD IS THE AWARD FOR THE BEST NEW WRITER. BUT IF I WERE TALKING TO A NEW WRITER COMING TO THE GENRE IN 2020, I WOULD TELL THEM: "WELL, IF YOU ARE AN AUTHOR OF COLOR, YOU WILL VERY LIKELY BE PAID ONLY A FRACTION OF THE ADVANCE THAT WHITE WRITERS ARE GETTING...

"YOU WILL BE PIGEONHOLED, YOU WILL BE MISCATEGORIZED, YOU WILL BE LUMPED IN WITH OTHER AUTHORS OF COLOR WHOSE WORK DOESN'T REMOTELY RESEMBLE YOURS. THE CHANCES ARE VERY HIGH THAT YOU WILL BE SEXUALLY HARASSED AT CONVENTIONS, OR THE TARGET OF RACIST MICROAGGRESSIONS, OR VERY OFTEN JUST OVERT RACISM. PEOPLE WILL MISPRONOUNCE YOUR NAME REPEATEDLY, AND IN PUBLIC, EVEN PEOPLE WHO ARE ON YOUR PUBLISHING TEAM!

"AND THE WAY PEOPLE TALK ABOUT YOU AND YOUR LITERATURE WILL BE TIED TO YOUR IDENTITY AND YOUR PERSONAL TRAUMA INSTEAD OF THE STORIES YOU ARE ACTUALLY TRYING TO TELL. AND IF I HAD KNOWN ALL OF THAT WHEN I WENT INTO THE INDUSTRY, I DON'T KNOW IF I WOULD HAVE DONE IT. SO I THINK THAT THE BEST WAY THAT WE CAN CELEBRATE NEW WRITERS IS TO MAKE THIS INDUSTRY MORE WELCOMING FOR EVERYONE!"

ANYWAY, TO SUM UP THIS GRADUAL REVOLUTION, ROD, CAN YOU PRODUCE A GENEALOGICAL CHART OF THE EVOLUTION OF ENGLISH-LANGUAGE WOMEN SF WRITERS, EVEN IF IT'S INCOMPLETE?

CERTAINLY, MS. MERRIL.

TEN CULT ANIME SERIES:

ASTRO BOY, 1963. THE FIRST WEEKLY JAPANESE ANIMATION.

UFO ROBO GRENDIZER, 1975. JAPAN'S BIGGEST CULT ROBOT IN FRANCE, ANCESTOR OF THE "MECHAS".

SPACE PIRATE CAPTAIN HARLOCK, 1978. THE KING OF ALL SPACE PIRATES?

CAPTAIN FUTURE, 1978. ADAPTED FROM THE NOVELS BY EDMOND HAMILTON.

ULYSSES 31, 1981. HOMER'S ODYSSEY IN SCI-FI STYLE!

MARY SHELLEY INVENTED SCIENCE FICTION.

CATHERINE LUCILLE MOORE CREATED THE JIREL OF JOIRY CHARACTER.

GERTRUDE BARROWS BENNETT WROTE *FRIEND ISLAND* (1918), WHERE THE WOMEN ARE SUPERIOR TO THE MEN.

EDNA MAYNE HULL WROTE WITH HER HUSBAND, ALFRED ELTON VAN VOGT.

VIRGINIA KIDD SET UP A LITERARY AGENCY TO REPRESENT WOMEN SCIENCE-FICTION WRITERS.

LEIGH BRACKETT WROTE FOR THE PULPS, AS WELL AS MOVIE SCRIPTS.

CELE GOLDSMITH EDITOR-IN-CHIEF OF *AMAZING STORIES*, PUBLISHED URSULA LE GUIN.

JUDITH MERRIL PUBLISHED FEMINIST SF STORY *SURVIVAL SHIP* IN 1951.

KATHERINE MACLEAN WROTE HARD SF WHEN IT WAS A MALE-DOMINATED GENRE.

MARION ZIMMER BRADLEY WROTE SCIENCE FANTASY AND THE *DARKOVER* SERIES. HELPED EMERGING WRITERS, E.G. MERCEDES LACKEY.

ZENNA HENDERSON *PILGRIMAGE: THE BOOK OF THE PEOPLE*, 1961. SHE IS OFTEN COMPARED TO CLIFFORD D. SIMAK.

CAROL EMSHWILLER URSULA LE GUIN DESCRIBED HER AS "ONE OF THE STRONGEST, MOST COMPLEX, MOST CONSISTENTLY FEMINIST VOICES IN FICTION".

JOANNA RUSS PUBLISHED ESSAYS ON WOMEN IN SCI-FI.

ANNE MCCAFFREY WROTE *THE DRAGON-RIDERS OF PERN*.

URSULA LE GUIN THE TRUE *GRANDE DAME* OF SF? FOR SURE! SIMPLY A MUST-READ!

ALICE SHELDON ACTIVE FROM THE 1960S TO THE 1980S, AND PUBLISHED UNDER THE PEN NAME OF JAMES TIPTREE, JR.

KATE WILHELM AN AUTHOR OF MAJOR IMPORTANCE TO SCIENCE FICTION. WON MANY AWARDS AND WAS FAMOUS FOR HER NOVEL *JUNIPER TIME*.

PAT CADIGAN CYBERPUNK AUTHOR OF *SYNNERS*, PUBLISHED IN 1991.

JOAN D. VINGE BEST KNOWN FOR HER WORKS *EYES OF AMBER* (1979) AND *PSION* (1982).

OCTAVIA BUTLER ONE OF THE PIONEERS OF AFROFUTURISM, WITH A FOCUS ON MINORITIES. READ *PARABLE OF THE SOWER* (1993).

CAROLYN JANICE CHERRYH WON THREE HUGO AWARDS. REVITALIZED SPACE OPERA WITH *DOWNBELOW STATION* (1981).

CONNIE WILLIS TIME-TRAVEL VIRTUOSO. READ *TO SAY NOTHING OF THE DOG* (1997).

NANCY KRESS HARD SF, ESPECIALLY CONCERNING GENETIC ENGINEERING. READ *MAXIMUM LIGHT* (1998).

MARGARET ATWOOD RENOWNED AUTHOR OF *THE HANDMAID'S TALE* (1985) AND *ORYX AND CRAKE* (2003).

LOIS MCMASTER BUJOLD READ THE *VORKOSIGAN SAGA*, AN INGENIOUS SPACE-OPERA SERIES.

KRISTINE KATHRYN RUSCH A TERRIFIC, MULTI-AWARD-WINNING NOVELIST.

LINDA NAGATA *LIMIT OF VISION*, 2001.

KAREN TRAVISS *CITY OF PEARL*, 2004.

ELIZABETH MOON *SPEED OF DARK*, 2002.

NNEDI OKORAFOR *WHO FEARS DEATH*, 2010.

BECKY CHAMBERS *THE LONG WAY TO A SMALL, ANGRY PLANET*, 2015.

JEANNETTE NG *UNDER THE PENDULUM SUN*, 2017.

KAMERON HURLEY *THE STARS ARE LEGION*, 2017.

RIVERS SOLOMON *AN UNKINDNESS OF GHOSTS*, 2017.

N. K. JEMISIN THE *BROKEN EARTH* TRILOGY, 2015.

AND THAT'S BUT A PARTIAL LIST? REMARKABLE.

WE HAD SOME CATCHING UP TO DO, HERBERT.

UNDERSTOOD. SO MANY NEW VOICES, SO MANY NEW POINTS OF VIEW...

THE GENRE CONTINUED TO EVOLVE. THE NEW WAVE HAD BROUGHT WITH IT NEW WAYS OF WRITING, READING, AND EVEN THINKING ABOUT SCIENCE FICTION.

ITS BOUNDARIES WERE EXPANDING. PERSPECTIVES WERE SHIFTING.

AS WITH J. G. BALLARD, WHOSE INTROSPECTIVE APPROACH FAVORED THE PSYCHOLOGICAL EFFECTS OF SOCIAL OR TECHNOLOGICAL DEVELOPMENTS, WHICH HE FOUND FAR MORE INTERESTING THAN THEIR MATERIAL CONSEQUENCES.

HOWEVER, WITH THE NEW WAVE WANING AND THE LARGER-SCALE PRINT RUNS OF THE NOVELS, CRITICS OFTEN CLAIMED THAT SF AUTHORS WERE LOSING SOME OF THEIR AMBITION, FAVORING COMMERCIAL WORK OVER ORIGINAL IDEAS.

WHILE SAMUEL DELANY STAYED TRUE TO HIS SPIRIT, ESPECIALLY WITH HIS CULT WORK DHALGREN, OTHERS--LIKE ZELAZNY WITH HIS LATER BOOKS--WERE ACCUSED BY CRITICS OF PANDERING TO MAINSTREAM AUDIENCES NONETHELESS, ZELAZNY'S INFLUENCE ON HIS SUCCESSORS WAS HEAVILY FELT.

SPACE ADVENTURE COBRA, 1982. AN ADVENTURER INSPIRED BY FRENCH ACTOR JEAN-PAUL BELMONDO.

JAYCE AND THE WHEELED WARRIORS, 1985. THEME: ALIEN PLANETS.

SPARTAKUS AND THE SUN BENEATH THE SEA, 1985. THEME: HOLLOW EARTH.

BATMAN: THE ANIMATED SERIES, 1992. GENRE: SUPERHEROES.

SPACE GOOFS, 1997. GENRE: COMEDY.

CERTAIN SUBGENRES OF SCIENCE FICTION FOUND RENEWAL. THROUGHOUT THE 1970S, SPACE OPERA--OR, MORE SPECIFICALLY, MILITARY SPACE OPERA--RE-EMERGED IN THE WORKS OF VIETNAM WAR VETERANS WHO FOUND THEIR COMBAT EXPERIENCE A GREAT SOURCE OF INSPIRATION.

DAVID DRAKE, AUTHOR OF THE *HAMMER'S SLAMMERS* SERIES, WAS ONE. HE CLAIMED THAT HE WROTE TO EDUCATE VOTERS AND POLICYMAKERS ABOUT THE HORRORS AND FUTILITY OF WAR.

IN 1974, VETERAN JOE HALDEMAN PUBLISHED THE FOREVER WAR...

...A NATURAL PROGRESSION OF THE WORKS OF HEINLEIN-- BUT WITH A TWIST.

IN THIS POWERFUL NOVEL, THE SOLDIER MANDELLA IS ENGAGED IN A WAR AGAINST THE TAURANS, AN ALIEN SPECIES THAT NO ONE HAS EVER OBSERVED BUT WHICH REGULARLY DESTROYS SHIPS FROM EARTH.

HALDEMAN WAS INSPIRED, IN PART, BY *STARSHIP TROOPERS*, BUT MOSTLY BY HIS OWN MILITARY SERVICE.

WHAT'S NOTEWORTHY IS THAT THE MESSAGES OF THE TWO NOVELS ARE DIAMETRICALLY OPPOSED. *THE FOREVER WAR*, WHICH IS NOT ANTI- MILITARIST, IS NEVERTHELESS A STORY THAT REFUSES TO DEPICT WAR AS A NOBLE PURSUIT.

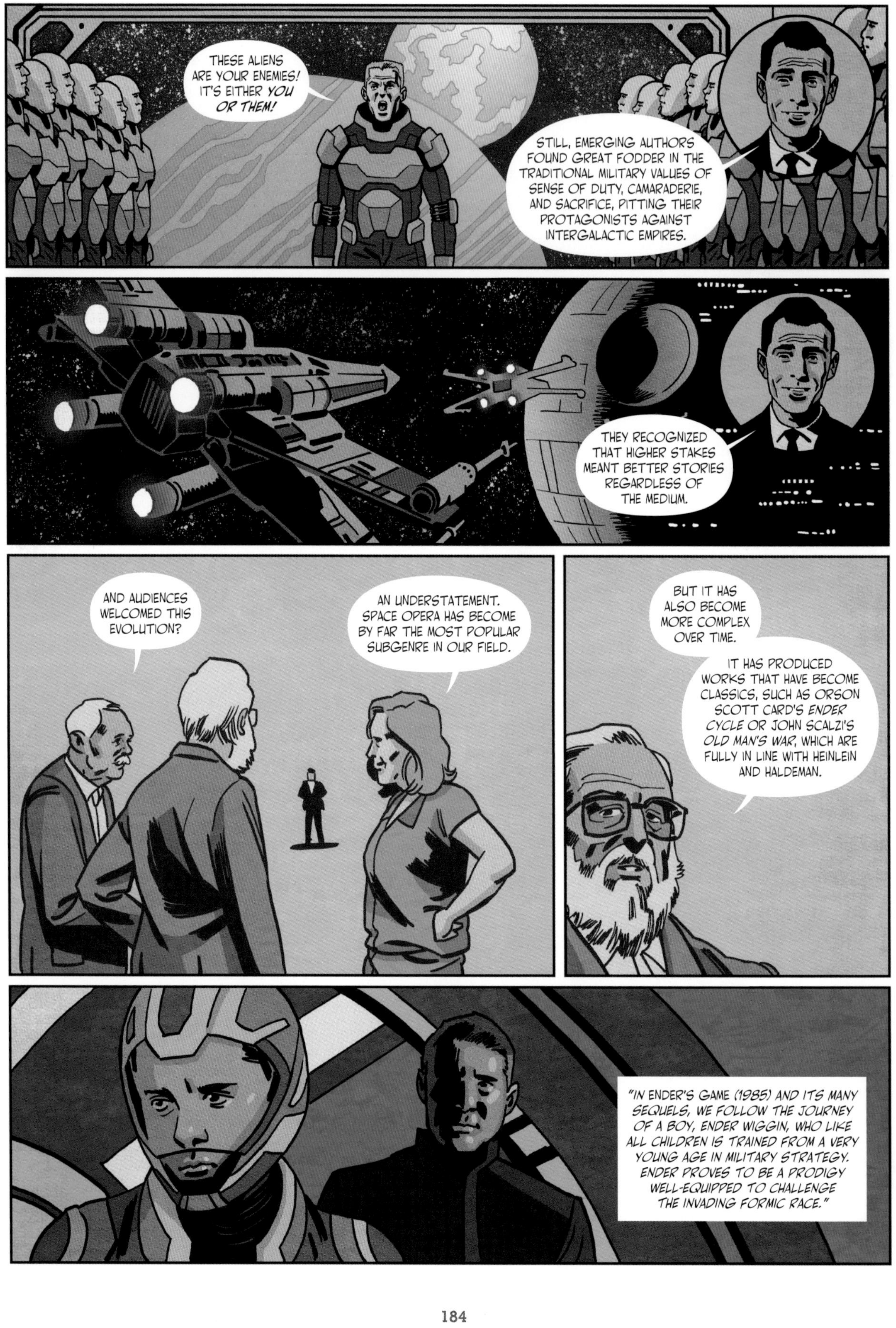
THESE ALIENS ARE YOUR ENEMIES! IT'S EITHER *YOU OR THEM!*
STILL, EMERGING AUTHORS FOUND GREAT FODDER IN THE TRADITIONAL MILITARY VALUES OF SENSE OF DUTY, CAMARADERIE, AND SACRIFICE, PITTING THEIR PROTAGONISTS AGAINST INTERGALACTIC EMPIRES.
THEY RECOGNIZED THAT HIGHER STAKES MEANT BETTER STORIES REGARDLESS OF THE MEDIUM.
AND AUDIENCES WELCOMED THIS EVOLUTION?
AN UNDERSTATEMENT. SPACE OPERA HAS BECOME BY FAR THE MOST POPULAR SUBGENRE IN OUR FIELD.
BUT IT HAS ALSO BECOME MORE COMPLEX OVER TIME.
IT HAS PRODUCED WORKS THAT HAVE BECOME CLASSICS, SUCH AS ORSON SCOTT CARD'S *ENDER CYCLE* OR JOHN SCALZI'S *OLD MAN'S WAR*, WHICH ARE FULLY IN LINE WITH HEINLEIN AND HALDEMAN.
"IN ENDER'S GAME (1985) AND ITS MANY SEQUELS, WE FOLLOW THE JOURNEY OF A BOY, ENDER WIGGIN, WHO LIKE ALL CHILDREN IS TRAINED FROM A VERY YOUNG AGE IN MILITARY STRATEGY. ENDER PROVES TO BE A PRODIGY WELL-EQUIPPED TO CHALLENGE THE INVADING FORMIC RACE."

JOHN SCALZI'S *OLD MAN'S WAR* WAS A 2006 HUGO AWARD FINALIST.

IT TELLS OF A 75-YEAR-OLD MAN, JOHN PERRY, WHO ENLISTS IN THE COLONIAL DEFENSE FORCES IN ORDER TO HAVE HIS CONSCIOUSNESS TRANSFERRED INTO A CLONE OF HIS YOUNGER BODY.

SCALZI WON THE HUGO IN 2013 WITH *REDSHIRTS*, A HUMOROUS SPACE OPERA THAT POKES AFFECTIONATE FUN AT TV SERIES SUCH AS *STAR TREK* AND *STARGATE*. CARD, FOR HIS EFFORTS, WON THE HUGO FOR BEST NOVEL IN 1986 FOR *ENDER'S GAME*.

HE WOULD WIN AGAIN THE NEXT YEAR FOR ITS SEQUEL, *SPEAKER FOR THE DEAD*. IN FACT, THE MAJORITY OF THE NOVELS AWARDED THE HUGO DURING THE 1980S AND 1990S, INCLUDING *HYPERION* (DAN SIMMONS), *THE UPLIFT WAR* (DAVID BRIN), *DOWNBELOW STATION* (C. J. CHERRYH), *A FIRE UPON THE DEEP* (VERNOR VINGE) AND *THE VOR GAME* (LOIS MCMASTER BUJOLD), COULD BE CLASSIFIED AS SPACE OPERA...

...AS COULD NEBULA WINNERS *STARTIDE RISING* (BRIN), *FALLING FREE* (BUJOLD), AND *FOREVER PEACE* (HALDEMAN). AS THE NEW CENTURY DAWNED, LET US NOT FORGET...

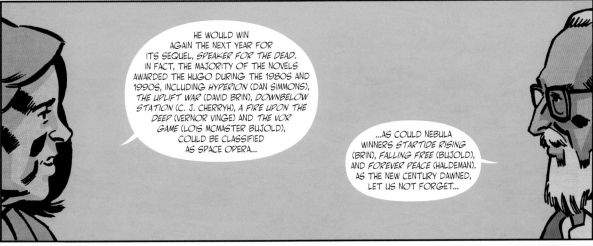

"...WRITER DAVID WEBER AND HIS HEROINE HONOR HARRINGTON..."

DAVID WEBER

JACK CAMPBELL

DAVID GUNN

"...JACK CAMPBELL AND HIS LOST FLEET SERIES..."

"...AND DAVID GUNN, WRITER OF THE IMPACTFUL *DEATH'S HEAD* AND ITS SEQUELS."

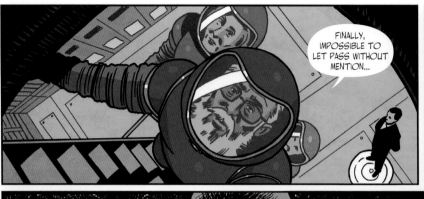

FINALLY, IMPOSSIBLE TO LET PASS WITHOUT MENTION...

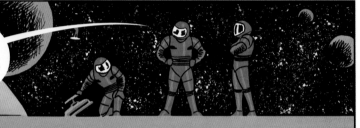

...THE VERY SUCCESSFUL SERIES OF NOVELS *THE EXPANSE*, BY DANIEL ABRAHAM AND TY FRANCK, WRITING UNDER THE JOINT PEN NAME JAMES S. A. COREY, WHICH HAS FOUND GREAT SUCCESS ADAPTED FOR TELEVISION.

"IN THIS SERIES, HUMANS HAVE COLONIZED THE SOLAR SYSTEM BY THE 24TH CENTURY, BUT THE RELATIONSHIP BETWEEN EARTH, MARS AND THE OUTER PLANETS HANGS IN PRECARIOUS BALANCE.

"THE EXPANSE FOLLOWS THE CREW OF THE SPACE FRIGATE ROCINANTE AND OTHERS AS THEY UNWITTINGLY PLACE THEMSELVES AT THE CENTER OF A VAST POLITICAL AND MILITARY CONSPIRACY."

AMERICAN AUTHORS, BY AND LARGE, CLING TO THE TRADITIONS OF OPTIMISM TOWARDS SCIENCE, THE EVOLUTION OF HUMANITY, AND PROGRESS.

BALLARD, ON THE OTHER HAND, THOUGHT OF THE FUTURE OF HUMANITY AS AN INEVITABLE DEVOLUTION, AS EXEMPLIFIED IN HIS SHORT STORY *THE VOICES OF TIME* (1960).

HOW VERY BRITISH!

MEANWHILE, THE OLDER GENERATIONS STAYED CONTEMPORARY BY ADAPTING THEIR STYLES, DRAWING ON NEW WAVE OR CUTTING-EDGE AUTHORS LIKE URSULA K. LE GUIN.

FOR EXAMPLES, WE NEED LOOK NO FURTHER THAN FREDERIK POHL WITH *GATEWAY* (1977), OR TO THE NOBEL PRIZE WINNER DORIS LESSING AND HER *CANOPUS IN ARGOS: ARCHIVES*, A SERIES OF NOVELS BEGUN IN 1979 AND FINISHED IN 1983.

OTHERS STAYED TRUE TO THEIR OWN MUSE, TAKING ADVANTAGE OF THEIR SUCCESS IN ORDER TO CONTINUE AND CONCLUDE THEIR SIGNATURE SERIES...

...INCLUDING ASIMOV WITH *FOUNDATION* AND FRANK HERBERT WITH *DUNE*.

SOME FOCUSED ON "HARD SCIENCE FICTION," CHARACTERIZED BY A CONCERN FOR SCIENTIFIC ACCURACY.

GREGORY BENFORD IS AN ASTROPHYSICIST WHOSE WORKS REFLECT THE RESEARCH HE DOES AS A PRACTICAL SCIENTIST. BENFORD'S CROWNING ACHIEVEMENT IN THE FIELD WAS INARGUABLY HIS 1980 NOVEL *TIMESCAPE*, WRITTEN WITH THE ASSISTANCE OF HIS SISTER-IN-LAW, HILARY FOISTER. *TIMESCAPE* CONNECTS A 1998 RAVAGED BY ECOLOGICAL DISASTERS WITH SCIENTISTS FROM THE 1960S WHO DECIPHER THEIR FUTURE'S TACHYON-BORNE WARNINGS. BENFORD'S REAL-WORLD CONTRIBUTIONS TO SCIENCE ARE NUMEROUS AND LEGENDARY.

GREG BEAR MADE A NAME FOR HIMSELF WITH HIS *THE WAY* TRILOGY (1985-1994), IN WHICH A MYSTERIOUS ASTEROID SETTLES INTO ORBIT AROUND THE EARTH, HEIGHTENING INTERNATIONAL TENSIONS. BEAR'S WORK OFTEN EXAMINES AND OFFERS ANSWERS TO CONTEMPORARY PROBLEMS IN CULTURE AND SCIENCE. HE WON THE HUGO AND NEBULA FOR 1983'S *BLOOD MUSIC*, SOMETIMES CREDITED AS THE FIRST ACCOUNT OF NANOTECHNOLOGY IN SCIENCE FICTION. BEAR WAS ALSO ONE OF THE CO-FOUNDERS OF THE ANNUAL SAN DIEGO COMIC-CON, WHICH CELEBRATES SCIENCE FICTION AND FANTASY ACROSS ALL MEDIA.

AS FOR KIM STANLEY ROBINSON, PERHAPS THE MOST FAMOUS OF THE THREE, HIS WORK OFTEN EXPLORES ECONOMIC AND SOCIAL JUSTICE, NATURE, AND ECOLOGICAL SUSTAINABILITY. HIS MANY AWARD-WINNING WORKS INCLUDE *THE BLIND GEOMETER* (1986) AND *THE YEARS OF RICE AND SALT* (2002), BUT HE IS BEST KNOWN FOR HIS *MARS* TRILOGY, TRANSLATED INTO OVER A DOZEN LANGUAGES. *RED MARS*, *GREEN MARS*, AND *BLUE MARS* TELL THE STORY OF EARTH'S COLONIZATION OF THE FIFTH PLANET, BEGINNING WITH A SMALL INTERNATIONAL EXPEDITION IN 2026 AND ENDING WITH THE FULL TERRAFORMATION OF MARS TWO CENTURIES LATER.

AUTHORS SUCH AS THESE THREE PAVED THE WAY FOR OTHER HARD SF WRITERS, LIKE STEPHEN BAXTER OR GREG EGAN, THE ENIGMATIC AUSTRALIAN AUTHOR AND GLOBAL FLAG-BEARER OF HARD SF. THE FIELD IS BROADENING.

THOUGH THERE IS STILL MUCH PROGRESS TO BE MADE AS OF THE 2020S, MORE BIPOC AND LGBTQIA VOICES ARE BEING HEARD IN SCIENCE FICTION AS WELL, OFTEN ASKING THE QUESTION "SUPPOSE THE INDIGNITIES KNOWN ALL TOO WELL TO THE MARGINALIZED HAPPENED TO PEOPLE IN POWER?" KEN LIU (*THE PAPER MENAGERIE*), TADE THOMPSON (*ROSEWATER*), AND FERNANDO FLORES (*TEARS OF THE TRUFFLEPIG*) ARE BUT THREE OF THOSE TORCH-BEARERS...

Cyberpunk--the last great revolution in science fiction?

...CHARLIE JANE ANDERS, V. E. SCHWAB, YOON HA LEE, AND MORE... ALL SIGNIFICANT.

AND THEN THERE ARE MORE RECENTLY EMERGENT TALENTS OF DISPARATE CULTURAL BACKGROUNDS WHO ARE FORGING A CONSIDERABLE LEGACY, SUCH AS TED CHIANG (*STORIES OF YOUR LIFE AND OTHERS*), RIVERS SOLOMON (*AN UNKINDNESS OF GHOSTS*), AND REBECCA ROANHORSE (*BLACK SUN*), TO NAME BUT A FEW.

EXTENSIVE DIVERSITY IN THE FIELD IS A DEVELOPMENT STILL IN PROCESS BUT AGGRESSIVELY OVERDUE. WITHOUT FRESH PERSPECTIVES, SCIENCE FICTION RISKS A DANGEROUS OSSIFICATION.

BEFORE THIS, DEAR JUDITH, YOU WERE TALKING ABOUT ANOTHER GREAT REVOLUTION...?

POSSIBLY THE LAST GREAT REVOLUTION IN SCIENCE FICTION, AND IT WAS VERY HIGH-TECH. I WAS REFERRING TO "CYBERPUNK" OF COURSE. I PRESUME ROD WILL BE ABLE TO TAKE US INTO "CYBERSPACE!"

INTO WHAT?

FOLLOW ME, AND YOU'LL SEE...

ALRIGHT, SO HERE WE ARE IN THE 1980S. A MAJOR SCIENCE-FICTION AUTHOR INVENTED THE TERM "CYBERSPACE" WHILE WATCHING THE KIDS IMMERSED IN THEIR ARCADE GAMES, THEN WENT ON TO ELABORATE THE CONCEPT OVER SEVERAL OF HIS SHORT STORIES.

William Gibson

Fragments of a Hologram Rose

Johnny Mnemonic

Burning Chrome

CYBERPUNK IS A MOVEMENT WHICH BEGAN TO CRYSTALLIZE IN THE LATE 1970S AND THE EARLY 1980S. IT WAS CENTERED AROUND A FEW ATYPICAL WRITERS, SOME OF WHOM TOOK INSPIRATION FROM VARIOUS THEMES PRESENTED BY AUTHORS SUCH AS DICK, BALLARD, BRUNNER, SPINRAD, AND YOU, MICHAEL...

YES, IT WAS THE NEXT LOGICAL WAY TO TURN, THOUGH THE BRAINS BEHIND THE MOVEMENT WAS ACTUALLY NOT GIBSON HIMSELF BUT THE WRITER BRUCE STERLING, WHO PUBLISHED A FANZINE TITLED *CHEAP TRUTH* AT THE START OF THE 1980S. IT FIRST MENTIONED A "MOVEMENT" MOCKING THE STAGNANT SCI-FI SCENE; A MOVEMENT THAT WAS YET TO BE BAPTIZED "CYBERPUNK..."

THE WRITERS WERE INTERESTED IN CYBERNETICS AND VIRTUAL REALITY, AS WELL AS GRIM, SOMBER MEGALOPOLISES AND ULTRA-LIBERAL CAPITALISTIC CYNICISM. GIBSON BECAME THE HIGH PRIEST OF THE NEW GENRE.

BUT HE WASN'T THE ONE WHO CAME UP WITH THE TERM CYBERPUNK. IT WAS THE TITLE OF A SHORT STORY BY BRUCE BETHKE FROM 1983. THE WORD WAS LATER POPULARIZED BY THE WRITER GARDNER DOZOIS IN A SERIES OF ARTICLES HE WROTE TO FORMALIZE THIS NEW MOVEMENT THAT WAS FAST BECOMING A PHENOMENON!

FIVE MAJOR CYBERPUNK BOOKS:

NEUROMANCER, WILLIAM GIBSON, 1984.

MIRRORSHADES: THE CYBERPUNK ANTHOLOGY, ED. BRUCE STERLING, 1986.

HARDWIRED, WALTER JON WILLIAMS, 1986.

SNOW CRASH, NEAL STEPHENSON, 1992.

SCHISMATRIX PLUS, BRUCE STERLING, 1996.

NONE OF THE ISSUES SURROUNDING CYBERNETICS AND VIRTUALITY WERE EXACTLY NEW, OF COURSE, AS PROVEN BY NOVELS SUCH AS MARTIN CAIDIN'S *CYBORG* (1972) AND, BEFORE THAT, *SIMULACRON-3* BY DANIEL GALOUYE (1964). THE FORMER WAS THE BASIS FOR THE SERIES *THE SIX MILLION DOLLAR MAN*, WHILE THE LATTER WAS A DISTANT ANCESTOR OF THE FILM *THE MATRIX*. BUT, AS FOR CYBERPUNK...

CYBERPUNK IS THE REALM WHERE THE COMPUTER HACKER AND THE ROCKER OVERLAP.

AND CYBERPUNK IS ALSO AN AESTHETIC THAT GIBSON WAS INSTRUMENTAL IN DEFINING. HE WAS HIGHLY SKILLED AT DREAMING UP AUDACIOUS, BUT NOT EXACTLY ACADEMIC, COMPUTER CONCEPTS THAT PLAYED OUT IN A POP-CULTURE-INSPIRED DÉCOR FEATURING THE MAFIA, PUNKS AND DRUGS IN AN ERA OF INFORMATION OVERLOAD.

THEN, IN 1984, WILLIAM GIBSON WROTE *NEUROMANCER*, A NOVEL COMMISSIONED BY THE EDITOR TERRY CARR. IT TYPIFIED HIS STYLE, CRAMMED WITH NEOLOGISMS, SLANG, AND STARK IMAGES. CLOAKED IN A PLOT STRAIGHT OUT OF A DASHIELL HAMMETT-STYLE HARDBOILED DETECTIVE NOVEL. IN A SOCIETY CONTROLLED BY INFORMATION AND VIRTUAL REALITY, GANGSTERS LAY DOWN THE LAW, WHETHER THEY COME FROM THE DREGS OF SOCIETY OR THE MEGA-CORPORATIONS THAT TOOK OVER THE WORLD WHEN GOVERNMENTS ALL COLLAPSED.

GIBSON HAD A WIDE SPECTRUM OF INFLUENCES, INCLUDING THOMAS PYNCHON (*GRAVITY'S RAINBOW*), ALFRED BESTER, AND WILLIAM BURROUGHS, WHOSE WORK TRULY IMPRESSED HIM.

AND SOME FRENCH CULTURE, TOO. JUST AS IT HAD LEFT ITS IMPRINT ON THE NEW WAVE, *MÉTAL HURLANT* MAGAZINE (AND ITS AMERICAN COUNTERPART *HEAVY METAL*) ALSO INFLUENCED CYBERPUNK (THE UBIQUITOUS ORIENTALIST AESTHETIC), NOT TO MENTION RIDLEY SCOTT'S *BLADE RUNNER* AND ITS BLEAK VISIONS OF URBAN DECAY...

GIBSON PUBLISHED TWO SEQUELS TO *NEUROMANCER*: *COUNT ZERO* AND *MONA LISA OVERDRIVE*. ALL THE BEST-KNOWN CYBERPUNK WORKS BY STERLING, STEPHENSON, WILLIAMS, AND CADIGAN WERE PUBLISHED IN THE AFTERMATH OF *NEUROMANCER'S* IMMENSE SUCCESS. THE ADVENT OF THIS NEW BRANCH OF SCIENCE FICTION WENT ON TO UTTERLY CHANGE THE VERY FACE OF THE GENRE.

SO, CYBERPUNK WAS A REAL TURNING POINT?

CYBERPUNK ALLOWED SCIENCE FICTION TO SHIFT INTO THE INFORMATION AGE OF COMPUTER TECH AND NETWORKING. IT ALSO OPENED UP THE PROSPECT OF VIRTUAL INNER WORLDS WHERE ANYTHING CAN HAPPEN, LIKE THE TECHNOLOGICAL SINGULARITY FORESEEN BY VERNOR VINGE.

TECHNOLOGICAL SINGULARITY? WHAT'S THAT?

THE UNCONTROLLABLE ADVANCE OF COMPUTER TECHNOLOGY WILL EVENTUALLY LEAD TO A CYCLE WHICH RESULTS IN A SUPER-INTELLIGENCE THAT SURPASSES ALL HUMAN ABILITIES.

AND HUMANITY WILL LOSE ITS DOMINANT POSITION?

ABSOLUTELY...

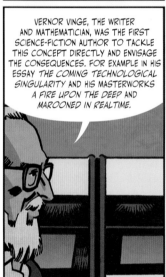

VERNOR VINGE, THE WRITER AND MATHEMATICIAN, WAS THE FIRST SCIENCE-FICTION AUTHOR TO TACKLE THIS CONCEPT DIRECTLY AND ENVISAGE THE CONSEQUENCES. FOR EXAMPLE IN HIS ESSAY *THE COMING TECHNOLOGICAL SINGULARITY* AND HIS MASTERWORKS *A FIRE UPON THE DEEP* AND *MAROONED IN REALTIME*.

VINGE FELT THAT THE AGE OF SUPER-INTELLIGENT MACHINES WOULD SPELL THE END OF THE HUMAN ERA.

HMM...ALL IN ALL, IT'S NOT MUCH WORSE THAN VICTOR FRANKENSTEIN TRYING TO CREATE A SUPERIOR BEING! BUT NEVER MIND... YOU WERE SAYING THAT CYBERPUNK HAD ALSO LEFT ITS MARK ELSEWHERE?

YES, IT BEGAN TO INFILTRATE CINEMA, TV SERIES, ROLE-PLAYING AND VIDEO GAMES, GRAPHIC NOVELS, AND EVEN MUSIC! HERE ARE A FEW EXAMPLES: THE WACHOWSKIS' *MATRIX* TRILOGY, THE SERIES *MAX HEADROOM*, THE *NEUROMANCER* ROLE-PLAYING GAME, THE VIDEO GAME *CYBERPUNK 2077*, THE MANGAS *AKIRA*, *GUNNM* AND *BLAME*, THE GRAPHIC NOVEL *RANXEROX* AND, IN MUSIC, BILLY IDOL'S *CYBERPUNK* ALBUM.

SO, WAS THAT THE END OF CLASSIC SCIENCE FICTION AND PULP CULTURE?

WELL, NOT QUITE. WE MUSTN'T FORGET STAR WARS.

OH YES? DO CARRY ON, MS. MERRIL, I'M ALL EARS!

IN 1977, STAR WARS EXPLODED ONTO OUR SCREENS AND ULTIMATELY BECAME ONE OF THE WORLD'S MOST POPULAR FRANCHISES EVER. IT WAS MODELED ON A WHOLE ARRAY OF PULP AND COMIC SOURCES, RANGING FROM ASIMOV, FLASH GORDON, AND EDMOND HAMILTON TO THE FRENCH VALERIAN AND LAURELINE GRAPHIC NOVELS BY MÉZIÈRES... SO MANY REFERENCES!

FINALLY, STAR WARS UNLEASHED A WHOLE WAVE OF SCIENCE-FICTION MOVIES THAT DEPENDED MORE ON EXCITEMENT AND SPECIAL EFFECTS, WHICH WERE RAPIDLY IMPROVING.

SO, DID THE CRITICS START THINKING THAT SCIENCE FICTION WAS MERELY THRILLS FOR TEENAGERS AGAIN?

WELL, THERE WERE A LOT OF EXCELLENT FEMALE AND MALE AUTHORS PRODUCING PLENTY OF QUALITY WRITING BETWEEN THE 1960S AND 2000S!

WE'VE LISTED THE FEMALE AUTHORS ALREADY, SO HERE ARE JUST A FEW OF THE MEN...

Gene Roddenberry - created the series Star Trek, Andromeda, and Earth: Final Conflict.

John Varley - The Ophiuchi Hotline (1977). A writer in the Heinlein tradition.

George R. R. Martin - Sandkings (1979). Nightflyers (1980).

Gregory Benford - Timescape (1980). Hard SF.

Tim Powers - The Anubis Gates (1983), a fundamental steampunk novel.

Orson Scott Card - Ender's Game (1985). Space opera.

Dan Simmons - Hyperion (1990). Space opera. Hugo Award 1990.

Kim Stanley Robinson - the Mars trilogy ((1992-1996). Hard SF.

Greg Egan - Axiomatic (1995). Short stories, Hard SF.

SPACE OPERA IS PROBABLY ONE OF THE MAIN SUB-GENRES IN WHICH CYBERPUNK BEGAN TO EXPAND AND BECOME A STAPLE. IN 2003, SEVERAL AUTHORS, INCLUDING KEN MACLEOD, PAUL MCAULEY, AND GWYNETH JONES, ANNOUNCED WHAT THEY TERMED THE "NEW SPACE OPERA" IN THE PAGES OF *LOCUS* MAGAZINE.

BUT WHAT WAS SO DIFFERENT ABOUT IT?

THEY WANTED TO REVISIT THE DARK SIDE OF CYBERPUNK, ADDING THEIR OWN DEFINITIONS, FOR EXAMPLE: "LITERARY, STIMULATING, DARK AND DISTURBING, FEATURING GRANDIOSE BACKDROPS, AS WELL AS ROMANCE, EXCITEMENT, AND BAGS OF SUSPENSE."

BUT "NEW" SPACE OPERA HAD ALREADY BEEN AROUND SINCE THE 1970S, WITH VARIOUS TALENTED AUTHORS SUCH AS MICHAEL JOHN HARRISON AND HIS *VIRICONIUM* SERIES, AND NOT FORGETTING THE SCOTS WRITER IAIN M. BANKS AND HIS *CULTURE* SERIES, WHICH CONTINUES TO BE A REFERENCE TODAY.

FOR THAT SERIES, HE DREAMED UP A TECHNOLOGICAL AND PHILOSOPHICAL UTOPIA IN THE MINUTEST DETAILS. A SOCIETY BASED ON ANARCHY, WITHOUT ANY LAWS, MONEY, OR HIERARCHIES!

IT'S REALLY EXCITING, MR. MOORCOCK. BUT ALL THIS INFORMATION MAKES MY HEAD SPIN. I THINK IT'S TIME FOR ME TO TAKE MY LEAVE.

I UNDERSTAND. MAYBE ONE DAY SOMEONE WILL WAKE YOU UP AGAIN...WITH THE SAME PASSION THAT DRIVES US!

BUT ENOUGH OF THE CHATTER, LET'S GET BACK TO WHERE WE FOUND YOU.

LATER, IN THE HOUSE OF SCIENCE FICTION...

HERE HE IS, BACK TO SLEEP. AS FOR US, WE CAN ALSO LEAVE.

BUT THE HOUSE OF SCIENCE FICTION IS SO VAST THAT WE COULD PROBABLY NEVER EXPLORE IT ALL!

WE HAVE PLENTY OF TIME, ROBERT, SO LET'S TAKE A GAMBLE AND PICK THE FIRST DOOR THAT WE COME TO!

OH, IT'S AS IF THE HOUSE IS LISTENING IN! IT'S JUST OPENED UP A PORTAL FOR US! IF THAT ISN'T SCIENCE FICTION, WHAT IS?!

BY THE WAY... IS THERE A PROPER, PRECISE DEFINITION OF SCIENCE FICTION?

RUSTY SOLENOIDS! IT'S DEEP THOUGHT, THE COMPUTER IN DOUGLAS ADAMS' THE HITCHHIKER'S GUIDE TO THE GALAXY! THIS IS WHERE HE WAS HIDING!

HE'LL BE ABLE TO GIVE US AN ANSWER!

O, DEEP THOUGHT, CAN YOU PROVIDE AN EXACT DEFINITION OF SCIENCE FICTION?

42!

READ THE HITCHHIKER'S GUIDE TO LEARN THE ANSWER TO THE GREAT QUESTION OF LIFE, THE UNIVERSE AND...SCIENCE FICTION!

END

index